Tess Gerritsen left a successful practice as a doctor to raise her children and concentrate on her writing. *Harvest* was her first novel. Her most recent novels, *The Surgeon*, *The Apprentice*, *The Sinner* and *Body Double*, have been worldwide and *Sunday Times* bestsellers. Her new novel, *Vanish*, is now available from Bantam Press.

She lives with her husband and two sons in Maine.

Acclaim for the novels of Tess Gerritsen:

'It's scary just how good Tess Gerritsen is – this is crime writing at its unputdownable, nerve-tingling best'
Harlan Coben

'If you've never read Gerritsen, figure in the price of electricity when you buy your first novel by her, 'cause baby, you are going to be up all night'
Stephen King

'Gerritsen is a better writer than such founders of the school as Kathy Reichs and Patricia Cornwell'
Observer

'[Gerritsen] has an imagination that allows her to conjure up depths of human behaviour so dark and frightening that she makes Edgar Allan Poe and H.P. Lovecraft seem like goody-two-shoes'
Chicago Tribune

'Her pages suffused from lividity, Doc Gerritsen's morgue slab awaits you, reader ... Glorious deaths bursting with the guilty glow of sex'
Kirkus Reviews

'Gerritsen has enough in the locker to seriously worry Michael Connelly, Harlan Coben and even the great Dennis Lehane. Brilliant'
Crime Time

HARVEST

Tess Gerritsen

BANTAM BOOKS

LONDON • TORONTO • SYDNEY • AUCKLAND • JOHANNESBURG

HARVEST
A BANTAM BOOK: 0553817728
9780553817720

Originally published in the United States by Simon & Schuster, Inc.
First published in Great Britain by Headline Limited

PRINTING HISTORY
Headline edition published 1996
Bantam edition published 2006

1 3 5 7 9 10 8 6 4 2

This is a work of fiction.
The New England Organ Bank (NEOB) is a not-for-profit agency
that recovers and distributes human organs and tissue for
transplant. The United Network for Organ Sharing (UNOS) maintains the
national transplant network under contract to the federal government and
monitors compliance with national rules for organ sharing and distribution.
Both NEOB and UNOS have systems in place to prevent unlawful recovery
of organs and to ensure equitable distribution of organs to recipients. It is
illegal to buy or sell organs. The use of their names and acronyms for their
names in this book is for the sake of the novel's atmosphere and plot.
In all other respects the characters, places and events are either the product
of the author's imagination or they are used entirely fictitiously. Any other
resemblance to actual events or locales or persons, living or dead,
is entirely coincidental.

Set in 11/12.5pt Sabon by
Falcon Oast Graphic Art Ltd.

Bantam Books are published by Transworld Publishers,
61–63 Uxbridge Road, London W5 5SA,
a division of The Random House Group Ltd,
in Australia by Random House Australia (Pty) Ltd,
20 Alfred Street, Milsons Point, Sydney, NSW 2061, Australia,
in New Zealand by Random House New Zealand Ltd,
18 Poland Road, Glenfield, Auckland 10, New Zealand
and in South Africa by Random House (Pty) Ltd,
Isle of Houghton, Corner of Boundary Road & Carse O'Gowrie,
Houghton 2198, South Africa.

Printed and bound in Great Britain by
Cox & Wyman Ltd, Reading, Berkshire.

Papers used by Transworld Publishers are natural, recyclable
products made from wood grown in sustainable forests. The
manufacturing processes conform to the environmental
regulations of the country of origin.

*To Jacob, my husband
and my very best friend*

Acknowledgments

A heartfelt thanks to Emily Bestler for her gentle and insightful editing; to David Bowman for sharing his expertise on the Russian mafia; to Transplant Coordinators Susan Pratt, at Penobscot Bay Medical Center, and Bruce White, at Maine Medical Center, for their invaluable insights into the organ donation process; to Patty Kahn for helping me navigate the medical library computer; to John Sargent of Rockland, Maine, for his locksmithing advice; and to Roger Pepper for faithfully sending research materials my way.

Above all, a very special thanks to Meg Ruley and Don Cleary of the Jane Rotrosen Agency. You made it happen.

Introduction

Before Jane Rizzoli, before Maura Isles, there was Abby DiMatteo.

Abby is the heroine of my very first thriller *Harvest*, which in 1996 launched my career as a suspense writer, and was my first novel to hit the *New York Times* bestseller list. The plot of *Harvest* was sparked by a disturbing dinner conversation I had with a retired policeman, who had been traveling in Russia. Moscow cops had told him that children were vanishing from the streets, and authorities there were convinced the kids were being sold around the world as organ donors.

I was horrified. Weeks later, still thinking about those children, I knew this would be the premise of my next book. I'm a physician, and in *Harvest*, I drew on my insider knowledge of the medical world. I bring you into the operating room, into the world of transplant surgery, and into the life of one particular young doctor, Abby DiMatteo. Immersed in the grinding fatigue of surgical training, Abby is thrilled to be working with Bayside Hospital's elite cardiac transplant team. But soon Abby discovers that Bayside hides a frightening secret. By revealing its horrors, she could very well pay the ultimate price.

This is also the story of Yakov, a plucky eleven-year-old Russian boy who finds himself aboard a freighter bound for America. He has been told he's going to an adoptive family. But as his ship rumbles its way across the Atlantic, the ever-inquisitive Yakov begins to suspect that, instead of a family, something terrible awaits him.

If you've enjoyed the forensic details of my Jane Rizzoli series, you'll find them in *Harvest* as well, from the slice of the surgeon's scalpel to the cut of the pathologist's knife, from the tension of the ER to the sights and smells of the autopsy room.

Here, in *Harvest*, is where the thrills began.

Tess Gerritsen, *Maine, 2006*

One

He was small for his age, smaller than the other boys who panhandled in the underpass at Arbats-Kaya, but at eleven years old he had already done it all. He had been smoking cigarettes for four years, stealing for three and a half, and turning tricks for two. This last vocation Yakov did not much care for, but it was something Uncle Misha insisted upon. How else were they to buy bread and cigarettes? Yakov, being the smallest and blondest of Uncle Misha's boys, bore the brunt of the trade. The customers always favored the young ones, the fair ones. They did not seem to care about Yakov's missing left hand; indeed, most did not even notice his withered stump. They were too enchanted by his smallness, his blondness, his unflinching blue eyes.

Yakov longed to grow out of the trade, to earn his keep by picking pockets like the bigger boys. Every morning when he woke up in Misha's flat, and every evening before he fell asleep, he would reach up with his one good hand and grasp the head bar of his cot. He'd stretch and stretch, hoping to add another fraction of a centimeter to his height. A useless exercise, Uncle Misha advised him. Yakov was small because he came from stunted stock. The woman who'd abandoned him in Moscow seven years ago had been stunted too. Yakov could scarcely remember the woman, nor could he remember much of anything else from his life before the city. He knew only what Uncle Misha told him, and he believed only half of it. At the tender age of eleven, Yakov was both diminutive and wise.

So it was with his natural skepticism that he now regarded the man and woman talking business with Uncle Misha over the dining table.

The couple had come to the flat in a large black car with dark windows. The man, named Gregor, wore a suit and tie and shoes of real leather. The woman Nadiya was a blonde dressed in a skirt and jacket of fine wool and she carried a hard-shelled valise. She was not Russian – that much was immediately evident to all four boys in the flat. She was American, perhaps, or English. She spoke in fluent but accented Russian.

While the two men conducted business over vodka, the woman's gaze wandered about the tiny flat, taking in the old army cots shoved up against the wall, the piles of dirty bedclothes, and the four boys huddled together in anxious silence. She had light gray eyes, pretty eyes, and she studied the boys each in turn. First she looked at Pyotr, the oldest at fifteen. Then she looked at Stepan, thirteen, and Aleksei, ten.

And finally, she looked at Yakov.

Yakov was accustomed to such scrutiny by adults, and he gazed back calmly. What he was not accustomed to was being so quickly passed over. Usually the adults ignored the other boys. This time it was gangly, pimply-faced Pyotr who garnered the woman's attention.

Nadiya said to Misha: 'You are doing the right thing, Mikhail Isayevich. These children have no future here. We offer them such a chance!' She smiled at the boys.

Stepan, the dullard, grinned back like an idiot in love.

'You understand, they speak no English,' said Uncle Misha. 'Only a word, here and there.'

'Children pick it up quickly. For them, it is effortless.'

'They will need time to learn. The language, the food—'

'Our agency is quite familiar with transitional needs. We work with so many Russian children. Orphans, like these. They will stay, for a while, in a special school to give them time to adjust.'

'And if they cannot?'

Nadiya paused. 'Every so often, there are exceptions. The ones with emotional difficulties.' Her gaze swept the four boys. 'Is there one in particular who concerns you?'

Yakov knew that *he* was the one with the difficulties of which they spoke. The one who seldom laughed and never cried, the one Uncle

Misha called his 'little stone boy.' Yakov did not know why he never cried. The other boys, when hurt, would shed fat and sloppy tears. Yakov would simply turn his mind blank, the way the television screen turned blank late at night after the stations shut off. No transmission, no images, just that comforting white fuzz.

Uncle Misha said, 'They are all good boys. Excellent boys.'

Yakov looked at the other three boys. Pyotr had a jutting brow and shoulders perpetually hunched forward like a gorilla's. Stepan had odd ears, small and wrinkled, between which floated a walnut for a brain. Aleksei was sucking his thumb.

And I, thought Yakov, looking down at his stump of a forearm, I have only one hand. Why do they say we are excellent? Yet that was precisely what Uncle Misha kept insisting. And the woman kept nodding. These were good boys, healthy boys.

'Even their teeth are good!' pointed out Misha. 'Not rotten at all. And look how tall my Pyotr is.'

'That one there looks undernourished.' Gregor pointed to Yakov. 'And what happened to his hand?'

'He was born without it.'

'The radiation?'

'It does not affect him otherwise. It's just the missing hand.'

'It should pose no problem,' said Nadiya. She rose from the chair. 'We must leave. It's time.'

'So soon?'

'We have a schedule to keep.'

'But – their clothes—'

'The agency will provide clothes. Better than what they're wearing now.'

'Is it to happen so quickly? We have no time to say goodbye?'

A ripple of irritation passed through the woman's eyes. 'A moment. We don't want to miss our connections.'

Uncle Misha looked at his boys, his four boys, related to him not by blood, nor even by love, but by mutual dependence. Mutual need. He hugged each of the boys in turn. When he came to Yakov, he held on a little longer, a little tighter. Uncle Misha smelled of onions and cigarettes, familiar smells. Good smells. But Yakov's instinct was to recoil from the closeness. He disliked being held or touched, by anyone.

'Remember your uncle,' Misha whispered. 'When you are rich in America. Remember how I watched over you.'

'I don't want to go to America,' said Yakov.

'It's for the best. For all of you.'

'I want to stay with you, Uncle! I want to stay here.'

'You have to go.'

'Why?'

'Because I have decided.' Uncle Misha grasped his shoulders and gave him a hard shake. 'I have decided.'

Yakov looked at the other boys, who were grinning at each other. And he thought: They are happy about this. Why am I the only one with doubts?

The woman took Yakov by the hand. 'I'll bring them to the car. Gregor can finish up here with the papers.'

'Uncle?' called Yakov.

But Misha had already turned away and was staring out the window.

Nadiya shepherded the four boys into the hallway and down the stairs. It was three flights to the street. All those clomping shoes, all that noisy boy energy, seemed to ricochet loudly through the empty stairwell.

They were already on the ground floor when Aleksei suddenly halted. 'Wait! I forgot Shu-Shu!' he cried and went tearing back up the stairs.

'Come back here!' called Nadiya. 'You can't go up there!'

'I can't leave him!' yelled Aleksei.

'Come back here *now*!'

Aleksei just kept thudding away up the steps. The woman was about to chase after him when Pyotr said, 'He won't leave without Shu-Shu.'

'Who the devil is Shu-Shu?' she snapped.

'His stuffed dog. He's had it forever.'

She glanced up the stairwell toward the fourth floor, and in that instant Yakov saw, in her eyes, something he did not understand.

Apprehension.

She stood as though poised between pursuit and abandonment of Aleksei. When the boy came running back down the stairs with the tattered

Shu-Shu clutched in his arms, the woman seemed to melt in relief against the banister.

'Got him!' crowed Aleksei, embracing the stuffed animal.

'Now we *go*,' the woman said, ushering them outside.

The four boys piled into the backseat of the car. It was cramped, and Yakov had to sit halfway on Pyotr's lap.

'Can't you put your bony ass somewhere else?' grumbled Pyotr.

'Where shall I put it? In your face?'

Pyotr shoved him. He shoved back.

'Stop it!' ordered the woman from the front seat. 'Behave yourselves.'

'But there's not enough room back here,' complained Pyotr.

'Then make room. And hush!' The woman glanced up at the building, toward the fourth floor. Toward Misha's flat.

'Why are we waiting?' asked Aleksei.

'Gregor. He's signing the papers.'

'How long will it take?'

The woman sat back and stared straight ahead. 'Not long.'

A close call, thought Gregor as the boy Aleksei left the flat for the second time and slammed the door behind him. Had the little bastard popped in a moment later, there would be hell to pay. What was that stupid Nadiya doing, letting the brat back upstairs? He had been against using Nadiya from the start. But Reuben had insisted on a woman. People would trust a woman.

The boy's footsteps receded down the stairwell, a loud clomp-clomp followed by the thud of the building door.

Gregor turned to the pimp.

Misha was standing at the window, staring down at the street, at the car where his four boys sat. He pressed his hand to the glass, his fat fingers splayed in farewell. When he turned to face Gregor, his eyes were actually misted with tears.

But his first words were about the money. 'Is it in the valise?'

'Yes,' said Gregor.

'All of it?'

'Twenty thousand American dollars. Five thousand per child. You did agree to the price.'

'Yes.' Misha sighed and ran a hand over his face. A face whose furrows showed only too well the effect of too much vodka, too many cigarettes. 'They will be adopted by proper families?'

'Nadiya will see to it. She loves children, you know. It's why she chose this work.'

Misha managed a weak smile. 'Perhaps she could find *me* an American family.'

Gregor had to get him away from the window. He pointed to the valise, which was resting on an end table. 'Go ahead. Check it if you wish.'

Misha went to the valise and unsnapped the catch. Inside were stacks of American bills, bound together in neat bundles. Twenty thousand dollars, enough for all the vodka a man would need to rot his liver. How cheap it is these days to buy a man's soul, thought Gregor. On the streets of this new Russia, one could barter for anything. A crate of Israeli oranges, an American television, the pleasure of a woman's body. Opportunity everywhere, for those with the talent to mine it.

Misha stood staring down at that money, his money, but not with a look of triumph. Rather, it was a look of disgust. He closed the valise and stood with head bowed, hands resting on the hard black plastic.

Gregor stepped up behind Misha's balding head, raised the barrel of a silenced automatic, and fired two bullets into the man's brain.

Blood and gray matter spattered the far wall. Misha collapsed facedown, toppling the end table as he fell. The valise thudded onto the rug beside him.

Gregor snatched up the valise before the pooling blood could reach it. There were clumps of human tissue on the side. He went into the bathroom, used toilet paper to wipe the splatters off the plastic, and flushed away the tissue. When he walked back into the room where Misha lay, the pool of blood had already crept across the floor and was soaking into another rug.

Gregor glanced around the room to assure himself that his work here was done and that no evidence remained. He was tempted to take the bottle of vodka with him, but decided against it. Explanations would be required as to why he had Misha's precious bottle, and Gregor had no patience for the questions of children. That was Nadiya's department.

He left the flat and went downstairs.

Nadiya and her charges were waiting in the car. She looked at him as he slid behind the wheel, the questions plain in her eyes.

'You have the papers all signed?' she asked.

'Yes. All of them.'

Nadiya sat back, exhaling an audible sigh of relief. She had no nerves for this, Gregor thought as he started the car. No matter what Reuben said, the woman was a liability.

There were sounds of scuffling from the backseat. Gregor glanced in the rearview mirror and saw that the boys were shoving each other back and forth. All except the smallest one, Yakov, who was staring straight ahead. In the mirror their gazes met, and Gregor had the eerie sensation that the eyes of an adult were staring out of that child's face.

Then the boy turned and punched his neighbor in the shoulder. Suddenly the backseat was a tangle of squirming bodies and flailing limbs.

'Behave yourselves!' said Nadiya. 'Can't you keep quiet? We have a long drive to Riga.'

The boys calmed down. For a moment there was silence in the backseat. Then, in the rearview mirror, Gregor saw the little one, the one with the adult eyes, jab an elbow at his neighbor.

That made Gregor smile. No reason to worry, he thought. They were, after all, merely children.

Two

It was midnight, and Karen Terrio was fighting to keep her eyes open. Fighting to stay on the road. She had been driving for the better part of two days now, had left right after Aunt Dorothy's funeral, and she hadn't stopped except to pull over for a quick nap or a hamburger and coffee. Lots of coffee. Her aunt's funeral had receded to a two-day-old blur of memories. Wilting gladioli. Nameless cousins. Stale finger sandwiches. Obligations, so damn many obligations.

Now all she wanted was to go home.

She knew she should pull off again, should try to catch another quick nap before pressing onward, but she was so close, only fifty miles from Boston. At the last Dunkin' Donuts, she'd tanked up on three more cups of coffee. That had helped, a little; it had given her just enough of a buzz to get from Springfield to Sturbridge. Now the caffeine was starting to wear off, and even though she thought she was awake, every so often her head would dip in a sharp bob, and she knew she'd fallen asleep, if only for a second.

A Burger King sign beckoned from the darkness ahead. She pulled off the highway.

Inside she ordered coffee and a blueberry muffin and sat down at a table. At this hour of night, there were only a few patrons in the dining room, all of them wearing the same pasty masks of exhaustion. Highway ghosts, thought Karen. The same tired souls who seemed to haunt every highway rest stop. It was eerily quiet in that dining room, everyone focused on trying to stay awake and get back on the road.

At the next table sat a depressed-looking woman with two small children, both of them quietly chewing on cookies. Those children, so well behaved, so blond, made Karen think of her own daughters. It was their birthday tomorrow. Tonight, asleep in their beds, she thought, they are only a day away from being thirteen. A day further from their childhood.

When you wake up, she thought, I'll be home.

She refilled her coffee cup, snapped on a plastic cover, and walked out to her car.

Her head felt clear now. She could make it. An hour, fifty miles, and she'd be walking in her front door. She started the engine and pulled out of the parking lot.

Fifty miles, she thought. Only fifty miles.

Twenty miles away, parked behind a 7-Eleven, Vince Lawry and Chuck Servis finished off the last six-pack. They'd been going at it for four straight hours, just a little friendly competition to see who could toss back the most Buds without puking it all up again. Chuck was ahead by one. They'd lost track of the total; they'd have to figure it out in the morning when they tallied up the beer cans mounded in the backseat.

But Chuck was definitely ahead, and he was gloating about it, which pissed Vince off, because Chuck was better at every fucking thing. And this wasn't a fair contest. Vince could've gone another round, but the Bud had run out, and now Chuck was wearing that eat-shit grin of his, even though he knew it wasn't a fair contest.

Vince shoved open the car door and climbed out of the driver's seat.

'Where you going?' asked Chuck.

'T'get some more.'

'You can't handle no more.'

'Fuck you,' said Vince, and stumbled across the parking lot toward the 7-Eleven's front door.

Chuck laughed. 'You can't even walk!' he yelled out the window.

Asshole, thought Vince. What the fuck, he could walk. See, he was walking fine. He'd just stroll into the 7-Eleven and pick up two more sixes. Maybe three. Yeah, he could do three, easy. His stomach was iron, and except for having to piss every few minutes, he didn't feel the effects at all.

He tripped going in the door – goddamn high threshold, they could get sued for that – but he picked himself right up. He got three six-packs from the cooler and swaggered over to the cash register. He plunked down a twenty-dollar bill.

The clerk looked at the money and shook his head. 'Can't take it,' he said.

'What do you mean, can't take it?'

'Can't sell beer to an intoxicated customer.'

'Are you saying I'm drunk?'

'That's right.'

'Look, it's money, isn't it? You don't want my fucking money?'

'I don't wanna get sued. You just put the beer back, son, OK? Better yet, why don't you buy a cup of coffee or something? A hot dog.'

'I don't want a fucking hot dog.'

'Then just walk on out, boy. Go on.'

Vince shoved one of the six-packs across the countertop. It slid off the edge and crashed to the floor. He was about to launch another six-pack off the counter when the clerk pulled out a gun. Vince stood staring at it, his body poised in mid-shove.

'Go on, get the hell out,' said the clerk.

'OK.' Vince stepped back, both hands raised in submission. 'OK, I hear you.'

He tripped on the damn threshold again as he went out the door.

'So where is it?' asked Chuck as Vince climbed back in the car.

'They're outta beer.'

'They can't be out of beer.'

'They're fucking *out*, OK?' Vince started the car and goosed the accelerator. They squealed out of the lot.

'Where we going now?' asked Chuck.

'Find another store.' He squinted ahead at the darkness. 'Where's the on-ramp? Gotta be around here somewhere.'

'Man, give it up. No way you'll go another round without puking.'

'Where's the fucking on-ramp?'

'I think you passed it.'

'No, there it is.' Vince veered left, tires squealing over the pavement.

'Hey,' said Chuck. 'Hey, I don't think—'

'Got twenty fucking bucks left to blow. They'll take it. Someone'll take it.'

'Vince, you're going the wrong way!'

'What?'

Chuck yelled, 'You're going the *wrong way*!'

Vince gave his head a shake and tried to focus on the road. But the lights were too bright and they were shining right in his eyes. They seemed to be getting brighter.

'Pull right!' screamed Chuck. 'It's a car! Pull right!'

Vince veered right.

So did the lights.

He heard a shriek, unfamiliar, unearthly.

Not Chuck's, but his own.

Dr Abby DiMatteo was tired, more tired than she'd ever been in her life. She had been awake for twenty-nine straight hours, if one didn't count her ten-minute nap in the X-ray lounge, and she knew her exhaustion showed. While washing her hands in the SICU sink she had glimpsed herself in the mirror and had been dismayed by the smudges of fatigue under her dark eyes, by the disarray of her hair, which now hung in a tangled black mane. It was already ten A.M., and she had not yet showered or even brushed her teeth. Breakfast had been a hard-boiled egg and a cup of sweet coffee, handed to her an hour ago by a thoughtful surgical ICU nurse. Abby would be lucky to find time for lunch, luckier still to get out of the hospital by five and home by six. Just to sink into a chair right now would be luxury.

But one did not sit during Monday morning attending rounds. Certainly not when the attending was Dr Colin Wettig, chairman of Bayside Hospital's surgical residency program. A retired army general, Dr Wettig had a reputation for crisp and merciless questions. Abby was terrified of the General. So were all the other surgical residents.

Eleven residents now stood in the SICU, forming a semicircle of white coats and green scrub suits. Their gazes were all trained on the residency chairman. They knew that any one of them could be ambushed with a question. To be caught without an answer was to be subjected to a prolonged session of personalized humiliation.

The group had already rounded on four postop patients, had discussed treatment plans and prognoses. Now they stood assembled beside SICU Bed 11. Abby's new admission. It was her turn to present the case.

Though she held a clipboard in her arms, she

did not refer to her notes. She presented the case from memory, her gaze focused on the General's unsmiling face.

'The patient is a thirty-four-year-old Caucasian female, admitted at one this morning via the trauma service after a high-speed head-on collision on Route Ninety. She was intubated and stabilized in the field, then airlifted here. On arrival to the ER, she had evidence of multiple trauma. There were compound and depressed skull fractures, fractures of the left clavicle and humerus, and severe facial lacerations. On my initial exam, I found her to be a well-nourished white female, medium build. She was unresponsive to all stimuli with the exception of some questionable extensor posturing—'

'Questionable?' asked Dr Wettig. 'What does that mean? Did she or did she not have extensor posturing?'

Abby felt her heart hammering. Shit, he was already on her case. She swallowed and explained, 'Sometimes the patient's limbs would extend on painful stimuli. Sometimes they wouldn't.'

'How do you interpret that? Using the Glasgow Coma Scale for motor response?'

'Well. Since a nil response is rated a one, and extensor posturing is a two, I suppose the patient could be considered a . . . one and a half.'

There was a ripple of uneasy laughter among the circle of residents.

'There is no such score as a one and a half,' said Dr Wettig.

'I'm aware of that,' said Abby. 'But this patient doesn't fit neatly into—'

'Just continue with your exam,' he cut in.

Abby paused and glanced around at the circle of faces. Had she screwed up already? She couldn't be sure. She took a breath and continued. 'Vital signs were blood pressure of ninety over sixty and pulse of a hundred. She was already intubated. She had no spontaneous respirations. Her rate was fully supported by mechanical ventilation at twenty-five breaths per minute.'

'Why was a rate of twenty-five selected?'

'To keep her hyperventilated.'

'Why?'

'To lower her blood carbon dioxide. That would minimize brain edema.'

'Go on.'

'Head exam, as I mentioned, revealed both depressed and compound skull fractures of the left parietal and temporal bones. Severe swelling and lacerations of the face made it difficult to evaluate facial fractures. Her pupils were mid-position and unreactive. Her nose and throat—'

'Oculocephalic reflexes?'

'I didn't test them.'

'You didn't?'

'No, sir. I didn't want to manipulate the neck. I was concerned about possible spinal dislocation.'

She saw, by his slight nod, that her answer had been acceptable.

She described the physical findings. The normal breath sounds. The unremarkable heart. The benign abdomen. Dr Wettig did not interrupt. By the time she'd finished describing the neurological findings, she was feeling more self-assured. Almost cocky. And why shouldn't she? She knew what the hell she'd been doing.

'So what was your impression?' asked Dr Wettig. 'Before you saw any X-ray results?'

'Based on the mid-position and unreactive pupils,' said Abby, 'I felt there was probable mid-brain compression. Most likely from an acute subdural or epidural hematoma.' She paused, and added with a quiet note of confidence, 'The CT scan confirmed it. A large left-sided subdural with severe midline shift. Neurosurgery was called in. They performed an emergency evacuation of the clot.'

'So you're saying your initial impression was absolutely correct, Dr DiMatteo?'

Abby nodded.

'Let's take a look at how things are this morning,' said Dr Wettig, moving to the bedside. He shone a penlight into the patient's eyes. 'Pupils unresponsive,' he said. He pressed a knuckle, hard, against the breastbone. She remained flaccid, unmoving. 'No response to pain. Extensor or otherwise.'

All the other residents had edged forward, but Abby remained at the foot of the bed, her gaze focused on the patient's bandaged head. While Wettig continued his exam, tapping on tendons with a rubber hammer, flexing elbows and knees, Abby felt her attention drift away on a tide of fatigue. She kept staring at the woman's head, recently shorn of hair. The hair had been a thick brown, she remembered, clotted with blood and glass. There had been glass ground into the clothes as well. In the ER, Abby had helped cut away the blouse. It was a blue and white silk with a Donna Karan label. That last detail was what seemed to linger in Abby's memory. Not the blood or the broken bones or the shattered face. It was that label. Donna Karan. A brand she herself had once purchased. She thought of how, sometime, somewhere, this woman must once have stood in a shop, flipping through blouses, listening to the hangers squeak as they slid across the rack . . .

Dr Wettig straightened and looked at the SICU nurse. 'When was the hematoma drained?'

'She came out of Recovery about four A.M.'

'Six hours ago?'

'Yes, that would make it six hours.'

Wettig turned to Abby. 'Then why has nothing changed?'

Abby stirred from her daze and saw that everyone was watching her. She looked down at the patient. Watched the chest rise and fall, rise and fall, with every wheeze of the ventilator bellows.

'There . . . may be some postop swelling,' she said, and glanced at the monitor. 'The intracranial pressure is slightly elevated at twenty millimeters.'

'Do you think that's high enough to cause pupillary changes?'

'No. But—'

'Did you examine her immediately postop?'

32

'No, sir. Her care was transferred to Neuro-surgery Service. I spoke to their resident after surgery, and he told me—'

'I'm not asking the neurosurgery resident. I'm asking you, Dr DiMatteo. You diagnosed a subdural hematoma. It's been evacuated. So why are her pupils still mid-position and unreactive six hours postop?'

Abby hesitated. The General watched her. So did everyone else. The humiliating silence was punctuated only by the whoosh of the ventilator.

Dr Wettig glanced imperiously at the circle of residents. 'Is there anyone here who can help Dr DiMatteo answer the question?'

Abby's spine straightened. 'I can answer the question myself,' she said.

Dr Wettig turned to her, his eyebrow raised. 'Yes?'

'The . . . pupillary changes – the extensor posturing of the limbs – they were high midbrain signs. Last night I assumed it was because of the sub-dural hematoma, pressing downwards on the midbrain. But since the patient hasn't improved, I . . . I guess that indicates I was mistaken.'

'You guess?'

She let out a breath. 'I was mistaken.'

'What's your diagnosis now?'

'A midbrain hemorrhage. It could be due to shearing forces. Or residual damage from the sub-dural hematoma. The changes might not show up yet on CT scan.'

Dr Wettig regarded her for a moment, his

33

expression unreadable. Then he turned to the other residents. 'A midbrain hemorrhage is a reasonable assumption. With a combined Glasgow Coma Scale of three' – he glanced at Abby – 'and a *half*,' he amended, 'the prognosis is nil. The patient has no spontaneous respirations, no spontaneous movements, and she appears to have lost all brain stem reflexes. At the moment, I have no suggestions other than life support. And consideration of organ harvest.' He gave Abby a curt nod. Then he moved on to the next patient.

One of the other residents gave Abby's arm a squeeze. 'Hey, DiMatteo,' he whispered. 'Flying colors.'

Wearily Abby nodded. 'Thanks.'

Chief surgical resident Dr Vivian Chao was a legend among the other residents at Bayside Hospital. As the story went, two days into her very first rotation as an intern, her fellow intern suffered a psychotic break and had to be carted off, sobbing uncontrollably, to the loony ward. Vivian was forced to pick up the slack. For twenty-nine straight days, she was the one and only orthopedic resident on duty, around the clock. She moved her belongings into the call room and promptly lost five pounds on an un- relenting diet of cafeteria food. For twenty-nine straight days, she did not step out of the hospital front doors. On the thirtieth day her rotation ended, and she walked out to her car, only to dis- cover that it had been towed away a week before.

The parking lot attendant had assumed it was abandoned.

Four days into the next rotation, vascular surgery, Vivian's fellow intern was struck by a city bus and hospitalized with a broken pelvis. Again, someone had to take up the slack.

Vivian Chao moved right back into the hospital call room.

In the eyes of the other residents, she had thus achieved honorary manhood, a lofty status that was later acknowledged at the yearly awards dinner when she was presented with a boxed pair of steel balls.

When Abby first heard the Vivian Chao stories, she'd had a hard time reconciling that steel-balls reputation with what she saw: a laconic Chinese woman who was so petite she had to stand on a footstool to operate. Though Vivian seldom spoke during attending rounds, she could always be found standing fearlessly at the very front of the group, wearing an expression of cool dispassion.

It was with her usual air of detachment that Vivian approached Abby in the SICU that afternoon. By then Abby was moving through a sea of exhaustion, every step a struggle, every decision an act of pure will. She didn't even notice Vivian was standing beside her until the other woman said, 'I hear you admitted an AB positive head trauma.'

Abby looked up from the chart where she'd been recording patient progress notes. 'Yes. Last night.'

'Is the patient still alive?'

Abby glanced toward Bed 11's cubicle. 'It depends what you mean by alive.'

'Heart and lungs in good shape?'

'They're functioning.'

'How old?'

'She's thirty-four. Why?'

'I've been following a medical patient on the teaching service. End-stage congestive failure. Blood type AB positive. He's been waiting for a new heart.' Vivian went over to the chart rack. 'Which bed?'

'Eleven.'

Vivian pulled the chart out of the rack and flipped open the metal cover. Her face betrayed no emotion as she scanned the pages.

'She's not my patient anymore,' said Abby. 'I transferred her to Neurosurgery. They drained a subdural hematoma.'

Vivian just kept reading the chart.

'She's only ten hours postop,' said Abby. 'It seems a little early to be talking harvest.'

'No neurologic changes so far, I see.'

'No. But there's a chance . . .'

'With a Glasgow Scale of three? I don't think so.' Vivian slid the chart back into the rack and crossed to Bed 11.

Abby followed her.

From the cubicle doorway she stood and watched as Vivian briskly performed a physical exam. It was the same way Vivian performed in the OR, wasting no time or effort. During Abby's first year – the year of her internship – she had often observed Vivian in surgery, and she had admired those small, swift hands, had watched in awe as those delicate fingers spun perfect knots. Abby felt clumsy by comparison. She had invested hours of practice and yards and yards of thread learning to tie surgical knots on the handles of her bureau drawers. Though she could manage the mechanics competently enough, she knew she would never have Vivian Chao's magical hands.

Now, as she watched Vivian examine Karen Terrio, Abby found the efficiency of those hands profoundly chilling.

'No response to painful stimuli,' Vivian observed.

'It's still early.'

'Maybe. Maybe not.' Vivian pulled a reflex hammer from her pocket and began tapping on tendons. 'This is a stroke of luck.'

'I don't see how you can call it that.'

'My patient in MICU is AB positive. He's been waiting a year for a heart. This is the best match that's come up for him.'

Abby looked at Karen Terrio and she remembered, once again, the blue and white blouse. She wondered what the woman had been thinking as she'd buttoned it up that last time. Mundane thoughts, perhaps. Certainly not mortal thoughts. Not thoughts of a hospital bed or IV tubes or machines pumping air into her lungs.

'I'd like to go ahead with the lymphocyte cross match. Make sure they're compatible,' said

Vivian. 'And we might as well start HL-A typing for the other organs. The EEG's been done, hasn't it?'

'She's not on my service,' said Abby. 'And anyway, I think this is premature. No one's even talked to the husband about it.'

'Someone's going to have to.'

'She has kids. They'll need time for this to sink in.'

'The organs don't have a lot of time.'

'I know. I know it's got to be done. But, as I said, she's only ten hours postop.'

Vivian went to the sink and washed her hands. 'You aren't really expecting a miracle, are you?'

An SICU nurse appeared at the cubicle door. 'The husband's back with the kids. They're waiting to visit. Will you be much longer?'

'I'm finished,' said Vivian. She tossed the crumpled paper towel into the trash can and walked out.

'Can I send them in?' the nurse asked Abby.

Abby looked at Karen Terrio. In that instant she saw, with painful clarity, what a child would see gazing at that bed. 'Wait,' said Abby. 'Not yet.' She went to the bed and quickly smoothed out the blankets. She wet a paper towel in the sink and wiped away the flecks of dried mucus from the woman's cheek. She transferred the bag of urine around to the side of the bed, where it would not be so visible. Then, stepping back, she took one last look at Karen Terrio. And she realized that nothing she could do, nothing anyone could do, would lessen the pain of what was to come for those children.

She sighed and nodded to the nurse. 'They can come in now.'

By four-thirty that afternoon, Abby could barely concentrate on what she was writing, could barely keep her eyes focused. She had been on duty thirty-three and a half hours. Her afternoon rounds were completed. It was, at last, time to go home.

But as she closed the last chart, she found her gaze drawn, once again, to Bed 11. She stepped into the cubicle. Here she lingered at the foot of the bed, gazing numbly at Karen Terrio. Trying to think of something else, anything else, that could be done.

She didn't hear the footsteps approaching from behind.

Only when a voice said: 'Hello, gorgeous,' did Abby turn and see brown-haired, blue-eyed Dr Mark Hodell smiling at her. It was a smile meant only for Abby, a smile she'd sorely missed seeing today. On most days, Abby and Mark managed to share a quick lunch together or, at the very least, exchange a wave in passing. Today, though, they had missed seeing each other entirely, and the sight of him now gave her a quiet rush of joy. He bent to kiss her. Then, stepping back, he eyed her uncombed hair and wrinkled scrub suit. 'Must've been a bad night,' he murmured sympathetically. 'How much sleep did you get?'

'I don't know. Half an hour.'

'I heard rumors you batted a thousand with the General this morning.'

She shrugged. 'Let's just say he didn't use me to wipe the floor.'

'That qualifies as a triumph.'

She smiled. Then her gaze shifted back to Bed 11 and her smile faded. Karen Terrio was lost in all that equipment. The ventilator, the infusion pumps. The suction tubes and monitors for EKG and blood pressure and intracranial pressure. A gadget to measure every bodily function. In this new age of technology, why bother to feel for a pulse, to lay hands on a chest? What use were doctors when machines could do all the work?

'I admitted her last night,' said Abby. 'Thirty-four years old. A husband and two kids. Twin girls. They were here. I saw them just a little while ago. And it's strange, Mark, how they wouldn't touch her. They stood looking. Just looking at her. But they wouldn't touch her. I kept thinking, *you have to. You have to touch her now because it could be your last chance. The last chance you'll ever have.* But they wouldn't. And I think, someday, they're going to wish . . .' She shook her head. Quickly she ran her hand across her eyes. 'I hear the other guy was driving the wrong way, drunk. You know what pisses me off, Mark? And it really pisses me off. He'll survive. Right now he's sitting upstairs in the orthopedic ward, whining about a few fucking broken bones.' Abby took another deep breath and with the sigh that followed, all

40

her anger seemed to dissipate. 'Jesus, I'm supposed to save lives. And here I am wishing that guy was smeared all over the highway.' She turned from the bed. 'It must be time to go home.'

Mark ran his hand down her back, a gesture of both comfort and possession. 'Come on,' he said. 'I'll walk you out.'

They left the SICU and stepped onto the elevator. As the doors slid shut, she felt herself wobble and melt against him. At once he took her into the warm and familiar circle of his arms. It was a place where she felt safe, where she'd always felt safe.

A year ago, Mark Hodell had seemed a far from reassuring presence. Abby had been an intern. Mark had been a thoracic surgery attending – not just any attending physician, but a key surgeon on the Bayside cardiac transplant team. They'd met in the OR over a trauma case. The patient, a ten-year-old boy, had been rushed in by ambulance with an arrow protruding from his chest – the result of a sibling argument combined with a bad choice in birthday presents. Mark had already been scrubbed and gowned when Abby entered the OR. It was only her first week as an intern, and she'd been nervous, intimidated by the thought of assisting the distinguished Dr Hodell. She'd stepped up to the table. Shyly she'd glanced at the man standing across from her. What she saw, above his mask, was a broad, intelligent forehead and a pair of beautiful blue eyes. Very direct. Very inquisitive.

Together they operated. The kid survived.

A month later, Mark asked Abby for a date. She turned him down twice. Not because she didn't *want* to go out with him, but because she didn't think she *should* go out with him.

A month went by. He asked her out again. This time temptation won out. She accepted.

Five and a half months ago, Abby moved into Mark's Cambridge home. It hadn't been easy at first, learning to live with a forty-one-year-old bachelor who'd never before shared his life – or his home – with a woman. But now, as she felt Mark holding her, supporting her, she could not imagine living with, or loving, anyone else.

'Poor baby,' he murmured, his breath warm in her hair. 'Brutal, isn't it?'

'I'm not cut out for this. What the hell do I think I'm doing here?'

'You're doing what you always dreamed about. That's what you told me.'

'I don't even remember what the dream *was* anymore. I keep losing sight of it.'

'I believe it had something to do with saving lives?'

'Right. And here I am wishing that drunk in the other car was dead.' She shook her head in self-disgust.

'Abby, you're going through the worst of it now. You've got two more days on trauma. You just have to survive two more days.'

'Big deal. Then I start thoracic—'

'A piece of cake in comparison. Trauma's

always been the killer. Tough it out like everyone else.'

She burrowed deeper into his arms. 'If I switched to psychiatry, would you lose all respect for me?'

'All respect. No doubt about it.'

'You're such a jerk.'

Laughing, he kissed the top of her head. 'Many people think it, but you're the only one allowed to say it.'

They stepped off on the first floor and walked out of the hospital. It was autumn already, but Boston was sweltering in the sixth day of a late-September heat wave. As they crossed the parking lot, she could feel her last reserves of strength wilting away. By the time they reached her car, she was scarcely able to drag her feet across the pavement. This is what it does to us, she thought. It's the fire we walk through to become surgeons. The long days, the mental and emotional abuse, the hours of pushing onward while bits and pieces of our lives peel away from us. She knew it was simply a winnowing process, ruthless and necessary. Mark had survived it; so would she.

He gave her another hug, another kiss. 'Sure you're safe driving home?' he asked.

'I'll just put the car on automatic pilot.'

'I'll be home in an hour. Shall I pick up a pizza?'

Yawning, she slid behind the wheel. 'None for me.'

'Don't you want supper?'

She started the engine. 'All I want tonight,' she sighed, 'is a bed.'

Three

In the night it came to her like the gentlest of whispers or the brush of fairy wings across her face: *I am dying.* That realization did not frighten Nina Voss. For weeks, through the changing shifts of three private duty nurses, through the daily visits of Dr Morissey with his ever-higher doses of furosemide, Nina had maintained her serenity. And why should she not be serene? Her life had been rich with blessings. She had known love, and joy, and wonder. In her forty-six years she had seen the sun rise over the temples of Karnak, had wandered the twilight ruins of Delphi, and climbed the foothills of Nepal. And she had known the peace of mind that comes with the acceptance of one's place in God's universe. She was left with only two regrets in her life. One was that she had never held a child of her own.

The other was that Victor would be alone.

All night her husband had maintained his vigil at her bedside, had held her hand through the long hours of labored breaths and coughing, through the changing of the oxygen tanks and the visits of Dr Morissey. Even in her sleep she had felt Victor's presence. Sometime near dawn, through the haze of her dreams, she heard him say: *She is so young. So very young. Can't something else, anything else, be done?*

Something! Anything! That was Victor. He did not believe in the inevitable.

But Nina did.

She opened her eyes and saw that night had finally passed, and that sunlight was shining through her bedroom window. Beyond that window was a sweeping view of her beloved Rhode Island Sound. In the days before her illness, before the cardiomyopathy had drained her strength, dawn would usually find Nina awake and dressed. She would step out onto their bedroom balcony and watch the sun rise. Even on mornings when fog cloaked the Sound, when the water seemed little more than a silvery tremor in the mist, she would stand and feel the earth tilting, the day spilling toward her. As it did today.

So many dawns have I known. I thank you, Lord, for every one of them.

'Good morning, darling,' whispered Victor.

Nine focused on her husband's face smiling down at her. Some who looked at Victor Voss saw the face of authority. Some saw genius or ruthlessness. But this morning, as Nina gazed at her husband, she saw only love. And weariness.

She reached out for his hand. He took it and

pressed it to his lips. 'You must get some sleep, Victor,' she said.

'I'm not tired.'

'But I can see you are.'

'No I'm not.' He kissed her hand again, his lips warm against her chilled skin. They looked at each other for a moment. Oxygen hissed softly through the tubes in her nostrils. From the open window came the sound of ocean waves sluicing across the rocks.

She closed her eyes. 'Remember the time . . .' Her voice faded as she paused to catch her breath.

'Which time?' he prompted gently.

'The day I . . . broke my leg . . .' She smiled.

It was the week they'd met, in Gstaad. He told her later that he'd first spotted her schussing down a double black diamond, had pursued her down the mountain, back up in the lift, and down the mountain again. That was twenty-five years ago.

Since then they had been together every day of their lives.

'I knew,' she whispered. 'In that hospital . . . when you stayed by my bed. I knew.'

'Knew what, darling?'

'That you were the only one for me.' She opened her eyes and smiled at him again. Only then did she see the tear trickle down his cheek. Oh, but Victor did not cry! She had never seen him cry, not once in their twenty-five years together. She had always thought of Victor as the strong one, the brave one. Now, as she looked at his

46

face, she realized how very wrong she had been.

'Victor,' she said and clasped his hand in hers. 'You mustn't be afraid.'

Quickly, almost angrily, he mopped his hand across his face. 'I won't let this happen. I won't lose you.'

'You never will.'

'No. That's not enough! I want you here on this earth. With me. With *me*.'

'Victor, if there's one thing . . . one thing I know . . .' She took a deep breath, a gasp for air. 'It's that this time . . . we have here . . . is a very small part . . . of our existence.'

She felt him stiffen with impatience, felt him withdraw. He rose from the chair and paced to the window, where he stood gazing out at the Sound. She felt the warmth of his hand fade from her skin. Felt the chill return.

'I'll take care of this, Nina,' he said.

'There are things . . . in this life . . . we cannot change.'

'I've already taken steps.'

'But Victor . . .'

He turned and looked at her. His shoulders, framed by the window, seemed to blot out the light of dawn. 'It will all be taken care of, darling,' he said. 'Don't you worry about a thing.'

It was one of those warm and perfect evenings, the sun just setting, ice cubes clinking in glasses, perfumed ladies floating past in silk and voile. It seemed to Abby, standing in the walled garden of

Dr Bill Archer, that the air itself was magical. Clematis and roses arched across a latticed pergola. Drifts of flowers swept broad strokes of color across the expanse of lawn. The garden was the pride and joy of Marilee Archer, whose loud contralto could be heard booming out botanical names as she shepherded the other doctors' wives from flowerbed to flowerbed.

Archer, standing on the patio with highball in hand, laughed. 'Marilee knows more goddamn Latin than I do.'

'I took three years of it in college,' said Mark. 'All I remember is what I learned in medical school.'

They were gathered next to the brick barbecue, Bill Archer, Mark, the General, and two surgical residents. Abby was the only woman in that circle. It was something she'd never grown accustomed to, being the lone female in a group. She might lose sight of it for a moment or two, but then she would glance around a room where surgeons were gathered, and she'd experience that familiar flash of discomfort with the realization that she was surrounded by men.

Tonight there were wives at Archer's house party, of course, but they seemed to move in a parallel universe seldom intersecting with that of their husbands. Abby, standing with the surgeons, would occasionally hear far-off snippets from the wives' conversations. Talk of damask roses, of trips to Paris, and meals savored. She would feel pulled both ways, as though she stood straddling

48

the divide between men and women, belonging to neither universe, yet drawn to both.

It was Mark who anchored her in this circle of men. He and Bill Archer, also a thoracic surgeon, were close colleagues. Archer, chief of the cardiac transplant team, had been one of the doctors who'd recruited Mark to Bayside seven years ago. It wasn't surprising the two men got along so well. Both of them were hard-driving, athletic, and fiercely competitive. In the OR they worked together as a team, but out of the hospital, their friendly rivalry extended from the ski slopes of Vermont to the waters of Massachusetts Bay. Both men kept their J-35 sailboats moored at Marblehead Marina, and so far this season, the racing score stood at six to five, Archer's *Red Eye* versus Mark's *Gimme Shelter*. Mark planned to even the score this weekend. He'd already recruited Rob Lessing, the other second-year resident, as crew.

What was it about men and boats? wondered Abby. This was gizmo talk, men and their sailing machines, high-tech conversation fueled by testosterone. In this circle, center stage belonged to the men with graying hair. To Archer, with his silver-threaded mane. To Colin Wettig, already a distinguished gray. And to Mark, who at forty-one was just starting to turn silver at the temples.

As the conversation veered toward hull maintenance and keel design and the outrageous price of spinnakers, Abby's attention drifted. That's when she noticed two late arrivals: Dr

Aaron Levi and his wife, Elaine. Aaron, the transplant team cardiologist, was a painfully shy man. Already he had retreated with his drink to a far corner of the lawn, where he stood stoop-shouldered and silent. Elaine was glancing around in search of a conversational beachhead.

This was Abby's chance to flee the boat talk. She slipped away from Mark and went to join the Levis.

'Mrs Levi? It's so nice to see you again.'

Elaine returned a smile of recognition. 'It's . . . Abby, isn't it?'

'Yes, Abby DiMatteo. I think we met at the residents' picnic.'

'Oh yes, that's right. There are so many residents, I have trouble keeping you all straight. But I do remember you.'

Abby laughed. 'With only three women in the surgery program, we do stick out.'

'It's a lot better than the old days, when there were no women at all. Which rotation are you on now?'

'I start thoracic surgery tomorrow.'

'Then you'll be working with Aaron.'

'If I'm lucky enough to scrub on any transplants.'

'You're bound to. The team's been so busy lately. They're even getting referrals from Massachusetts General, which tickles Aaron pink.' Elaine leaned toward Abby. 'They turned him down for a fellowship years ago. Now they're sending *him* patients.'

'The only thing Mass Gen has over Bayside is their Harvard mystique,' said Abby. 'You know Vivian Chao, don't you? Our chief resident?'

'Of course.'

'She graduated top ten at Harvard Med. But when it came time to apply for residency, Bayside was her number one choice.'

Elaine turned to her husband. 'Aaron, did you hear that?'

Reluctantly he looked up from his drink. 'Hear what?'

'Vivian Chao picked Bayside over Mass Gen. Really, Aaron, you're already at the top here. Why would you want to leave?'

'Leave?' Abby looked at Aaron, but the cardiologist was glaring at his wife. Their sudden silence was what puzzled Abby most. From across the lawn came the sound of laughter, the echoing drifts of conversation, but in this corner of the garden, nothing was said.

Aaron cleared his throat. 'It's just something I've toyed with,' he said. 'You know. Getting away from the city. Moving to a small town. Everyone daydreams about small towns, but no one really wants to move there.'

'I don't,' said Elaine.

'I grew up in a small town,' said Abby. 'Belfast, Maine. I couldn't wait to get out.'

'That's how I imagine it would be,' said Elaine. 'Everyone clawing to get to civilization.'

'Well, it wasn't *that* bad.'

'But you're not going back. Are you?'

Abby hesitated. 'My parents are dead. And both my sisters have moved out of state. So I don't have any reason to go back. But I have a lot of reasons to stay here.'

'It was just a fantasy,' said Aaron, and he took a deep gulp of his drink. 'I wasn't really thinking about it.'

In the odd silence that followed, Abby heard her name called. She turned and saw Mark waving to her.

'Excuse me,' she said, and crossed the lawn to join him.

'Archer's giving the tour of his inner sanctum,' said Mark.

'What inner sanctum?'

'Come on. You'll see.' He took her hand and led her across the terrace and into the house. They climbed the staircase to the second floor. Only once before had Abby been upstairs in the Archer house, and that was to view the oil paintings hung in the gallery.

Tonight was the first time she'd been invited into the room at the end of the hall.

Archer was already waiting inside. In a grouping of leather chairs were seated Drs Frank Zwick and Raj Mohandas. But Abby scarcely noticed the people; it was the room itself that commanded her attention.

She was standing in a museum of antique medical instruments. In display cases were exhibited a variety of tools both fascinating and frightening. Scalpels and bloodletting basins.

Leech jars. Obstetrical forceps with jaws that could crush an infant's skull. Over the fireplace hung an oil painting: the battle between Death and the Physician over the life of a young woman. A Brandenburg Concerto was playing on the stereo.

Archer turned down the volume, and the room suddenly seemed very quiet, with only the whisper of music in the background.

'Isn't Aaron coming?' asked Archer.

'He knows about it. He'll be on his way up,' said Mark.

'Good.' Archer smiled at Abby. 'What do you think of my little collection?'

She studied the contents of a display case. 'This is fascinating. I can't even tell you what some of these things are.'

Archer pointed to an odd contraption of gears and pulleys. 'That device over there is interesting. It was meant to generate a weak electrical current, which was applied to various parts of the body. Said to be helpful for anything from female troubles to diabetes. Funny, isn't it? The nonsense medical science would have us believe?'

Abby stopped before the oil painting and gazed at the black-robed image of Death. Doctor as hero, Doctor as conqueror, she thought. And of course the object of rescue is a woman. A beautiful woman.

The door opened.

'Here he is,' said Mark. 'We wondered if you'd forgotten about it, Aaron.'

Aaron came into the room. He said nothing, only nodded as he sat down in a chair.

'Can I refill your drink, Abby?' said Archer, gesturing to her glass.

'I'm fine.'

'Just a splash of brandy? Mark's driving, right?'

Abby smiled. 'All right. Thanks.'

Archer touched up Abby's drink and handed it back to her. The room had fallen strangely quiet, as though everyone was waiting for this formality to be completed. It struck her then: she was the only resident in the room. Bill Archer threw this sort of party every few months, to welcome another batch of house staff to the thoracic and trauma rotations. At this moment, there were six other surgical residents circulating downstairs in the garden. But here, in Archer's private retreat, there was only the transplant team.

And Abby.

She sat down on the couch next to Mark and sipped her drink. Already she was feeling the brandy's heat, and the warmth of this special attention. As an intern, she'd viewed these five men with awe, had felt privileged just to assist in the same OR with Archer and Mohandas. Though her relationship with Mark had brought her into their social circle, she never forgot who these men were. Nor did she forget the power they held over her career.

Archer sat down across from her. 'I've been hearing some good things about you, Abby. From the General. Before he left tonight, he paid you some wonderful compliments.'

'Dr Wettig did?' Abby couldn't help a surprised laugh. 'To be honest, I'm never quite sure what he thinks about my performance.'

'Well, that's just the General's way. Spreading a little insecurity around in the world.'

The other men laughed. Abby did too.

'I do respect Colin's judgment,' said Archer. 'And I know he thinks you're one of the best Level Two residents in the program. I've worked with you, so I know he's right.'

Abby shifted uneasily on the couch. Mark reached for her hand and gave it a squeeze. That gesture was not missed by Archer, who smiled.

'Obviously, Mark thinks you're pretty special. And that's part of the reason we thought we should have this discussion. I know it may seem a little premature, but we're long-range planners, Abby. We think it never hurts to scout out the territory in advance.'

'I'm afraid I don't quite follow you,' said Abby.

Archer reached for the brandy decanter and poured himself a scant refill. 'Our transplant team's interested in only the best. The best credentials, the best performance. We're always looking over the residents for fellowship material. Oh, we have a selfish motive, of course. We're grooming people for the team.' He paused. 'And we were wondering if you might have an interest in transplant surgery.'

Abby flashed Mark a startled look. He nodded. 'It's not something you have to decide anytime soon,' said Archer. 'But we want you to think about it. We have the next few years to get to know each other. By then, you may not even want a fellowship. It may turn out transplant surgery's not something you're even vaguely interested in.'

'But it is.' She leaned forward, her face flushing with enthusiasm. 'I guess I'm just . . . surprised by this. And flattered. There are so many good residents in the program. Vivian Chao, for instance.'

'Yes, Vivian is good.'

'I think she'll be looking for a fellowship next year.'

Mohandas said, 'There's no question that Dr Chao's surgical technique is outstanding. I can think of several residents with excellent technique. But you have heard the saying? One can teach a monkey how to operate. The trick is teaching him *when* to operate.'

'I think what Raj is trying to say is, we're looking for good clinical judgment,' said Archer. 'And a sense of teamwork. We see you as someone who works well with a team. Not at cross-purposes. That's something we insist on, Abby, teamwork. When you're sweating it out in the OR, all sorts of things can go wrong. Equipment fails. Scalpels slip. The heart gets lost in transit. We have to be able to pull together, come hell or high water. And we do.'

'We help each other out, too,' said Frank Zwick. 'Both in the OR and outside of it.'

'Absolutely,' said Archer. He glanced at Aaron. 'Wouldn't you agree?'

Aaron cleared his throat. 'Yes, we help each other out. It's one of the benefits of joining this team.'

'One of the many benefits,' added Mohandas.

For a moment no one spoke. The Brandenburg Concerto played softly in the background. Archer said, 'I like this part,' and turned up the volume. As the sound of violins spilled from the speakers, Abby found herself gazing, once again, at Death versus the Physician. The battle for a patient's life, a patient's soul.

'You mentioned there were . . . other benefits,' said Abby.

'For example,' offered Mohandas, 'when I completed my surgery residency, I had a number of student loans to pay off. So that was part of my recruitment package. Bayside helped me pay off my loans.'

'Now that's something we can talk about, Abby,' said Archer. 'Ways we can make this attractive to you. Young surgeons nowadays, they come out of residency at thirty years old. Most of them are already married with maybe a kid or two. And they owe – what? A hundred thousand dollars in loans. They don't even own a house yet! It'll take 'em ten years just to get out of debt. By then they're forty, and worried about college for their kids!' He shook his head. 'I don't know why anyone goes into medicine these days. Certainly not to make money.'

'If anything,' agreed Abby, 'it's a hardship.'

'It doesn't have to be. That's where Bayside can

help. Mark mentioned to us that you were on financial aid all the way through medical school.'

'A combination of scholarships and loans. Mostly loans.'

'Ouch. That sounds painful.'

Abby nodded ruefully. 'I'm just beginning to feel the pain.'

'College loans as well?'

'Yes. My family had financial problems,' Abby admitted.

'You make it sound like something to be ashamed of.'

'It was more a case of . . . bad luck. My younger brother was hospitalized for a number of months and we weren't insured. But then, in the town where I grew up, a lot of people weren't insured.'

'Which only confirms how hard you must have worked to beat the odds. Everyone here knows what that's like. Raj here was an immigrant, didn't speak English until he was ten. Me, I'm the first in my family to go to college. Believe me, there are no goddamn Boston Brahmins in this room. No rich daddies or handy little trust funds. We know about beating the odds because we've all done it. That's the kind of drive we're looking for in this team.'

The music swelled to its finale. The last chord of trumpets and strings faded away. Archer shut off the stereo and looked at Abby.

'Anyway. It's something for you to think about,' he said. 'We're not making any firm offers, of course. It's more like talking about a, uh . . .' Archer grinned at Mark. 'First date.'

'I understand,' said Abby.

'One thing you should know. You're the only resident we've approached. The only one we're really considering. It would be wise if you didn't mention this to the rest of the house staff. We don't want to stir up any jealousy.'

'Of course not.'

'Good.' Archer looked around the room. 'I think we're all in agreement about this. Right, gentlemen?'

There was a general nodding of heads.

'We have consensus,' said Archer. And, smiling, he reached once again for the brandy decanter. 'This is what I call a real team.'

'So what do you think?' Mark asked as they drove home.

Abby threw back her head and shouted deliriously. 'I'm floating! God, what a night!'

'You're happy about it, huh?'

'Are you kidding? I'm terrified.'

'Terrified? Of what?'

'That I'll screw up. And blow it all.'

He laughed and gave her knee a squeeze. 'Hey, we've worked with all the other residents, okay? We know we're recruiting the best.'

'And just how much of this was your influence, Dr Hodell?'

'Oh, I put in my two cents' worth. The others just happened to be in complete agreement.'

'Right.'

'It's true. Believe me, Abby, you're our number

one choice. And I think you'd find it a terrific arrangement, too.'

She sat back, smiling. Imagining. Until tonight, she'd had only a fuzzy notion of where she'd be working in three and a half years. Toiling in an HMO, most likely. Private practice was in its dying days; she saw no future in it, at least, not in the city of Boston. And Boston was where she wanted to stay.

Where Mark was.

'I want this so badly,' she said. 'I just hope I don't disappoint you all.'

'Not a chance. The team knows what it wants. We're all together on this.'

She fell silent for a moment. 'Even Aaron Levi?' she asked.

'Aaron? Why wouldn't he be?'

'I don't know. I was talking to his wife tonight. Elaine. I got the feeling Aaron isn't very happy. Did you know he was thinking of leaving?'

'What?' Mark glanced at her in surprise.

'Something about moving to a small town.'

He laughed. 'It'll never happen. Elaine's a Boston girl.'

'It wasn't Elaine. It was Aaron who was thinking about it.'

For a while Mark drove without saying a word. 'You must have misunderstood,' he said at last.

She shrugged. 'Maybe I did.'

'Light, please,' said Abby.

A nurse reached up and adjusted the overhead

lamp, focusing the beam on the patient's chest. The operative site had been drawn on the skin in black marker, two tiny X's connected by a line tracing along the top of the fifth rib. It was a small chest, a small woman. Mary Allen, eighty-four years old and a widow, had been admitted to Bayside a week ago complaining of weight loss and severe headaches. A routine chest X-ray had turned up an alarming find: multiple nodules in both lungs. For six days she'd been probed, scanned, and X-rayed. She'd had a bronchoscope down her throat, needles punched through her chest wall, and still the diagnosis was unclear.

Today they'd know the answer.

Dr Wettig picked up the scalpel and stood with blade poised over the incision site. Abby waited for him to make the cut. He didn't. Instead he looked at Abby, his eyes a hard, metallic blue over the mask.

'How many open lung biopsies have you assisted on, DiMatteo?' he asked.

'Five, I think.'

'You're familiar with this patient's history? Her chest films?'

'Yes, sir.'

Wettig held out the scalpel. 'This one's yours, Doctor.'

Abby looked in surprise at the scalpel glittering in his hand. The General seldom relinquished the blade, even to his upper-level residents.

She took the scalpel, felt the weight of stainless steel settle comfortably in her grasp. With steady hands, she made her incision, stretching the skin taut as she sliced a line along the rib's upper edge. The patient was thin, almost wasted; there was scant subcutaneous fat to obscure the landmarks. Another, slightly deeper incision parted the intercostal muscles.

She was now in the pleural cavity.

She slipped a finger through the incision and could feel the surface of the lung. Soft, spongy. 'Everything all right?' she asked the anesthesiologist.

'Doing fine.'

'Okay, retract,' said Abby.

The ribs were spread apart, widening the incision. The ventilator pumped another burst of air, and a small segment of lung tissue ballooned out of the incision. Abby clamped it, still inflated.

Again she glanced at the anesthesiologist. 'Okay?'

'No problem.'

Abby focused her attention on the exposed segment of lung tissue. It took only a glance to locate one of the nodules. She ran her fingers across it. 'Feels pretty solid,' she said. 'Not good.'

'No surprise,' said Wettig. 'She looked like a chemotherapy special on X-ray. We're just confirming cell type.'

'The headache? Brain metastases?'

Wettig nodded. 'This one's aggressive. Eight months ago she had a normal X-ray. Now she's a cancer farm.'

'She's eighty-four,' said one of the nurses. 'At least she had a long life.'

But what kind of life? wondered Abby as she resected the wedge of lung containing the nodule. Yesterday, she had met Mary Allen for the first time. She had found the woman sitting very quiet and still in her hospital room. The shades had been drawn, the bed cast in semidarkness. It was the headaches, Mary said. *The sun hurts my eyes. Only when I sleep does the pain go away. So many different kinds of pain . . .*

Please, Doctor, couldn't I have a stronger sleeping pill?

Abby completed the resection and sutured the cut edge of lung. Wettig offered no comment. He merely watched her work, his gaze as chilly as ever. The silence was compliment enough; she'd learned long ago that just to escape the General's criticism was a triumph.

At last, the chest closed, the drain tube in place, Abby stripped off her bloodied gloves and deposited them in the bin labeled CONTAMINATED.

'Now comes the hard part,' she said, as the nurses wheeled the patient out of the OR. 'Telling her the bad news.'

'She knows,' said Wettig. 'They always do.'

They followed the squeak of the gurney wheels to Recovery. Four postop patients in various states of consciousness occupied the curtained stalls. Mary Allen, in the last stall, was just beginning to stir. She moved her foot. Moaned. Tried to pull her hand free of the restraint.

With her stethoscope, Abby took a quick listen to the patient's lungs, then said: 'Give her five milligrams of morphine, IV.'

The nurse injected an IV bolus of morphine sulfate. Just enough to dull the pain, yet allow a gentle return to consciousness. Mary's groaning ceased. The tracing on the heart monitor remained steady and regular.

'Postop orders, Dr Wettig?' the nurse asked.

There was a moment's silence. Abby glanced at Wettig, who said, 'Dr DiMatteo's in charge here.' And he left the room.

The nurses looked at each other. Wettig always wrote his own postop orders. This was another vote of confidence for Abby.

She took the chart to the desk and began to write: *Transfer to 5 East, Thoracic Surgery Service. Diagnosis: Postop open lung biopsy for multiple pulmonary nodules. Condition: stable.* She wrote steadily, orders for diet, meds, activity. She reached the line for code status. Automatically she wrote: *Full code.*

Then she looked across the desk at Mary Allen, lying motionless on the gurney. Thought about what it would be like to be eight-four years old and riddled with cancer, the days numbered, each one filled with pain. Would the patient choose a kinder, swifter death? Abby didn't know.

'Dr DiMatteo?' It was a voice over the intercom.

'Yes?' said Abby.

'You had a call from Four East about ten minutes ago. They want you to come by.'

'Neurosurg? Did they say why?'

'Something about a patient named Terrio. They want you to talk to the husband.'

'Karen Terrio's not my patient any longer.'

'I'm just passing the message along, Doctor.'

'Okay, thanks.'

Sighing, Abby rose to her feet and went to Mary Allen's gurney for one last check of the cardiac monitor, the vital signs. The pulse was running a little fast, and the patient was moving, groaning again. Still in pain.

Abby looked at the nurse. 'Another two milligrams of morphine,' she said.

The blip on the EKG monitor traced a slow and steady rhythm.

'Her heart's so strong,' murmured Joe Terrio. 'It doesn't want to give up. She doesn't want to give up.'

He sat at his wife's bedside, his hand clasping hers, his gaze fixed on that green line squiggling across the oscilloscope. He looked bewildered by all the gadgetry in the room. The tubes, the monitors, the suction pump. Bewildered and afraid. He focused every ounce of attention on the EKG monitor, as though, if he could somehow master the secrets of that mysterious box, he could master everything else. He could understand why and how he had come to be sitting at the bedside of the woman he loved, the woman whose heart refused to stop beating.

It was three P.M., sixty-two hours since a drunk driver had slammed into Karen Terrio's car. She was thirty-four years old, HIV negative, cancer free, infection free. She was also brain-dead. In short, she was a living supermarket of healthy donor organs. Heart. Lungs. Kidneys. Pancreas. Liver. Bone. Corneas. Skin. With one terrible harvest, half a dozen different lives could be saved or changed for the better.

Abby pulled up a stool and sat down across from him. She was the only doctor who'd actually spent much time talking with Joe, so she was the one the nurses had called to speak to him now. To convince him to sign the papers and allow his wife to die. She sat quietly with him for a moment. Karen Terrio's body stretched between them, her chest rising and falling at a preselected twenty breaths per minute.

'You're right, Joe,' said Abby. 'Her heart is strong. It could keep going for some time. But not forever. Eventually the body knows. The body understands.'

Joe looked across at her, his eyes red-rimmed with tears and sleeplessness. 'Understands?'

'That the brain is dead. That there's no reason for the heart to keep beating.'

'How would it know?'

'We need our brains. Not just to think and feel, but also to give the rest of our body a purpose. When that purpose is gone, the heart, the lungs, they start to fail.' Abby looked at the ventilator. 'The machine is breathing for her.'

'I know.' Joe rubbed his face with his hands. 'I know, I know. I know . . .'

Abby said nothing. Joe was rocking back and forth in his chair now, his hands in his hair, his throat squeezing out little grunts and whimpers, the closest thing to sobs a man could allow himself. When he raised his head again, clumps of his hair stood up damp and stiff with tears.

He looked up at the monitor again. The one spot in the room he seemed to feel safe to stare at. 'It all seems too soon.'

'It isn't. There's only a certain amount of time before the organs start to go bad. Then they can't be used. And no one is helped by that, Joe.'

He looked at her, across the body of his wife. 'Did you bring the papers?'

'I have them.'

He scarcely looked at the forms. He merely signed his name at the bottom and handed the papers back. An ICU nurse and Abby witnessed the signature. Copies of the form would go into Karen Terrio's record, to the New England Organ Bank, and Bayside's transplant coordinator files. Then the organs would be harvested.

Long after Karen Terrio was buried, bits and pieces of her would go on living. The heart that she'd once felt thudding in her chest when she'd played as a five-year-old, married as a twenty-year-old, and strained at childbirth as a twenty-one-year-old, would go on beating in the chest of a stranger. It was as close as one could come to immortality.

But it was scarcely much comfort to Joseph Terrio, who continued his silent vigil at the bedside of his wife.

* * *

Abby found Vivian Chao undressing in the OR locker room. Vivian had just emerged from four hours of emergency surgery, yet not a single blot of sweat stained the discarded scrub clothes lying on the bench beside her.

Abby said, 'We have consent for the harvest.'

'The papers are signed?' asked Vivian.

'Yes.'

'Good. I'll order the lymphocyte cross match.' Vivian reached for a fresh scrub top. She was dressed only in her bra and underpants, and every rib seemed to stand out on her frail, flat chest. Honorary manhood, thought Abby, is a state of mind, not body. 'How are her vitals?' asked Vivian.

'They're holding steady.'

'Have to keep her blood pressure up. Kidneys perfused. It's not every day a nice pair of AB-positive kidneys comes along.' Vivian pulled on a pair of drawstring trousers and tucked in her shirt. Every movement she made was precise. Elegant.

'Will you be scrubbing in on the harvest?' asked Abby.

'If my patient gets the heart, I will. The harvest is the easy part. It's reattaching the plumbing that gets interesting.' Vivian closed the locker door and snapped the padlock shut. 'You have a minute? I'll introduce you to Josh.'

'Josh?'

'My patient on the teaching service. He's in MICU.'

They left the locker room and headed down the hall toward the elevator. Vivian made up for her short legs by her quick, almost fierce stride. 'You can't judge the success of a heart transplant until you've seen the before *and* the after,' said Vivian. 'So I'm going to show you the before. Maybe it'll make things easier for you.'

'What do you mean?'

'Your woman has a heart but no brain. My boy has a brain and practically no heart.' The elevator door opened. Vivian stepped in. 'Once you get past the tragedy, it all makes sense.'

They rode the elevator in silence.

Of course it makes sense, thought Abby. *It makes perfect sense. Vivian sees it clearly. But I can't seem to get past the image of two little girls standing by their mother's bed. Afraid to touch her . . .*

Vivian led the way to the Medical ICU.

Joshua O'Day was asleep in Bed 4.

'He's sleeping a lot these days,' whispered the nurse, a sweet-faced blonde with HANNAH LOVE, R.N. on her name tag.

'Change in meds?' asked Vivian.

'I think it's depression.' Hannah shook her head and sighed. 'I've been his nurse for weeks. Ever since he was admitted. He's such a terrific kid, you know? Really nice. A little goofy. But lately, all he does is sleep. Or stare at his trophies.' She nodded at the bedside stand, where a display of various awards and ribbons had been lovingly arranged. One ribbon went all the way back to the third grade – an honorable mention for a Cub Scout Pinewood Derby. Abby knew about Pinewood Derbies. Like Joshua O'Day, her brother had been a Cub Scout.

Abby moved to the bedside. The boy looked much younger than she had expected. Seventeen, according to the birthdate on Hannah Love's clipboard. He could have passed for fourteen. A thicket of plastic tubes surrounded his bed, IVs and arterial and Swan-Ganz lines. The last was used to monitor pressures in the right atrium and pulmonary artery. On the screen overhead, Abby could read the right atrial pressure. It was high. The boy's heart was too weak to pump effectively, and blood had backed up in his venous system. Even without the monitor, she could have reached that conclusion by a glance at his neck veins. They were bulging.

'You're looking at Redding High School's baseball star from two years ago,' said Vivian. 'I'm not into the game so I don't really know how to judge his batting average. But his dad seems pretty proud of it.'

'Oh, his dad *is* proud,' said Hannah. 'He was in here the other day with a ball and mitt. I had to kick him out when they started a game of catch.' Hannah laughed. 'The dad's as crazy as the kid!'

'How long has he been sick?' asked Abby.

'He hasn't been to school in a year,' said Vivian. 'The virus hit him about two years ago. Coxsackievirus B. Within six months, he was in congestive heart failure. He's been in the ICU for a

70

month now, just waiting for a heart.' Vivian paused. And smiled. 'Right, Josh?'

The boy's eyes were open. He was looking at them as though through layers of gauze. He blinked a few times, then smiled at Vivian. 'Hey, Dr Chao.'

'I see some new ribbons on display,' said Vivian.

'Oh. Those.' Josh rolled his eyes. 'I don't know where my mom digs those up. She keeps everything, you know. She even has this plastic bag with all my baby teeth. I think it's pretty gross.'

'Josh, I brought someone along to meet you. This is Dr DiMatteo, one of our surgical residents.'

'Hello, Josh,' said Abby.

It seemed to take the boy a moment to fully refocus his gaze. He didn't say anything.

'Is it okay for Dr DiMatteo to examine you?' asked Vivian.

'Why?'

'When you get your new heart, you'll be like that crazy Road Runner on TV. We won't be able to tie you down long enough for an exam.'

Josh smiled. 'You're so full of it.'

Abby moved to the bedside. Already, Josh had pulled up his gown and bared his chest. It was white and hairless, not a teenager's chest but a boy's. She laid her hand over his heart and felt it fluttering like a bird's wings against the cage of ribs. She laid her stethoscope against it and listened to the heartbeat, the whole time aware of the boy's gaze, wary and untrusting. She had seen such looks from children who had been too long in pediatric wards, children who'd learned that every new pair of hands brings a new variety of pain. When she finally straightened and slipped her stethoscope back into her pocket, she saw the look of relief in the boy's face.

'Is that all?' he said.

'That's all.' Abby smoothed down his hospital gown. 'So. Who's your favorite team, Josh?'

'Who else?'

'Ah. Red Sox.'

'My dad taped all their games for me. We used to go to the park together, my dad and me. When I get home, I'm going to watch 'em all. All those tapes. Three straight days of baseball . . .' He took a deep breath of oxygen-infused air and looked up at the ceiling. Softly he said, 'I want to go home, Dr Chao.'

'I know,' said Vivian.

'I want to see my room again. I miss my room.' He swallowed, but he couldn't hold back the sob. 'I want to see my room. That's all. I just want to see my room.'

At once Hannah moved to his side. She gathered the boy into her arms and held him, rocked him. He was fighting not to cry, his fists clenched, his face buried in her hair. 'It's okay,' murmured Hannah. 'Baby, you just go ahead and cry. I'm right here with you. I'm going to stay right here, Josh. As long as you need me. It's okay.' Hannah's gaze met Abby's over the boy's shoulder. The tears on the nurse's face weren't Josh's, but hers.

In silence, Abby and Vivian left the room.

At the MICU nurses' station, Abby watched as Vivian signed in duplicate the order for the lymphocyte cross match between Josh O'Day's and Karen Terrio's blood.

'How soon can he go to surgery?' asked Abby.

'We could be scrubbed and ready to cut by tomorrow morning. The sooner the better. The kid's had three episodes of V. tach in just the last day. With a heart rhythm that unstable, he doesn't have much time.' Vivian swiveled around to face Abby. 'I'd really like that boy to see another Red Sox game. Wouldn't you?'

Vivian's expression was as calm and unreadable as ever. She might be soft as slush inside, thought Abby, but Vivian would never show it.

'Dr Chao?' said the ward clerk.

'Yes?'

'I just called SICU about that lymphocyte cross match. They said they're already running a match against Karen Terrio.'

'Great. For once my intern's on the ball.'

'But Dr Chao, the cross match isn't with Josh O'Day.'

Vivian turned and looked at the clerk. 'What?'

'SICU says they're running it on someone else. Some private patient named Nina Voss.'

'But Josh is critical! He's at the top of the list.'

'All they said was the heart's going to that other patient.'

Vivian shot to her feet. In three quick steps she

was at the telephone, punching in a number. A moment later, Abby heard her say:

'This is Dr Chao. I want to know who ordered that lymphocyte cross match on Karen Terrio.' She listened. Then, frowning, she hung up.

'Did you get the name?' asked Abby.

'Yes.'

'Who ordered it?'

'Mark Hodell.'

Four

Abby and Mark had made reservations that night for Casablanca, a restaurant just down the road from their Cambridge house. Though it was meant to be a celebration, to mark the six-month anniversary of their moving in together, the mood at their table was anything but cheerful.

'All I want to know,' said Abby, 'is who the hell is Nina Voss?'

'I told you, I don't know,' said Mark. 'Now can we drop the subject?'

'The boy's critical. He's coding practically twice a day. He's been on the recipient list for a year. Now an AB-positive heart finally becomes available, and you're bypassing the registry system? Giving the heart to some private patient who's still living at home?'

'We're not *giving* it away, OK? It was a clinical decision.'

'Whose decision was it?'

'Aaron Levi's. He called me this afternoon. Told me that Nina Voss was being admitted tomorrow.

He asked me to order the screening labs on the donor.'

'That's all he told you?'

'Essentially.' Mark reached for the bottle of wine and refilled his glass, sloshing burgundy onto the tablecloth. 'Now can we change the subject?'

She watched him sip the wine. He wasn't looking at her, wasn't meeting her gaze.

'Who is this patient?' she asked. 'How old is she?'

'I don't want to talk about it.'

'You're the one taking her to surgery. You must know how old she is.'

'Forty-six.'

'From out of state?'

'Boston.'

'I heard she was flying in from Rhode Island. That's what the nurses told me.'

'She and her husband live in Newport during the summer.'

'Who's her husband?'

'Some guy named Victor Voss. That's all I know about him, his name.'

She paused. 'How did Voss get his money?'

'Did I say anything about money?'

'A summer home in Newport? Give me a break, Mark.'

He still wouldn't look at her, still wouldn't lift his gaze from that glass of wine. So many times before, she'd looked across a table at him and seen all the things that had first attracted her. The direct gaze. The forty-one years of laugh lines.

The quick smile. But tonight, he wasn't even looking at her.

She said, 'I didn't realize it was so easy to buy a heart.'

'You're jumping to conclusions.'

'Two patients need a heart. One is a poor, uninsured kid on the teaching service. The other has a summer home in Newport. So which one gets the prize? It's pretty obvious.'

He reached again for the wine bottle and poured himself another glass – his third. For a man who prided himself on his temperate lifestyle, he was drinking like a lush. 'Look,' he said. 'I spend all day in the hospital. The last thing I feel like doing is talking about it. So let's just drop the subject.'

They both fell silent. The subject of Karen Terrio's heart was like a blanket snuffing out the sparks of any other conversation. *Maybe we've already said everything there is to say to each other*, she thought. Maybe they'd reached that dismal phase of a relationship when their life stories had been told and the time had come to dredge up new material. *We've been together only six months, and already the silences have started.*

She said: 'That boy makes me think of Pete. Pete was a Red Sox fan.'

'Who?'

'My brother.'

Mark said nothing. He sat with shoulders hunched in obvious discomfort. He'd never been at ease with the subject of Pete. But then, death

77

was not a comfortable subject for doctors. Every day we play a game of tag with that word, she thought. We say 'expired' or 'could not resuscitate' or 'terminal event.' But we seldom use that word: *died*.

'He was crazy about the Red Sox,' she said. 'He had all these baseball cards. He'd save his lunch money to buy them. And then he'd spend a fortune on little plastic covers to keep them safe. A five-cent cover for a one-cent piece of card-board. I guess that's the logic of a ten-year-old for you.'

Mark took a sip of wine. He sat wrapped in his discomfort, insulated against her attempts at conversation.

The celebration dinner was a bust. They ate with scarcely another word between them.

Back in the house, Mark retreated behind his stack of surgical journals. That was the way he always reacted to their disagreements – withdrawal. Damn it, *she* didn't mind a good, healthy fight. The DiMatteo family, with its three head-strong daughters and little Pete, had weathered more than its share of adolescent conflicts and sibling rivalries, but their love for each other had never been in doubt. Oh yes, Abby could deal with a healthy argument.

It was silence she couldn't stand.

In frustration she went into the kitchen and scrubbed the sink. *I'm turning into my mother*, she thought in disgust. *I get angry and what do I do? I clean the kitchen*. She wiped the stovetop, then dismantled the burners and scrubbed those as well. She had the whole damn kitchen sparkling by the time she heard Mark finally head upstairs to the bedroom.

She followed him.

In darkness they lay side by side, not touching. His silence had rubbed off on her and she could think of no way to break through it without seeming like the needy one, the weak one. But she couldn't stand it any longer.

'I hate it when you do this,' she said.

'Please, Abby. I'm tired.'

'So am I. We're both tired. It seems like we're always tired. But I can't go to sleep this way. And neither can you.'

'All right. What do you want me to say?'

'Anything! I just want you to keep talking to me.'

'I don't see the point of talking things to death.'

'There are things I *need* to talk about.'

'Fine. I'm listening.'

'But you're doing it through a wall. I feel like I'm in confession. Talking through a grate to some guy I can't see.' She sighed and stared up at the darkness. She had the sudden, dizzying sensation that she was floating free, unattached. Unconnected. 'The boy's in MICU,' she said. 'He's only seventeen.'

Mark said nothing.

'He reminds me so much of my brother. Pete was a lot younger. But there's this sort of fake courage that all boys have. That Pete had.'

79

'It's not my decision alone,' he said. 'There are others involved. The whole transplant team. Aaron Levi, Bill Archer. Even Jeremiah Parr.'

'Why the hospital president?'

'Parr wants our statistics to look good. And all the research shows that outpatients are more likely to survive a transplant.'

'Without a transplant, Josh O'Day's not going to survive at all.'

'I know it's a tragedy. But that's life.'

She lay very still, stunned by his matter-of-fact tone.

He reached out to touch her hand. She pulled away.

'You could change their minds,' she said. 'You could talk them into—'

'It's too late. The team's decided.'

'What *is* this team, anyway? God?'

There was a long silence. Quietly, Mark said: 'Be careful what you say, Abby.'

'You mean about the holy team?'

'The other night, at Archer's, we all meant what we said. In fact, Archer told me later that you're the best fellowship material he's seen in three years. But Archer's careful about which people he recruits, and I don't blame him. We need people who'll work with us. Not against us.'

'Even if I don't agree with the rest of you?'

'It's part of being on a team, Abby. We all have our points of view. But we make the decisions together. And we stick by them.' He reached out again to touch her hand. This time she didn't pull

80

away. Neither did she return his squeeze. 'Come on, Abby,' he said softly. 'There are residents out there who'd kill for a transplant fellowship at Bayside. Here you're practically handed one on a platter. It *is* what you want, isn't it?'

'Of course it's what I want. It scares me how much I want it. The crazy thing is, I never knew I did, not until Archer raised the possibility . . .' She took a deep breath, released it in a long sigh. 'I hate the way I keep wanting more. Always wanting more. There's something that keeps pulling me and pulling me. First it was getting into college, then med school. Then a surgery residency. And now, it's this fellowship. It's moved so far from where I started. When I just wanted to be a doctor . . .'

'It's not enough anymore. Is it?'

'No. I wish it was. But it isn't.'

'Then don't blow it, Abby. Please. For both our sakes.'

'You make it sound as if *you're* the one with everything to lose.'

'I'm the one who suggested your name. I told them you're the best choice they could make.' He looked at her. 'I still think so.'

For a moment they lay without talking, only their hands in contact. Then he reached over and caressed her hip. Not a real embrace, but an attempt at one.

It was enough. She let him take her into his arms.

* * *

81

The simultaneous squeal of half a dozen pocket pagers was followed by the curt announcement over the hospital speaker system:

Code Blue, MICU, Code Blue, MICU.

Abby joined the other surgical residents in a dash for the stairway. By the time she'd jogged into the MICU, a crowd of medical personnel was already thronging the area. A glance told her there were more than enough people here to deal with a Code Blue. Most of the residents were starting to drift out of the room. Abby, too, would have left.

Had she not seen that the code was in Bed 4. Joshua O'Day's cubicle.

She pushed into the knot of white coats and scrub suits. At their center lay Joshua O'Day, his frail body fully exposed to the glare of overhead lights. Hannah Love was administering chest compressions, her blond hair whipping forward with every thrust. Another nurse was frantically rummaging through the crash cart drawers, pulling out drug vials and syringes and passing them to the medical residents. Abby glanced up at the cardiac monitor screen.

Ventricular fibrillation. The pattern of a dying heart.

'Seven and a half ET tube!' a voice yelled.

Only then did Abby notice Vivian Chao crouched behind Joshua's head. Vivian already had the laryngoscope ready.

The crash cart nurse ripped the plastic cover off an ET tube and passed it to Vivian.

'Keep bagging him!' Vivian ordered.

The respiratory tech, holding an anesthesia mask to Josh's face, continued squeezing the balloonlike reservoir a few times, manually pumping oxygen into the boy's lungs.

'OK,' said Vivian. 'Let's intubate.'

The tech pulled the mask away. Within seconds, Vivian had the ET tube in place, the oxygen connected.

'Lidocaine's in,' said a nurse.

The medical resident glanced up at the monitor. 'Shit. Still in V. fib. Let's have the paddles again. Two hundred joules.' A nurse handed him the defibrillator paddles. He slapped them onto the chest. The placement was already marked by conductive gel pads: one paddle near the sternum, the other outside the nipple. 'Everyone back.'

The burst of electricity shot through Joshua O'Day's body, jolting every muscle into a simultaneous spasm. He gave a grotesque jerk and then lay still.

Everyone's gaze shot to the monitor screen.

'Still in V. fib,' someone said. 'Bretylium, two-fifty.'

Hannah automatically resumed chest compressions. She was flushed, sweating, her expression numb with fear.

'I can take over,' Abby offered.

Nodding, Hannah stepped aside.

Abby climbed onto the footstool and positioned her hands on Joshua's chest, her palm on the lower third of the sternum. His chest felt thin and brittle, as though it would crack under a few vigorous thrusts; she was almost afraid to lean against it.

She began to pump. It was a task that required no mental exertion. Just that repetitive motion of lean forward, release, lean forward, release. The alpha rhythm of CPR. She was a participant in the chaos yet she was apart from it, her mind pulling back, withdrawing. She could not bring herself to look at the boy's face, to watch as Vivian taped the ET tube in place. She could only focus on his chest, on that point of contact between his sternum and her clasped hands. Sternums were anonymous. This could be anyone's chest. An old man's. A stranger's. *Lean, release.* She concentrated. *Lean, release.*

'Everyone back again!' someone yelled.

Abby pulled away. Another jolt of the paddles, another grotesque spasm.

Ventricular fibrillation. The heart signaling that it cannot hold on.

Abby crossed her hands and placed them again on the boy's chest. Lean, release. *Come back, Joshua,* her hands were saying to him. *Come back to us.*

A new voice joined in the bedlam. 'Let's try a bolus of calcium chloride. A hundred milligrams,' said Aaron Levi. He was standing near the foot-board, his gaze fixed on the monitor.

'But he's on digoxin,' said the medical resident.

'At this point, we've got nothing to lose.'

A nurse filled a syringe and handed it to the resident. 'One hundred milligrams calcium chloride.'

The bolus was injected into the IV line. A penny toss into the chemical wishing well.

'OK, try the paddles again,' said Aaron. 'Four hundred joules this time.'

'Everyone back!'

Abby pulled away. The boy's limbs jerked, fell still.

'Again,' said Aaron.

Another jolt. The tracing on the monitor shot straight up. As it settled back to baseline, there was a single blip – the jagged peak of a QRS complex. At once it deteriorated back to V. fib.

'One more time!' said Aaron.

The paddles were slapped on the chest. The body thrashed under the shock of 400 joules. There was a sudden hush as everyone's gaze shot to the monitor.

A QRS blipped across. Then another. And another.

'We're in sinus,' said Aaron.

'I'm getting a pulse!' said a nurse. 'I feel a pulse!'

'BP seventy over forty . . . up to ninety over fifty . . .'

A collective sigh seemed to wash through the room. At the foot of the bed, Hannah Love was crying unashamedly. *Welcome back, Josh*, Abby thought, her gaze blurred with tears.

Gradually the other residents filed out, but Abby couldn't bring herself to leave; she felt too drained to move on. In silence she helped the nurses gather up the used syringes and vials, all the bits of glass and plastic that are the aftermath of every Code Blue. Working beside her, Hannah Love sniffled as she wiped away the electrode paste, her washcloth stroking lovingly across Josh's chest.

It was Vivian who broke the silence.

'He could be getting that heart right now,' she said. Vivian was standing by the tray table of Joshua's trophies. She picked up the Cub Scout ribbon. Pinewood Derby, third grade. 'He could've gone to the OR this morning. Had the transplant by ten o'clock. If we lose him, it's your fault, Aaron.' Vivian looked at Aaron Levi, whose pen had frozen in the midst of signing the code sheet.

'Dr Chao,' said Aaron quietly. 'Would you care to talk about this in private?'

'I don't care who's listening! The match is perfect. I wanted Josh on the table this morning. But you wouldn't give me a decision. You just delayed. And delayed. And fucking *delayed*.' She took a deep breath and looked down at the award ribbon she was holding. 'I don't know what the hell you think you're doing. Any of you.'

'Until you calm down, I'm not going to discuss this with you,' said Aaron. He turned and walked out.

'You are. You are going to,' said Vivian, following him out of the cubicle.

Through the open doorway, Abby could hear Vivian's pursuit of Aaron across the MICU. Her angry questions. Her demands for an explanation.

Abby bent down and picked up the Pinewood

Derby ribbon that Vivian had dropped on the floor. It was green – not a winner's ribbon, but merely an honorable mention for the hours spent laboring over a small block of wood, sanding it, painting it, greasing the axles, pounding in the lead fishing weights to make it tumble faster. All that effort must be rewarded. Little boys need their tender egos soothed.

Vivian came back into the cubicle. She was white-faced, silent. She stood at the foot of Josh's bed, staring down at the boy, watching his chest rise and fall with each whoosh of the ventilator.

'I'm transferring him,' she said.

'What?' Abby looked at her in disbelief. 'Where?'

'Massachusetts General. Transplant Service. Get Josh ready for the ambulance. I'm going to make the calls.'

The two nurses didn't move. They were staring at Vivian.

Hannah protested, 'He's in no condition to be moved.'

'If he stays here, we're going to lose him,' said Vivian. '*We are going to lose him.* Are you willing to let that happen?'

Hannah looked down at the frail chest rising and falling beneath her washcloth. 'No,' she said. 'No. I want him to live.'

'Ivan Tarasoff was my professor at Harvard Med,' said Vivian. 'He's head of their transplant team. If our team won't do it, then Tarasoff will.'

'Even if Josh survives the transfer,' said Abby, 'he still needs a donor heart.'

'Then we'll have to get him one.' Vivian looked straight at Abby. 'Karen Terrio's.'

That's when Abby understood exactly what she had to do. She nodded. 'I'll talk to Joe Terrio now.'

'It has to be in writing. Make sure he signs it.'

'What about the harvest? We can't use the Bayside team.'

'Tarasoff likes to send his own man for the harvest. We'll assist. We'll even deliver to his doorstep. There can't be any delay. We have to do it fast, before anyone here can stop us.'

'Wait a minute,' said the other nurse. 'You can't authorize a transfer to Mass Gen.'

'Yes I can,' said Vivian. 'Josh O'Day is on teaching service. Which means the chief residents are in charge. I'll take full responsibility. Just follow my orders and get him ready for ambulance transfer.'

'Absolutely, Dr Chao,' said Hannah. 'In fact, I'll ride with him.'

'You do that.' Vivian looked at Abby. 'Okay, DiMatteo,' she snapped. 'Go get us a heart.'

Ninety minutes later, Abby was scrubbing in. She completed her final rinse and, elbows bent, backed through the swinging door into OR 3.

The donor lay on the table, her pale body washed in fluorescent light. A nurse-anesthetist was changing IV bottles. No need for anesthesia on this patient; Karen Terrio could feel no pain.

Vivian, gowned and gloved, stood at one side of

the table. Dr Lim, a kidney surgeon, stood on the other. Abby had worked with Lim on previous cases. A man of few words, he was known for his swift, silent work.

'Signed and sealed?' asked Vivian.

'In triplicate. It's in the chart.' She herself had typed up the directed-donation consent, a statement specifying that Karen Terrio's heart be given to Josh O'Day, age seventeen.

It was the boy's age that had swayed Joe Terrio. He'd been sitting at his wife's bedside, holding her hand, and had listened in silence as Abby told him about a seventeen-year-old boy who loved baseball. Without saying a word, Joe had signed the paper.

And then he'd kissed his wife goodbye.

Abby was helped into a sterile gown and size six and a half gloves. 'Who's doing the harvest?' she asked.

'Dr Frobisher, from Tarasoff's team. I've worked with him before,' said Vivian. 'He's on his way now.'

'Any word about Josh?'

'Tarasoff called ten minutes ago. They've got his blood typed and crossed and an OR cleared. They're standing by.' She looked down impatiently at Karen Terrio. 'Jesus, I could do the heart myself. Where the hell's Frobisher?'

They waited. Ten minutes, fifteen. The intercom buzzed with a call from Tarasoff at Mass Gen. Was the harvest proceeding?

'Not yet,' said Vivian. 'Any minute now.'

Five minutes later, the OR door swung open and Frobisher pushed in, his hefty arms dripping water. 'Size nine gloves,' he snapped.

At once the atmosphere in the room stretched taut. No one except Vivian had ever worked with Frobisher before, and his fierce expression did not invite any conversation. With silent efficiency, the nurses helped him gown and glove.

He stepped to the table and critically eyed the prepped operative site. 'Causing trouble again, Dr Chao?' he said.

'As usual,' said Vivian. She gestured to the others standing at the table. 'Dr Lim will do the kidneys. Dr DiMatteo and I will assist as needed.'

'History on this patient?'

'Head injury. Brain-dead, donor forms all signed. She's thirty-four, previously healthy, and her blood's been screened.'

He picked up a scalpel and paused over the chest. 'Anything else I should know?'

'Not a thing. NEOB confirms it's a perfect match. Trust me.'

'I hate it when people tell me that,' muttered Frobisher. 'Okay, let's take a quick look at our heart, make sure it's in good shape. Then we'll move aside and let Dr Lim do his thing first.' He touched the scalpel blade to Karen Terrio's chest. In one swift slice, he cut straight down the center, exposing the breastbone. 'Sternal saw.'

The scrub nurse handed him the electric saw. Abby took hold of the retractor. As Frobisher cut through the sternum, Abby couldn't help turning away. She felt vaguely nauseated by the whine of the blade, the smell of bone dust, neither of which seemed to bother Frobisher, whose hands moved with swift skill. In moments he was in the chest cavity, his scalpel poised over the pericardial sac.

Cutting through the sternum had seemed an act of brute force. What lay ahead was a far more delicate task. He slit open the membrane.

At his first glance at the beating heart, he gave a soft murmur of satisfaction. Glancing across at Vivian, he asked: 'Opinion, Dr Chao?'

With almost reverential silence, Vivian reached deep into the chest cavity. She seemed to caress the heart, her fingers stroking the walls, tracing the course of each coronary artery. The organ pulsed vigorously in her hands. 'It's beautiful,' she said softly. Eyes shining, she looked across at Abby. 'It's just the heart for Josh.'

The intercom buzzed. A nurse's voice said: 'Dr Tarasoff's on the line.'

'Tell him the heart looks fine,' said Frobisher. 'We're just starting the kidney harvest.'

'He wants to talk to one of the doctors. He says it's extremely urgent.'

Vivian glanced at Abby. 'Go ahead and break scrub. Take the call.'

Abby peeled off her gloves and went to pick up the wall phone. 'Hello, Dr Tarasoff? This is Abby DiMatteo, one of the residents. The heart looks great. We should be at your doorstep in an hour and a half.'

'That may not be soon enough,' answered Tarasoff. Over the line, Abby could hear a lot of background noise: a rapid-fire exchange of voices, the clank of metal instruments. Tarasoff himself sounded tense, distracted. She heard him turn away, talk to someone else. Then he was back on the line. 'The boy's coded twice in the last ten minutes. Right now we've got him back in sinus rhythm. But we can't wait any longer. Either we get him on the bypass machine now or we lose him. We may lose him in any event.' Again he turned from the receiver, this time to listen to someone. When he came back on line, it was only to say: 'We're going to cut. Just get here, okay?'

Abby hung up and said to Vivian: 'They're putting Josh on bypass. He's coded twice. They need that heart now.'

'It'll take me an hour to free up the kidneys,' said Dr Lim.

'Screw the kidneys,' snapped Vivian. 'We go straight for the heart.'

'But—'

'She's right,' said Frobisher. He called to the nurse: 'Iced saline! Get the Igloo ready. And someone better call an ambulance for transport.'

'Shall I scrub in again?' asked Abby.

'No.' Vivian reached for the retractor. 'We'll be done in a few minutes. We need you for a delivery.'

'What about my patients?'

'I'll cover for you. Leave your beeper at the OR desk.'

One nurse began to pack an Igloo cooler with ice. Another was arranging buckets of cold saline next to the operating table. Frobisher didn't need to issue any more orders; these were cardiac nurses. They knew exactly what to do.

Already, Frobisher's scalpel was moving swiftly, freeing up the heart in preparatory dissection. The organ was still pumping, each beat squeezing oxygen-rich blood into the arteries. Now it was time to stop it, time to shut down the last vestiges of life in Karen Terrio.

Frobisher injected five hundred cc's of a high-potassium solution into the aortic root. The heart beat once. Twice.

And it stopped. It was now flaccid, its muscles paralyzed by the sudden infusion of potassium. Abby couldn't help glancing at the monitor. There was no EKG activity. Karen Terrio was finally, and clinically, dead.

A nurse poured a bucket of the iced solution into the chest cavity, quickly chilling the heart. Then Frobisher got to work, ligating, cutting.

Moments later, he lifted the heart out of the chest and slid it gently into a basin. Blood swirled in the cold saline. A nurse stepped forward, holding open a plastic bag. Frobisher gave the heart a few more swishes in the liquid, then eased the rinsed organ into the bag. More iced saline was poured in. The heart was double-bagged and placed in the Igloo.

'It's yours, DiMatteo,' said Frobisher. 'You ride in the ambulance. I'll follow in my car.'

Abby picked up the Igloo. She was already pushing out the OR doors when she heard Vivian's voice calling after her:

'Don't drop it.'

Five

I'm holding Josh O'Day's life in my hands, thought Abby as she clutched the Igloo in her lap. Boston traffic, heavy as always at the noon hour, parted like magic before the flashing ambulance lights. Abby had never before ridden in an ambulance. Under other circumstances, she might have enjoyed this ride, the exhilarating experience of watching Boston drivers – the rudest in the world – finally yield the right of way. But at the moment, she was too focused on the cargo she held in her lap, too aware that every second that ticked by was another second drained from the life of Josh O'Day.

'Got yourself a live one in there, huh Doc?' said the ambulance driver. G. Furillo, according to his name tag.

'A heart,' said Abby. 'A nice one.'

'So who's it going to?'

'Seventeen-year-old boy.'

Furillo maneuvered the ambulance around a row of stalled traffic, his loose-jointed arms steering with almost casual grace. 'I've done kidney runs, from the airport. But I have to tell you, this is my first heart.'

'Mine too,' said Abby.

'It stays good – what, five hours?'

'About that.'

Furillo glanced at her and grinned. 'Relax, I'll get you there with four and a half hours to spare.'

'It's not the heart I'm worried about. It's the kid. Last I heard, he wasn't doing so well.'

Furillo focused his gaze more intently on the traffic. 'We're almost there. Five minutes, tops.'

A voice crackled over the radio. 'Unit Twenty-three, this is Bayside. Unit Twenty-three, this is Bayside.'

Furillo picked up the microphone. 'Twenty-three, Furillo.'

'Twenty-three, please return to Bayside ER.'

'Impossible. I'm transporting live organ to Mass Gen. Do you copy? I'm en route to Mass Gen.'

'Twenty-three, your instructions are to return to Bayside immediately.'

'Bayside, try another unit, okay? We have live organ on board—'

'This order is specific for Unit Twenty-three. Return immediately.'

'Who's ordering this?'

'Comes direct from Dr Aaron Levi. Do not proceed to Mass Gen. Do you copy?'

Furillo glanced at Abby. 'What the hell's this all about?'

They found out, thought Abby. *Oh God,*

96

they found out. And they're trying to stop us . . .

She looked down at the Igloo containing Karen Terrio's heart. She thought about all the months and years of living that should lie ahead for a boy of seventeen.

She said, 'Don't turn around. Keep going.'

'What?'

'I said, *keep going.*'

'But they're ordering me—'

'Unit Twenty-three, this is Bayside,' the radio cut in. 'Please respond.'

'Just get me to Mass Gen!' said Abby. '*Do it.*'

Furillo glanced at the radio. 'Jesus H.,' he said. 'I don't know—'

'Okay, then let me off!' ordered Abby. 'I'll walk the rest of the way!'

The radio said: 'Unit Twenty-three, this is Bayside. Please respond immediately.'

'Oh, fuck you,' Furillo muttered to the radio.

And he stepped on the gas.

A nurse in green scrubs was waiting at the ambulance dock. As Abby stepped out carrying the Igloo, the nurse snapped: 'From Bayside?'

'I have the heart.'

'Follow me.'

Abby had time for only a last wave of thanks to Furillo, then she was following the nurse through the ER. Moving at a near-jog, Abby caught a fast-forward view of corridors and busy hallways. They stepped into an elevator, and the nurse inserted the emergency key.

'How's the boy doing?' asked Abby.

'He's on bypass. We couldn't wait.'

'He coded again?'

'He doesn't *stop* coding.' The nurse glanced at the Igloo. 'That's his last chance you've got there.'

They stepped off the elevator, made another quick jog through a set of automatic doors, into the surgery wing.

'Here. I'll take the heart,' said the nurse.

Through the suite window, Abby saw a dozen masked faces turn to look as the container was passed through the door to a circulating nurse. The Igloo was immediately opened, the heart lifted from its bed of ice.

'If you put on fresh scrubs, you can go in,' said a nurse. 'Women's locker room's down the hall.'

'Thanks. I think I will.'

By the time Abby had donned new greens, cap, and shoe covers, the team in the OR had already removed Josh O'Day's diseased heart. Abby slipped in among the throng of personnel, but found she couldn't see a thing over all those shoulders. She could hear the surgeons' conversation, though. It was relaxed, even congenial. All ORs looked alike, the same stainless steel, the same blue-green drapes and bright lights. What varied was the atmosphere for the people working in that room, and the atmosphere was determined by the senior surgeon's personality.

Judging by the easy conversation, Ivan Tarasoff was a comfortable surgeon to work with.

Abby eased around to the head of the table and stood beside the anesthesiologist. Overhead, the cardiac monitor showed a flat line. There was no heart beating in Josh's chest; the bypass machine was doing all the work. His eyelids had been taped shut to protect the corneas from drying, and his hair was covered by a paper cap. One dark tendril had escaped, curling over his forehead. *Still alive*, she thought. *You can make it, kid.*

The anesthesiologist glanced at Abby. 'You from Bayside?' he whispered.

'I'm the courier. How's it going so far?'

'Touch and go for a while. But we're over the worst of it. Tarasoff's fast. He's already on the aorta.' He nodded toward the chief surgeon.

Ivan Tarasoff, with his snowy eyebrows and mild gaze, was the image of everyone's favorite grandfather. His requests for a fresh suture needle, for more suction, were spoken in the same gentle tone with which one might ask for another cup of tea, please. No showmanship, no high-flying ego, just a quiet technician laboring at his job.

Abby looked up again at the monitor. Still a flat line.

Still no sign of life.

Josh O'Day's parents were crying in the waiting room, sobs mingled with laughter. Smiles all around. It was six P.M., and their ordeal was finally over.

'The new heart's working just fine,' said Dr Tarasoff. 'In fact, it started beating before we expected it to. It's a good strong heart. It should last Josh for a lifetime.'

'We didn't expect this,' said Mr O'Day. 'All we heard was that they moved him here. That there was some kind of emergency. We thought – we thought—' He turned away, wrapped his arms around his wife. They clung together, not speaking. Not able to speak.

A nurse said, gently, 'Mr and Mrs O'Day? If you'd like to see Josh, he's starting to wake up.'

A smiling Tarasoff watched as the O'Days were led toward the Recovery Room. Then he turned and looked at Abby, his blue eyes glistening behind the wire-rim glasses. 'That's why we do it,' he said softly. 'For moments like that.'

'It was close,' said Abby.

'Too damn close.' He shook his head. 'And I'm getting too damn old for this excitement.'

They went into the surgeons' lounge, where he poured them both cups of coffee. With his cap off, his gray hair in disarray, he looked more the part of the rumpled professor than the renowned thoracic surgeon. He handed Abby a cup. 'Tell Vivian to give me a little more warning next time,' he said. 'I get one phone call from her, and suddenly this kid's on our doorstep. *I'm* the one who almost coded.'

'Vivian knew what she was doing. Sending the kid to you.'

He laughed. 'Vivian Chao always knows what she's doing. She was like that as a medical student.'

'She's a great chief resident.'

'You're in the Bayside surgery program?'

100

Abby nodded and sipped the hot coffee. 'Second year.'

'Good. Not enough women in the field. Too many macho blades. All they want to do is cut.'

'That doesn't sound like a surgeon talking.'

Tarasoff glanced at the other doctors gathered near the coffee pot. 'A little blasphemy,' he whispered, 'is a healthy thing.'

Abby drained her coffee and glanced at the time. 'I've got to get back to Bayside. I probably shouldn't have stayed for the surgery. But I'm glad I did.' She smiled at him. 'Thanks, Dr Tarasoff. For saving the boy's life.'

He shook her hand. 'I'm just the plumber, Dr DiMatteo,' he said. 'You brought the vital part.'

It was after seven when the taxi delivered Abby to Bayside's lobby entrance. As she walked in the door, the first thing she heard was her name being paged on the overhead. She picked up the in-house phone.

'This is DiMatteo,' she said.

'Doctor, we've been paging you for hours,' said the operator.

'Vivian Chao was supposed to cover for me. She's carrying my beeper.'

'We have your beeper here at the operator's desk. Mr Parr's the one who's been paging you.'

'Jeremiah Parr?'

'His extension is five-six-six. Administration.'

'It's seven o'clock. Is he still there?'

'He was there five minutes ago.'

Abby hung up, her stomach fluttering with a sense of alarm. Jeremiah Parr, the hospital president, was an administrator, not a physician. She'd spoken to him only once before, at the annual welcoming picnic for new house staff. They'd shaken hands, exchanged a few pleasantries, and then Parr had moved on to greet the other residents. That brief encounter had left her with a vivid impression of a man who was unflappable. And he wore great suits.

She'd seen him since the picnic, of course. They'd smile and nod in recognition whenever they met in elevators or passed in hallways, but she doubted he remembered her name. Now he was paging her at seven o'clock in the evening.

This can't be good, she thought. *This can't be good at all.*

She picked up the phone and dialed Vivian's house. Before she spoke to Parr, she had to know what was going on. Vivian would know.

There was no answer.

Abby hung up, her sense of alarm more acute than ever. *Time to face the consequences. We made a decision; we saved a boy's life. How can they fault us for that?*

Heart thudding, she rode the elevator to the second floor.

The Administration wing was only dimly lit by a single row of fluorescent ceiling panels. Abby walked beneath the strip of light, her footsteps noiseless on the carpet. The offices on either side of her were dark, the secretaries' desks deserted.

But at the far end of the hall, light was shining under a closed door. Someone was inside the conference room.

She went to the door and knocked.

It swung open. Jeremiah Parr stood gazing at her, his backlit face unreadable. Behind him, seated at the conference table, were half a dozen men. She glimpsed Bill Archer, Mark, and Mohandas. The transplant team.

'Dr DiMatteo,' said Parr.

'I'm sorry, I didn't know you were trying to reach me,' said Abby. 'I was out of the hospital.'

'We know where you were.' Parr stepped out of the room. Mark came out right behind him, both men confronting Abby in the dim hallway. They'd left the door ajar and she saw Archer rise from his chair and shut the door against her gaze.

'Come into my office,' said Parr. The instant they stepped inside, he slammed the door and said, 'Do you understand the damage you've done? Do you have any idea?'

Abby looked at Mark, but his face told her nothing. That's what scared her most: that she could not see past the mask, to the man she loved.

'Josh O'Day's alive,' she said. 'The transplant saved his life. I can't consider that any kind of mistake.'

'The mistake lies in *how* it was done,' said Parr.

'We were standing over his bed. Watching him die. A boy that young shouldn't have to—'

'Abby,' said Mark. 'We're not questioning your

instincts. They were good, of course they were good.'

'What's this crap about instincts, Hodell?' snapped Parr. 'They stole a goddamn heart! They knew what they were doing, and they didn't care who they dragged into it! Nurses. Ambulance drivers. Even Dr Lim got suckered in!'

'Following the orders of her chief resident is exactly what Abby was supposed to do. And that's all she did. Obey orders.'

'There have to be repercussions. Firing the chief resident isn't enough.'

Fired? Vivian? Abby looked at Mark for confirmation.

'Vivian admitted everything,' Mark said. 'She admits that she coerced you and the nurses to go along with her.'

'I hardly think Dr DiMatteo is so easily coerced,' said Parr.

'What about Lim?' said Mark. 'He was in the OR too. Are you going to kick him off the staff?'

'Lim had no idea what was going on,' said Parr. 'He was just there to harvest the kidneys. All he knew was that Mass Gen had a recipient on the table. And there was a directed-donation form in the chart.' Parr turned to Abby. 'Drawn up and witnessed by *you*.'

'Joe Terrio signed it willingly,' said Abby. 'He agreed the heart should go to the boy.'

'Which means no one can be accused of organ theft,' Mark pointed out. 'It was perfectly legal, Parr. Vivian knew exactly which strings to pull and she pulled them. Including Abby's.'

Abby started to speak, to defend Vivian, but then she saw the cautionary look in Mark's eyes. *Careful. Don't dig yourself a grave.*

'We have a patient who came in for a heart. And now we have no heart to give her. What the hell am I supposed to tell her husband? "Sorry, Mr Voss, but the heart got *misplaced*?"' Parr turned to Abby, his face rigid with anger. 'You are just a resident, Dr DiMatteo. You took a decision into your own hands, a decision that wasn't yours to make. Voss has already found out about it. Now Bayside's going to have to pay for it. Big time.'

'Come on, Parr,' said Mark. 'It hasn't reached that point.'

'You think Victor Voss *won't* call his lawyers?'

'On what basis? There's a directed-donation consent. The heart *had* to go to the boy.'

'Only because *she* coerced the husband into signing!' said Parr, pointing angrily at Abby.

'All I did was tell him about Josh O'Day,' said Abby. 'I told him the boy was only seventeen—'

'That alone is enough to get you fired,' said Parr. He glanced at his watch. 'As of seven-thirty – that's right now – you're out of the residency program.'

Abby stared at him in shock. She started to protest, but found her throat had closed down, strangling the words.

'You can't do that,' said Mark.

'Why not?' said Parr.

'For one thing, it's a decision for the program

director. Knowing the General, I don't think he'll take to having his authority usurped. For another thing, our surgical house staff is already stretched thin. We lose Abby, that means thoracic service rotates call every other night. They'll get tired, Parr. They'll make mistakes. If you want lawyers on your doorstep, *that's* how to do it.' He glanced at Abby. 'You're on call tomorrow night, aren't you?'

She nodded.

'So what do we do now, Parr?' said Mark. 'You know of some other second-year resident who can just step right in and take her place?'

Jeremiah Parr glared at Mark. 'This is temporary. Believe me, this is only temporary.' He turned to Abby. 'You'll hear more about this tomorrow. Now get out of here.'

On unsteady legs, Abby somehow managed to walk out of Parr's office. She felt too numb to think. She made it halfway down the hallway and stopped. Felt the numbness give way to tears. She would have broken down and cried right then and there, had it not been for Mark, who came up beside her.

'Abby.' He turned her around to face him. 'It's been a battlefield here all afternoon. What the hell did you think you were doing today?'

'I was saving a boy's life. That's what I thought I was doing!' Her voice cracked, shattered into sobs. 'We saved him, Mark. It's exactly what we *should* have done. I wasn't following orders. I was following my own instincts. *Mine.*' She made an angry swipe at her tears. 'If Parr wants to get back at me, then let him. I'll present the facts to any ethics committee. A seventeen-year-old boy versus some rich man's wife. I'll lay it all out, Mark. Maybe I'll still get fired. But I'll go down kicking and screaming.' She turned and continued down the hall.

'There's another way. An easier way.'

'I can't think of one.'

'Listen to me.' Again he caught her arm. 'Let Vivian take the fall! She'll do it anyway.'

'I did more than just follow her orders.'

'Abby, take a gift when it's offered! Vivian accepted the blame. She did it to protect you and the nurses. Leave it at that.'

'And what happens to her?'

'She's already resigned. Peter Dayne's taking over as chief resident.'

'And where does Vivian go?'

'That's her concern, not Bayside's.'

'She did exactly what she should have done. She saved her patient's life. You don't fire someone for that!'

'She violated the number one rule here. And that's play with the team. This hospital can't afford loose cannons like Vivian Chao. A doctor's either with us or against us.' He paused. 'Where does that put you?'

'I don't know.' She shook her head. Felt the tears beginning to fall again. 'I don't know anymore.'

'Consider your options, Abby. Or your lack of

them. Vivian's finished her five years of residency. She's already board-eligible. She could find a job, open a surgical practice. But all you've got is an internship. You get fired now, you'll never be a surgeon. What're you going to do? Spend the rest of your life doing insurance physicals? Is that what you want?'

'No.' She took a breath and let it out in a rush of despair. 'No.'

'What the hell *do* you want?'

'I know exactly what I want!' She wiped her face with a furious swipe of her hand. Took another deep breath. 'I knew it today. This afternoon. When I watched Tarasoff in the OR. I saw him pick up the donor heart and it's limp, like a handful of dead meat. And there's the boy on the table. He connects the two and the heart starts beating. And suddenly there's life again . . .' She paused, swallowing back another surge of tears. 'That's when I knew what I wanted. I want to do what Tarasoff does.' She looked at Mark. 'Graft a piece of life onto kids like Josh O'Day.'

Mark nodded. 'Then you have to make it happen. Abby, we can still make this work. Your job. The fellowship. Everything.'

'I don't see how.'

'I'm the one who pushed your name for the transplant team. You're still my number one choice. I can talk to Archer and the others. If we all stick by you, Parr will have to back down.'

'That's a big if.'

'You can help make it happen. First, let Vivian

take the blame. She was chief resident. She made a bad judgment call.'

'But she didn't!'

'You saw only half the picture. You didn't see the other patient.'

'What other patient?'

'Nina Voss. She was admitted at noon today. Maybe you should take a look at her now. See for yourself that the choice wasn't so clear. That it's possible you *did* make a mistake.'

Abby swallowed. 'Where is she?'

'Fourth floor. Medical ICU.'

Even from the hallway, Abby could hear the commotion in the MICU: the cacophony of voices, the whine of a portable X-ray machine, two telephones ringing at once. The instant she walked through the doorway, she felt a hush descend on the room. Even the telephones suddenly went silent. A few of the nurses were staring at her; most were pointedly looking the other way.

'Dr DiMatteo,' said Aaron Levi. He had just emerged from Cubicle 5, and he stood staring at her with a look of barely suppressed rage. 'Perhaps you should come and see this,' he said.

The throng of personnel silently moved aside to let Abby approach Cubicle 5. She went to the window. Through the glass, she saw a woman lying in the bed, a fragile-looking woman with white-blond hair and a face as colorless as the sheets. An ET tube had been inserted down her throat and was hooked up to a ventilator. She was fighting the machine, her chest moving spasmodically as she tried to suck in air. The machine wasn't cooperating. Alarms buzzed as it fed her breaths at its own preset rhythm, ignoring the patient's desperate inhalations. Both the woman's hands were restrained. A medical resident was inserting an arterial line into one of the patient's wrists, piercing deep under the skin and threading a plastic catheter into the radial artery. The other wrist, tied to the bed, looked like a pincushion of IV lines and bruises. A nurse was murmuring to the patient, attempting to calm her down, but the woman, fully conscious, stared up with an expression of sheer terror. It was the look of an animal being tortured.

'That's Nina Voss,' said Aaron.

Abby remained silent, stunned by the horror she saw in the woman's eyes.

'She was admitted eight hours ago. Almost from the moment she arrived, her condition deteriorated. At five o'clock she coded. Ventricular tachycardia. Twenty minutes ago, she coded again. That's why she's intubated. She was scheduled for surgery tonight. The team was ready. The OR was ready. The patient was more than ready. Then we find out the donor went to surgery hours ahead of schedule. And the heart that should have gone to this woman has been stolen. *Stolen*, Dr DiMatteo.'

Still Abby said nothing. She was transfixed by the ordeal she was witnessing in Cubicle 5. At that instant, Nina Voss's eyes lifted to hers. It was only a brief meeting of gazes, an appeal for mercy. The pain in those eyes left Abby shaken.

'We didn't know,' Abby whispered. 'We didn't know her condition was critical . . .'

'Do you realize what will happen now? Do you have any idea?'

'The boy—' She turned to Aaron. 'The boy's alive.'

'What about this woman's life?'

There was no reply Abby could make. No matter what she said, how she defended herself, she could not justify the suffering beyond that window.

She scarcely noticed the man crossing toward her from the nurses' station. Only when he said 'Is this Dr DiMatteo?' did she focus on the man's face. He was in his sixties, tall and well dressed, the sort of man whose very presence demands attention.

Quietly she answered, 'I'm Abby DiMatteo.' Only as she said it did she realize what she saw in the man's eyes. It was hatred, pure and poisonous. She almost backed away as the man stepped toward her, his face darkening in rage.

'So you're the other one,' he said. 'You and that chink doctor.'

'Mr Voss. Please,' said Aaron.

'You think you can fuck around with me?' Voss yelled at Abby. 'With my wife? There'll be consequences, Doctor. Damn you, I'll see there are consequences!' Hands clenched, he took another step toward Abby.

'Mr Voss,' said Aaron. 'Believe me, we'll deal with Dr DiMatteo in our own way.'

'I want her out of this hospital! I don't want to see her face again!'

'Mr Voss,' said Abby. 'I'm so sorry. I can't tell you how sorry I am—'

'Just get her the hell *away* from me!' roared Voss.

Aaron quickly moved between them. He took Abby firmly by the arm and pulled her away from the cubicle. 'You'd better leave,' he said.

'If I could just talk to him – explain—'

'The best thing you can do right now is leave the ICU.'

She glanced at Voss, who stood squarely in front of Cubicle 5 as though guarding his wife from attack. Never before had Abby seen such a look of hatred. No amount of talking, of explanation, could ever get past that.

Meekly she nodded to Aaron. 'All right,' she said softly. 'I'll leave.'

And she turned and walked out of the MICU.

Three hours later, Stewart Sussman pulled up at the curb on Tanner Avenue, and from his car he studied number 1451. The house was a modest cape with dark shutters and a covered front porch. A white picket fence surrounded the property. Though it was too dark for Sussman to see much of the yard, instinct told him the grass would be trim and the flowerbeds free of weeds. The faint perfume of roses hung in the air.

Sussman left his car and walked through the gate and up the porch steps to the front door. The occupants were home. The lights were on, and he could see movement through the curtained windows.

He rang the bell.

A woman answered. Tired face, tired eyes, her shoulders sagging under some terrible psychic weight. 'Yes?' she said.

'I'm sorry to disturb you. My name is Stewart Sussman. I wonder if I might have a word with Joseph Terrio?'

'He'd rather not speak to anyone right now. You see, we've just had a . . . loss in the family.'

'I understand, Mrs . . .'

'Terrio. I'm Joe's mother.'

'I know about your daughter-in-law, Mrs Terrio. And I'm very, very sorry. But it's important I speak to your son. It has to do with Karen's death.'

The woman hesitated only a moment. Then she said: 'Excuse me,' and shut the door. He could hear her call: 'Joe?'

A moment later the door opened again and a man appeared, eyes red-rimmed, every movement sluggish with grief. 'I'm Joe Terrio,' he said.

Sussman extended his hand. 'Mr Terrio, I've been sent here by someone who's very concerned about the circumstances surrounding your wife's death.'

'Circumstances?'

'She was a patient at Bayside Medical Center. Is that correct?'

'Look, I don't understand what this is all about.'

'It's about your wife's medical care, Mr Terrio. And whether any mistakes were made. Mistakes that may have proved fatal.'

'Who are you?'

'I'm an attorney with Hawkes, Craig and Sussman. My specialty is medical malpractice.'

'I don't need any attorney. I don't want any god-damn ambulance chaser bothering me tonight.'

'Mr Terrio—'

'Get the hell out of here.' Joe started to close the door, but Sussman put out a hand to stop it.

'Mr Terrio,' Sussman said quietly. Calmly. 'I have reason to believe one of Karen's doctors made an error. A terrible error. It's possible your wife didn't have to die. I can't be certain of that yet. But with your permission, I can look at the record. I can uncover the facts. All of the facts.'

Slowly Joe let the door swing open again. 'Who sent you? You said somebody sent you. Who was it?'

Sussman gazed back with a look of sympathy. 'A friend.'

Six

Never before had Abby dreaded going to work, but as she walked into Bayside Hospital that morning, she felt she was walking straight into the fire. Last night Jeremiah Parr had threatened repercussions; today she'd have to face them. But until Wettig actually stripped her of her hospital privileges, she was determined to carry on as usual with her duties. She had patients to round on and cases scheduled for the OR. Tonight she was on call. Damn it, she was going to do her job, and do it well. She owed it to her patients – and to Vivian. Only an hour ago, they had spoken on the phone, and Vivian's last words to her were: 'Someone there has to speak up for the Josh O'Days. Stay with it, DiMatteo. For both of us.'

The moment Abby walked into the SICU, she heard the instantaneous lowering of voices. By now, everyone must know about Josh O'Day. Though no one said a word to Abby, she could hear the nurses' quiet murmurings, could see their uneasy looks. She went to the rack and gathered her patients' charts for rounds. It took every ounce of concentration for her to complete that one task. She placed the charts in a rolling cart and wheeled it out of the station, to the cubicle of the first patient on her list. It was a relief just to step inside, away from everyone's gaze. She shut the curtains, blocking the view through the doorway, and turned to the patient.

Mary Allen lay on the bed, her eyes closed, her sticklike arms and legs drawn up in a fetal position. Mary's open lung biopsy two days ago had been followed by two brief episodes of hypotension, so she'd been kept in the SICU for close observation. According to the nurse's notes, Mary's blood pressure had remained stable for the past twenty-four hours and no abnormal cardiac rhythms had been noted. Chances were, Mary could be transferred today to an unmonitored room in the surgery ward.

Abbey went to the bedside and said, 'Mrs Allen?'

The woman stirred awake. 'Dr DiMatteo,' she murmured.

'How are you feeling today?'

'Not so good. It still hurts, you know.'

'Where?'

'My chest. My head. Now my back. It hurts all over.'

Abby saw from the chart that the nurses had been giving morphine around the clock. Obviously it wasn't enough; Abby would have to order a higher dose.

116

'We'll give you more medicine for the pain,' said Abby. 'As much as you need to keep you comfortable.'

'To help me sleep, too. I can't sleep.' Mary gave a sigh of profound weariness and closed her eyes. 'I just want to go to sleep, Doctor. And not wake up . . .'

'Mrs Allen? Mary?'

'Couldn't you do that for me? You're my doctor. You could make it so easy. So simple.'

'We can make the pain go away,' said Abby.

'But you can't take away the cancer. Can you?' The eyes opened again, and regarded Abby with a look that pleaded for undiluted honesty.

'No,' said Abby. 'We can't take that away. The cancer's spread to too many places. We can give you chemotherapy, to slow it down. Gain some time for you.'

'Time?' Mary gave a resigned laugh. 'What do I need time for? To lie here another week, another month? I'd rather have it done and over with.'

Abby took Mary's hand. It felt like bones wrapped in parchment, no flesh at all. 'Let's take care of the pain first. If we do that, it could make everything else seem different.'

In answer, Mary simply turned on her side, away from Abby. She was closing her off, shutting her out. 'I suppose you want to listen to my lungs,' was all she said.

They both knew the exam was merely a formality. It was a useless ceremony, the stethoscope on the chest, on the heart. Abby went through the motions anyway. She had little else to offer Mary Allen except this laying on of hands. When she was finished, her patient still lay with her back turned.

'We'll be transferring you out of the SICU,' said Abby. 'You can go to a room on the ward. It'll be quieter there. Not so many disturbances.'

No answer. Just a deep breath, a long sigh.

Abby left the cubicle feeling more defeated, more useless than ever. There was so little she could do. An absence of pain was the best she had to offer. That, and a promise to let nature take its course.

She opened Mary's chart and wrote: 'Patient expresses wish to die. Will increase morphine sulfate for pain control and change code status to Do Not Resuscitate.' She wrote the transfer orders and handed them to Cecily, Mary's nurse.

'I want her kept comfortable,' said Abby. 'Titrate the dose to her pain. Give her as much as she needs to sleep.'

'What's our upper limit?'

Abby paused, considered the fine line between comfort and unconsciousness, between sleep and coma. She said, 'No upper limit. She's dying, Cecily. She wants to die. If the morphine makes it easier, then that's what we should give her. Even if it means the end comes a little sooner.'

Cecily nodded, a look of unspoken agreement in her eyes.

As Abby started toward the next cubicle, she heard Cecily call out: 'Dr DiMatteo?'

Abbey turned. 'Yes?'

'I . . . just wanted to tell you. I think you should know that, well . . .' Nervously Cecily glanced around the SICU. She saw that some of the other nurses were watching. Waiting. Cecily cleared her throat. 'I wanted you to know that we think you and Dr Chao did the right thing. Giving the heart to Josh O'Day.'

Abby blinked away an unexpected flash of tears. She whispered, 'Thank you. Thank you so much.'

Only then, as Abby looked around the room, did she see all the nods of approval.

'You're one of the best residents we've ever had, Dr D.,' said Cecily. 'We wanted you to know that, too.'

In the hush that followed, a pair of hands started clapping. Another joined in, then another. Abby stood speechless, clutching a chart to her chest, as all the SICU nurses burst out in loud and spontaneous applause. They were applauding *her*. It was a standing ovation.

'I want her off the staff and out of this hospital,' said Victor Voss. 'And I'll do whatever the hell it takes to accomplish that.'

Jeremiah Parr had faced numerous crises during his eight-year tenure as president of Bayside Medical Center. He'd dealt with two nursing strikes, several multimillion-dollar malpractice suits, and militant Right-to-Lifers rampaging through the lobby, but never had he faced such outright fury as he saw now in the face of Victor Voss. At ten A.M., Voss, flanked by his two attorneys, had marched into Parr's office and demanded a conference. It was now close to noon and the group had expanded to include Surgical Residency Director Colin Wettig and Susan Casado, the attorney representing Bayside. Calling Susan was Parr's idea. As yet there was no talk of any legal action, but Parr couldn't be too cautious. Especially when dealing with someone as powerful as Victor Voss.

'My wife is dying,' said Voss. 'Do you understand? *Dying*. She may not survive another night. I lay the blame squarely on those two residents.'

'Dr DiMatteo is only in her second year,' said Wettig. 'She wasn't the one who made the decision. Our chief resident did. Dr Chao is no longer in our program.'

'I want Dr DiMatteo's resignation as well.'

'She hasn't offered it.'

'Then find a reason to fire her.'

'Dr Wettig,' said Parr, calmly. Reasonably. 'We must be able to find some basis for termination.'

'There's no basis at all,' said Wettig, stubbornly holding his ground. 'All her evaluations have been outstanding and they're all on record. Mr Voss, I know this is a painful situation for you. I know it's only normal to want to lay blame somewhere. But I think your anger is misdirected. The real problem lies in the shortage of organs. Thousands of people need new hearts and there are only a few to go around. Consider what would happen if we did fire Dr DiMatteo. She could lodge an appeal. The matter would go to higher review. They look at this case and they'll ask questions. They'll ask why a seventeen-year-old boy didn't get that heart from the beginning.'

There was a pause. 'Jesus,' murmured Parr.

'You understand what I'm saying?' said Wettig. 'It looks bad. It makes the hospital look bad. This isn't the sort of thing we want to see in the newspapers. Hints of class warfare. The poor getting the short end of the stick. That's how they'll play it up. Whether or not it's true.' Wettig looked questioningly around the table. No one said a thing.

Our silence speaks volumes, thought Parr.

'Of course we can't allow people to get the wrong impression,' said Susan. 'Outrageous as it may seem, even the appearance of human organ deals would kill us in the press.'

'I'm just telling you how it looks,' said Wettig.

'I don't care how it looks,' said Voss. 'They stole that heart.'

'It was a directed donation. Mr Terrio had every right to specify the recipient.'

'My wife was guaranteed that heart.'

'Guaranteed?' Wettig frowned at Parr. 'Is there something I don't know about?'

'It was decided before her admission,' Parr said. 'The match was perfect.'

'So was the boy's,' countered Wettig.

Voss shot to his feet. 'Let me explain something to you people. My wife is dying because of Abby

DiMatteo. Now, you people don't know me very well. But let me tell you, no one screws me or my family and gets away with—'

'Mr Voss,' interjected one of his attorneys. 'Perhaps we should discuss this in—'

'Goddamn it! Let me *finish*!'

'Please, Mr Voss. This isn't in your best interests.'

Voss glared at his attorney. With apparent effort, he broke off his attack and sat back down. 'I want something done about Dr DiMatteo,' he said. And he looked straight at Parr.

By now Parr was sweating. God, it would be so easy just to fire that resident. Unfortunately, the General wasn't going to play ball with them. Damn these surgeons and their egos; they resented anyone else calling the shots. Why was Wettig being so stubborn about this?

'Mr Voss,' said Susan Casado in her silkiest voice. Her tame-the-savage-beast voice. 'May I suggest we all take some time to think this over? Rushing into legal action is seldom the best course. In a few days, we may be able to resolve your concerns.' Susan looked pointedly at Wettig.

The General just as pointedly ignored her.

'In a few days,' said Voss, 'my wife may be dead.' He rose to his feet and regarded Parr with a look of contempt. 'I don't need to think this over. I want something done about Dr DiMatteo. And I want it done soon.'

* * *

'I see the bullet,' said Abby.

Mark redirected the light beam, focusing it on the posterior reaches of the thoracic cavity. Something metallic glinted back at them, then vanished behind the inflating lung.

'Sharp eyes, Abby. Since you spotted it, you want to do the honors?'

Abbey took a pair of needle forceps off the instrument tray. The lungs had expanded again, blocking off her view of the cavity. 'I need deflation. Just for a sec.'

'You got it,' said the anesthesiologist.

Abby plunged her hand deep into the thorax, following the inner curve of the ribs. As Mark gently retracted the right lung, Abby clamped the forceps tips around the metal fragment and carefully withdrew it from the cavity.

The bullet, a flattened twenty-two, clattered into the metal basin.

'No bleeding. Looks like we can close,' said Abby.

'This is one lucky guy,' Mark said, eyeing the probable trajectory. 'Entry hole just right of the sternum. Rib must have deflected it or something. And it tumbled free along the pleural space. All he gets is a pneumothorax.'

'Hope he learned his lesson,' said Abby.

'What lesson?'

'Never piss off your wife.'

'*She* was the shooter?'

'Hey, we've come a long way, baby.'

They were closing the chest now, working

together with the companionable ease of two people who know each other well. It was four P.M. Abby had been on duty since seven that morning. Already her calves ached from standing all day, and she had another twenty-four hours on duty to go. But she was on a high right now, buoyed by the success of this operation – and by the chance to operate with Mark. This was exactly how she'd pictured their future together: working hand in hand, confident of themselves and each other. Mark was a superb surgeon, swift yet meticulous. From the very first day she'd scrubbed in with him, Abby had been impressed by the comfortable atmosphere in his OR. Mark never lost his cool, never yelled at a nurse, never even raised his voice. She'd decided then that if *she* ever had to go under the knife, Mark Hodell was the one surgeon she'd want to be holding the scalpel.

Now she was working right beside him, her gloved hand brushing against his, their heads bent close. This was the man she loved, the work she loved. Just for this moment, she could forget Victor Voss and the crisis shadowing her career. Perhaps the crisis was over. No ax had yet fallen, no ominous message had been issued from Parr's office. In fact, Colin Wettig had taken her aside this morning to tell her, in his usual gruff way, that she'd received outstanding evaluations for trauma rotation.

It will all work out, she thought as she watched the patient wheeled out to Recovery. *Somehow, this will all turn out just fine.*

'Excellent job, DiMatteo,' said Mark, stripping off his OR gown.

'I bet you say that to all the residents.'

'Here's something I never say to the other residents.' He leaned toward her and whispered: 'Meet me in the call room.'

'Uh . . . Dr DiMatteo?'

Abby and Mark, both flushing, turned and looked at the circulating nurse, who'd just poked her head in the door.

'There's a call for you from Mr Parr's secretary. They want to see you in Administration.'

'Now?'

'They're waiting for you,' said the nurse, and she left.

Abby shot Mark a look of apprehension. 'Oh God. Now what?'

'Don't let 'em rattle you. I'm sure it'll be OK. Want me to come with you?'

She thought it over a moment, then shook her head. 'I'm a big girl. I should be able to handle this.'

'If there's any problem, page me. I'll be right there.' He gave her hand a squeeze. 'That's a promise.'

She managed to return the thinnest of smiles. Then she pushed through the OR door and headed grimly for the elevator.

With the same feeling of dread she'd felt last night, she stepped off onto the second floor and headed up the carpeted hall to Jeremiah Parr's office. Parr's secretary directed her to the meeting room. Abby knocked on the door.

'Come in,' she heard Parr say.

Taking a shaky breath, she stepped inside.

Parr rose from his seat at the conference table. Also in the room were Colin Wettig and a woman whom Abby did not recognize, a fortyish brunette in a nicely tailored blue suit. Nothing she saw in those faces gave Abby the slightest clue as to the purpose of this meeting, but every instinct told her this session would not be a pleasant one.

'Dr DiMatteo,' said Parr, 'let me introduce you to Susan Casado, the hospital's corporate attorney.'

An attorney? This is not good.

The two women shook hands. Ms Casado's grip felt unnaturally warm against Abby's icy skin.

Abby took a chair next to Wettig. There was a brief silence, punctuated by the lawyer's rattling of papers and Wettig's gruff throat clearing.

Then Parr said, 'Dr DiMatteo, perhaps you could tell us what you recall about your role in the care of a Mrs Karen Terrio.'

Abby frowned. This was not at all what she'd expected. 'I performed the initial evaluation on Mrs Terrio,' she said. 'Then I referred her to Neurosurgery. They took over her case.'

'So how long was she under your care?'

'Officially? About two hours. More or less.'

'And during those two hours, what did you do, exactly?'

'I stabilized her. Ordered the necessary labs. It would be in the medical record.'

'Yes, we have a copy,' said Susan Casado. She patted the chart lying on the table.

'You'll find it all documented in there,' said Abby. 'My admitting notes and orders.'

'Everything you did?' said Susan.

'Yes. Everything.'

'Do you remember anything you did that might have negatively affected the patient's course?'

'No.'

'Anything you *should* have done? In retrospect?'

'No.'

'I understand the patient expired.'

'She'd suffered massive head trauma. A motor vehicle accident. She was declared brain-dead.'

'After you cared for her.'

In frustration, Abby glanced around the table. 'Could someone please tell me what's going on?'

'What's going on,' said Parr, 'is that our insurance carrier, Vanguard Mutual – that's your carrier as well – received written notification just a few hours ago. It was hand-delivered and signed by an attorney from Hawkes, Craig and Sussman. I'm sorry to tell you this, Dr DiMatteo, but it appears as if you – and Bayside – are about to be sued for malpractice.'

The air went out of Abby's lungs in a sickening rush. She found herself gripping the table, fighting the sudden nausea rising in her stomach. She knew they were waiting for her to respond, but all she could manage was a shocked look and a disbelieving shake of her head.

'I take it you weren't expecting this,' said Susan Casado.

'I . . .' Abby swallowed. 'No. No.'

'It's only a preliminary notification,' said Susan Casado. 'You understand, of course, that there are a number of formalities that lead up to any actual trial. First, the case will be reviewed by a state screening panel to determine whether or not this is, in fact, malpractice. If the panel decides there was none, this whole thing may stop right there. But the plaintiff still has the right to proceed to trial, regardless.'

'The plaintiff,' murmured Abby. 'Who is the plaintiff?'

'The husband. Joseph Terrio.'

'There has to be a mistake. A misunderstanding—'

'Damn right there's a misunderstanding,' said Wettig. Everyone looked at the General, who had, until then, sat in stony silence. 'I've reviewed the record myself. Every page of it. There's no malpractice there. Dr DiMatteo did everything she should have done.'

'Then why is she the only doctor named in the lawsuit?' said Parr.

'I'm the only one?' Abby looked at the attorney. 'What about Neurosurgery? The emergency room? No one else was named?'

'Just you, Doctor,' said Susan. 'And your employer. Bayside.'

Abby sat back, stunned. 'I don't believe this . . .'

'Neither do I,' said Wettig. 'This isn't the way

it's done and we all know it. Damn lawyers usually take the shotgun approach, name every M.D. who came within a mile of the patient. There's something wrong here. Something else is going on.'

'It's Victor Voss,' said Abby softly.

'Voss?' Wettig gave a dismissive wave. 'He has no stake in this case.'

'He's out to ruin me. That's his stake.' She looked around the table. 'Why do you think I'm the only doctor named? Somehow Voss has gotten to Joe Terrio. Convinced him I did something wrong. If I could just talk to Joe—'

'Absolutely not,' said Susan. 'It would be a sign of desperation. A tip-off to the plaintiff that you know you're in trouble.'

'I *am* in trouble!'

'No. Not yet. If there's really no malpractice here, it will all blow over sooner or later. Once the panel rules in your favor, chances are the other side will drop the suit.'

'What if they insist on going to trial anyway?'

'It would make no sense. The legal expenses alone would—'

'Don't you see, *Voss* must be footing the bill. He doesn't care about winning or losing! He could pay an army of lawyers, just to keep me running scared. Joe Terrio may be only the first lawsuit. Victor Voss could track down every patient I've ever cared for. Convince every single one of them to file suit against me.'

'And we're her employer. Which means they'll

129

file suit against Bayside as well,' said Parr. He looked ill. Almost as ill as Abby felt.

'There's got to be a way to defuse this,' said Susan. 'Some way to approach Mr Voss and cool down the situation.'

No one said anything. But Abby, looking at Parr's face, could read the thought going through his head: *The fastest way to cool this down is to fire you.*

She waited for the blow to fall, expected it to fall. It didn't. Parr and Susan merely exchanged glances.

Then Susan said, 'We're still early in the game. We have months to maneuver. Months to plan a response. In the meantime . . .' She looked at Abby. 'You'll be assigned counsel by Vanguard Mutual. I suggest you meet with their attorney as soon as possible. You may also consider hiring your own private counsel.'

'Do you think I need to?'

'Yes.'

Abby swallowed 'I don't know how I'm going to afford to hire an attorney . . .'

'In your particular situation, Dr DiMatteo,' said Susan, 'you can't afford not to.'

For Abby, being on call that night was a blessing in disguise. A flurry of calls and pages kept her on the run all evening, attending to everything from a pneumothorax in the medical ICU to a postop fever in the surgical ward. There was little time for her to brood over Joe Terrio's lawsuit. But every so often, when there was a lull in the phone calls, she would find herself hovering dangerously close to tears. Of all the grieving spouses she'd comforted and counseled, Joe Terrio was the last one she'd expected to sue her. *What did I do wrong?* she wondered. *Could I have been more compassionate? More caring?*

Damn it, Joe, what else did you want from me?

Whatever it was, she knew she could not have given more of herself. She'd done the very best job she could have done. And for all her anguish over Karen Terrio, she was being rewarded with a slap in the face.

She was angry now, at the attorneys, at Victor Voss, even at Joe. She felt sorry for Joe Terrio, but she also felt betrayed by him. By the very man whose suffering she had so acutely felt.

At ten o'clock she was finally free to retreat to the on-call room. Too upset to read her journals, too demoralized to talk to anyone, even Mark, she lay down on the bed and stared at the ceiling. Her legs felt paralyzed, her whole body lifeless. *How the hell do I get through this night*, she wondered, *when I can't even bring myself to move from this bed?*

But move she did when, at ten-thirty, the phone rang. She sat up and reached for the receiver. 'Dr DiMatteo.'

'This is the OR. Drs Archer and Hodell need you up here.'

'Now?'

'ASAP. They've got a case brewing.'

'I'll be there.' Abby hung up. Sighing, she ran both her hands through her hair. Any other time, any other evening, she'd already be on her feet and raring to scrub. Tonight she could barely stand the thought of facing Mark and Archer across an operating table.

Damn it, you're a surgeon, DiMatteo. So act like one!

It was self-disgust that finally propelled her to her feet and out of the call room.

She found Mark and Archer upstairs in the surgeons' lounge. They were standing by the microwave, their voices lowered in quiet conversation. She knew, just by the way their heads jerked up as she entered, that their conversation was meant to be private. But the instant they saw her, both of them smiled.

'There you are,' said Archer. 'All quiet in the trenches?'

'For the moment,' said Abby. 'I hear you two have a case coming up.'

'Transplant,' said Mark. 'The team's coming in now. Trouble is, we can't get hold of Mohandas. A fifth-year resident's going to be standing in for him, but we may need you to assist as well. Feel up to scrubbing in?'

'On a heart transplant?' The quick shot of adrenaline was exactly what Abby needed to shake off her depression. She gave Mark an emphatic nod. 'I'd be thrilled.'

'There's only one small problem,' said Archer. 'The patient is Nina Voss.'

Abby stared at him. 'They found her a heart so soon?'

'We got lucky. The heart's coming in from Burlington. Victor Voss would probably have a stroke if he knew we were using you. But we're calling the shots right now. And we may need another pair of hands in that OR. On such short notice, you're the obvious choice.'

'Are you still up for it?' asked Mark.

Abby didn't even hesitate. 'Absolutely,' she said.

'OK,' said Archer. 'Looks like we got our assistant.' He nodded to Mark. 'Meet you both in OR 3. Twenty minutes.'

At eleven-thirty P.M., they got the call from the thoracic surgeon at Wilcox Memorial Hospital in Burlington, Vermont. The donor harvest was completed; the organ appeared to be in excellent shape and was being rushed to the airport. Preserved at four degrees centigrade, its beating temporarily paralyzed by a concentrated potassium flush, the heart could be kept viable for only four to five hours. Without blood flow to the coronary arteries, every minute that passed – ischemic time – could result in the death of a few more myocardial cells. The longer the ischemic time, the less likely the heart would function in Nina Voss's chest.

The flight, by emergency charter, was expected to take a maximum of an hour and a half.

By midnight, the Bayside Hospital transplant team was assembled and dressed in surgical greens. Along with Bill Archer, Mark, and anesthesiologist Frank Zwick, there was a small army of support staff: nurses, a perfusion technician, cardiologist Aaron Levi, and Abby.

Nina Voss was wheeled to OR 3.

At one-thirty, the call came in from Logan International: the plane had landed safely.

That was the cue for the surgeons to head to the scrub area. As Abby washed her hands at the sink, she could look through the window into OR 3, where the rest of the transplant team was already busy with preparations. The nurses were laying out instrument trays and tearing open packets of sterile drapes. The perfusionist was recalibrating the cabinetlike bypass machine. A fifth-year resident, already scrubbed in, stood by waiting to prep the surgical site.

On the operating table, at the center of a tangle of EKG wires and IV lines, lay Nina Voss. She seemed oblivious to the activity around her. Dr Zwick stood at Nina's head, murmuring to her gently as he injected a bolus of pentobarb into her IV line. Her eyelids flickered shut. Zwick placed the mask over her mouth and nose. With the ambubag he pumped a few breaths of oxygen in quick succession, then removed the mask.

The next step had to be performed swiftly. The patient was unconscious now, unable to breathe on her own. Tilting her head back, Zwick slipped a curved laryngoscope blade into her throat, located the vocal cords, and inserted the plastic endotracheal tube. An air-inflated cuff would keep the tube in place in her trachea. Zwick connected the tube to the ventilator and her chest began to rise and fall with the whoosh of the bellows. The intubation had taken less than thirty seconds.

The operating lights were turned on and directed at the table. Bathed in that brilliant glow, Nina seemed unearthly. Spectral. A nurse pulled off the sheet draping Nina's body and exposed the torso, the ribs arching beneath pale skin, the breasts small, almost shrunken. The resident proceeded to disinfect the operative site, painting broad strokes of iodine across the skin.

The OR doors banged open as Mark, Archer, and Abby, freshly scrubbed, walked in with hands held up, elbows dripping water. They were greeted with sterile towels, gowns, and gloves. By the time everyone was fully garbed, Nina Voss had been prepped and draped.

Archer moved to the operating table. 'Is it here yet?' he asked.

'Still waiting for it,' said a nurse.

'It's only a twenty-minute drive from Logan.'

'Maybe they got caught in a traffic jam.'

'At two in the morning?'

'Jesus,' said Mark. 'That's all we need now. An accident.'

Archer peered up at the monitors. 'Happened at Mayo. Had a kidney flown in all the way from Texas. Right out of the airport, ambulance hits a truck. Organ gets squashed. Perfectly matched one, too.'

'You're kidding,' said Zwick.

'Hey, would I kid about a kidney?'

The fifth-year resident glanced up at the wall clock. 'We're going on three hours since harvest.'

'Wait. Just wait,' said Archer.

The phone rang. Everyone's head swiveled to watch as the nurse answered it. Seconds later she hung up and announced: 'It's downstairs. The courier's on his way up from the ER.'

'OK,' snapped Archer. 'Let's cut.'

From where Abby stood, she caught only a slanted glimpse of the procedure, and even then her view was intermittent, cut off by Mark's shoulder. Archer and Mark were working swiftly and in concert, making a midline sternotomy incision, exposing fascia, then bone.

The wall intercom buzzed. 'Dr Mapes from the harvest team is here with a special delivery,' came the message from the OR front desk.

'We're cannulating,' said Mark. 'Have him join the fun.'

Abby glanced toward the OR door. Through the viewing window, she could see the scrub area beyond, where a man stood waiting. Beside him, on a gurney, was a small Igloo cooler. The same sort of cooler in which she'd transported Karen Terrio's heart.

'He'll be in,' said the desk nurse. 'As soon as he changes clothes.'

Moments later, Dr Mapes entered, now wearing greens. He was a small man with an almost Neanderthal brow and a nose that jutted out

136

like a hawk's beak under the surgical mask.

'Welcome to Boston,' said Archer, glancing up at the visitor. 'I'm Bill Archer. This is Mark Hodell.'

'Leonard Mapes. I scrubbed with Dr Nicholls at Wilcox.'

'Good flight, Len?'

'Could've used a beverage service.'

Archer cracked a smile, visible even through his mask. 'So what'd you bring us for Christmas, Len?'

'Nice one. I think you'll be pleased.'

'Let me finish cannulating and I'll take a look.'

Cannulation of the ascending aorta was the first step to connecting the patient to the bypass machine. That squat box, under control of the perfusion technician, would temporarily assume the job of the heart and lungs, collecting venous blood, replenishing its oxygen, and pumping it back into the patient's aorta.

Archer, using silk sutures, sewed two concentric 'purse strings' in the wall of the ascending aorta. With a scalpel tip he made a tiny stab in the vessel. Bright blood spurted out. Swiftly he inserted the arterial cannula into the incision and tightened the purse strings. The bleeding slowed to an ooze, then stopped as he sewed the cannula tip in place. The other end of the cannula was connected to the bypass machine's arterial line.

Mark, with Abby retracting, was already starting on the venous cannulation.

'OK,' said Archer, moving from the table. 'Let's unwrap our present.'

A nurse unpacked the Igloo cooler and lifted out the organ, wrapped in two ordinary plastic bags. She untwisted the ties and slid the naked organ into a basin of sterile saline.

Gently Archer lifted the chilled heart from its bath. 'Nice excision job,' he noted. 'You guys did good work.'

'Thanks,' said Mapes.

Archer ran his gloved finger over the surface. 'Arteries soft and smooth. Clean as a whistle.'

'Seems a bit on the small side, doesn't it?' said Abby, glancing across the table. 'How big was the donor?'

'Forty-four kilograms,' said Dr Mapes.

Abby frowned. 'Adult?'

'An adolescent, previously healthy. A boy.'

Abby caught the flicker of distress in Archer's eyes. She remembered then that he had two teenage sons. Gently he lay the organ back in its bath of chilled saline.

'We won't let this one go to waste,' he said. And he turned his attention back to Nina.

By then, Mark and Abby were already finishing up the venous cannulation. Two Tygon tubes fitted with metal baskets at the end were inserted through stab wounds in the right atria, and secured by purse-string sutures. Venous blood would be collected by these cannulae and directed to the pump-oxygenator.

Working together now, Archer and Mark snared shut the inferior and superior venae cavae, cutting off return blood to the heart.

'Cross-clamping aorta,' announced Mark as he closed off the ascending aorta.

The heart, cut off from both venous inflow and arterial outflow, was now a useless sac. Nina Voss's circulation was under the complete control of the perfusionist and her magical machine. Also under control was the body temperature. By chilling the fluids, the body could be slowly cooled down to twenty-five degrees centigrade – profound hypothermia. This would preserve the newly implanted myocardial cells and lessen the body's oxygen consumption.

Zwick turned off the ventilator. The rhythmic wheeze of the bellows ceased. There was no need to pump air into the lungs when the bypass machine was doing the work.

Transplantation could now proceed.

Archer cut the aorta and pulmonary arteries. Blood gushed out into the chest, spilled onto the floor. At once a nurse threw a towel down to soak up the mess. Archer kept working, oblivious to the sweat beading his forehead, to the lights burning down. Next he transected the atria. More blood, darker, splashed Archer's gown. He reached elbow-deep into the chest cavity. Nina Voss's sick heart, pale and flabby, was now lifted away and dropped into a basin. What remained was a gaping hollow.

Abby glanced up at the monitor screen and felt an automatic rush of alarm at the flat EKG line. Of course there was no tracing. There was no heart. In fact, all the classic signs of life had ceased. The lungs were still. The heart was gone. Yet the patient still lived.

Mark lifted the donor heart from the basin and lowered it into the chest. 'Some folks call this procedure a glorified plumbing job,' he said, rotating the heart to match up the left atrial chambers. 'They think it's like stitching together a stuffed animal or something. But you let your attention slip for a minute, and before you realize it, you're sewing the heart in backwards.'

The fifth-year resident laughed.

'Not funny. It's happened.'

'Saline,' said Archer, and a nurse poured a basin of chilled saline over the heart to keep it cold under the lights.

'A hundred things can go wrong,' said Mark, his suture needle taking deep, almost savage bites into the left atrium. 'Drug reaction. Anesthetic disasters. And damn it, the surgeon always gets the blame.'

'Lot of blood pooling in here,' said Archer. 'Suction, Abby.'

The hiss of the suction machine gave way to a tense silence as the surgeons worked more quickly now. There was only the whir of the pump-oxygenator and the click of the needle clamps as the serrated jaws snapped shut with each new stitch. Despite Abby's repeated suctioning, blood kept soaking into the drapes and dribbling onto the floor. The towels at their feet were saturated. The surgeons kicked them aside and new towels were thrown down.

Archer snipped away the suture needle. 'Right atrial anastomosis done.'

'Perfusion catheter,' said Mark.

A nurse handed him the catheter. He introduced it into the left atrium and infused four-degree-centigrade saline. The flood of chilled liquid cooled down the ventricle and flushed out any air pockets inside.

'Okeydoke,' said Archer, repositioning the heart to sew the aortic anastomosis. 'Let's hook up these pipes.'

Mark glanced up at the wall clock. 'Look at that. We're ahead of schedule, folks. What a team.'

The intercom buzzed. It was the OR desk nurse. 'Mr Voss wants to know how his wife is doing.'

'Fine,' called Archer. 'No problems.'

'How much longer, do you think?'

'An hour. Tell him to hang in there.'

The intercom shut off. Archer glanced across at Mark. 'He rubs me the wrong way.'

'Voss?'

'Likes to be in control.'

'No kidding.'

Archer's suture needle curved in and out of the glistening aortic wall. 'But then, I guess if I had his money, I'd call the shots too.'

'Where does his money come from?' asked the fifth-year resident.

Archer glanced at him in surprise. 'You don't know about Victor Voss? VMI International? Everything from chemicals to robotics.'

'Is that what the V stands for in VMI?'

'You got it.' Archer tied off and snipped the last suture. 'Aorta done. Cross clamp off.'

'Perfusion catheter coming out,' said Mark, and turned to Abby. 'Get those two pacing wires ready for insertion.'

Archer picked up a fresh suture needle from the tray and began the pulmonary anastomosis. He was just tying off when he noticed the organ balling up. 'Look at that!' he said. 'Ice cold and already a spontaneous contraction. This baby's rarin' to go.'

'Pacing wires on,' said Mark.

'Isuprel infusion going in,' said Zwick. 'Two micrograms.'

They watched and waited for the Isuprel to take effect, for the heart to repeat the contraction.

It lay inert as a limp sac.

'Come on,' said Archer. 'Don't let me down.'

'Defibrillator?' asked a nurse.

'No, give it a chance.'

Slowly the heart tightened into a fist-sized knot, then fell flaccid.

Zwick said, 'Increasing Isuprel to three mics.'

There was one more contraction. Then nothing.

'Go on,' said Archer. 'Flog it a little more.'

'Four mics,' said Zwick, dialing up the IV infusion.

The heart tightened, relaxed. Contracted, relaxed.

Zwick glanced up at the monitor. QRS spikes

were now tracing across the screen. 'Rate's up to fifty. Sixty-four. Seventy . . .'

'Titrate to one-ten,' said Mark.

'That's what I'm doing,' said Zwick, adjusting the Isuprel.

Archer said to the circulation nurse: 'Get on the intercom, will you? Tell Recovery we're about to close.'

'Rate's one-ten,' said Zwick.

'OK,' said Mark. 'Let's take her off bypass. Get those cannulae out.'

Zwick flipped on the ventilator. Everyone in the room seemed to exhale a simultaneous sigh of relief.

'Let's just hope she and this heart get along,' said Mark.

'We know how close the HL-A match is?' asked Archer. He turned around to look at Dr Mapes.

There was no one standing behind him.

Abby had been so focused on the operation, she hadn't noticed the man had left.

'He walked out twenty minutes ago,' one of the nurses said.

'Just like that?'

'Maybe he had a plane to catch,' she said.

'Didn't even get a chance to shake his hand,' said Archer. He turned back to the patient on the table. 'OK. Let's close.'

Seven

Nadiya had had enough. All the whining, all the demands, all the pent-up boy energy that regularly erupted into swearing and shoving, had sucked away her strength. That, and now the seasickness. Gregor, the big ape, was sick as well, as were most of the boys. On the roughest days, when the ship's hull pounded like a hammer on the anvil of the North Sea, they all lay groaning in their bunks, the sounds and smells of their wretchedness penetrating even to the decks above. On such days, the mess hall below remained dark and half-deserted, the passageways were empty, and the ship was like some great and moaning ghost vessel, guided by the hands of a spirit crew.

Yakov had never had such a good time.

Unstricken by even the faintest twinge of nausea, he roamed freely throughout the ship. No one stopped him. Indeed, the crew seemed to enjoy his presence. He would visit Koubichev in the engine room, and in that noisy hell of grinding pistons and diesel fumes, the two of them played chess. Sometimes, Yakov even won. When he got hungry, Yakov would wander into the galley where Lubi, the cook, would offer him tea and beet soup and medivnyk, the fragrant spiced honey cake from his native Ukraine. Lubi never said much. 'More?' and 'Enough, eh?' was the extent of his conversation. The food he served was eloquence enough. Then there was the dusty cargo hold to explore, and the radio room with its dials and knobs, and the deck with its tarp-covered lifeboats to hide in. The only place he could not wander was the far aft section. He could not find any passage to get in there.

His favorite place of all was the bridge. Captain Dibrov and the navigator would greet Yakov with indulgent smiles and allow him to sit at the chart table. There he'd trace with the index finger of his one hand the course they had already sailed. From the port of Riga, down the Baltic Sea, through the channel past Malmö and Copenhagen, around the top of Denmark, and across the North Sea with its stepping stones of oil platforms with names like Montrose and Forties and Piper. The North Sea was bigger than he'd imagined. It was not just a little puddle of blue, the way it seemed on the chart. It was two days of water. And soon, the navigator told him, they'd be crossing an even bigger sea, the Atlantic Ocean.

'They won't live that long,' Yakov predicted.

'Who won't?'

'Nadiya and the other boys.'

'Of course they will,' said the navigator.

'Everyone gets sick in the North Sea. After a while their stomachs settle. It has to do with the inner ear.'

'What does the ear have to do with the stomach?'

'It senses motion. Too much motion makes it confused.'

'How?'

'I don't really understand it. But that's how it works.'

'I'm not sick. Is there something different about my inner ear?'

'You must be a born sailor.'

Yakov looked down at the stump of his left arm and shook his head. 'I don't think so.'

The navigator smiled. 'You have a good brain. Brains are far more important. You will need them, where you're going.'

'Why?'

'In America, if you're clever, you can become rich. You want to be rich, don't you?'

'I don't know.'

Both the navigator and the captain laughed.

'Maybe the boy doesn't have any brains after all,' said the captain.

Yakov looked at them without smiling.

'It was just a joke,' said the navigator.

'I know.'

'Why don't you ever laugh, boy? I never see you laugh.'

'I never feel like it.'

The captain snorted. 'Lucky little bastard's

going to some rich family in America. And he doesn't feel like laughing? What's wrong with him?'

Yakov shrugged and looked back at the chart. 'I don't cry, either.'

Aleksei was curled up on the lower bunk, clutching Shu-Shu to his chest. He was startled awake as Yakov sat down on the mattress.

'Aren't you ever going to get up?' asked Yakov.

Aleksei closed his eyes. 'I'm sick.'

'Lubi made lamb dumplings for supper. I ate nine of them.'

'Don't talk about it.'

'Aren't you hungry?'

'Of course I'm hungry. But I'm too sick to eat.'

Yakov sighed and looked around the cabin. There were eight bunk beds in the room, and six of them were occupied by boys too ill to play. Yakov had already visited the adjoining quarters and found the other boys equally incapacitated. Would it be this way all across the Atlantic?

'It's all because of your inner ear,' said Yakov.

'What are you talking about?' moaned Aleksei.

'Your ear. It's making your stomach sick.'

'My ears are fine.'

'You've been sick four days now. You've got to get up and eat.'

'Oh, leave me alone.'

Yakov grabbed Shu-Shu and yanked it away.

'Give him back!' wailed Aleksei.

'Come and get him.'

'Just give him back!'

'First you get up. Come on.' Yakov scurried away from the bunk as Aleksei made a futile swipe for the stuffed dog. 'You'll feel better if you're out of bed.'

Aleksei sat up. For a moment he huddled at the edge of his mattress, his head swaying with every tilt of the ship. Suddenly he clapped his hand to his mouth, lurched to his feet, and scrambled across the cabin. He vomited into the sink. Groaning, he crawled back into his bunk.

Solemnly, Yakov handed back Shu-Shu.

Aleksei hugged the stuffed dog against his chest. 'I told you I was sick. Now go away.'

Yakov left the boys' quarters and wandered into the corridor. At Nadiya's stateroom door, he knocked. There was no answer. He moved on to Gregor's stateroom and knocked again.

'Who is it?' came a growl.

'It's me. Yakov. Are you still sick as well?'

'Get the fuck away from my door.'

Yakov left. He wandered around the ship for a while, but Lubi had retired for the night. The captain and the navigator were too busy to talk to him. As usual, Yakov was on his own.

He went down to visit Koubichev in the engine room.

They set up the chessboard. Yakov drew the first move, pawn to king four.

'Have you ever been to America?' Yakov asked over the rumble of the pistons.

'Twice,' said Koubichev, moving his queen's pawn forward.

'Did you like it there?'

'Wouldn't know. They always order us confined to quarters as soon as we get into port. I never see a fucking thing.'

'Why does the captain order this?'

'The captain doesn't. It's those people in the aft cabin.'

'What people? I've never seen them.'

'No one ever does.'

'Then how do you know they're there?'

'Ask Lubi. He cooks for them. Someone's eating the food he sends up. Now are you going to move a piece or what?'

With great concentration, Yakov advanced another pawn. 'Why don't you just leave the ship when we get there?' he asked.

'Why would I?'

'To stay in America and get rich.'

Koubichev grunted. 'They pay me enough. I can't complain.'

'How much do they pay you?'

'You're too nosy.'

'Is it a lot?'

'It's more than I used to make. More than a lot of men make. And just to go back and forth, back and forth across this damned Atlantic.'

Yakov moved out his queen. 'So it's a good job? To be a ship's engineer?'

'That's a stupid move, bringing out your queen. Why did you make it?'

'I'm trying new things out. Should I be a ship's engineer some day?'

'No.'

'But you get paid a lot.'

'It's only because I work for the Sigayev Company. They pay very well.'

'Why?'

'I keep my mouth shut.'

'Why?'

'How the hell should I know?' Koubichev reached across the board. 'My knight takes your queen. See, I told you it was a stupid move.'

'It was an experiment,' said Yakov.

'Well, I hope you learned something from it.'

A few days later, on the bridge, Yakov asked the navigator: 'What's the Sigayev Company?'

The navigator shot him a look of surprise. 'How did you hear that name?'

'Koubichev told me.'

'He shouldn't have.'

'So you don't talk about it either,' said Yakov.

'That's right.'

For a moment, Yakov didn't say anything. He watched the navigator fuss with his electronics equipment. There was a small screen where little numbers kept flashing, and the navigator would write the numbers in a book, then look in his chart.

'Where are we?' asked Yakov.

'Here.' The navigator pointed to a tiny X on the chart. It was in the middle of the ocean.

'How do you know?'

'By the numbers. I read them on the screen. The latitude and longitude. See?'

'You have to be very clever to be a navigator, don't you?'

'Not so clever, really.' The man was moving two plastic rulers across the chart now. They were connected by hinges, and he'd clack them together as he slid them to the compass rose at the edge of the chart.

'Are you doing something illegal?' asked Yakov.

'What?'

'Is that why you're not supposed to talk about it?'

The navigator sighed. 'My only responsibility is to guide this ship from Riga to Boston and back to Riga.'

'Do you always carry orphans?'

'No. Usually we carry cargo. Crates. I don't ask what's in them. I don't ask questions, period.'

'So you could be doing something illegal.'

The navigator laughed. 'You are a little devil, aren't you?' He began to write again in his notebook, recording numbers in neat columns.

The boy watched him for a while in silence. Then he said, 'Do you think anyone will adopt me?'

'Of course someone will.'

'Even with this?' Yakov raised his stump of an arm.

The navigator looked at him, and Yakov recognized the flicker of pity in the man's eyes. 'I know for a fact someone will adopt you,' he said.

'How do you know?'

'Someone's paid for your passage, haven't they?
Arranged for your papers.'

'I've never seen my papers. Have you?'

'It's none of my business. My only job is to get
this ship to Boston.' He waved Yakov aside. 'Why
don't you go back to the other boys? Go on.'

'They're still not feeling well.'

'Well, go play somewhere else.'

Reluctantly Yakov left the bridge and went out
on deck. He was the only one there. He stood by
the rail and stared down at the water splintering
before the bow. He thought of the fish swimming
somewhere below in their gray and turbid world,
and suddenly he found he couldn't breathe; the
image of swirling water was suffocating. Yet he
didn't move. He stayed at the rail, gripping it with
his one hand, letting the panicky thoughts of cold,
deep water wash through him. Fear was something he had not felt in a very long time.

He was feeling it now.

Eight

She had the same dream two nights in a row. The nurses told her it was because of all the medications she'd been taking. The methylprednisolone and the cyclosporine and the pain pills. The chemicals were scrambling her brain. And after days of hospitalization, of course she'd be having bad dreams. Everyone did. It was nothing to worry about. The dreams would, eventually, fade away.

But that morning, as Nina Voss lay in her ICU bed, the tears fresh in her eyes, she knew the dream would not go away, would never go away. It was part of her now. Just as this heart was part of her.

Softly, she touched her hand to the bandages on her chest. It had been two days since the operation, and though the soreness was just starting to ease, it still awakened her at night, a reminder of the gift she'd received. It was a good, strong heart. She had known that within a day of the surgery. During the long months of her illness, she'd forgotten what it was like to have a strong heart. To walk without gasping for air. To feel the blood pump, warm and vital, to her muscles. To look down at her own fingers and marvel at the rosy flush of her capillaries. She had lived so long waiting for death, accepting death, that life itself had become foreign to her. But now she could see it in her own hands. Could feel it in her fingertips.

And in the beating of this new heart.

It did not yet feel as if it belonged to her. Perhaps it never would.

As a child, she would often inherit her older sister's clothing, Caroline's good wool sweaters, her scarcely worn party dresses. Although the garments had unquestionably passed to Nina's ownership, she had never stopped thinking of them as her sister's. In her mind, they would always be *Caroline's* dresses, *Caroline's* skirts.

And whose heart are you? she thought, her hand gently touching her chest.

At noon, Victor came to sit by her bed.

'I had the dream again,' she told him. 'The one about the boy. It was so clear to me this time! When I woke up, I couldn't stop crying.'

'It's the steroids, darling,' said Victor. 'They warned you about that side effect.'

'I think it means something. Don't you see? I have this part of him inside me. A part that's still alive. I can feel him . . .'

'That nurse should never have told you it was a boy's.'

'I asked her.'

'Still, she shouldn't have told you. It does no one any good to release that information. Not you. Not the boy.'

'No,' she said softly. 'Not the boy. But the family – if there's a family—'

'I'm sure they don't wish to be reminded. Think about it, Nina. It's a strictly confidential process. There's a reason for it.'

'Would it be so bad? To send the family a thank-you letter? It would be completely anonymous. Just a simple—'

'No, Nina. Absolutely not.'

Nina sank back quietly on the pillows. She was being foolish again. Victor was right. Victor was always right.

'You're looking wonderful today, darling,' he said. 'Have you been up in a chair yet?'

'Twice,' said Nina. Suddenly the room seemed very, very cold to her. She looked away and shivered.

Pete was sitting in a chair by Abby's bed, looking at her. He wore his blue Cub Scout uniform, the one with all the little patches sewn on the sleeves and the plastic beads dangling from the breast pocket, one bead for each achievement. He was not wearing his cap. Where is his cap? she wondered. And then she remembered that it was lost, that she and her sisters had searched and searched the roadside but had not found it anywhere near the mangled remains of his bicycle.

He had not visited in a long time, not since the

night she'd left for college. When he did visit, it was always the same. He would sit looking at her, not speaking.

She said, 'Where have you been, Pete? Why did you come if you're not going to say anything?'

He just sat watching her, his eyes silent, his lips unmoving. The collar of his blue shirt was starched and stiff, just the way their mother had pressed it for the burial. He turned and looked toward another room. A musical note seemed to be calling to him; he was starting to shimmer, like water that has been stirred.

She said, 'What did you come to tell me?'

The waters were churning now, beaten to a froth by all those musical notes. Another bell-like jangle led to total disintegration. There was only darkness.

And the ringing telephone.

Abby reached for the receiver. 'DiMatteo,' she said.

'This is the SICU. I think maybe you'd better come down.'

'What's happening?'

'It's Mrs Voss in Bed Fifteen. The transplant. She's running a fever, thirty-eight point six.'

'What about her other vitals?'

'BP's a hundred over seventy. Pulse is ninety-six.'

'I'll be there.' Abby hung up and switched on the lamp. It was two A.M. The chair by her bed was empty. No Pete. Groaning, she climbed out of bed and stumbled across the room to the sink,

156

where she splashed cold water on her face. Its temperature didn't even register. She felt the water as though through anesthesia. Wake up, wake up, she told herself. You have to know what the hell you're doing. A postop fever. A three-day-old transplant. First step, check the wound. Examine the lungs, the abdomen. Order a chest X-ray and cultures.

And keep your cool.

She couldn't afford to make any mistakes. Not now, and certainly not with this patient.

Every morning for the past three days, she'd walked into Bayside not knowing if she still had a job. And every afternoon at five o'clock she'd heaved a sigh of relief that she'd survived another twenty-four hours. With each day that passed, the crisis seemed a little dimmer and Parr's threats more remote. She knew she had Wettig on her side, and Mark as well. With their help maybe – just maybe – she'd keep her job. She didn't want to give Parr any reason to question her performance as a doctor, so she'd been especially meticulous at work, had checked and rechecked every lab result, every physical finding. And she'd been careful to steer clear of Nina Voss's hospital room. Another angry encounter with Victor Voss was the last thing she needed.

But now Nina Voss was running a fever and Abby was the resident on the spot. She couldn't avoid this; she had a job to do.

She pulled on her tennis shoes and left the on-call room.

Late at night, a hospital is a surreal place. Hallways stretch empty, the lights are too bright, and through tired eyes, all those white walls seem to curve and sway like moving tunnels. She was weaving through one of those tunnels now, her body still numb, her brain still struggling to function. Only her heart had fully responded to the crisis; it was pounding.

She turned a corner, into the SICU.

The lights were dimmed for the night – modern technology's concession to the diurnal needs of human patients. In the gloom of the nurses' station, the electrical patterns of sixteen patients' hearts traced across sixteen screens. A glance at Screen 15 confirmed that Mrs Voss's pulse was running fast. A rate of 100.

The monitor nurse picked up the ringing telephone, then said: 'Dr Levi's on the line. He wants to talk to the on-call resident.'

'I'll take it,' said Abby, reaching for the receiver. 'Hello, Dr Levi? This is Abby DiMatteo.'

There was a silence. 'You're on call tonight?' he said, and she heard a distinct note of dismay in his voice. She understood at once the reason for it. Abby was the last person he wanted to lay hands on Nina Voss. But tonight there was no alternative; she was the senior resident on call.

She said: 'I was just about to examine Mrs Voss. She's running a fever.'

'Yes, they told me about it.' Again there was a pause.

She plunged into that void, determined to keep

their conversation purely professional. 'I'll do the usual fever workup,' she said. 'I'll examine her. Order a CBC and cultures, urine, and chest X-ray. As soon as I have the results I'll call you back.'

'All right,' he finally said. 'I'll be waiting for your call.'

Abby donned an isolation gown and stepped into Nina Voss's cubicle. A single lamp had been left on, and it shone dimly above the bed. Under that soft cone of light, Nina Voss's hair was a silvery streak across the pillow. Her eyelids were shut, her hands crossed over her body in a strange semblance of holy repose. *The princess in the sepulcher*, thought Abby.

She moved to the side of the bed and said softly: 'Mrs Voss?'

Nina opened her eyes. Slowly her gaze focused on Abby. 'Yes?'

'I'm Dr DiMatteo,' said Abby. 'I'm one of the surgical residents.' She saw the flicker of recognition in the other woman's eyes. *She knows my name*, thought Abby. *She knows who I am.* The grave robber. The body thief.

Nina Voss said nothing, merely looked at her with those fathomless eyes.

'You have a fever,' explained Abby. 'We need to find out why. How are you feeling, Mrs Voss?'

'I'm . . . tired. That's all,' whispered Nina. 'Just tired.'

'I'll have to check your incision.' Abby turned up the lights and gently peeled the bandages off the chest wound. The incision looked clean, no redness, no swelling. She pulled out her stethoscope and moved on to the rest of the fever workup. She heard the normal rush of air in and out of the lungs. Felt the abdomen. Peered into the ears, nose, and throat. She found nothing alarming, nothing that would cause a fever. Through it all, Nina remained silent, her gaze following Abby's every move.

At last Abby straightened and said: 'Everything seems to be fine. But there must be a reason for the fever. We'll be getting a chest X-ray and collecting three different blood samples for cultures.' She smiled apologetically. 'I'm afraid you're not going to get much sleep tonight.'

Nina shook her head. 'I don't sleep much, anyway. All the dreams. So many dreams . . .'

'Bad dreams?'

Nina took in a breath, slowly let it out. 'About the boy.'

'Which boy, Mrs Voss?'

'This boy.' Softly she touched her hand to her chest. 'They told me it was a boy's. I don't even know his name. Or how he died. All I know is, this was a boy's.' She looked at Abby. 'It was. Wasn't it?'

Abby nodded. 'That's what I heard in the operating room.'

'You were there?'

'I assisted Dr Hodell.'

A small smile formed on Nina's lips. 'Strange. That you should be there, after . . .' Her voice faded.

Neither one of them spoke for a moment, Abby silenced by guilt, Nina Voss by . . . what? The irony of this meeting? Abby dimmed the lights. Once again the cubicle took on its sepulchral gloom.

'Mrs Voss,' said Abby. 'What happened a few days ago. The other heart, the first heart . . .' She looked away, unable to meet the other woman's gaze. 'There was a boy. Seventeen. Boys that age, they want cars or girlfriends. But this boy, all he wanted was to go home. Nothing else, just to go home.' She sighed. 'In the end, I couldn't let it happen. I didn't know you, Mrs Voss. You weren't the one lying in that bed. He was. And I had to make a choice.' She blinked, felt tears wet her lashes.

'He lived?'

'Yes. He lived.'

Nina nodded. Again she touched her own chest. She seemed to be conferring with her heart. Listening, communicating. She said, 'This boy. This boy's alive, too. I'm so aware of his heart. Every beat. Some people believe that the heart is where the soul lives. Maybe that's what his parents believe. I think about them, too. And how hard it must be. I never had a son. I never had a child.' She closed her hand into a fist, pressed it against the bandages. 'Don't you think it would be a comfort, to know that some part of him is still alive? If it was my son, I'd want to know. I'd want to know.' She was crying now, the tears a sparkling trickle down her temple.

Abby reached for the woman's hand and was startled by the force of Nina's grasp, the skin feverish, the fingers tight with need. Nina was looking up at her, a gaze that seemed to shine with its own strange fire. *If I had known you then*, thought Abby, *If I had watched you dying in one bed and Josh O'Day in another, which one of you would I have chosen?*

I don't know.

Above the bed, a line skipped across the green glow of the oscilloscope. The heart of an unknown boy, beating a hundred times a minute, pumping fevered blood through a stranger's veins.

Abby, holding Nina's hand, could feel the throb of a pulse. A slow, steady pulse.

Not Nina's, but her own.

It took twenty minutes for the X-ray tech to arrive and shoot the portable chest film, and another fifteen minutes before Abby had the developed X-ray in hand. She clipped it to the SICU viewing box and examined it for signs of pneumonia. She saw none.

It was three A.M. She called Aaron Levi's house.

Aaron's wife answered, her voice husky with sleep. 'Hello?'

'Elaine, this is Abby DiMatteo. I'm sorry to bother you at this hour. May I speak with Aaron?'

'He left for the hospital.'

'How long ago?'

'Uh . . . it was just after the second phone call. Isn't he there?'

162

'I haven't seen him,' said Abby.

There was silence on the other end of the line. 'He left home an hour ago,' said Elaine. 'He should be there.'

'I'll page his beeper. Don't worry about it, Elaine.' Abby hung up, then dialed Aaron's beeper and waited for the phone to ring.

By three-fifteen, he still hadn't answered.

'Dr D?' said Sheila, Nina Voss's nurse. 'The last blood culture's been drawn. Is there anything else you want to order?'

What have I missed? thought Abby. She leaned forward against the desk and massaged her temples, struggling to stay awake. Think. A postop fever. Where was the infection coming from? What had she overlooked?

'What about the organ?' said Sheila.

Abby looked up. 'The heart?'

'It was just something that occurred to me. But I guess it's not very likely . . .'

'What are you thinking, Sheila?'

The nurse hesitated. 'I've never seen it happen here. But before I came to Bayside, I used to work with a renal transplant service in Mayo. I remember we had this patient. A kidney recipient with postop fevers. We didn't figure out what his infection was until after he died. It turned out to be fungal. Later they tracked down the donor record and found out the donor's blood cultures were positive, but the results didn't come back until a week after the kidney was harvested. By then it was too late for the recipient. Our patient.'

163

Abby thought it over for a moment. She looked at the bank of monitors, at the heart tracing of Bed 15 dancing across the screen.

'Where's the donor information kept?' asked Abby.

'It would be in the transplant coordinator's office downstairs. The nursing supervisor has the key.'

'Could you ask her to get the file for me?'

Abby reopened Nina Voss's chart. She turned to the New England Organ Bank donor form – the sheet that had accompanied the heart from Vermont. Recorded there was the ABO blood type, HIV status, syphilis antibody titers, and a long list of other lab screens for various viral infections. The donor was not identified.

Fifteen minutes later, the phone rang. It was the nursing supervisor, calling for Abby.

'I can't find the donor file,' she said.

'Isn't it under Nina Voss's name?'

'They're filed under the recipient's medical record number. There's nothing here under Mrs Voss's number.'

'Could it be misfiled?'

'I've looked in all the kidney and liver transplant files too. And I double-checked that record number. Are you sure it isn't somewhere up in the SICU?'

'I'll ask them to look. Thanks.' Abby hung up and sighed. Missing paperwork. It was the last thing she felt like dealing with at this time of the morning. She looked at the SICU records shelf, where files from current patients' previous hospitalizations were kept. If the missing file was buried somewhere in *that*, she could be searching for an hour.

Or she could call the donor hospital directly. They could pull the record, tell her the donor's medical history and lab tests.

Directory assistance gave her the number for Wilcox Memorial. She dialed the number and asked for the nursing supervisor.

A moment later a woman answered: 'Gail DeLeon speaking.'

'This is Dr DiMatteo calling from Bayside Hospital in Boston,' said Abby. 'We have a heart transplant recipient here who's running a postop fever. We know the donor heart came from your OR. I need a little more information on the donor's medical history. I wonder if you might know the patient's name.'

'The organ harvest was done here?'

'Yes. Three days ago. The donor was a boy. An adolescent.'

'Let me check the OR log. I'll call you back.'

Ten minutes later, she did – not with an answer but with a question: 'Are you sure you have the right hospital, Doctor?'

Abby glanced down at Nina's chart. 'It says right here. Donor hospital was Wilcox Memorial. Burlington, Vermont.'

'Well, that's us. But I don't see a harvest on the log.'

'Can you check your OR schedule? The date

would have been . . .' Abby looked at the form. 'September twenty-fourth. The harvest would've been done sometime around midnight.'

'Hold on.'

Over the receiver, Abby heard the sound of turning pages and the nurse's intermittent throat clearing. The voice came back. 'Hello?'

'I'm here,' said Abby.

'I've checked the schedule for September twenty-third, twenty-fourth, and twenty-fifth. There are a couple of appendectomies, a cholecystectomy, and two cesareans. But there's no organ harvest anywhere.'

'There has to be. We got the heart.'

'We're not the ones who sent it.'

Abby scanned the OR nurses' notes and saw the notation: *0105: Dr Leonard Mapes arrived from Wilcox Memorial.* She said, 'One of the surgeons who scrubbed on the harvest was Dr Leonard Mapes. That's the same guy who delivered it.'

'We don't have any Dr Mapes on our staff.'

'He's a thoracic surgeon—'

'Look, there's no Dr Mapes here. In fact, I don't know of any Dr Mapes practicing anywhere in Burlington. I don't know where you're getting your info, Doctor, but it's obviously wrong. Maybe you should check again.'

'But—'

'Try another hospital.'

Slowly Abby hung up.

For a long time she sat staring at the phone. She

thought about Victor Voss and his money, about all the things that money could buy. She thought about the amazing confluence of events that had granted Nina Voss a new heart. A matched heart.

She reached, once again, for the telephone.

Nine

'You're overreacting,' said Mark, flipping through Nina Voss's SICU chart. 'There has to be a reasonable explanation for all of this.'

'I'd like to know what it is,' said Abby.

'It was a good excision. The heart came packed right, delivered right. And there *were* donor papers.'

'Which now seem to be missing.'

'The transplant coordinator will be in at nine. We can ask her about the papers then. I'm sure they're around somewhere.'

'Mark, there's one more thing. I called the donor hospital. There's no surgeon named Leonard Mapes practicing there. In fact, there's no such surgeon practicing in Burlington.' She paused. Softly she said, 'Do we really know where that heart came from?'

Mark said nothing. He seemed too dazed, too tired to be thinking straight. It was four-fifteen. After Abby's phone call, he'd dragged himself out of bed and driven to Bayside. Postop fevers required immediate attention, and although he trusted Abby's findings, he had wanted to see the patient for himself. Now Mark sat in the gloom of the SICU, struggling to make sense of the paperwork in Nina Voss's chart. A bank of heart monitors faced him on the countertop, and three bright green lines traced across the reflection in his glasses. In the semidarkness nurses moved like shadows and spoke in hushed voices.

Mark closed the chart. Sighing, he pulled off his glasses and rubbed his eyes. 'This fever. What the hell is causing the fever? That's what really concerns me.'

'Could it be an infection passed from the donor?'

'Unlikely. I've never seen it happen with a heart.'

'But we don't know anything about the donor. Or his medical history. We don't even know which hospital that heart came from.'

'Abby, you're going off the deep end here. I know Archer spoke on the phone to the harvesting surgeon. I also know there were papers. They came in this brown envelope.'

'I remember seeing it.'

'All right. Then we saw the same thing.'

'Where's the envelope now?'

'Hey, I was the one operating, OK? I'm up to my elbows in blood. I can't keep track of some goddamn envelope.'

'Why is there all this secrecy about the donor, anyway? We don't have records. We don't know his name.'

'That's standard procedure. Donor records are confidential. They're always kept separate from the recipient's chart. Otherwise you'd have families contacting each other. The donor side would expect undying gratitude, the recipient side would either resent it or feel guilty. It leads to one giant emotional mess.' He sank back in his chair. 'We're wasting time on this issue. It'll all be resolved in a few hours. So let's concentrate on the fever.'

'All right. But if there's any question about this, New England Organ Bank wants to discuss it with you.'

'How did NEOB get involved?'

'I called them. They have this twenty-four-hour line. I told them you or Archer would get back to them.'

'Archer can handle it. He'll be here any minute.'

'He's coming in?'

'He's worried about the fever. And we can't seem to get hold of Aaron. Have you paged him again?'

'Three times. No answer. Elaine told me he was driving in.'

'Well, I know he got here. I just saw his car down in the parking lot. Maybe he got busy on the medical floor.' Mark flipped through Nina Voss's chart to the order sheets. 'I'm going to move on this without him.'

Abby glanced toward Nina Voss's cubicle. The patient's eyes were closed, her chest rising and falling with the gentle rhythm of sleep.

'I'm starting antibiotics,' said Mark. 'Broad-spectrum.'

'What infection are you treating?'

'I don't know. It's just a temporary bridge until the cultures come back. As immunosuppressed as she is, we can't take a chance she's infected somewhere.' In frustration, Mark rose from the chair and walked over to the cubicle window. He stood there a moment, staring in at Nina Voss. The sight of her seemed to calm him. Abby came to stand beside him. They were very close, almost touching each other, and yet separated by the gulf of this crisis. On the other side of the window, Nina Voss slept peacefully.

'It could be a drug reaction,' said Abby. 'She's on so many things. Any one of them could cause a fever.'

'That's a possibility. But not likely on steroids and cyclosporine.'

'I couldn't find any source of infection. Anywhere.'

'She's immunosuppressed. We miss something, she's dead.' He turned to pick up the chart. 'I'm starting the bug juice.'

At six A.M. the first dose of IV Azactam was dripping into Nina's vein. A stat infectious disease consult was requested, and at seven-fifteen the consultant, Dr Moore, arrived. He concurred with Mark's decision. A fever in an immunosuppressed patient was too dangerous to go untreated.

At eight o'clock, a second antibiotic, piperacillin, was infused.

By then Abby was making morning SICU rounds, her wheeled cart piled six-deep with charts. It had been a bad call night – just one hour of sleep before that two A.M. phone call, and not a moment's rest since then. Fueled by two cups of coffee and a view of the end in sight, she pushed her cart along the row of cubicles, thinking: *Four hours and I'm out of here. Only four more hours until noon.* She passed by Bed 15, and she glanced through the cubicle window.

Nina was awake. She saw Abby and weakly managed a beckoning wave.

Abby left her charts by the door, donned an isolation gown, and stepped into the cubicle.

'Good morning, Dr DiMatteo,' murmured Nina. 'I'm afraid you didn't get much sleep because of me.'

Abby smiled. 'That's okay. I slept last week. How are you feeling?'

'Like quite the center of attention.' Nina glanced up at the bottle of IV antibiotics hanging over the bed. 'Is that the cure?'

'We hope so. You're getting a combination of piperacillin and Azactam. Broad-spectrum antibiotics. If you have an infection, that should take care of it.'

'And if this isn't an infection?'

'Then the fever won't respond. And we'll try something else.'

'So you don't really know what's causing this.'

Abby paused. 'No,' she admitted. 'We don't. It's more of an educated shot in the dark.'

Nina nodded. 'I thought you'd tell the truth. Dr Archer wouldn't, you know. He was here this morning, and he kept telling me not to worry. That everything was taken care of. He never admitted he didn't know.' Nina gave a soft laugh, as though the fever, the antibiotics, all these tubes and machines were part of some whimsical illusion.

'I'm sure he didn't want to worry you,' said Abby.

'But the truth doesn't scare me. Really it doesn't. Doctors don't tell the truth often enough.' She looked straight at Abby. 'We both know that.'

Abby found her gaze shifting automatically to the monitors. She saw that all the lines tracing across the screen were in the normal ranges. Pulse. Blood pressure. Right atrial pressure. It was pure habit, that focus on the numbers. Machines didn't pose difficult questions, didn't expect painfully truthful answers.

She heard Nina say, softly: 'Victor.'

Abby turned. Only then, as she faced the doorway, did she realize Victor Voss had just stepped into the cubicle.

'Get out,' he said. 'Get out of my wife's room.'

'I was only checking on her.'

'I said, get *out*!' He took a step toward her and grabbed a handful of the isolation gown.

Reflexively Abby resisted, pulling free. The cubicle was so tiny there was no more room to back away, no space to retreat to.

He lunged at her. This time he caught hold of her arm with a grip that was meant to hurt.

'Victor, don't!' said Nina.

Abby gave a cry of pain as she was wrenched forward. He thrust her out of the cubicle. The force of his shove sent her backward against the wheeled cart. She felt herself falling as the cart slid away. She landed hard on her buttocks. The cart, still rolling, slammed against a counter and charts thudded to the floor. Abby, stunned by the impact, looked up to see Victor Voss standing over her. He was breathing hard, not from exertion but from fury.

'Don't you go near my wife again,' he said. 'Do you hear me, Doctor? *Do you hear me?*' Voss turned his gaze to the shocked personnel standing around the SICU. 'I don't want this woman near my wife. I want that written in the chart and posted on the door. I want it done now.' He gave Abby one last look of disgust, then he walked into his wife's cubicle and yanked the curtain across the window.

Two of the nurses hurried over to help Abby to her feet.

'I'm okay,' said Abby, waving them away. 'I'm fine.'

'He's crazy,' one of the nurses whispered. 'We should report him to Security.'

'No, don't,' said Abby. 'Let's not make things worse.'

'But that was assault! You could press charges.'

'I just want to forget about it, okay?' Abby went

over to the cart. Her charts were on the floor, loose pages and lab slips scattered everywhere. Face burning, she gathered up all the papers and set them back in the cart. By then she was fighting to hold back tears. *I can't cry*, she thought. *Not here. I won't cry.* She looked up.

Everyone was watching her.

She left the cart right where it was and walked out of the SICU.

Mark found her three hours later, in the cafeteria. She was sitting at a corner table, hunched over a cup of tea and a blueberry muffin. The muffin had only one bite taken out of it, and the teabag had been left soaking so long the water was black as coffee.

Mark pulled out a chair across from her and sat down. 'Voss was the one who threw the tantrum, Abby. Not you.'

'I'm just the one who landed on her butt in front of everyone.'

'He shoved you. That's something you can use. Leverage against any more of those nutty lawsuits.'

'You mean I charge him with assault?'

'Something like that.'

She shook her head. 'I don't want to think about Victor Voss. I don't want to have anything to do with him.'

'There were half a dozen witnesses. They saw him push you.'

'Mark, let's forget the whole thing.' She picked up the muffin, took an unenthusiastic bite, and put it back down again. She sat staring at it, desperately wanting to change the subject.

Finally she said, 'Did Aaron agree about starting antibiotics?'

'I haven't seen Aaron all day.'

She looked up, frowning. 'I thought he was here.'

'I beeped him but he never answered.'

'Did you call his home?'

'I got the housekeeper. Elaine left for the weekend, visiting their kid at Dartmouth.' Mark shrugged. 'It's Saturday. This isn't Aaron's weekend to make rounds anyway. He probably decided to take a vacation from all of us.'

'A vacation,' Abby sighed and rubbed her face. 'God, that's what I want. A beach and a few palm trees and a piña colada.'

'Sounds good to me, too.' Reaching across the table, he took her hand. 'Mind if I join you?'

'You don't even like piña coladas.'

'But I like beaches and palm trees. And you.' He gave her hand a squeeze. That was just what she needed at that moment. His touch. It felt as solid and dependable as the man himself.

He leaned across the table. Right there, in the cafeteria, he kissed her. 'Look at us. Creating another public spectacle,' he whispered. 'You'd better go home, before we get everyone's attention.'

She glanced at her watch. It was twelve o'clock, and a Saturday. The weekend, at last, had begun.

He walked her out of the cafeteria and across

176

the hospital lobby. As they pushed through the doors he said, 'I almost forgot to tell you. Archer called Wilcox Memorial and spoke to some thoracic surgeon named Tim Nicholls. Turns out Nicholls assisted on the harvest. He confirmed the patient was theirs. And that Dr Mapes did the excision.'

'Then why isn't Mapes listed on the Wilcox staff?'

'Because Mapes was flown in by private jet from Houston. We knew nothing about it. Apparently, Mr Voss didn't trust just any Yankee surgeon to do the job. So he had a specialist flown in.'

'All the way from Texas?'

'With his money, Voss could've flown in the whole Baylor team.'

'So the harvest *was* done at Wilcox Memorial.'

'Nicholls says he was there. Whatever nurse you spoke to last night must've been looking at the wrong log sheet. If you'd like me to call and confirm it again—'

'No, just forget it. It all seems so stupid now. I don't know what I was thinking.' She sighed and looked across at her car, parked in its usual spot at the far end of the lot. Outer Siberia, the residents called their assigned parking area. Then again, slave labor was lucky to get assigned parking at all. 'I'll see you at home,' she said. 'If I'm still awake.'

He put his arms around her, tipped her head back, and kissed her, one tired body clinging to another. 'Careful driving home,' he whispered. 'I love you.'

She walked across the lot, dazed by fatigue and by the sound of those three words still echoing in her head.

I love you.

She stopped and looked back to wave at him, but he had already vanished through the lobby doors.

'I love you too,' she said, and smiled.

She turned to her car, her keys already out of her purse. Only then did she notice that the lock button was up. Jesus, what an idiot. She'd left the car unlocked all night.

She opened the door.

At the first foul whiff of air, she backed away, gagging on the stench. And repulsed by the sight of what lay on the front seat.

Loops of rotting intestine were coiled around the gear shift and one end hung like a grotesque streamer from the bottom of the steering wheel. A hacked-up mass of unidentifiable tissue was smeared across the passenger seat. And on the driver's side, propped up against the cushion, was a single bloody organ.

A heart.

The address was in Dorchester, a run-down neighborhood in southeast Boston. He parked across the street and eyed the boxy house, the weedy lawn. There was a kid of about twelve bouncing a basketball in the driveway, every so often flinging it at a hoop over the garage, and missing every time. No athletic scholarship for that one. Judging by the junker of a car parked in the garage and the general shabbiness of the home, a scholarship would certainly come in handy.

He got out of his car and crossed the street. As he walked up the driveway, the boy suddenly fell still. Hugging the ball to his chest, he eyed the visitor with obvious suspicion.

'I'm looking for the Flynt residence.'

'Yeah,' said the boy. 'This is it.'

'Are your parents at home?'

'My dad is. Why?'

'Maybe you could let him know he has a visitor.'

'Who are you?'

He handed the boy his business card. The boy read it with only vague interest, then tried to hand it back.

'No, keep it. Show it to your father.'

'You mean right now?'

'If he's not busy.'

'Yeah. Okay.' The boy went into the house, the screen door slapping shut behind him.

A moment later a man came to the door, big-bellied, unsmiling. 'You looking for me?'

'Mr Flynt, my name is Stewart Sussman. I'm with the law firm of Hawkes, Craig and Sussman.'

'Yeah?'

'I understand you were a patient at Bayside Medical Center six months ago.'

'I was in an accident. Other guy's fault.'

'You had your spleen removed. Is that correct?'

'How do you know all this?'

'I'm here in your best interests, Mr Flynt. You had major surgery, did you not?'

'They said I coulda died. I guess that makes it major.'

'Was one of your doctors a woman resident named Abigail DiMatteo?'

'Yeah. She saw me every day. Real nice lady.'

'Did she or any of the other doctors tell you the consequences of having your spleen removed?'

'They said I could have bad infections if I'm not careful.'

'Fatal infections. Did they say that?'

'Uh . . . maybe.'

'Did they mention anything about an accidental nick during surgery?'

'What?'

'A scalpel slipping, cutting the spleen. Causing a lot of bleeding.'

'No.' The man was leaning toward him now, with a look of intense worry. 'Did something like that happen to me?'

'We'd like to confirm the facts. All we need is your consent to obtain your medical record.'

'Why?'

'It would be in your interest, Mr Flynt, to know if the loss of your spleen was, in fact, due to surgical error. If a mistake was made, then you've suffered unnecessary damage. And you should be compensated.'

Mr Flynt said nothing. He looked at the boy,

who was listening to the conversation. Probably understanding none of it. Then he looked at the pen that was being offered to him.

'By compensation, Mr Flynt,' said the attorney, 'I was referring to money.'

The man took the pen and signed his name.

Back in his car, Sussman slipped the signed records request form in his briefcase and reached once again for the list. There were four more names, four more signatures to obtain. He should have no problem. Greed and retribution were a powerful combination.

He crossed off the name *Flynt, Harold*, and started the car.

Ten

'It was a pig's heart. They probably left it in my car the night before, where it baked all day in the heat. I still can't get rid of the smell.'

'The man is mindfucking you,' said Vivian Chao. 'I say you should fuck him right back.'

Abby and Vivian pushed through the front doors and crossed the lobby to the elevators. It was Sunday noon at Massachusetts General, and the public elevator was already crammed tight with visitors and get-well balloons bobbing overhead. The doors slid shut and the scent of carnations was instantly overpowering.

'We don't have any proof,' murmured Abby. 'We can't be sure he's the one doing this.'

'Who else would it be? Look what he's done already. Manufacturing lawsuits. Shoving you in public. I'm telling you, DiMatteo, it's time to press charges. Assault. Terroristic threatening.'

'The problem is, I understand why he's doing it. He's upset. His wife's having a rocky postop course.'

'Do I detect a note of guilt?'

Abby sighed. 'It's hard not to feel guilty every time I pass her bed.'

They stepped off the elevator onto the fourth floor and headed up the hall toward the cardiac surgery wing.

'He has the money to make your life hell for a very long time,' said Vivian. 'You've got one law-suit against you already. There'll probably be more.'

'I think there already are. Medical Records told me they've had six more chart requests from Hawkes, Craig and Sussman. That's the law firm representing Joe Terrio.'

Vivian stopped and stared at her. 'Jesus. You're going to be in court for the rest of your natural life.'

'Or until I resign. Like you.'

Vivian began walking again, her stride as fierce as ever. The little Asian Amazon, afraid of nothing.

'How come *you* aren't fucking back?' said Abby.

'I'm trying to. The problem is, the man we're up against is Victor Voss. When I mentioned that name to my attorney, she turned a few shades whiter. Which is an amazing feat for a black woman.'

'What was her advice?'

'To walk away from it. And call myself lucky that I'm already a board-eligible surgeon. At least I can find another job. Or open up my own practice.'

'Voss scares her that much?'

'She wouldn't admit it, but yes. He scares a lot of people. I'm in no position to fight, anyway. I was the one in charge, so it's my head that rolls. We stole a heart, DiMatteo. There's no way around that. If it had been anyone else but Victor Voss, we might have gotten away with it. Now it's costing me.' She looked at Abby. 'But not as much as it could cost you.'

'At least I still have my job.'

'For how long? You're only a second-year resident. You've got to start fighting back, Abby. Don't let him ruin you. You're too good a doctor to be forced out.'

Abby shook her head. 'Sometimes I wonder if it was all worth it.'

'Worth it?' Vivian stopped outside Room 417. 'Take a look. You tell me.' She knocked on the door, then stepped into the room.

The boy was sitting up in bed, fussing with a TV remote. If not for the Red Sox cap on his head, Abby might not have recognized Josh O'Day, so transformed was his appearance by the rosy flush of health. At his first glimpse of Vivian, he grinned hugely.

'Hey, Dr *Chao*!' he whooped. 'Geez, I wondered if you were *ever* coming to see me.'

'I did come by,' said Vivian. 'Twice. But you were always asleep.' She shook her head in mock disgust. 'Typical lazy teenager.'

They both laughed. There was a brief silence. Then, almost shyly, Josh opened his arms for a hug.

For a moment Vivian didn't move. It was as if she didn't know how to respond. Then she suddenly snapped free of some invisible restraint and stepped toward him. The embrace was brief and clumsy. Vivian seemed almost relieved when it was over.

'So how are you?' she asked.

'Real good. Hey, didja see?' He pointed to the TV. 'My dad brought me all those baseball tapes. But we can't figure out how to hook up the VCR. You know how to do it?'

'I'd probably blow up the TV.'

'And you're a doctor?'

'Okay. Next time you need surgery, buster, you call a TV repairman.' She nodded toward Abby. 'You remember Dr DiMatteo, don't you?'

Josh looked uncertainly at Abby. 'I think so. I mean . . .' He shrugged. 'I forgot some things, you know? Things that happened last week. It's almost like I got dumb or something.'

'That's nothing to worry about,' said Vivian. 'When your heart stops, Josh, you don't get enough blood to your brain. You can forget a few things.' She touched his shoulder. It was not the sort of thing Vivian Chao would normally do. But there she was, actually making contact. 'At least you didn't forget me,' she said. And added with a laugh, 'Though you may have tried.'

Josh looked down at the bedspread. 'Dr Chao,' he said softly, 'I don't ever want to forget you.'

Neither one spoke for a moment. They seemed frozen by embarrassment in that awkward pose,

Vivian's hand on the boy's shoulder. The boy looking downward, his face hidden under the bill of his cap.

Abby had to turn away and focus on something else. The trophies. They were all there, all the ribbons and plaques, arranged on the nightstand. No longer an altar to a dying boy, but a celebration of life. Of rebirth.

There was a knock on the door and a woman called out: 'Joshie?'

'Hey, Mom,' said Josh.

The door swung open and the room was invaded by parents and siblings and aunts and uncles, sweeping in with them a forest of helium balloons and the smell of McDonald's fries. They swarmed around the bed, assaulted Josh with hugs and kisses and exclamations of 'Look at him!' 'He looks so good.' 'Doesn't he look good?' Josh bore it all with an expression of sheepish delight. He didn't seem to notice that Vivian had slipped away from his bedside, to make room for the noisy army of O'Days.

'Josh, honey, we brought Uncle Harry from Newbury. He knows all about VCRs. He can hook it up, can't you, Harry?'

'Oh, sure. I do all my neighbors' VCRs.'

'Did you bring the right wires, Harry? You sure you got all the wires you need?'

'You think I'd forget the wires?'

'Look, Josh. Three extra-large orders of fries. It's okay, isn't it? Dr Tarasoff didn't say you couldn't have fries?'

'Mom, we forgot the camera! I was gonna take a picture of Josh's scar.'

'You don't want a picture of his scar.'

'My teacher said it'd be cool.'

'Your teacher's too old to use words like cool. No pictures of scars. That's an invasion of privacy.'

'Hey Josh, you need any help eating those fries?'

'So Harry, you think you can hook it up?'

'Gee, I don't know. This is a pretty old TV . . .'

Vivian had managed at last to sidle around to where Abby was standing. There was another knock on the door, and a fresh spurt of relatives pushed into the room, with more cries of 'He looks so good!' 'Doesn't he look good?' Through the crowd of O'Days, Abby caught a fleeting glimpse of Josh. He was looking their way. He gave them a helpless smile, a wave.

Quietly Abby and Vivian left the room. They stood in the hallway, listening to the voices beyond the door. And Vivian said, 'So, Abby. To the question of *Was it worth it?*, that's your answer.'

At the nurses' station, they asked to speak to Dr Ivan Tarasoff. The ward clerk suggested they look in the surgeons' lounge. That's exactly where Abby and Vivian found him, sipping coffee and scribbling in his charts. With his drooping glasses and tweed jacket, Dr Tarasoff looked more like some puttering English gentleman than the renowned cardiac surgeon.

'We just saw Josh,' said Vivian.

Tarasoff looked up from his coffee-splattered notes. 'And what do you think, Dr Chao?'

'I think you do good work. The kid looks fantastic.'

'He has a little postcode amnesia. Otherwise, he's bounced back the way kids always do. He'll be out of here in a week. If the nurses don't kick him out sooner.' Tarasoff closed the chart and looked at Vivian. His smile faded. 'I have a very big bone to pick with you, Doctor.'

'Me?'

'You know what I'm talking about. That other transplant patient at Bayside. When you shipped us the boy, you didn't tell me the whole story. Then I find out the heart was already assigned.'

'It wasn't. There was a directed-donation consent.'

'Obtained through a certain amount of subterfuge.' He frowned over his glasses at Abby. 'Your administrator, Mr Parr, told me all the details. So did Mr Voss's attorney.'

Vivian and Abby glanced at each other.

'His attorney?' said Vivian.

'That's right.' Tarasoff's gaze shifted back to Vivian. 'Were you *trying* to get me sued?'

'I was trying to save the boy.'

'You withheld information.'

'And now he's alive and well.'

'I'm only going to say it once. Don't ever do anything like this again.'

Vivian seemed about to reply, but then thought better of it. Instead she gave a solemn nod. It was her deferential Asian act, eyes downcast, head dipping in a faint bow.

Tarasoff didn't buy it. He regarded her with a look of mild vexation. Then, unexpectedly, he laughed. Turning back to his charts, he said: 'I should have expelled you from Harvard. When I had the chance.'

'Ready about. Hard a lee!' Mark yelled, and shoved the tiller.

The bow of *Gimme Shelter* turned into the wind, sails crackling, ropes lashing the deck. Raj Mohandas scurried across to the starboard winch and began cranking the jib sheet. With a loud *whap*, the sail filled, and *Gimme Shelter* heeled to starboard, sending off a clatter of soft drink cans in the cabin below.

'Upwind rail, Abby!' Mark yelled. 'Get to the upwind rail!'

Abby scrambled across the deck to the port side, where she clung to the lifeline and offered up another fervent vow of *never again*. What was it about men and their boats? she wondered. What was it about the sea that made them yell?

They were *all* yelling, all four of them, Mark and Mohandas and Mohandas's eighteen-year-old son Hank, and Pete Jaegly, a third-year resident. Yelling about sheets that needed tightening and spinnaker poles and wasted wind puffs. They were yelling about Archer's boat, *Red Eye*, which was gaining on them. And, every so often, they would yell at Abby. She actually had a role in this race, a role known politely as *ballast*. Dead weight. A job that could be performed by sandbags. Abby was a sandbag with legs. They'd yell and she'd run across to the opposite rail, where, with some regularity, she'd throw up. The men weren't throwing up. They were too busy scampering around in their expensive boat shoes and yelling.

'Coming up on the mark! One more tack. Ready about!'

Mohandas and Jaegly resumed their frantic deck dance.

'Hard a lee!'

Gimme Shelter turned through the wind and heeled to port. Abby scrambled to the other side. Sails flapped, ropes thrashed. Mohandas cranked the winch, the muscles of his brown arm rippling with each turn of the handle.

'She's coming up on us!' Hank called.

Behind them, *Red Eye* had gained another half boat length. They could hear Archer yelling at *his* crew, exhorting them to *Come up, come up!*

Gimme Shelter rounded the buoy and started her downwind course. Jaegly struggled with the spinnaker pole. Hank pulled down the jib.

Abby was throwing up over the side.

'Shit, he's right on our tail!' yelled Mark. 'Get the fucking spinnaker up! Go, go, *go!*'

Jaegly and Hank hoisted the spinnaker. The wind filled it with a thunderous *whomp* and *Gimme Shelter* suddenly surged ahead.

'That's it, baby!' Mark whooped. 'Baby, baby, here we go!'

190

'Look,' said Jaegly, pointing aft. 'What the hell's happening?'

Abby managed to raise her head and look back, toward Archer's boat.

Red Eye was no longer in pursuit. It had turned around near the buoy and was now heading back to port.

'They've started their motor,' said Mark.

'Think they're conceding defeat?'

'Archer? Not a chance.'

'So why're they going back?'

'I guess we'd better find out. Get the spinnaker down.' Mark started the engine. 'We're heading back too.'

Thank you, God! thought Abby.

Her nausea was already subsiding by the time they motored into the marina. *Red Eye* was tied up at the dock and her crew was busy folding up sails and coiling ropes.

'Ahoy *Red Eye*!' yelled Mark as they glided past. 'What's going on?'

Archer waved his cellular phone. 'Got a call from Marilee! She told us to come in. It's something serious. She's waiting for us in the yacht club.'

'Okay. Meet you at the bar,' said Mark. He looked at his own crew. 'Let's tie up. We'll have a drink and take her back out again.'

'You'll have to do it without your ballast,' said Abby. 'I'm jumping ship.'

Mark glanced at her in surprise. 'Already?'

'Didn't you see me hanging over the side? I wasn't admiring the scenery.'

'Poor Abby! I'll make it up to you, okay? Promise. Champagne. Flowers. Restaurant of your choice.'

'Just get me off this goddamn boat.'

Laughing, he steered toward the dock. 'Aye aye, first mate.'

As *Gimme Shelter* glided alongside the visitor's dock, Mohandas and Hank stepped onto the pier and tied fast the bow and stern lines. Abby was off the boat in a flash. Even the dock seemed to be swaying.

'Just leave her rigged,' said Mark. 'Until we find out what's up with Archer.'

'He's probably got the party started already,' said Mohandas.

Oh Lord, Abby thought as she and Mark walked up the pier, his arm slung possessively around her shoulder. More boat talk coming up. Tanned men standing around with their gin and tonics and their polo shirts and their booming laughter.

They went inside the club, stepping from sunlight into shadow. The first thing she noticed was the silence. She saw Marilee standing at the bar with a drink in her hand. Saw Archer sitting by himself at a table, no drink, just a paper coaster in front of him. *Red Eye*'s crew was gathered around the bar, no one moving, no one saying a thing. The only sound in the room was the clatter of ice cubes in Marilee's glass as she lifted the drink to her lips, took a sip and set it back down again on the counter.

Mark said, 'Is something wrong?'

Marilee looked up and blinked, as if noticing

Mark for the first time. Then she looked back down at the counter. At her drink.

'They found Aaron,' she said.

It was the grinding of the Stryker bone saw that usually did it; that or the smell. This one smelled pretty bad.

Homicide Detective Bernard Katzka glanced across the autopsy table and saw that the stench had gotten to Lundquist. His younger partner was turned partially away from the table, gloved hand cupped over his nose and mouth, his movie-star good looks twisted into a squint of nausea. Lundquist had not yet developed the stomach for autopsies; most cops never did. While the cutting open of dead bodies was not Katzka's favorite spectator sport, over the years he had trained himself to view the procedure as an intellectual exercise, to focus not on the humanity of the victim but on the purely organic nature of death. He had seen bodies cooked in fires, bodies scraped off the pavement after twenty-story free falls, bodies shot or stabbed or both, bodies gnawed by rodents. Except for the children, which always upset him, one body was like any other on the table, a specimen stripped, examined, and cataloged. To view them any other way was to invite nightmares.

Bernard Katzka was forty-four years old and a widower. Three years ago, he had watched his wife die of cancer. Katzka had already lived his worst nightmare.

He focused impassively on the body now being autopsied. The corpse was a fifty-four-year-old white male, married with two college-aged children, a cardiologist by profession. His identity had been confirmed by fingerprints as well as visual ID by the widow. The experience must have been profoundly upsetting to her. Viewing the corpse of a loved one is difficult enough. When that loved one has been hanging by the neck for two days in a warm and unventilated room, the sight would be truly horrifying.

The widow, he'd been told, had fainted dead away on the morgue floor.

And no wonder, thought Katzka, looking down at the corpse of Aaron Levi. The face was a bloodless white; its arterial supply had been cut off by the pressure of the leather belt looped around the neck. The protruding tongue was a scaly black, its mucous surface dried out by two days' exposure to air. The eyelids were only partially closed. The slitted openings revealed scleral hemorrhages that had turned the whites of the eyes a frightening blood-red. Below the neck, where the belt had imprinted its ligature mark, the skin showed the classic pattern of dependent pooling, a bruiselike discoloration of the lower legs and arms as well as pinpoint hemorrhages, called Tardieu spots, where vessels had ruptured. All of this was consistent with death by hanging. The only visible injury, aside from the ligature marks around the neck, was a coin-shaped bruise on the left shoulder.

Dr Rowbotham and his assistant, both gowned,

gloved, and wearing protective goggles, completed the thoraco-abdominal incision. It was Y-shaped with two diagonal incisions starting at the shoulders and joining at the lower end of the sternum, then a vertical slice down the abdomen to the pubic bone. Rowbotham had served thirty-two years with the ME's office, and very little seemed to surprise or excite him. If anything, he looked slightly bored as he cut into the body. He was dictating in his usual monotone as his foot clicked on and off the recording pedal. Now he lifted off the triangular shield of rib and breastbone and exposed the pleural cavity.

'Take a look, Slug,' he said to Katzka. The nickname had nothing to do with Katzka's appearance, which was average in every way. Rather, it was a reflection of Katzka's unflappable nature. Among his fellow cops, the running joke was that if you shot Bernard Katzka on a Monday, he might react by Friday. But only if he was pissed.

Katzka leaned forward to peer inside the chest cavity, his expression every bit as flat as Rowbotham's. 'I don't see anything unusual.'

'Exactly. Maybe a little pleural congestion. Probably due to capillary leakage from hypoxia. But it's all consistent with asphyxiation.'

'So I guess we're out of here, huh?' said Lundquist. Already he was sliding away from the table, away from the smell, impatient to get on to other things. He was like all the other young bucks, eager to cut to the chase. Any chase.

Suicide by hanging was not something he wanted to waste his time on.

Katzka did not move from the table.

'We really need to watch the rest of this, Slug?' asked Lundquist.

'They're just starting.'

'It's a suicide.'

'This one feels different to me.'

'The findings are classic. You just heard it.'

'He got out of bed in the middle of the night. He got up, got dressed, and climbed in his car. Think about it. Getting out of your nice warm bed to go hang yourself on the top floor of a hospital.'

Lundquist glanced at the body, then looked away again.

By now Rowbotham and his assistant had severed the trachea and the great vessels and were removing the heart and lungs in one floppy bundle. Rowbotham dropped them onto a hanging scale. The steel cradle bounced a few times, squeaking with the weight of the organs.

'It's your only chance to view it,' said Rowbotham, his scalpel now at work on the spleen. 'We finish up here, and it goes straight to burial. Family request.'

'Any particular reason?' asked Lundquist.

'Jewish. You know, quick interment. All the organs have to be returned to the body.' Rowbotham dropped the spleen onto the scale and watched as the indicator needle quivered, then came to a rest.

Lundquist yanked off his autopsy gown, revealing shoulders bulky with muscle. It was all those hours in the gym, pumping and sweating. He had restless energy and he was showing it now. Always on to bigger and better things, that was Lundquist. Katzka still had to work on him, and the lesson today ought to be the fallibility of first impressions – not an easy thing to get across to a young cop who had all that confidence, all those good looks. That and a full head of hair.

Rowbotham continued with the disembowelment. He cut free the intestines, pulling out what seemed like endless loops of bowel. The liver, pancreas, and stomach were removed in a single mass. Finally, the kidneys and bladder were dissected out and dropped onto that squeaky scale. Another weight was called out, recorded. A few more mutterings into the tape recorder. What was left was a gaping cavity.

Now Rowbotham circled around to the corpse's head. He made an incision behind one ear and cut straight across the back of the scalp. He peeled the scalp forward in one flap, doubling it over the face. Then he peeled the other flap back over the neck, exposing the base of the skull. He picked up the oscillating saw. His expression twisted into a grimace as the bone dust began to fly. No one was talking at this point. The saw was too noisy, and the procedure had turned sickening. Cutting into a chest and abdomen, though grotesque, was somehow impersonal. Like butchering a cow. But peeling a man's scalp over his face was mutilating the most human, the most personal aspect of a corpse.

Lundquist, looking a little green, suddenly sat down in a chair by the sink and dropped his head in his hands. Many a cop had made use of that particular chair.

Rowbotham put down the saw and removed the skull cap. Now he freed up the brain for removal. He cut the optic nerves and severed the blood vessels and spinal cord. Then, gingerly, he lifted the brain out in one quivering mass. 'Nothing unusual,' he said, and slid it into a pail of formalin.

'Now we get down to the nitty-gritty. The neck.'

Everything that had come before this was merely preliminary to this stage. The removal of viscera and brain had allowed drainage of fluids out the cranial and chest cavities. The neck dissection could proceed with a minimum of obscuring blood and fluids.

The belt ligature had been removed from the neck early in the autopsy. Rowbotham now examined the furrow left behind on the skin.

'Your classic inverted V shape,' he noted aloud. 'See here, Slug, you've got parallel ligature marks which match the edges of the belt. And at the back here, you see this?'

'Looks like a mark from the buckle.'

'Right. No surprises so far.' Rowbotham picked up his scalpel and began the neck dissection.

By now Lundquist had recovered and was back at the table, looking a little humble. Nausea, thought Katzka, was so satisfyingly democratic. It brought down even muscle-bound cops with full heads of hair.

Rowbotham's blade had already sliced through the skin of the anterior neck. He cut deeper, exposing the pearly white superior horns of the thyroid cartilage.

'No fractures. You've got some hemorrhage over here, in the strap muscles. But the thyroid cartilage and hyoid bone both seem intact.'

'Meaning?'

'Not a thing. Hanging doesn't necessarily cause much internal neck damage. Death results purely from interruption of the blood supply to the brain. All that's needed is compression of the carotid arteries. It's a relatively painless way to kill yourself.'

'You seem pretty sure it's suicide.'

'The only other possibility is accidental. Autoerotic asphyxiation. But you say there was no evidence of that.'

Lundquist said, 'His cock was still zipped up. Didn't look like he'd been jerking off.'

'So we're talking suicide. Homicidal hanging is almost unheard of. If someone was strangled first, you'd see a different ligature pattern. Not this inverted V. And forcing a man's head in a noose, well, that would almost certainly leave other injuries. He'd fight back.'

'There's that bruise on the upper arm.'

Rowbotham shrugged. 'He could have hurt himself in any number of ways.'

'What if he was drugged and unconscious before he was hanged?'

'We'll do a tox screen, Slug, just to make you happy.'

Lundquist cut in with a laugh, 'And we do have to keep Slug happy.' He moved away from the table. 'It's four o'clock. You coming, Slug?'

'I'd like to see the rest of the neck dissection.'

'Whatever turns you on. I say we just call it a suicide and leave it.'

'I would. Except for the lights.'

'What lights?' said Rowbotham, his eyes finally registering interest behind the protective goggles.

'Slug's hung up on the lights in that room,' said Lundquist.

'Dr Levi was found hanging in an unused patient room of the hospital,' explained Katzka. 'The workman who found the body was almost certain the lights were off.'

'Go on,' said Rowbotham.

'Well, your time-of-death finding correlates with what we think happened – that Dr Levi died very early Saturday morning. Well before sunrise. Which means he either hung himself in the dark. Or someone else turned off the lights.'

'Or the workman didn't remember what the fuck he saw,' said Lundquist. 'The guy was puking his guts into the toilet. You think he'd remember if the light switch was up or down?'

'It's just a detail that concerns me.'

Lundquist laughed. 'Doesn't bother me,' he said, and tossed his gown into the laundry bag.

* * *

It was nearly six o'clock that evening when Katzka pulled his Volvo into a parking space at Bayside Hospital. He got out, walked into the lobby, and took the elevator to the thirteenth floor. That was as far as it would take him without a pass key. He had to leave the elevator and climb the emergency stairwell to reach the top level.

The first thing he noticed as he emerged from the stairwell was the silence. The sense of emptiness. For months, this area had been undergoing renovations. No construction workers had come in today, but their equipment was everywhere. The air smelled of sawdust and fresh paint . . . and something else. An odor he recognized from the autopsy room. Death. Decay. He walked past ladders and a Makita saw, and turned the corner.

Halfway down the next corridor, yellow police tape was plastered across one of the doorways. He ducked under the tape and pushed through the closed door.

In this room, the renovations had been completed. There was new wallpaper, custom cabinetry, and a floor-to-ceiling window with a view over the city. A penthouse hospital suite for that special patient with a bottomless wallet. He went into the bathroom and flicked on the wall switch. More luxury. A marble vanity, brass fixtures, a mirror with cosmetic lighting. A thronelike toilet. He turned off the lights and walked back out of the bathroom.

He went to the closet.

This was where Dr Aaron Levi had been found hanging. One end of the leather belt had been tied to the closet dowel. The other end had been looped around Levi's neck. Apparently, he had simply let his legs go limp, causing the belt to tighten around his throat, cutting off carotid blood flow to the brain. If he had changed his mind at the last moment, all he had to do was set his feet back on the floor, stand up, and loosen the belt. But he had not done so. He had hung there for the five to ten seconds it had taken for consciousness to fade.

Thirty-six hours later, on a Sunday afternoon, one of the workmen had come into this room to finish grouting the bathtub. He had not planned on finding a dead body.

Katzka crossed to the window. There he stood looking over the city of Boston. Dr Aaron Levi, he thought, what could've gone so wrong in your life?

A cardiologist. A wife, a nice home, a Lexus. Two kids, grown and in college. For one irrational moment, Katzka felt a flash of rage at Aaron Levi. What the hell had *he* known about despair and hopelessness? What possible reason did he have to end his life? Coward. Coward. Katzka turned away from the window, shaken by his own anger. By his disgust at anyone who chose such an end. And why *this* end? Why hang yourself in this lonely room where no one might find you for days?

There were other ways to commit suicide. Levi

was a doctor. He had access to narcotics, barbiturates, any number of drugs that could be ingested in fatal doses. Katzka knew exactly how much phenobarb it took to end a life. He had made it his business to know. Once, he had counted out the right number of pills, calculated for his own body weight. He had laid them on his dining room table, had contemplated the freedom they represented. An end to grief, to despair. An easy but irreversible way out, once his affairs were in order. But the time had never been quite right. He had too many responsibilities to take care of first. Annie's funeral arrangements. Paying off her hospital bills. Then there'd been a trial that required his testimony, then a double homocide in Roxbury, and the last eight car payments to complete, and then a triple homicide in Brookline, and another trial requiring his testimony.

In the end, Slug Katzka had simply been too busy to kill himself.

Now it was three years later and Annie was buried and those phenobarb pills had long since been disposed of. He never thought about suicide these days. Every so often, though, he'd think about the pills lying on his dining room table, and he would wonder why he had ever been tempted. How he had ever come so close to surrender. He had no sympathy for the Slug of three years ago. Nor did he have sympathy for anyone else with a bottle of pills and a terminal case of self-pity.

And what was your reason, Dr Levi?

He looked at that glowing view of Boston, and

he thought about how it must have been in the last hour of Aaron Levi's life. He tried to imagine climbing out of bed at three in the morning. Driving to the hospital. Riding the elevator to the thirteenth floor and then climbing the last flight of steps to the fourteenth. Walking into this room. Tying the belt over the closet dowel and slipping your head into the loop.

Katzka frowned.

He crossed to the light switch and flipped it up. The lights came on. They worked just fine. So who had turned them off? Aaron Levi? The workman who'd found the body?

Someone else?

Details, thought Katzka. It was the details that drove him crazy.

Eleven

'I can't believe it,' Elaine kept saying. 'I just can't believe it.' She was not crying, had sat dry-eyed through the burial, a fact that greatly disturbed her mother-in-law, Judith, who had wept loudly and unashamedly while the Kaddish was recited over the grave. Judith's pain was as public as the ceremonial slash in her blouse, a symbol of a heart cut by grief. Elaine had not slashed her blouse. Elaine had not shed tears. She now sat in a chair in her living room, a plate of canapés on her lap, and she said, again: 'I can't believe he's gone.'

'You didn't cover the mirrors,' Judith said. 'You should cover them. All the mirrors in your house.'

'Do what you want,' said Elaine.

Judith left the room in search of sheets for the mirrors. A moment later, all the guests gathered in the living room could hear Judith opening and closing closets upstairs.

'It must be a Jewish thing,' whispered Marilee Archer as she passed another tray of finger sandwiches to Abby.

Abby took an olive sandwich and passed the tray along. It moved from hand to hand down a succession of guests. No one was really eating. A polite nibble, a sip of soda, was all that anyone seemed to have stomach for. Abby didn't feel much like eating either. Or talking. At least two dozen people were in the room, seated solemnly on couches and chairs or standing around in small groups, but no one was saying much.

Upstairs, a toilet flushed. Judith, of course. Elaine gave a little wince of embarrassment. Here and there, subdued smiles appeared among the guests. Behind the couch where Abby was seated, someone began to talk about how late autumn was this year. It was October already, and the leaves were just beginning to turn. The silence, at last, had been breached. Now new conversations stirred to life, murmurings about fall gardens and how do you like Dartmouth? and wasn't it warm for October? Elaine sat at the center of it all, not conversing, but obviously relieved that others were.

The sandwich platter had made its rounds and now came back, empty, to Abby. 'I'll refill it,' she said to Marilee, and she rose from the couch and went into the kitchen. There she found the marble countertops covered with platters of food. No one would go hungry today. She was unwrapping a tray of smoked salmon when she looked out the kitchen window and noticed Archer, Raj Mohandas, and Frank Zwick standing outside on the flagstone terrace. They were talking, shaking their heads. Leave it to the men to retreat, she thought. Men had no patience for grieving widows or long silences; they left that ordeal to their wives in the house. They'd even brought a bottle of Scotch outside with them. It sat on the umbrella table, positioned for easy refills. Zwick reached around for the bottle and poured a splash into his glass. As he recapped the bottle, he caught sight of Abby. He said something to Archer. Now Archer and Mohandas were looking at her as well. They all nodded and gave a quick wave. Then the three men crossed the terrace and walked away, into the garden.

'So much food. I don't know what I'm going to do with all of it,' said Elaine. Abby hadn't noticed that she had come into the kitchen. Elaine stood gazing at the countertop and shaking her head. 'I told the caterer forty people, and this is what she brings me. It's not like a wedding. Everyone eats at a wedding. But no one eats much after a funeral.' Elaine looked down at one of the trays and picked up a radish, carved into a tiny rosette. 'Isn't it pretty, how they do it? So much work for something you just put in your mouth.' She set it back down again and stood there, not talking, admiring in silence that radish rosette.

'I'm so sorry, Elaine,' said Abby. 'If only there was something I could say to make it easier.'

'I just wish I could understand. He never said anything. Never told me he . . .' She swallowed and shook her head. She carried the platter of food to the refrigerator, slid it onto a shelf, and shut the door. Turning, she looked at Abby. 'You spoke to him that night. Was there anything you talked about – anything he might have said . . .'

'We discussed one of our patients. Aaron wanted to make sure I was doing all the right things.'

'That's all you talked about?'

'Just the patient. Aaron didn't seem any different to me. Just concerned. Elaine, I never imagined he would . . .' Abby fell silent.

Elaine's gaze drifted to another platter. To the garnish of green onions, the leaves slitted and curled into lacy puffs. 'Did you ever hear anything about Aaron that . . . you wouldn't want to tell me?'

'What do you mean?'

'Were there ever rumors about other women?'

'Never.' Abby shook her head. And said again, with more emphasis, 'Never.'

Elaine nodded, but seemed to take little comfort from Abby's reassurance. 'I never really thought it was a woman,' she said. She picked up another tray and carried it to the refrigerator. When she'd closed the door she said, 'My mother-in-law blames me. She thinks it must be something I did. A lot of people must be wondering.'

'No one makes another person commit suicide.'

'There was no warning. Nothing at all. Oh, I know he wasn't happy about his job. He kept talking about leaving Boston. Or quitting medicine entirely.'

'Why was he so unhappy?'

'He wouldn't talk about it. When he had his own practice in Natick, we'd talk about his work all the time. Then the offer came in from Bayside, and it was too good to refuse. But after we moved here, it was as if I didn't know him anymore. He'd come home and sit down like a zombie in front of that damn computer. Playing video games all evening. Sometimes, late at night, I'd wake up and hear those weird beeps and clicks. And it was Aaron, sitting up all alone, playing some game.' She shook her head and stared down at the countertop. At yet another platter of untouched food. 'You're one of the last people who spoke to him. Isn't there anything you remember?'

Abby gazed out the kitchen window, trying to piece together that last conversation with Aaron. She could think of nothing to distinguish it from any other late-night phone call. They all seemed to blur together, a chorus of monotonous voices demanding action from her tired brain.

Outside, the three men were returning from their garden walk. She watched them cross the terrace to the kitchen door. Zwick was carrying the bottle of Scotch, now half-empty. They entered the house and nodded to her in greeting.

'Nice little garden,' said Archer. 'You should go out and take a tour, Abby.'

'I'd like to,' she said. 'Elaine, maybe you'd come out and show me . . .' She paused.

There was no one standing by the refrigerator. She glanced around the kitchen, saw the platters of food on the counter and an open carton of plastic wrap, a glassy sheet hanging out and fluttering in the air.

Elaine had left the room.

A woman was praying by Mary Allen's bed. She had been sitting there for the last half hour, head bowed, hands clasped together as she murmured aloud to the good Lord Jesus, imploring him to rain down miracles upon the mortal shell of Mary Allen. Heal her, strengthen her, purify her body and her unclean soul so that she might finally accept His word in all its glory.

'Excuse me,' said Abby. 'I'm sorry to intrude, but I need to examine Mrs Allen.'

The woman kept praying. Perhaps she had not heard her. Abby was about to repeat the request, when the woman at last said, 'Amen,' and raised her head. She had unsmiling eyes and dull brown hair with the first streaks of gray. She regarded Abby with a look of irritation.

'I'm Dr DiMatteo,' said Abby. 'I'm taking care of Mrs Allen.'

'So am I,' the woman said, rising to her feet. She made no attempt to shake hands with Abby, but stood with arms cradling the Bible to her chest. 'I'm Brenda Hainey. Mary's niece.'

'I didn't know Mary had a niece. I'm glad you're able to visit.'

'I only heard about her illness two days ago. No one bothered to call me.' Her tone of voice implied that this oversight was somehow Abby's fault.

'We were under the impression Mary had no close relatives.'

'I don't know why. But I'm here now.' Brenda looked at her aunt. 'And she'll be fine.'

Except for the fact she's dying, thought Abbey. She moved to the bedside and said softly: 'Mrs Allen?'

Mary opened her eyes. 'I'm awake, Dr D. Just resting.'

'How are you feeling today?'

'Still nauseated.'

'It could be a side effect of the morphine. We'll give you something to settle your stomach.'

Brenda interjected: 'She's getting morphine?'

'For the pain.'

'Aren't there other ways to relieve her pain?'

Abby turned to the niece. 'Mrs Hainey, could you leave the room please? I need to examine your aunt.'

'It's Miss Hainey,' said Brenda. 'And I'm sure Aunt Mary would rather have me stay.'

'I still have to ask you to leave.'

Brenda glanced at her aunt, obviously expecting a protest. Mary Allen stared straight ahead, silent.

Brenda clutched the Bible tighter. 'I'll be right outside, Aunt Mary.'

'Dear Lord,' whispered Mary, as the door shut behind Brenda. 'This must be my punishment.'

'Are you referring to your niece?'

Mary's tired gaze focused on Abbey. 'Do you think my soul needs saving?'

'I'd say that's entirely up to you. And no one

else.' Abby took out her stethoscope. 'Can I listen to your lungs?'

Obediently Mary sat up and lifted her hospital gown.

Her breath sounds were muffled. By tapping down Mary's back, Abby could hear the change between liquid and air, could tell that more fluid had accumulated in the chest since the last time she'd examined her.

Abby straightened. 'How's your breathing?'

'It's fine.'

'We may need to drain some more fluid pretty soon. Or insert another chest tube.'

'Why?'

'To make your breathing easier. To keep you comfortable.'

'Is that the only reason?'

'Comfort is a very important reason, Mrs Allen.'

Mary sank back on the pillows. 'Then I'll let you know when I need it,' she whispered.

When Abby emerged from the room, she found Brenda Hainey waiting right outside the door. 'Your aunt would like to sleep for a while,' said Abby. 'Maybe you could come back some other time.'

'There's a matter I need to discuss with you, Doctor.'

'Yes?'

'I was just checking with the nurse. About that morphine. Is it really necessary?'

'I think your aunt would say so.'

'It's making her drowsy. All she does is sleep.'

'We're trying to keep her as pain free as possible. The cancer's spread everywhere. Her bones, her brain. It's the worst kind of pain imaginable. The kindest thing we can do for her is to help her go with a minimum of discomfort.'

'What do you mean, help her go?'

'She's dying. There's nothing we can do to change that.'

'You used those words. *Help her go.* Is that what the morphine's for?'

'It's what she wants and needs right now.'

'I've confronted this sort of issue before, Doctor. With other relatives. I happen to know for a fact it's not legal to medically assist a suicide.'

Abby felt her face flush with anger. Fighting to control it, she said as calmly as she could manage: 'You misunderstand me. All we're trying to do is keep your aunt comfortable.'

'There are other ways to do it.'

'Such as?'

'Calling on higher sources of help.'

'Are you referring to prayer?'

'Why not? It's helped me through difficult times.'

'You're certainly welcome to pray for your aunt. But if I recall, there's nothing against morphine in the Bible.'

Brenda's face went rigid. Her retort was cut off by the sound of Abby's beeper.

'Excuse me,' said Abby coolly, and she walked away, leaving the conversation unfinished. A good thing, too; she'd been on the verge of saying something really sarcastic. Something like: *While you're praying to your God, why don't you ask Him for a cure?* That would surely have pissed off Brenda. With Joe Terrio's lawsuit lurking on the horizon, and Victor Voss determined to get her fired, the last thing she needed was another complaint lodged against her.

She picked up a phone in the nurses' station and dialed the number on her beeper readout.

A woman's voice answered: 'Information Desk.'

'This is Dr DiMatteo. You paged me?'

'Yes, Doctor. There's a Bernard Katzka standing here at the desk. He's wondering if you could meet him here in the lobby.'

'I don't know anyone by that name. I'm sort of busy up here. Could you ask him what his business is?'

There was a background murmur of conversation. When the woman came back on, her voice sounded oddly reticent. 'Dr DiMatteo?'

'Yes.'

'He's a policeman.'

The man in the lobby looked vaguely familiar. He was in his mid-forties, medium height, medium build, with the sort of face that was neither handsome nor homely and not particularly memorable. His hair, a dark brown, was starting to thin at the top, a fact he made no effort to conceal the way some men did with a sideways combing of camouflaging strands. As she approached him, she had the impression that he recognized her as well. His gaze had, in fact, singled her out the moment she stepped off the elevator.

'Dr DiMatteo,' he said. 'I'm Detective Bernard Katzka. Homicide.'

Just hearing that word startled her. What was this all about? They shook hands. Only then, as she met his gaze, did she remember where she'd seen him. The cemetery. Aaron Levi's funeral. He'd been standing slightly apart from everyone, a silent figure in a dark suit. During the service, their gazes had intersected. She'd understood none of the Hebrew being recited, and her attention had wandered to the other mourners. That's when she'd become aware that someone else was scanning the gathering. They had looked at each other, only for a second, and then he'd looked away. At the time, she'd registered almost no impression of the man. Looking up at his face now, she found herself focusing on his eyes, which were a calm, unflinching gray. If not for the intelligence of those eyes, one might never notice Bernard Katzka.

She said, 'Are you a friend of the Levi family?'

'No.'

'I saw you at the cemetery. Or am I mistaken?'

'I was there.'

She paused, waiting for an explanation, but all he said was, 'Is there somewhere we can talk?'

'Can I ask what this is all about?'

'Dr Levi's death.'

She glanced at the lobby doors. The sun

was shining and she had not been outside all day.

'There's a little courtyard with a few benches,' she said. 'Why don't we go out there?'

It was warm outside, a perfect October afternoon. The courtyard garden was in its chrysanthemum phase, the circular bed planted with blooms of rust, orange, and yellow. At the center a fountain poured out a quietly comforting trickle of water. They sat down on one of the wooden benches. A pair of nurses occupying the other bench rose and walked back toward the building, leaving Abby and the detective alone. For a moment nothing was said. The silence made Abby uneasy, but it did not appear to disturb her companion in the least. He seemed accustomed to long silences.

'Elaine Levi gave me your name,' he said. 'She suggested I talk to you.'

'Why?'

'You spoke to Dr Levi early Saturday morning. Is that correct?'

'Yes. On the phone.'

'Do you remember what time that was?'

'Around two A.M., I guess. I was at the hospital.'

'He made the call?'

'Well, he called the SICU and asked to speak to the upper-level resident. I happened to be it that night.'

'Why was he calling?'

'About a patient. She was running a postop fever, and Aaron wanted to discuss a plan of action. Which labs we should order, which X-rays.

216

Do you mind telling me what this is all about?'

'I'm trying to establish the chronology of events. So Dr Levi called the SICU at two A.M. and you came on the line.'

'That's right.'

'Did you talk to him again? After that two A.M. call?'

'No.'

'Did you try to call him?'

'Yes, but he'd already left the house. I spoke to Elaine.'

'What time was that?'

'I don't know. Maybe three o'clock, three-fifteen. I wasn't paying a lot of attention to the clock.'

'You didn't call his house any other time that morning?'

'No. I tried paging his beeper several times, but he never answered. I knew he was somewhere in the building, because his car was in the parking lot.'

'What time did you see it there?'

'I didn't. My boyfriend – Dr Hodell – he saw it when he drove in around four A.M. Look, why is Homicide investigating this?'

He ignored her question. 'Elaine Levi says there was a call around two-fifteen. Her husband answered the phone. A few minutes later he got dressed and left the house. Do you know anything about that call?'

'No. It could have been one of the nurses. Doesn't Elaine know?'

'Her husband took the phone into the bathroom. She didn't hear the conversation.'

'It wasn't me. I spoke to Aaron only once. Now I'd really like to know why you're asking me these questions. This can't possibly be a routine thing you do.'

'No. It's not routine.'

Abby's beeper went off. She recognized the number on the readout. It was the residency office – not an emergency, but she was getting fed up with this conversation anyway. She rose to her feet. 'Detective, I've got work to do. Patients to see. I don't have time to answer a lot of vague questions.'

'My questions are quite specific. I'm trying to establish who made calls at what time that morning. And what was said during those calls.'

'Why?'

'It may have a bearing on Dr Levi's death.'

'Are you saying someone talked him into hanging himself?'

'I'd just like to know who did talk to him.'

'Can't you pull it off the phone company computer or something? Don't they keep records?'

'The two-fifteen call to Dr Levi was made from Bayside Hospital.'

'So it could have been a nurse.'

'Or anyone else in the building.'

'Is that your theory? That someone from Bayside called Aaron and told him something so upsetting that he killed himself?'

'We're considering possibilities other than suicide.'

She stared at him. He had said it so quietly, she wondered if she had understood him correctly. Slowly she sank back down on the bench. Neither one spoke for a moment.

A nurse pushed a woman in a wheelchair across the courtyard. The pair lingered by the flowerbed, admiring the chrysanthemums, then moved on. The only sound in the courtyard was the musical splash of the fountain.

'Are you saying he might have been murdered?' said Abby.

He didn't answer immediately. And she couldn't tell, looking at his face, what his answer might be. He sat motionless, revealing nothing by his posture, his hands, his expression.

'*Did* Aaron hang himself?' she asked.

'The autopsy findings were consistent with asphyxia.'

'That's what you'd expect. It sounds like a suicide.'

'It very well could be.'

'Then why aren't *you* convinced?'

He hesitated. For the first time she saw uncertainty in his eyes, and she knew he was weighing his next words. This was the sort of man who made no move without considering all the ramifications. The sort of man for whom spontaneity itself was a planned action.

He said, 'Two days before he died, Dr Levi brought home a brand new computer.'

'That's all? That's the basis for your questions?'

'He used it to do several things. First, he made

219

plane reservations for two to St. Lucia in the Caribbean. Leaving around Christmas time. Also, he sent an e-mail to his son at Dartmouth, discussing plans for Thanksgiving break. Think about it, Doctor. Two days before committing suicide, this man is making plans for the future. He has a nice vacation on the beach to look forward to. But at two-fifteen A.M., he climbs out of his bed and drives to the hospital. Takes an elevator, then the stairwell, to a deserted floor. Ties a belt to the closet dowel, loops the other end around his neck, and simply lets his legs go limp. Consciousness wouldn't fade at once. There would be five, maybe ten seconds left to change his mind. He has a wife, kids, and a beach on St. Lucia to look forward to. But he chooses to die. Alone, and in the dark.' Katzka's gaze held hers. 'Think about it.'

Abby swallowed. 'I'm not sure I want to.'

'I have.'

She looked at his quiet gray eyes and she wondered: What other nightmarish things do you think about? What kind of man chooses a job that requires such terrible visions?

'We know Dr Levi's car was found in its usual parking spot here at the hospital. We don't know why he drove here. Or why he left the house at all. Except for that two-fifteen caller, you're the last person we know of who spoke to Dr Levi. Did he say anything about leaving for the hospital?'

'He was concerned about our patient. He might

have decided to come in and see to the problem himself.'

'As opposed to letting you deal with it?'

'I'm a second-year resident, Detective Katzka, not the attending physician. Aaron was the transplant team internist.'

'I understood he was a cardiologist.'

'He was also an internist. When there was a medical problem, like a fever, the nurses would usually contact him. And he'd call in other consultants if he needed them.'

'During that phone call, did he say he was coming into the hospital?'

'No. It was just a game plan discussion. I told him what I was going to do. That I'd examine the patient and order some blood work and X-rays. He approved.'

'That was it?'

'That was the extent of our conversation.'

'Did anything he say strike you as not quite right?'

Again she thought about it. And she remembered that initial pause in their phone conversation. And how dismayed Aaron had sounded when she'd first come on the line.

'Dr DiMatteo?'

She looked up at Katzka. Though he'd said her name quietly, his expression had taken on new alertness.

'Do you remember something?' he asked.

'I remember he didn't sound very happy that I was the resident on duty.'

'Why not?'

'Because of the particular patient involved. Her husband and I – we'd had a conflict. A serious one.' She looked away, feeling a little queasy at the thought of Victor Voss. 'I'm sure Aaron would've preferred that I stay miles away from Mrs Voss.'

Katzka's silence made her look up again.

'Mrs *Victor* Voss?' he said.

'Yes. You know the name?'

Katzka sat back, exhaling softly. 'I know he founded VMI International. What surgery did his wife have?'

'A heart transplant. She's doing much better now. The fever resolved after a few days of antibiotics.'

Katzka was staring at the fountain, where sprays of sunlit water sparkled like gold chain. Abruptly he rose to his feet.

'Thank you for your time, Dr DiMatteo,' he said. 'I may call you again.'

She started to reply 'Any time,' but he had already turned and was swiftly walking away. The man had gone from absolute motionlessness to the speed of sound. Amazing.

Her beeper chirped. It was the residency office again. She silenced it. When she looked up, Katzka was nowhere in sight. The magical disappearing cop. Still puzzling over his questions, she returned to the lobby and picked up the house phone.

A secretary answered her call. 'Residency office.'

'This is Abby DiMatteo. You paged me?'

'Oh, yes. Two things. You had an outside call from Helen Lewis at New England Organ Bank. She wanted to know if you ever got an answer to your question about that transplant. You didn't answer your page, so she hung up.'

'If she calls again, let her know my question's already been answered. What was the second thing?'

'You have a certified letter up here. I signed for it. I hope that's okay.'

'Certified?'

'It was delivered a few minutes ago. I thought you'd want to know.'

'Who sent it?'

There was a sound of shuffling papers. Then, 'It's from Hawkes, Craig and Sussman. Attorneys at Law.'

Abby's stomach went into free fall. 'I'll be right there,' she said, and hung up. The Terrio lawsuit again. The wheels of justice would surely grind her to dust. Her hands were sweating as she rode the elevator to the administrative floor. *Dr DiMatteo, known for her calmness in the OR, is a nervous wreck.*

The residency office secretary was on the telephone. She saw Abby and pointed at the mail cubicles.

There was one envelope in Abby's slot. *Hawkes, Craig and Sussman* was printed in the upper left-hand corner. She ripped it open.

At first she didn't understand what she was reading. Then she focused on the plaintiff's name, and the meaning at last sank in. Her stomach had ended its free fall. It had crashed. This letter wasn't about Karen Terrio at all. It was about another patient, a Michael Freeman. An alcoholic, he had unexpectedly ruptured a swollen blood vessel in his esophagus and bled to death in his hospital room. Abby had been the intern on his case. She remembered it as a shockingly gruesome end. Now Michael Freeman's wife was suing, and she had retained Hawkes, Craig and Sussman to represent her. Abby was the defendant. The only defendant named in the lawsuit.

'Dr DiMatteo? Are you all right?'

Abby suddenly realized that she was leaning against the mail cubicles and that the room wasn't quite steady. The secretary was frowning at her.

'I'm . . . fine,' said Abby. 'I'm okay.'

By the time Abby made it out of the room, she was in full retreat. She fled straight to the on-call room, locked herself inside, and sat down on the bed. Then she unfolded the letter and read it again. And again.

Two lawsuits in two weeks. Vivian was right. Abby would be in court for the rest of her natural life.

She knew she should call her attorney, but she couldn't bring herself to deal with that right now. So she remained sitting on the bed, staring at that letter on her lap. Thinking about all the years, all the work it had taken, just to get to this point in her career. She thought about the nights she'd fallen asleep on her books while everyone else in the dorm was out on dates. The weekends she'd worked double shifts as a hospital phlebotomist, drawing tubes and tubes of blood to earn her tuition. She thought about the hundred and twenty thousand dollars in student loans she still had to pay off. The dinners of peanut butter sandwiches. The movies and concerts and plays she had never seen.

And she thought about Pete, who'd been the reason for it all. The brother she'd wanted to save, and hadn't been able to. Most of all, she thought of Pete, eternally ten years old.

Victor Voss was winning. He'd said he would destroy her and that was exactly what he was going to do.

Fight back. It was time to fight back. Only she couldn't think of any way to do it. She wasn't clever enough. The letter burned like acid in her hands. She thought and thought about how to stop him, but she had nothing with which to fight back except that shove he'd given her in the SICU. A charge of assault and battery. It was not enough, not nearly enough to stop him.

Fight back. You have to think of a way.

The beeper went off. It was a page from the surgical ward. She was in no mood to take any goddamn calls. She reached for the phone and stabbed in the numbers. 'DiMatteo,' she snapped.

'Doctor, we're having a problem here with Mary Allen's niece.'

'What is it?'

225

'We're trying to give the four o'clock morphine dose, but Brenda won't let us. Maybe you could—'

'I'm on my way.' Abby slammed the receiver down. Fuck Brenda, she thought, shoving the attorney's letter in her pocket. She used the stairwell, running the two flights down. By the time she emerged on the ward she was breathing hard, not from exertion, but from rage. She stormed straight into Mary Allen's room.

Two nurses were inside, talking with Brenda. Mary Allen was awake in bed, but she looked too weak and in pain to contribute a word.

'She's doped up enough as it is,' Brenda was saying. 'Look at her. She can't even talk to me.'

'Maybe she doesn't want to talk to you,' said Abby.

The nurses turned to Abby with expressions of relief. The voice of authority had arrived.

'Please leave the room, Miss Hainey,' said Abby.

'The morphine isn't necessary.'

'I'll determine that. Now leave the room.'

'She hasn't got much time left. She needs all her faculties.'

'For what?'

'To fully accept the Lord. If she dies before accepting Him—'

Abby held her hand out to the nurse. 'Give me the morphine. I'll administer it.'

At once the syringe was handed to her. Abby stepped over to the IV line. As she uncapped the needle, she saw Mary Allen's weak nod of gratitude.

'You give her that dope and I'll call an attorney,' said Brenda.

'Do that,' said Abby. She slipped the needle into the IV injection port. She was just pushing the plunger when Brenda surged forward and pulled the catheter out of her aunt's arm. Blood dribbled from the puncture site onto the floor. Those bright red drops spattering the linoleum were the final outrage.

A nurse clapped gauze to Mary Allen's arm. Abby turned to Brenda and said: 'Get out of this room.'

'You left me no choice, Doctor.'

'*Get out!*'

Brenda's eyes widened. She took a step backward.

'Do you want me to call Security to throw you out?' Abby was yelling now, moving toward Brenda, who continued to back away into the hall. 'I don't want you anywhere near my patient! I don't want you harassing her with your Bible bullshit!'

'I'm her relative!'

'*I don't give a fuck who you are!*'

Brenda's jaw dropped open. Without another word she spun around and walked away.

'Dr DiMatteo, can I speak to you?'

Abby turned and saw the nursing supervisor, Georgina Speer.

'That was very inappropriate, Doctor. We don't speak to the public that way.'

'She just pulled the IV out of my patient's arm!'

227

'There are better ways to handle it. Call Security. Call for any assistance. But profanity is definitely not the way we do it in this hospital. Do you understand?'

Abby took a deep breath. 'I understand,' she said. And added, in a whisper, 'I'm sorry.'

After she'd restarted Mary Allen's IV, Abby retreated to the on-call room and lay listlessly on the bed. Staring up at the ceiling, she wondered: What the hell is wrong with me? She'd never lost control like that before, never even come close to cursing at a patient or relative. I'm going crazy, she thought. The stress is finally breaking me. Maybe I'm not fit to be a doctor.

Her beeper went off. God, would they never leave her alone? What she'd give to go a whole day, a whole week, without being beeped or phoned or harassed. It was the hospital operator paging her. She picked up the phone and dialed zero.

'Outside call for you, Doctor,' said the operator. 'Let me put it through.' There were a few transfer clicks, then a woman said:

'Dr Abby DiMatteo?'

'Speaking.'

'This is Helen Lewis at New England Organ Bank. You left a message last Saturday about a heart donor. We expected someone at Bayside to call back, but no one did. So I thought I should check back.'

'I'm sorry. I should have called you, but things have been crazy around here. It turns out it was just a misunderstanding.'

'Well that makes it easy. Since I couldn't find the information anyway. If you have any other questions, just give me a—'

'Excuse me,' Abby cut in. 'What did you just say?'

'I couldn't find the information.'

'Why not?'

'The data you requested isn't in our system.'

For a solid ten seconds Abby was silent. Then she asked, slowly, 'Are you absolutely certain it's not there?'

'I've searched our computer files. On the date you gave for the harvest, we have no record of a heart donor. Anywhere in Vermont.'

Twelve

'Here it is,' said Colin Wettig, laying open the *Directory of Medical Specialists*. 'Timothy Nicholls. BA, University of Vermont. MD, Tufts. Residency, Massachusetts General. Specialty: Thoracic Surgery. Affiliated with Wilcox Memorial, Burlington, Vermont.' He slid the book onto the conference table for anyone in the room to look at. 'So there really is a thoracic surgeon named Tim Nicholls practicing in Burlington. He's not some figment of Archer's imagination.'

'When I spoke to him on Saturday,' said Archer, 'Nicholls claimed he was there at the harvest. And he said it took place at Wilcox Memorial. Unfortunately, I haven't been able to find anyone else who was in the OR with him. And now I can't get hold of Nicholls. His office staff tells me he's taken a prolonged leave of absence. I don't know what's going on, Jeremiah, but I sure as hell wish we'd had nothing to do with it. Because it's starting to smell pretty rotten.'

Jeremiah Parr shifted uneasily in his chair and glanced at attorney Susan Casado. He didn't bother to look at Abby, who was sitting at the far end of the table, next to the transplant co-ordinator, Donna Toth. Maybe he didn't *want* to look at her. Abby, after all, was the one who had brought this mess to everyone's attention. The one who had initiated this meeting.

'What exactly *is* going on here?' Parr asked.

Archer said, 'I think Victor Voss arranged to keep the donor out of the registry system. To shunt the heart directly to his wife.'

'Could he do that?'

'Given enough money – probably.'

'And he certainly has the money,' said Susan. 'I just saw the latest list in *Kiplinger*'s. The fifty wealthiest people in America. He's moved up to number fourteen.'

'Maybe you'd better explain to me how donor assignments are *supposed* to work,' said Parr. 'Because I don't understand how this happened.'

Archer looked at the transplant coordinator. 'Donna usually handles it. Why don't we let her explain?'

Donna Toth nodded. 'The system's pretty straightforward,' she said. 'We have both a regional and a national waiting list of patients needing organs. The national system's the United Network for Organ Sharing, or UNOS for short. The regional list is maintained by New England Organ Bank. Both systems rank patients in order of need. The list has nothing to do with wealth,

231

race, or social status. Only how critical their conditions are.' She opened a folder and took out a sheet of paper. She passed it to Parr. 'That's what the latest regional list looks like. I had it faxed over from the NEOB office in Brookline. As you can see, it gives each patient's medical status, organ required, the nearest transplant center, and the phone number to contact, which is usually the transplant coordinator's.'

'What're these other notations here?'

'Clinical information. Minimum and maximum height and weight acceptable for the donor. Whether the patient's had any previous transplants, which would make cross matching more difficult because of antibodies.'

'You said this list is in order of need?'

'That's right. The number one name is the most critical.'

'Where was Mrs Voss?'

'On the day she received her transplant, she was number three on the AB blood type list.'

'What happened to the first two names?'

'I checked with NEOB. Both names were reclassified as Code Eights a few days later. Permanently inactive and off the list.'

'Meaning they died?' Susan Casado asked softly.

Donna nodded. 'They never got their transplants.'

'Jesus,' groaned Parr. 'So Mrs Voss got a heart that should have gone to someone else.'

'That seems to be what happened. We don't know how it was arranged.'

'How did *we* get notified of the donor?' asked Susan.

'A phone call,' said Donna. 'That's how it usually happens. The transplant coordinator at the donor hospital handles it. He or she will check the latest NEOB waiting list and call the contact number for the first patient on the list.'

'So you were called by Wilcox Memorial's transplant coordinator?'

'Yes. I've spoken to him before on the phone, about other donors. So I had no reason to question this particular donation.'

Archer shook his head. 'I don't know how Voss managed this. Every step of the way, it looked legal and aboveboard to us. Someone at Wilcox obviously got paid off. My bet is, it's their transplant coordinator. So Voss's wife gets the heart. And Bayside gets suckered into a cash-for-organs arrangement. And we don't have any of the donor paperwork to double-check this.'

'It's still missing?' asked Parr.

'I haven't been able to find it,' said Donna. 'The donor records aren't anywhere in my office.'

Victor Voss, thought Abby. *Somehow, he's made the papers disappear.*

'The worst part,' said Wettig, 'is the kidneys.'

Parr frowned at the General. 'What?'

'His wife didn't need the kidneys,' said Wettig. 'Or the pancreas or the liver. So what happened to those? If they never made it to the registry?'

'They must have gotten dumped,' said Archer.

'Right. That's three, four lives that could have been saved. And got tossed instead.'

There was a ballet of shaking heads, dismayed expressions.

'What are we going to do about this?' said Abby.

Her question was met with a momentary silence.

'I'm not sure what we should do,' said Parr. He looked at the attorney. 'Are we obligated to follow up on this?'

'Ethically, yes,' said Susan. 'However, there's a consequence, if we report this. I can think of several consequences, in fact. First, there's no way we can keep this from the press. A cash-for-organs deal, especially involving Victor Voss, is a juicy story. Second, we're going to be, in a sense, breaching patient confidentiality. That's not going to sit well with a certain segment of our patient population.'

Wettig snorted. 'Meaning the bloody rich ones.'

'The ones who keep this hospital alive,' corrected Parr.

'Exactly.' Susan continued. 'If they hear that Bayside spurred the investigation of someone like Victor Voss, they're not going to trust us to keep *their* records private. We could lose all our private-pay transplant referrals. Finally, what if this somehow gets turned around? Made to look like we were *part* of the conspiracy? We'd lose our credibility as a transplant center. If it turns out Voss really did keep that donor out of the registry system, we'll be tainted as well.'

Abby glanced at Archer, who looked stunned by the possibility. This could destroy the Bayside transplant program. It could destroy the team.

'How much of this has already gotten out?' asked Parr. He looked, at last, at Abby. 'What did you tell NEOB about this, Dr DiMatteo?'

'When I spoke to Helen Lewis, I wasn't sure what was going on. Neither of us were. We were just trying to figure out why the donor hadn't been entered in their system. That's how we left it. Unresolved. Immediately after the call, I told Archer and Dr Wettig about it.'

'And Hodell. You must have told Hodell.'

'I haven't spoken to Mark yet. He's been in surgery all day.'

Parr sighed with relief. 'All right. So it's just in this room. And all Mrs Lewis knows is that you're not sure what happened.'

'Correct.'

Susan Casado shared Parr's look of relief. 'We've still got a shot at damage control. I think what needs to be done now is, Dr Archer should call NEOB. Reassure Mrs Lewis that we've cleared up the misunderstanding. Chances are, she'll leave it at that. We'll continue to make inquiries, but discreetly. We should try reaching Dr Nicholls again. He might be able to clear things up.'

'No one seems to know when Nicholls is coming back from his leave of absence,' said Archer.

'What about the other surgeon?' asked Susan. 'The guy from Texas?'

'Mapes? I haven't tried calling him yet.'

'Someone should.'

Parr cut in: 'I disagree. I don't think we should be contacting anyone else about this.'

'Your reason, Jeremiah?'

'The less we know about it, the less involved we'll be in this mess. We should stay miles away from it. Tell Helen Lewis that it was a directed donation. And that's why it never went through NEOB. Then let's just move on.'

'In other words,' said Wettig, 'stick our goddamn heads in the sand.'

'See no evil, hear no evil.' Parr glanced around the table. He seemed to take the lack of response as a sign of general assent. 'Needless to say, we don't talk about it outside this room.'

Abby couldn't hold her silence. 'The problem is,' she said, 'the evil doesn't go away. Whether or not we hear about it or see it, it's still *there*.'

'Bayside's the innocent party,' said Parr. 'We shouldn't have to suffer. And we certainly shouldn't expose ourselves to unfair scrutiny.'

'What about the ethical obligations? This could happen again.'

'I really doubt Mrs Voss will be needing another heart any time soon. It's an isolated incident, Dr DiMatteo. A desperate husband bent the rules to save his wife. It's done with. We just need to install safeguards to ensure it doesn't happen again.' Parr looked at Archer. 'Can we do that?'

Archer nodded. 'We're damn well going to have to.'

'What happens to Victor Voss?' said Abby. By the silence that followed, she knew the answer: nothing would happen to him. Nothing ever happened to men like Victor Voss. He could beat the system and buy a heart, buy a surgeon, buy an entire hospital. And he could buy lawyers, too, a whole army of them, enough to turn a lowly surgical resident's dreams into scorched earth.

She said, 'He's out to ruin me. I thought it would ease up after his wife's transplant, but it hasn't. He's dumped offal in my car. He's initiated two lawsuits, with more on the way, I'm sure of it. It's hard for me to see no evil, hear no evil, when he's resorting to tactics like those.'

'Can you prove it's Voss doing these things?' asked Susan.

'Who else would it be?'

'Dr DiMatteo,' said Parr, 'this hospital's reputation is on the line. We need everyone to be on the same team, everyone to pull together. Including you. This is your hospital too.'

'What if it all comes out anyway? What if it hits the front page of the *Globe*? Bayside's going to be accused of a coverup. And this'll blow up in all your faces.'

'That's why it can't leave this room,' said Parr.

'It could get out anyway.' She lifted her chin. 'It probably will.'

Parr and Susan exchanged nervous glances.

Susan said: 'That's a risk we'll have to take.'

Abby stripped off her OR gown, tossed it in the laundry hamper, and pushed through the double doors. It was nearly midnight. The patient, a stabbing victim, was now in Recovery, the postop orders were being written by the intern, and the ER had nothing coming down the pike. All was quiet in the trenches.

She wasn't sure she welcomed the lull. It gave her too much time to brood over what had been said at that afternoon meeting.

My one chance to fight back, she thought, and I can't. Not if I'm going to be a team player. Not if I'm going to keep Bayside's interests at heart.

And her own interests as well. That she was still considered part of the team was a good sign. It meant she had a chance of staying on here, a chance of actually completing her residency. It came down to a deal with the devil. Keep her mouth shut, and hang on to the dream. If Victor Voss would let her.

If her conscience would let her.

Several times that evening, she'd been on the verge of picking up the phone and calling Helen Lewis. That's all it would take, one phone call, to get NEOB into the picture. One phone call to expose Victor Voss. Now, as she headed back to the on-call room, she was still mulling over what she should do. She unlocked the door and stepped inside.

It was the fragrance she noticed first, even before she turned on the lights. The perfume of roses and lilies. She switched on the lamp and stared in wonder at the vase of flowers on the desk.

A rustle of sheets drew her gaze to the bed. 'Mark?' she said.

He came awake with a start. For a moment he seemed unsure of where he was. Then he saw her and smiled. 'Happy birthday.'

'God. I completely forgot.'

'I didn't,' he said.

She went to the bed and sat down beside him. He'd fallen asleep in his surgical scrubs and when she bent down to kiss him, she could smell that familiar on-call scent of Betadine and fatigue. 'Ouch. You need a shave.'

'I need another kiss.'

She smiled and obliged him. 'How long have you been here?'

'What time is it?'

'Midnight.'

'Two hours.'

'You've been waiting here since ten?'

'I didn't actually plan it this way. I guess I just fell asleep.' He moved aside to make room for her on the narrow mattress. She pulled off her shoes and lay down beside him. At once she felt comforted by the warmth of the bed, and of the man. She thought of telling him about the meeting this afternoon, about the second lawsuit, but she didn't want to talk about any of it. All she wanted was to be held.

'Sorry I forgot the cake,' he said.

'I can't believe I forgot my own birthday. Maybe I wanted to forget it. Twenty-eight already.'

Laughing, he wrapped an arm around her. 'Such a decrepit old lady.'

'I *feel* old. Especially tonight.'

'Yeah, well then, I feel ancient.' He kissed her, softly, on the ear. 'And I'm not getting any younger. So maybe now's the time.'

'Time for what?'

'To do what I should have done months ago.'

'Which is?'

He turned her toward him and cupped her face in his hand. 'Ask you to marry me.'

She stared at him, unable to say a word, but so filled with happiness she knew the answer must be plain in her eyes. She was suddenly, joyfully, aware of his every aspect. His hand warming her cheek. His face, tired and no longer young, but far more dear to her because of that.

'I knew, a couple of nights ago, that this was what I wanted,' he said. 'You were on call. And there I was at home, eating dinner out of a carton. I went up to bed, and I saw your things on the dresser. Your hairbrush. Jewelry box. That bra that you never seem to put away.' Softly he laughed. So did she. 'Anyway, that's when I knew. I never want to live anywhere without your stuff lying on my dresser. I don't think I could. Not anymore.'

'Oh, Mark.'

'The crazy thing is, you're hardly ever home. And when you are home, I'm not. We sort of wave to each other in the hallways. Or hold hands in the elevator if we're lucky. What matters to me is knowing that, when I do go home, I see your things on that dresser. I know you've been there, or you will be there. And that's enough.'

Through tears, she saw him smile. And she felt his heart thudding as though in fear.

'So what do you think, Dr D?' he whispered. 'Can we fit a wedding into our tight schedules?'

Her answer was half sob, half laughter. 'Yes. Yes, yes, *yes*!' And rising up, she rolled on top of him, her arms thrown around his neck, her mouth finding his. They were both laughing, kissing, while the mattress springs gave horrible squeaks. The bed was far too small; they'd never be able to sleep in it together.

But for the purpose of lovemaking, it suited just fine.

She had been beautiful once. Sometimes, when Mary Allen looked at her own hands and saw the wrinkles and brown stains of age, she would wonder with a start: Whose hands are these? A stranger's, certainly; an old woman's. Not my hands, not pretty Mary Hatcher's. Then the flash of confusion would pass, and she'd look around the hospital room and realize she'd been dreaming again. Not a true dream that came with true sleep, but a sort of mist that drifted through her brain and lingered there, even into wakefulness. It was the morphine. She was grateful for the morphine. It took away her pain and it opened some secret gate in her mind, allowing images to flow in, images of a remembered life, almost over now. She had heard life described as a circle, a returning to the point of one's beginning, but her own life did not seem nearly so organized. Rather, it was like a tapestry of unruly threads, some broken, some raveled, none of them straight and true.

But woven with so many, many colors.

She closed her eyes and that secret gate swung open. A path to the sea. Hedges of beach roses, pink and sweet smelling. Warm sand swallowing up her toes. Waves tumbling in from the bay. The luxury of hands skimming lotion down her body.

Geoffrey's hands.

The gate swung wider, and he stepped in, a memory fully rendered. Not as he was, on that beach, but as she'd first seen him, in his uniform, dark hair ruffled, his face turning toward her in mid-laugh. Their first look at each other. It had been on a Boston street. She was carrying a sack of groceries, looking every inch the efficient young housewife on her way home to cook her husband his evening meal. Her dress had been an exceedingly ugly shade of brown; it was wartime, and one had to make do with what was available in the shops. She had not done up her hair, and the wind was whipping it into a witch's mane. She thought she looked quite hideous. But there was that young man, smiling at her, his gaze following her as she passed him on the sidewalk.

The next day, he would be there again, and they

would look at each other, not strangers this time, but something more.

Geoffrey. Another lost thread. Not one that merely frayed and weakened until it broke, like her husband, but one that had been ripped too early from the tapestry, tearing an empty furrow that ran all the way down to the final weaving.

She heard a door swing open. A real door. Heard footsteps. Softly they approached her bed.

Suspended in her morphine daze, she had to struggle just to open her eyes. When at last she did, she found the room was dark except for one small circle of light hovering nearby. It was the light she tried to focus on. It danced like a firefly, then steadied to a single bright pinpoint on her bedsheet. She focused harder and made out a patch of darkness that had materialized by her bed. Something not quite solid, not quite real. She wondered if this, too, was a morphine dream. Some unwelcome memory come through the gate to haunt her. She heard the sheets slither aside and felt a hand grasp her arm with a touch that was cold and rubbery.

Her breath come out in a rush of fear. This was not a dream. This was real. *Real*. The hand was here to lead her somewhere, to take her away.

In panic she thrashed, managed to pull free from that grip.

A voice said, softly: 'It's all right, Mary. It's all right. It's just time for you to sleep.'

Mary fell still. 'Who are you?'

'I'm taking care of you tonight.'

'Is it already time for my medicine?'

'Yes. It's time.'

Mary saw the penlight playing, once again, on her arm. Her IV. She watched as the gloved hand produced a syringe. The plastic cap was removed and something glittered in the thin beam of light. A needle.

Mary felt a fresh stirring of alarm. Gloves. Why were the hands wearing gloves?

She said, 'I want to see my nurse. Please call my nurse.'

'There's no need.' The needle tip pierced the IV injection port. The plunger began its slow and steady descent. Mary felt a warmth flush through her vein and then up her arm. She realized that the syringe was very full, that the plunger was taking far longer than usual to deliver its dose of painless oblivion. Not right, she thought, as the syringe emptied its contents into her vein. Something is not right.

'I want my nurse,' she said. She managed to lift her head and call out, weakly, 'Nurse! Please! I need—'

A gloved hand closed over her mouth. It shoved her head back to the pillow with such force Mary felt as though her neck had snapped. She reached up to pry away the hand, but could not. It was clamped too tightly over her mouth, muffling her cries. She thrashed, felt the IV rip loose, felt the disconnected tubing dribbling saline. Still the hand would not release her mouth. By now the liquid warmth had spread from her arm to her chest and was rushing toward her brain. She tried to move her legs and found she couldn't.

Found, suddenly, that she didn't care.

The hand slid away from her face.

She was running. She was a girl again, her hair long and brown and flying around her shoulders. The sand was warm under her bare feet, and the air smelled of beach roses and the sea.

The gate hung wide open before her.

The ringing telephone pulled Abby from a place that was both warm and safe. She stirred awake and found an arm wrapped around her waist. Mark's. Somehow, despite the small bed, they'd managed to fall asleep together. Gently she disentangled herself from his embrace and reached for the ringing telephone.

'DiMatteo.'

'Dr D, this is Charlotte on Four West. Mrs Allen just expired. The interns are all busy at the moment, so we wondered if you could come down and pronounce the patient.'

'Right. I'll be there.' Abby hung up and lay back down on the bed for a moment, allowing herself the luxury of slowly coming awake. Mrs Allen. Dead. It had happened sooner than she'd expected. She felt relieved that the ordeal was finally over, and guilty that she should experience such relief at all. At three in the morning, a patient's death seems less a tragedy and more a nuisance, just another reason for lost sleep.

Abby sat up on the side of the bed and pulled on

her shoes. Mark was snoring softly, oblivious to ringing telephones. Smiling, she leaned over and gave him a kiss. 'I do,' she whispered in his ear. And she left the room.

Charlotte met her at the Four West nurses' station. Together they walked to Mary's room, at the far end of the hall.

'We found her at two A.M. rounds. I checked her at midnight, and she was sleeping, so it happened sometime after that. At least she went peacefully.'

'Have you called the family?'

'I called the niece. The one listed in the chart. I told her she didn't have to come in, but she insisted. She's on her way now. We've been cleaning things up for the visit.'

'Cleaning?'

'Mary must have pulled her IV out. There was saline and blood spilled on the floor.' Charlotte opened the door to the patient's room, and they both entered.

By the light of a bedside lamp, Mary Allen lay in a serene pose of sleep, her arms at her sides, the bedsheets neatly folded back across her chest. But she was not sleeping, and that was readily apparent. Her eyelids hung partially open. A washcloth had been rolled up and placed under her chin to prop up the sagging jaw. Relatives paying their last respects did not want to stare into a loved one's gaping mouth.

Abby's task took only moments. She placed her fingers on the carotid artery. No pulse. She lifted the gown and lay her stethoscope on the chest. She listened for ten seconds. No respirations, no heart-beat. She shone a penlight into the eyes. Pupils mid-position and fixed. A pronouncement of death was merely a matter of paperwork. The nurses had already recognized the obvious; Abby's role was simply to confirm the nurses' findings and record the event in the chart. It was one of those responsibilities they never explained to you in medical school. Newly minted interns, asked to pronounce their first dead patient, often had no idea what they were supposed to do. Some made impromptu speeches. Or called for a Bible, thus earning an exalted place in the nurses' annals of Stupid Doctor stories.

A death in a hospital is not an occasion for a speech, but for signatures and paperwork. Abby picked up Mary Allen's chart and completed the task. She wrote: 'No spontaneous respirations or pulse. Auscultation reveals no heart sounds. Pupils fixed and mid-position. Patient pronounced expired at 0305.' She closed the chart and turned to leave.

Brenda Hainey was standing in the doorway.

'I'm sorry, Miss Hainey,' said Abby. 'Your aunt passed away in her sleep.'

'When did it happen?'

'Sometime after midnight. I'm sure she was comfortable.'

'Was anyone with her when it happened?'

'There were nurses on duty in the ward.'

'But no one was here. In the room?'

Abby hesitated. Decided that the truth was

247

always the best answer. 'No, she was alone. I'm sure it happened in her sleep. It was a peaceful way to go.' She stepped away from the bed. 'You can stay with her for a while, if you want. I'll ask the nurses to give you some privacy.' She started past Brenda, toward the door.

'Why was nothing done to save her?'

Abby turned back to look at her. 'Nothing could be done.'

'You can shock a heart, can't you? Start it up again?'

'Under certain circumstances.'

'Did you do that?'

'No.'

'Why not? Because she was too old to save?'

'Age had nothing to do with it. She had terminal cancer.'

'She came into the hospital only two weeks ago. That's what she told me.'

'She was already very sick.'

'I think you people made her sicker.'

By now Abby's stomach was churning. She was tired, she wanted to go back to bed, and this woman wouldn't let her. Abuse heaped on abuse. But she had to take it. She had to stay calm.

'There was nothing we could do,' Abby repeated.

'Why wasn't her heart shocked, at least?'

'She was a no-code. That means we don't shock her. And we don't put her on a breathing machine. It was your aunt's request, and we honored it. So should you, Miss Hainey.' She left before Brenda

248

could say anything else. Before *she* could say anything she regretted.

She found Mark still asleep in the on-call room. She crawled in bed, turned on her side with her back to his chest, and pulled his arm over her waist. She tried to burrow back into that safe, warm haven of unconsciousness, but she kept seeing Mary Allen, the washcloth stuffed under her sagging chin, the eyelids drooping over glassy corneas. A body in its first stages of decay. She realized she knew almost nothing at all about Mary Allen's life, what she had thought, whom she had loved. Abby was her doctor, and all she knew about Mary Allen was the way she had died. Asleep, in her bed.

No, not quite. Sometime before her death, Mary had pulled out her IV. The nurses had found blood and saline on the floor. Had Mary been agitated? Confused? What had induced her to tug the line out of her vein?

It was one more detail about Mary Allen that she would never know.

Mark sighed and nestled closer to her. She took his hand and clasped it to her chest. To her heart. *I do.* She smiled, in spite of the sadness. It was the beginning of a new life, hers and Mark's. Mary Allen's was over, and theirs was about to start. The death of an elderly patient was a sad thing, but here, in the hospital, was where lives passed on.

And where new lives began.

* * *

It was ten A.M. when the taxi dropped Brenda Hainey off at her house in Chelsea. She had not eaten breakfast, had not slept since that call from the hospital, but she felt neither tired nor hungry. If anything, she felt immensely serene.

She had prayed at her aunt's bedside until five A.M., when the nurses had come to take the body to the morgue. She had left the hospital intending to come straight home, but during the taxi ride, she had been troubled by a sense of unfinished business. It had to do with Aunt Mary's soul, and where it might be at this moment in its cosmic journey. If, indeed, it was in transit at all. It could be stuck somewhere, like an elevator between floors. Whether it was headed upward or downward, Brenda could not be certain, and that was what troubled her.

Aunt Mary had not made things easy for herself. She had not joined in prayer, had not asked Him for forgiveness, had not even glanced at the Bible Brenda had left at her bedside. Aunt Mary had been entirely too indifferent, Brenda thought. One could not be indifferent in such a situation.

Brenda had seen it before, in other dying friends and relatives, that mindless serenity as the end approached. She was the only one who dared address the salvation of their souls, the only one who seemed at all concerned about which way their elevator might be heading. And a good thing she was concerned. So concerned, in fact, she had made it her business to know who in the family might be seriously ailing. Wherever they were in the country, she would go to them, stay with them until the end. It had become her calling, and there were those who considered her the family saint because of it. She was too modest to accept such a title. No, she was simply doing His bidding, as any good servant would do.

In Aunt Mary's case, though, she had failed. Death had come too soon, before her aunt had accepted Him into her heart. That was why, as the taxi pulled away from Bayside Hospital at five forty-five A.M., Brenda had felt such a sense of failure. Her aunt was dead, her soul beyond salvation. She, Brenda, had not been persuasive enough. If Aunt Mary had lived only another day, perhaps there would have been time.

The taxi passed a church. It was an Episcopal church, not Brenda's denomination, but it was a church all the same.

'Stop,' she'd ordered the driver. 'I want to get off here.'

And so, at six A.M., Brenda had found herself sitting in a pew at St Andrew's. She sat there for two and a half hours, her head bent, her lips moving silently. Praying for Aunt Mary, praying that the woman's sins, whatever they might be, would be forgiven. That her aunt's soul would no longer be stuck between floors and that the elevator she was riding would be heading not down, but up. When at last Brenda raised her head, it was eight-thirty. The church was still empty. Morning light was cascading down in a mosaic of blues and golds through the stained glass windows. As she focused on the altar, she saw the shape of Christ's head emblazoned there. It was just the projected figure from the window, she knew that, but it seemed at that moment to be a sign. A sign that her prayers had been answered.

Aunt Mary was saved.

Brenda had risen from the bench feeling light-headed with hunger, but joyous. Another soul turned to the light, and all because of her efforts. How fortunate that He had listened!

She'd left St Andrew's feeling wondrously buoyant, as though there were little cloud slippers on her feet. Outside, she found a taxi that just happened to be idling at the curve, waiting for her. Another sign.

She rode home in a trance of contentment.

Climbing the steps to her front porch, she looked forward to a quiet breakfast and then a long and deserved nap. Even His servants needed rest. She unlocked the door.

A scattering of mail lay on the floor, deposited that morning through the door slot. Bills and church newsletters and appeals for donations. So many needy people in the world! Brenda gathered up the mail and shuffled through the stack as she went into the kitchen. At the very bottom of the pile, she found an envelope with her name on it. That's all that was written there, just her name. No return address.

She broke the seal and unfolded the enclosed slip of paper. There was one typewritten line:

Your aunt did not die a natural death.

It was signed: A friend.

The stack of mail slipped from Brenda's grasp, the bills and newsletters scattering across the kitchen floor. She sank into a chair. She was no longer hungry, no longer serene.

She heard a cawing outside her window. She looked up and saw a crow perched on a nearby tree branch, its yellow eye staring straight at her.

It was another sign.

Thirteen

Frank Zwick glanced up from the patient on the operating table and said, 'I understand congratulations are in order.'

Abby, her hands dripping from the obligatory ten-minute scrub, had just walked into the OR to find Zwick and the two nurses grinning at her.

'I never thought that one would get hooked. Not in a million years,' said the scrub nurse, handing Abby a towel. 'Just goes to show you, bachelorhood *is* a curable illness. When did he pop the question, Dr D?'

Abby slipped her arms into the sterile gown and snapped on gloves. 'Two days ago.'

'You kept it a secret for two whole days?'

Abby laughed. 'I wanted to make sure he wasn't going to suddenly change his mind.' *And he hasn't. If anything, we're more sure of each other than ever before.* Smiling, she moved to the table. The patient, already anesthetized, lay with chest exposed and skin stained a yellow-brown from Betadine. It was to be a simple thoracotomy, a wedge resection of a peripheral pulmonary nodule. Her hands moved through the preop routine with the ease of one who's done it many times before. She lay down sterile cloths. Fastened clamps. Lay down the blue drapes and fastened more clamps.

'So when's the big day?' asked Zwick.

'We're still talking about it.' In fact, she and Mark had done little *but* talk about it. How big a wedding? Whom to invite. Outdoors or indoors? Only one thing had been decided for certain. Their honeymoon would be spent on a beach. Any beach, as long as there were palm trees in the vicinity.

She could feel her smile broadening at the prospect of warm sand and blue water. And Mark.

'I bet Mark's thinking *boat*,' said Zwick. 'That's where he'll want to get married.'

'Not the boat.'

'Uh-oh. That sounds definite.'

She finished draping the patient and looked up as Mark, freshly scrubbed, pushed through the doors. He donned gown and gloves and took his place across the table from her.

They grinned at each other. Then she picked up the scalpel.

The intercom buzzed. A voice over the speaker said, 'Is Dr DiMatteo in there?'

'Yes she is,' said the circulating nurse.

'Could you have her break scrub and come out?'

'They're just about to open. Can't this wait till later?'

There was a pause. Then: 'Mr Parr needs her out of the OR.'

'Tell him we're in surgery!' said Mark.

'He knows that. We need Dr DiMatteo out here,' repeated the intercom. 'Now.'

Mark looked at Abby. 'Go ahead. I'll have them call one of the interns to assist.'

Abby backed away from the table and nervously stripped off her gown. Something was wrong. Parr wouldn't pull her out of surgery unless there was some kind of crisis.

Her heart was already racing as she pushed through the OR doors and walked to the front desk.

Jeremiah Parr was standing there. Beside him were two hospital security guards and the nursing supervisor. No one was smiling.

'Dr DiMatteo,' said Parr, 'could you come with us?'

Abby looked at the guards. They had fanned out to either side of her. The nursing supervisor, too, had shifted position, taking a step back.

'What's this all about?' said Abby. 'Where are we going?'

'Your locker.'

'I don't understand.'

'It's just a routine check, Doctor.'

There's nothing routine about this. Flanked by the two guards, Abby had no choice but to follow Parr up the hall to the women's locker room. The nursing supervisor went in first, to clear the area of personnel. Then she beckoned Parr and the others inside.

'Your locker is number seventy-two?' said Parr.

'Yes.'

'Could you open it please?'

Abby reached for the combination padlock. She made one spin of the dial, then stopped and turned to Parr. 'I want to know what this is all about first.'

'It's just a check.'

'I think I'm a little beyond the stage of high school locker inspections. What are you looking for?'

'Just *open the locker*.'

Abby glanced at the guards, then at the nursing supervisor. They were watching her with heightened suspicion. She thought: I can't win this one. If I refuse to open it, they'll think I'm hiding something. The best way to defuse this crazy situation was to cooperate.

She reached for the lock, spun the combination, and tugged it open.

Parr stepped closer. So did the guards. They were standing right beside him as she swung open the locker door.

Inside were her street clothes, her stethoscope, her purse, a flowered toilet bag for on-call nights, and the long white coat she used for attending rounds. They wanted cooperation, she'd damn well give them cooperation. She unzipped the flowered bag and held it open for everyone to see. It was a show and tell of intimate feminine toiletries. Toothbrush and tampons and Midol. One of the male guards flushed. He'd gotten his thrill for the day. She zipped up the bag and opened her purse. No surprises in there either. A wallet, checkbook, car keys, more tampons. Women and their specialized plumbing. The guards were looking uncomfortable now, and a little sheepish.

Abby was starting to enjoy this.

She put the purse back in the locker and took the white coat off the hook. The instant she did, she knew there was something different about it. It was heavier. She reached into the pocket and felt something cylindrical and smooth. A glass vial. She took it out and stared at the label.

Morphine sulfate. The vial was almost empty.

'Dr DiMatteo,' said Parr, 'please give that to me.'

She looked up at him. Slowly she shook her head. 'I don't know what it's doing there.'

'Give me the vial.'

Too stunned to think of an alternative action, she simply handed it to him. 'I don't know how it got there,' she said. 'I've never seen it before.'

Parr handed the vial to the nursing supervisor. Then he turned to the guards. 'Please escort Dr DiMatteo to my office.'

'This is bullshit,' said Mark. 'Someone set her up and we all know it.'

'We don't know any such thing,' said Parr.

'It's part of the same pattern of harassment! The lawsuits. The bloody organs in her car. And now this.'

258

'This is entirely different, Dr Hodell. This is a dead patient.' Parr looked at Abby. 'Dr DiMatteo, why don't you just tell us the truth and make things easier for all of us?'

A confession was what he wanted. A clean and simple admission of guilt. Abby glanced around the table, at Parr and Susan Casado and the nursing supervisor. The only person she couldn't look at was Mark. She was afraid to look at him, afraid to see any doubt in his eyes.

She said, 'I told you, I don't know anything about it. I don't know how the morphine got in my locker. I don't know how Mary Allen died.'

'You pronounced her death,' said Parr. 'Two nights ago.'

'The nurses found her. She'd already expired.'

'That was the night you were on call.'

'Yes.'

'You were in the hospital all night.'

'Of course. That's what being on call *means*.'

'So you were here on the very night Mrs Allen expired of a morphine OD. And today we find this in your locker.' He set the vial on the table where it sat, center stage, on the gleaming mahogany surface. 'A controlled substance. Just the fact it's in your possession is serious enough.'

Abby stared at Parr. 'You just said Mrs Allen died of a morphine OD. How do you know that?'

'A postmortem drug level. It was sky-high.'

'She was on a therapeutic dose, titrated to comfort.'

'I have the report right here. It came back this

259

morning. Four-tenths milligram per liter. A level of two-tenths is considered fatal.'

'Let me see that,' said Mark.

'Certainly.'

Mark scanned the lab slip. 'Why would anyone order a postmortem morphine level? She was a terminal cancer patient.'

'It was ordered. That's all you need to know.'

'I need to know a hell of a lot more.'

Parr looked at Susan Casado, who said: 'There was reason to suspect this was not a natural death.'

'What reason?'

'That's not the point of this—'

'*What* reason?'

Susan released a sharp breath. 'One of Mrs Allen's relatives asked us to look into it. She received some kind of note implying the death was suspicious. We notified Dr Wettig, of course, and he ordered an autopsy.'

Mark handed Abby the lab slip. She stared at it, recognizing the indecipherable scrawl on the line *Ordering Physician*. It was, indeed, the General's signature. He'd ordered a quantitative drug screen at eleven A.M. yesterday morning. Eight hours after Mary Allen's death.

'I had nothing to do with this,' said Abby. 'I don't know how she got all this morphine. It could be a lab error. A nursing error—'

'I can speak for my staff,' said the nursing supervisor. 'We follow strict controls on narcotics administration. You all know that. There's no nursing error here.'

'Then what you're saying,' said Mark, 'is that the patient was deliberately overdosed.'

There was a long silence. Parr said, 'Yes.'

'This is ridiculous! I was *with* Abby that night, in the call room!'

'All night?' said Susan.

'Yes. It was her birthday, and we, uh . . .' Mark cleared his throat and glanced at Abby. *We slept together* was what they were both thinking. 'We celebrated,' he said.

'You were together the whole time?' said Parr.

Mark hesitated. He doesn't really know, thought Abby. He'd slept through all her phone calls, hadn't even stirred when she'd left to pronounce Mrs Allen at three o'clock, nor when she'd left again to restart an IV at four. He was about to lie for her, and she knew that it wouldn't work because Mark had no idea what she'd done that night. Parr did. He had it from the nurses. From the notes and orders she'd written, each one recorded with the time.

She said, 'Mark was in the call room with me. But he slept all night.' She looked at him. *We have to stick to the truth. It's the only thing that'll save me.*

'What about you, Dr DiMatteo?' said Parr. 'Did you stay in the room?'

'I was called to the wards several times. But you know that already, don't you?'

Parr nodded.

'You think you know everything!' said Mark. 'So tell me this. Why would she do it? Why would she kill her own patient?'

'It's no secret she has sympathies with the euthanasia movement,' said Susan Casado.

Abby stared at her. '*What?*'

'We've spoken with the nurses. On one occasion, Dr DiMatteo was heard to say, quote' – Susan flipped through the pages of a yellow legal pad – ' "If the morphine makes it easier, then that's what we should give her. Even if it makes the end come sooner." Unquote.' Susan looked at Abby. 'You did say that, didn't you?'

'That had nothing to do with euthanasia! I was talking about pain control! About keeping a patient comfortable.'

'So you did say it?'

'Maybe I did! I don't remember.'

'Then there was the exchange with Mrs Allen's niece, Brenda Hainey. It was witnessed by several nurses, as well as Mrs Speer here.' She nodded toward the nursing supervisor. And again she glanced at her legal pad. 'It was an argument. Brenda Hainey felt her aunt was getting too much morphine. And Dr DiMatteo disagreed. To the point of using obscenities.'

It was a charge Abby couldn't deny. She *had* argued with Brenda. She *had* used an obscenity. It was all crashing in on her now, wave after giant wave. She felt unable to breathe, unable to move, as the waves just kept slamming her down.

There was a knock and Dr Wettig walked in and

carefully shut the door behind him. He didn't say anything for a moment. He just stood at the end of the table and looked at Abby. She waited for the next wave to crash.

'She says she knows nothing about it,' said Parr.

'I'm not surprised,' Wettig said. 'You really don't know anything about this, do you, DiMatteo?'

Abby met the General's gaze. It had never been easy for her to look directly at those flat blue eyes. She saw too much power there, and it was power over her future. But she was looking straight at him now, determined to make him see that she had nothing to hide.

'I didn't kill my patient,' she said. 'I swear it.'

'That's what I thought you'd say.' Wettig reached in his lab coat pocket and produced a combination padlock. He set it down with a thud on the table.

'What's this?' said Parr.

'It's from Dr DiMatteo's locker. In the last half hour, I've become something of an expert on combination padlocks. I called a locksmith. He says it's a spring-loaded model, a piece of cake to get open. One sharp blow is all it takes. And it'll snap open. Also, there's a code on the back. Any registered locksmith can use that code to obtain the combination.'

Parr glanced at the lock, then gave a dismissive shrug. 'That doesn't prove anything. We're still left with a dead patient. And *that*.' He pointed to the vial of morphine.

'What's wrong with you people?' said Mark. 'Can't you see what's happening here? An anonymous note. Morphine conveniently planted in her locker. Someone's setting her up.'

'To what purpose?' said Susan.

'To discredit her. Get her fired.'

Parr snorted. 'You're suggesting someone actually murdered a patient just to ruin Dr DiMatteo's career?'

Mark started to answer, then seemed to think better of it. It was an absurd theory and they all knew it.

'You have to agree, Dr Hodell, that a conspiracy is pretty far-fetched,' said Susan.

'Not as far-fetched as what's already happened to me,' said Abby. 'Look at what Victor Voss has already done. He's mentally unstable. He assaulted me in the SICU. Putting bloody organs in my car is something only a sick mind would think of. And then there are the lawsuits – two of them already. And that's just the beginning.'

There was a silence. Susan glanced at Parr. 'Doesn't she know?'

'Apparently not.'

'Know *what*?' said Abby.

'We got a call from Hawkes, Craig and Sussman just after lunch,' said Susan. 'The lawsuits against you have been dropped. Both of them.'

Abby reeled back in her chair. 'I don't understand,' she murmured. 'What is he doing? What is Voss doing?'

'If Victor Voss *was* trying to harass you, it

appears he's stopped. This has nothing to do with Voss.'

'Then how else do we explain this?' said Mark.

'Look at the evidence.' Susan pointed to the vial.

'There are no witnesses, nothing to link that particular vial with the patient's death.'

'Nevertheless, I think we can all draw the same conclusion.'

The silence was suffocating. Abby saw that no one was looking at her, not even Mark.

At last Wettig spoke. 'What do you propose to do, Parr? Call in the police? Turn this mess into a media circus?'

Parr hesitated. 'It would be premature . . .'

'You either make your accusations stick, or you withdraw them. Anything else would be unfair to Dr DiMatteo.'

'My God, General. Let's keep the police out of this,' said Mark.

'If you people want to call this murder, then the police *should* be involved,' said Wettig. 'Call in a few reporters as well, put your PR people to work. They could use a little excitement. Get it all out in the open, that's the best policy.' He looked directly at Parr. '*If* you're going to call this murder.'

It was a dare.

Parr was the one to back down. He cleared his throat and said to Susan, 'We can't be absolutely certain that's what it is.'

'You'd better be certain it's murder,' said Wettig. 'You'd better be *damn* certain. Before you call the police.'

'The matter's still being looked into,' said Susan. 'We have to interview a few more nurses on that ward. Find out if there's something we've missed.'

'You do that,' said Wettig.

There was another pause. No one was looking at Abby. She had faded from view, the invisible woman no one wanted to acknowledge.

They all seemed startled when Abby spoke. She scarcely recognized her own voice; it sounded like a stranger's, calm and steady. 'I'd like to return to my patients now. If I may,' she said.

Wettig nodded. 'Go ahead.'

'Wait,' said Parr. 'She can't go back to her duties.'

'You haven't proved anything,' said Abby, rising from her chair. 'The General's right. Either you make the charges stick, or you withdraw them.'

'We have one charge that's indisputable,' said Susan. 'Illegal possession of a controlled substance. We don't know how you obtained the morphine, Doctor, but the fact you had it in your locker is serious enough.' She looked at Parr. 'We don't have a choice. The potential for liability is sky-high. If something goes wrong with *any* of her patients, and people find out we knew about this morphine business, we're dead.' She turned to Wettig. 'So's the reputation of your residency program, General.'

Susan's warning had its intended effect. Liability was something they all worried about. Wettig, like every other doctor, dreaded lawyers and lawsuits. This time, he didn't argue.

'What does this mean?' said Abby. 'Am I being fired?'

Parr rose to his feet, a signal that the meeting was over, the decision now made. 'Dr DiMatteo, until further notice, you're on suspension. You're not to go on the wards. You're not to go anywhere near a patient. Do you understand?'

She understood. She understood perfectly.

Fourteen

Yakov had not dreamed of his mother in years, had scarcely thought of her in months, so he was bewildered when, on his thirteenth day at sea, he awakened with a memory of her so vivid he could almost smell her scent still lingering in the air. His last glimpse of her, as the dream faded, was her smile. A wisp of blond hair tracing her cheek. Green eyes that seemed to be looking through him, beyond him, as though *he* were the one who was not real, not flesh. Her face was so instantly familiar to him that he knew this must surely be his mother. Over the years he had tried hard to remember her, but her face had never quite come to him. Yakov had no photographs, no mementos. But somehow, through the years, he must have carried the memory of her face stored like a seed in the dark but fertile soil of his mind. Last night, it had finally blossomed.

He remembered her, and she was beautiful.

That afternoon, the sea turned flat as glass and the

sky darkened to the same cold gray as the water. Standing on the deck, looking over the railing, Yakov could not tell where the sea ended and the sky began. They were adrift in a giant gray fishbowl. He'd heard the cook say there was bad weather ahead, that by tomorrow no one would be keeping down much more than bread and soup. Today, though, the sea was calm, the air heavy and metallic with the taste of rain. Yakov was finally able to coax Aleksei from his bunk to go exploring.

The first place Yakov took him was Hell. The engine room. They wandered for a while in the clanking darkness until Aleksei complained the smell of fuel was making him sick. Aleksei had the stomach of a baby – always puking. So Yakov took him up to the bridge, where the captain was too busy to talk to them. So was the navigator. Yakov could not even demonstrate his special status as a regular and accepted visitor.

Next they headed to the galley, but the cook was in a cranky mood and did not offer them even a slice of bread. He had a meal to prepare for the aft passengers, the people no one ever saw. They were a demanding pair, he complained, requiring far too much of his time and attention. He grumbled as he set two glasses and a wine bottle on a tray and slid it into the dumbwaiter. He pressed a button and sent it whirring upward, to their private quarters. Then he turned back to the stove, where a pan was sizzling and pots were steaming. He lifted one of the pot lids, releasing the fragrance of butter and onions. He stirred the contents with a wooden spoon.

'Onions have to be cooked slowly,' he said. 'It makes them sweet as milk. It takes patience to cook well, but no one has patience these days. Everyone wants things done at once. Stick it in the microwave! Might as well eat old leather.' he closed the pot lid, then lifted the lid to the frying pan. Browning inside were six tiny birds, each one no bigger than a boy's fist. 'Like morsels from heaven,' he said.

'Those are the smallest chickens I've ever seen,' marveled Aleksei.

The cook laughed. 'They're quail, idiot.'

'Why do we never eat quail?'

'Because you're not in the aft cabin.' The cook arranged the steaming birds on a platter and drizzled them with chopped parsley. Then he stepped back, his face red and sweating as he admired his creation. 'This they cannot complain about,' he said, and slid the platter into the dumbwaiter, which by then had returned empty.

'I'm hungry,' said Yakov.

'You're always hungry. Go, cut yourself a slice of bread. The loaf is stale, but you can toast it.'

The two boys rummaged in drawers for the bread knife. The cook was right; the loaf was dry and stale. Holding down the loaf with the stump of his left arm, Yakov sawed off two slices and carried them across to the toaster.

'Look what you're doing to my floor!' said the cook. 'Dropping crumbs all over. Pick them up.'

'You pick them up,' Yakov told Aleksei.

'You dropped them. I didn't.'

'I'm making the toast.'

'But I didn't drop the crumbs.'

'All right then. I'll just throw away your slice.'

'*Someone* pick them up!' roared the cook.

Aleksei instantly dropped to his knees and picked up the crumbs.

Yakov slid the first piece of bread into the toaster. A furry ball of gray suddenly popped out of one of the slots and leaped to the floor.

'A mouse!' shrieked Aleksei. 'There's a mouse!'

The gray ball was scampering around Aleksei's dancing feet now, chased in one direction by Yakov, then in the other direction by the cook who threw a pot lid at it for good measure. The mouse skittered halfway up Aleksei's leg, eliciting such a scream of terror it immediately changed course. It dropped back to the floor and shot off, vanishing under a cabinet.

Something was burning on the stove. Cursing, the cook ran to turn off the flame. He cursed some more as he scraped blackened onions from the pot, the onions he'd been so tenderly nursing along in butter. 'A mouse in my kitchen! And look at this! Ruined. I'll have to start over again. Bloody fucking mouse.'

'He was in the toaster,' said Yakov. Suddenly he felt a little sick. He thought about that mouse crawling, scratching around inside.

'Probably left it full of his shit,' said the cook. 'Bloody mouse.'

Yakov cautiously peered into the toaster. No more mice, but lots of mysterious brown specks.

He slid the toaster toward the sink, intending to dump out the crumbs.

The cook gave a shout. 'Hey! Are you stupid? What are you doing?'

'I'm cleaning out the toaster.'

'There's water in that sink! And look, the thing is still plugged in. If you put that in there and you touch the water, you're dead. Didn't anyone ever teach you that?'

'Uncle Misha never had a toaster.'

'It's not just toasters. It's anything that plugs in, anything with an electric cord. You're as stupid as all the others.' He waved his arms, shoving them toward the door. 'Go on, get out of here, both of you. You're a nuisance.'

'But I'm hungry,' said Yakov.

'You wait for supper like everyone else.' He threw a fresh slab of butter into a saucepan. Glancing at Yakov, he barked: 'Go!'

The boys left.

They played on deck for a while, until they grew chilled. They tried the bridge again, but were shooed from there as well. Sheer boredom took them, at last, to the one place in the boat where Yakov knew they would bother no one, and no one would bother them. It was his secret place, and he'd meant to show it to Aleksei only as a reward, and only if Aleksei could manage, for once, not to be a crybaby. He had found it on his third day of exploring, when he had spotted the closed door in the engine room corridor. He had opened that door and found it led to a stairwell shaft.

Wonderland.

The shaft soared three levels. A circular staircase spiraled up and up, and leading off the second level was a flimsy steel walkway that clattered and shook if you jumped up and down on it. The blue door leading aft from the walkway was always kept locked. Yakov had stopped even bothering to try it.

They climbed up to the top level. There, with the floor a dizzying drop below them, it was easy to scare Aleksei with a few noisy jumps.

'Stop it!' Aleksei cried. 'You're making it move!'

'That's the ride. The Wonderland ride. Don't you like it?'

'I don't want to take a ride!'

'You never want to do anything.' Yakov would have kept jumping up and down, shaking the walkway, but Aleksei was on the verge of hysteria. He had one hand clenched around the railing, the other hugging Shu-Shu.

'I want to go back down,' Aleksei whimpered.

'Oh, all right.'

They went down the staircase, setting off lovely clatters. At the bottom they played for a while under the steps. Aleksei found some old rope and tied one end to the lowest walkway railing. He used it to swing back and forth like the ape man. It was only a foot off the ground; not very exciting.

Then Yakov showed him the empty crate, the one he'd found shoved into a nook under the stairs. They crawled inside. There they lay in darkness among the wood shavings and listened to the engines rumble in Hell. The sea felt very close here, a great, dark cradle that rocked the hull of the ship.

'This is my secret place,' said Yakov. 'You can't tell anyone about it. Swear to me you won't tell.'

'Why should I? It's a disgusting place. It's cold and wet. And I bet there are mice in here somewhere. We're probably lying right now in mouse shit.'

'There's no mouse shit in here.'

'How do you know? You can't see anything.'

'If you don't like it, you can get out. Go on.' Yakov gave him a kick through the wood shavings. Stupid Aleksei. He should have known better than to bring him here. Anyone who carried a filthy stuffed dog everywhere could not be expected to enjoy adventures. 'Go on! You're no fun anyway.'

'I don't know the way back.'

'You think I'm going to show you?'

'You brought me here. You have to bring me back.'

'Well I'm not going to.'

'You bring me back or I tell everyone about your stupid secret place. Disgusting place, full of mouse shit.' Aleksei was climbing out of the crate now, kicking up shavings in Yakov's face. 'Bring me back now or—'

'Shut *up*,' said Yakov. He grabbed Aleksei by the shirt and yanked him backward. Both boys tumbled together into the shavings.

'You asshole,' said Aleksei.

'Listen. *Listen!*'

'What?'

Somewhere above, a door squealed and clanged shut. The walkway was rattling now, the sound of every footstep shattering to a thousand echoes in the stairway shaft.

Yakov crawled to the opening and peered out of the crate at the walkway above. Someone was knocking at the blue door. A moment later the door opened, and he caught a glimpse of blond hair as the woman vanished inside. The door closed behind her.

Yakov retreated back into the crate. 'It's just Nadiya.'

'Is she still out there?'

'No, she went in the blue door.'

'What's in there?'

'I don't know.'

'I thought you were the great explorer.'

'And you're the great asshole.' Yakov gave another kick, but only succeeded in tossing up a puff of shavings. 'It's always locked. Someone's living in there.'

'How do you know?'

'Because Nadiya knocked, and they let her in.'

Aleksei retreated deeper into the crate, having changed his mind about venturing out quite yet. He whispered: 'It's the quail people.'

Yakov thought of the tray with the wine bottle and the two glasses, the onions sizzling in butter, the six tiny birds blanketed in gravy. His stomach suddenly gave a rumble.

'Listen to this,' said Yakov. 'I can make really sick noises with my stomach.' He sucked in and thrust out his belly. Anyone else would have been impressed by the symphony of gurgles.

Aleksei just said, 'That's disgusting.'

'Everything's disgusting to you. What's wrong with you, anyway?'

'I don't like disgusting things.'

'You used to like them.'

'Well, I don't anymore.'

'It's because of that Nadiya. She's turned you all soft and gooey. You're sweet on her.'

'Am not.'

'Are too.'

'Am *not*!' Aleksei threw a handful of shavings, catching Yakov full in the face. Suddenly both boys were grappling, rolling against one side of the crate, then the other, cursing, kicking. There was not much room to move, so they could not really hurt each other. Then Aleksei lost Shu-Shu somewhere in the shavings and began scrabbling around in the darkness, searching for his dog. Yakov was tired of fighting anyway.

So they both stopped.

For a while they rested side by side, Aleksei clutching Shu-Shu, Yakov trying to coax new and more repulsive sounds from his stomach. Soon he tired of even that. They lay immobilized by boredom, by the sleep-inducing rumble of the engines, and by the sway of the sea.

Aleksei said, 'I'm not sweet on her.'

'I don't care if you are.'

'But the other boys like her. Haven't you noticed how they talk about her?' Aleksei paused. And added: 'I like the way she smells. Women smell different. They smell soft.'

'Soft doesn't make a smell.'

'Yes it does. You smell a woman like that, and you know, when you touch her, she'll be soft. You just know it.' Aleksei stroked Shu-Shu. Yakov could hear his hand skimming the tattered fabric.

'My mother smelled that way,' said Aleksei.

Yakov remembered his dream. The woman, the smile. The wisp of blond hair tracing across a cheek. Yes, Aleksei was right. In his dream, his mother had indeed worn the scent of softness.

'It sounds stupid,' said Aleksei. 'But I remember that. Some things I still remember about her.'

Yakov stretched, and his feet touched the other end of the crate. Have I grown? he wondered. If only. If only I could grow big enough to kick my feet right through that wall.

'Don't you ever think about your mother?' asked Aleksei.

'No.'

'You wouldn't remember her anyway.'

'I remember she was a beauty. She had green eyes.'

'How would you know? Uncle Misha says you were a baby when she left.'

'I was four. That's not a baby.'

'I was six when my mother left and I hardly remember anything.'

'I'm telling you, she had green eyes.'

'So she had green eyes. So what?'

The clang of a door made them both fall silent. Yakov squirmed over to the crate opening and looked up. It was Nadiya again. She'd just come out of the blue door and was crossing the walkway. She vanished through the forward hatch.

'I don't like her,' said Yakov.

'I do. I wish she was *my* mother.'

'She doesn't even like children.'

'She told Uncle Misha she dedicates her life to us.'

'You believe that?'

'Why would she say it if it isn't true?'

Yakov tried to think of an answer, but could not come up with one. Even if he had, it would make no difference to Aleksei. Stupid Aleksei. Stupid everyone. Nadiya had them all fooled. Eleven boys, and each and every one of them was in love with her. They fought to sit beside her at supper. They watched her, studied her, sniffed at her like puppies. At night, in their bunks, they whispered about Nadiya this and Nadiya that. What foods she preferred, what she'd eaten at lunch. They speculated about everything from how old she was to what undergarments she wore under her gray skirts. They discussed whether or not Gregor, whom everyone despised, was her lover, and unanimously decided he was not. They pooled their knowledge about feminine anatomy, the older boys explaining, in lurid detail, the function of tampons and how and where they are inserted, thus transforming forever the way the younger boys would view women – as creatures with dark and mysterious holes. This only increased their fascination with Nadiya.

Yakov shared that fascination, but his was not adoration. He was afraid of her.

It was all because of the blood tests.

On their fourth day at sea, when the boys were still puking and moaning in their bunks, Gregor and Nadiya had come around carrying a tray of needles and tubes. It will be only a small prick, they'd said, a small tube of blood to confirm you are healthy. No one will adopt you if they cannot be assured you are healthy. The pair had moved from boy to boy, weaving a bit from the rough sea, the glass tubes clattering on the tray. Nadiya had looked sick, on the verge of throwing up. Gregor had been the one to draw the blood. At each bunk they'd asked the boy his name and fitted him with a plastic bracelet on which they'd written a number. Then Gregor tied a giant rubber band around the boy's arm and slapped the skin a few times, to make the vein swell. Some of the boys cried, and Nadiya had to hold their hand and comfort them while Gregor drew the blood.

Yakov was the only boy whom she was unable to comfort. No matter how she tried, she could not make him hold still. He did not want that needle in his arm, and he had given Gregor a kick to emphasize the point. That's when the real Nadiya took over. She pinned Yakov's one arm to the bed, holding it there with a grasp that pinched and twisted at the same time. As Gregor drew the blood, she had kept her gaze fixed on Yakov, had spoken quietly, even sweetly to him as the needle pierced his skin and the blood streamed into the tube. Everyone else in that room, listening to Nadiya's voice, heard only murmured words of reassurance. But Yakov, staring into those pale eyes of hers, saw something entirely different.

Afterward, he had gnawed off his plastic bracelet.

Aleksei still wore his. Number 307. His certification of good health.

'Do you think she has children of her own?' asked Aleksei.

Yakov gave a shudder. 'I hope not,' he said, and crawled to the crate opening. He looked up and saw the deserted walkway and the empty stairway, coiling above like a serpent's skeleton. The blue door, as always, was shut.

Brushing off the wood shavings, he scrambled out of their hiding place. 'I'm hungry,' he said.

As the cook had predicted, that gray and oppressive afternoon was soon followed by heavy seas – not a severe storm, but rough enough to confine the passengers, both children and adults, to their cabins. And that was precisely where Aleksei intended to stay. All the coaxing in the world would not budge him from his bunk. It was cold and wet outside, and the floor was rocking, and he had no interest in poking around the dark, damp corners that seemed to fascinate Yakov so. Aleksei liked it in his bed. He liked the coziness of a blanket pulled up around his shoulders, liked the drafts of warmth that puffed at his face when he turned or wiggled, liked the smell of Shu-Shu sleeping beside him on the pillow.

All morning, Yakov tried to drag Aleksei out of bed, to tempt him with another visit to Wonderland. Finally he gave up and went off on his own. He came back once or twice to see if Aleksei had changed his mind, but Aleksei slept all afternoon, through supper, and straight into the evening.

In the night, Yakov awakened and sensed at once that something was different. At first he could not decide what it was. Perhaps just the passing of the storm? He could feel the ship had steadied. Then he realized it was the engines that had changed. That ceaseless rumble had muffled to a soft growl.

He crawled out of his bunk and went to give Aleksei a shake. 'Wake up,' he whispered.

'Go away.'

'Listen. We've stopped moving.'

'I don't care.'

'I'm going up to take a look. Come with me.'

'I'm sleeping.'

'You've been sleeping a whole day and night. Don't you want to see land? We must be near land. Why would the ship stop in the middle of the ocean?' Yakov bent closer to Aleksei, his whispers softly enticing. 'Maybe we can see the lights. America. You'll miss it unless you come with me.'

Aleksei sighed, stirred a bit, not quite certain what he wanted to do.

Yakov threw out the ultimate lure. 'I saved a potato from supper,' he said. 'I'll give it to you. But only if you come up with me.'

Aleksei had missed supper, and lunch as well. A potato would be heaven. 'All right, all right.' Aleksei sat up and began buckling on his shoes. 'Where's the potato?'

'First we go up.'

'You're an asshole, Yakov.'

They tiptoed past the double bunks of sleeping boys and climbed the stairway, to the deck.

Outside, a soft wind was blowing. They looked over the railing, straining for a view of city lights, but the stars met only a black and formless horizon.

'I don't see anything,' said Aleksei. 'Give me my potato.'

Yakov produced the treasure from his pocket. Aleksei squatted down and devoured it right there, cold, like a wild animal.

Yakov turned and looked up toward the bridge. He could see the greenish glow of the radar screen through the window, and the silhouette of a man standing watch. The navigator. What did he see from that lonely perch of his?

Aleksei had finished his potato. Now he stood up and said: 'I'm going to bed.'

'We can look for more food in the galley.'

'I don't want to see another mouse.' Aleksei began to feel his way across the deck. 'Besides, I'm cold.'

'I'm not cold.'

'Then *you* stay out here.'

They had just reached the stairway when they heard a series of sharp thuds. Suddenly the deck was ablaze with light. Both boys froze, blinking at the unexpected glare.

Yakov grabbed Aleksei's hand and tugged him under the bridge stairway, where they crouched, peering out between the steps. They heard voices and saw two men walk into the circle of flood-lights. Both men were wearing white overalls. Together they bent down and gave something a tug. There was a scrape of metal as some kind of cover was forced aside. It revealed a new light, this one blue. It shone at the center of the floodlit circle, like the forbidding iris of an eye.

'Bloody mechanics,' one of the men said. 'They'll never get this repaired.'

Both men straightened and looked up at the sky. Toward the distant growl of thunder.

Yakov, too, looked up. The thunder was moving closer. No longer just a growl, it deepened to a rhythmic *whup-whup*. The two men retreated from the floodlights. The sound drew right over-head, churning the night like a tornado.

Aleksei clapped his hands over his ears and shrank deeper into the shadows. Yakov did not. He watched, unflinching, as the helicopter descended into the wash of light and touched down on the deck.

One of the men in overalls reappeared, running bent at the waist. He swung open the helicopter door. Yakov could not see what was inside; the stairway post was blocking his direct view. He eased out from the shadows, moving out onto the deck just far enough to see around the post. He caught a glimpse of the pilot and one passenger – a man.

'Hey!' came a shout from overhead. 'You! Boy!'

Yakov glanced straight up and saw the navigator peering down at him from the bridge deck.

'What are you doing down there? You come up here right now, before you get hurt! Come on!'

The man in overalls had spotted the boys too, and was crossing toward them. He did not look pleased.

Yakov scurried up the stairway. Aleksei, in a panic, was right on his heels.

'Don't you know enough to stay off the main deck when a chopper's landing?' yelled the navigator. He gave Aleksei a whack on the rump and pulled them inside, into the wheelhouse. He pointed to two chairs. 'Sit. Both of you.'

'We were just watching,' said Yakov.

'You two are supposed to be in bed.'

'I *was* in bed,' whimpered Aleksei. 'He made me come out.'

'Do you know what a chopper rotor can do to a boy's head? Do you?' The navigator slashed a hand across Aleksei's skinny neck. 'Just like that. Your head goes flying straight off. And blood shoots everywhere. Quite spectacular. You think I'm joking, don't you? Believe me, I don't go down there when the chopper comes. I stay the hell away. But if you want your stupid heads sliced off, be my guests. Go on.'

Aleksei sobbed, 'I *wanted* to stay in bed!'

The roar of the helicopter made them all turn to look. They watched as it lifted into the sky, the rotor wash whipping the overalls of the two men standing on deck. It made a slow ninety-degree turn, then veered off, to be swallowed by the night. Only a soft rumble lingered, fading away like retreating thunder.

'Where does it go?' asked Yakov.

'You think they tell me?' said the navigator. 'They just call me when it's coming in for a pickup and I turn the bow into the wind. That's all.' He reached for one of the panel switches and flicked it.

The floodlights were instantly extinguished. The main deck vanished into darkness.

Yakov pressed close to the bridge window. The chopper rumble was gone now. In every direction stretched the blackness of the sea.

Aleksei was still crying.

'Stop it now,' said the navigator. He gave Aleksei a scolding slap on the shoulder. 'A boy your age, acting like a woman.'

'But what does it come for? The helicopter?' asked Yakov.

'I told you. A pickup.'

'What does it pick up?'

'I don't ask. I just do what they tell me.'

'Who?'

'The passengers in the aft cabin.' He tugged Yakov away from the window and gave him a push toward the door. 'Go back to your bunks. Can't you see I have work to do?'

Yakov was following Aleksei to the door when his gaze lit on the radar screen. So many times before, he'd stared at that screen, transfixed by the hypnotic sweep of the line tracing its three-hundred-sixty-degree arc. Now he stood before it again, watching the line circle around and around. He saw it at once, a small white sliver at the edge of the screen.

'Is it another ship?' Yakov asked. 'There, on the radar.' He pointed to the sliver, which suddenly pulsed whiter as the line swept over it.

'What else would it be? Get out of here.'

The boys went outside and clattered down the bridge stairway to the main deck. Yakov glanced up and saw, against the green glow of the bridge window, the navigator's silhouette. Watching. Always watching.

And he said: 'Now I know where the helicopter goes.'

Pyotr and Valentin were not at breakfast. By then the news of their departure during the night had already spread to Yakov's cabin, so when he sat down at the table that morning and faced the row

286

of boys sitting across from him, he knew the reason for their silence. They did not understand, any of them, why Pyotr and Valentin should be the first to leave the ship, the first to be chosen. Pyotr, they'd all thought from the start, would be among the leftovers, or would be consigned to some unlikely family who favored idiot children. Valentin, who'd joined the group in Riga, had been clever enough, handsome enough, but he had a secret perversion known to the younger boys. After the lights went out at night, he would crawl into their bunks without his underwear, would whisper: 'Feel that? Feel how big I am?' And he would grab their hands and force them to touch him.

But Valentin was gone now, he and Pyotr. Gone to new parents who'd chosen them, Nadiya said.

The rest of them were the leftovers.

In the afternoon, Yakov and Aleksei climbed to the deck and stretched out on the spot where the helicopter had landed. They lay gazing up at the hard blue glare of the sky. No clouds, no helicopters. The deck was warm and, like two kittens on a radiator, they began to feel drowsy.

'I've been thinking,' said Yakov, his eyes closed against the sun. 'If my mother is alive, I don't want to be adopted.'

'She's not.'

'She could be.'

'Why didn't she come back for you, then?'

'Maybe she's looking for me right now. And here I am, in the middle of the sea where no one can find me. Except with radar. I'm going to tell Nadiya to take me back. I don't want a new mother.'

'I do,' said Aleksei. He was quiet for a moment. Then he said, 'Do you think there's something wrong with me?'

Yakov laughed. 'You mean besides the fact you're retarded?'

When Aleksei didn't answer, Yakov squinted up at his friend and was puzzled to see the boy had his hands over his face, and his shoulders were shaking.

'Hey,' said Yakov. 'Are you crying?'

'No.'

'You are, aren't you?'

'No.'

'You're such a baby. I didn't mean it. You're not retarded.'

Aleksei had folded into a ball of arms and legs. He was crying all right. Though he didn't make a sound, Yakov could see his chest spasmodically sucking in gulps of air. Yakov didn't know what to make of this or what to say. A fresh insult was what automatically came to mind. *Stupid girl. Crybaby.* But then he thought better of it. He had never seen Aleksei this way, and he felt a little guilty, a little scared. It was just a joke. Why couldn't Aleksei see it was a joke?

'Let's go down and swing on the rope,' said Yakov. He gave Aleksei a poke in the ribs.

Aleksei lashed back with an angry shove and jumped up, his face red and wet.

'What's the matter with you anyway?' said Yakov.

'Why did they choose that stupid Pyotr instead of me?'

'They didn't choose me either,' said Yakov.

'But there's nothing wrong with *me*!' cried Aleksei. He ran from the deck.

Yakov sat very still. He looked down at the stump of his left arm. And he said, 'There's nothing wrong with me either.'

'Knight to bishop three,' said Koubichev, the engineer.

'You always do that. Don't you ever try anything new?'

'I believe in the tried and true. It's beaten you every time. Your move. Don't take all day.'

Yakov rotated the chessboard and studied it first from one angle, then another. He got on his knees and peered down the row of pawns. Imagined black-armored soldiers standing in formation, awaiting orders.

'What the hell are you doing now?' said Koubichev.

'Did you ever notice the queen has a beard?'

'What?'

'She has a beard. Look.'

Koubichev grunted. 'That's just her neck ruffle. Now will you make your move?'

Yakov set the queen back on the board and reached for a knight. He set it down, picked it up. Set it down in a different place and again picked it up. All around them rumbled the engines of Hell.

Koubichev was no longer watching. He'd opened a magazine and was flipping through the pages, eyeing a succession of glamorous faces. The one hundred most beautiful women in America. Every so often he'd grunt and say, 'You call *that* beautiful?' or 'I wouldn't let my dog fuck that one.'

Yakov picked up the queen again and set her down on bishop four. 'There.'

Koubichev regarded Yakov's latest move with a snort. 'Why do you always repeat the same mistake? Moving your queen out too early?' He tossed the magazine down and leaned forward to move his pawn. That's when Yakov spotted the face on the magazine page. It was a woman. Blond hair, with one wisp curling over the cheek. A melancholy smile. Eyes that seemed to be gazing not at you, but beyond you.

'It's my mother,' said Yakov.

'What?'

'It's her. It's my *mother*!' He lunged for the magazine, knocking against the crate that served for a table. The chessboard toppled. Pawns and bishops and knights flew in every direction.

Koubichev snatched the magazine out of reach. 'What the hell is wrong with you?'

'Give it to me!' screamed Yakov. He was clawing at the man's arm now, frantic to claim his mother's photo. 'Give it!'

'You crazy boy, it's not your mother!'

'It is! I remember her face! She looked like that, just like that!'

'Stop scratching me. Get away, do you hear?'

'Give it to me!'

'All right, all right. Here, I'll show you. It's not your mother.' Koubichev slapped the magazine down on the crate. 'See?'

Yakov stared at the face. Every detail was exactly as he'd dreamed it. The way the head was tilted, the way her skin dimpled near the corners of her mouth. Even the way the light fell on her hair. He said, 'It's her. I've seen her face.'

'Everyone's seen her face.' Koubichev pointed to the name on the photo. 'Michelle Pfeiffer. She's an actress. American. Not even the name is Russian.'

'But I know her! I had a dream about her!'

Koubichev laughed. 'You and every other horny boy.' He glanced around at the scattered chess pieces. 'Look at this mess. We'll be lucky to find all the pawns. Come on, you knocked it over. Now pick them up.'

Yakov didn't move. He stood staring at the woman, remembering the way she had smiled at him.

Koubichev, grumbling, dropped to his hands and knees and began to crawl about, retrieving chess pieces from underneath machinery. 'You've probably seen her face somewhere. The TV, or maybe some magazine, and you forgot about it. Then you have a dream about her, that's all.' He set two bishops and a queen on the board, then heaved himself back onto the chair. His face was flushed, his barrel chest panting heavily. He tapped his head. 'The brain is a mysterious thing. It takes real life and spins it into dreams, and we can't tell what's made up and what's real. Sometimes I have this dream where I'm sitting at a table with all this wonderful food, everything I could want to eat. Then I wake up and I'm still on this fucking boat.' He reached for the magazine and tore out the page with Michelle Pfeiffer. 'Here. It's yours.'

Yakov took the page but didn't say anything. He just held it. Looked at it.

'If you want to pretend that's your mother, go ahead. A boy could do worse. Now pick up the pieces. Hey! Hey, boy! Where do you think you're going?'

Yakov, still clutching the page, fled Hell.

Up on deck he stood at the rail, his face to the sea. The page was wrinkled now, flapping and crackling in the wind. He looked at it, saw that he'd been holding it so tightly a crease now cut across those half-smiling lips.

He grasped one corner with his teeth and ripped the page in two. It was not enough. Not enough. He was breathing hard, close to crying, but no sound came out. He ripped the page again and again, using his teeth like an animal tearing at real flesh, letting the pieces fly off into the wind.

When he'd finished, he was still holding on to one scrap of the page. It was an eye. Just beneath it, pinched by his fingers, was a star-shaped crease. Like the sparkle of a single teardrop.

He threw the scrap over the rail and watched it flutter away and fall into the sea.

Fifteen

She was in her late forties, with the thin, dry face of a woman who had long ago lost her estrogenic glow. In Bernard Katzka's opinion, that alone did not make a woman unattractive. A woman's appeal lay not in the luster of her skin and hair, but in what was revealed by her eyes. In that regard, he had met a number of fascinating seventy-year-olds, among them his maiden aunt Margaret, whom he'd grown particularly close to since Annie's death. That Katzka actually looked forward to his weekly coffee chats with Aunt Margaret would probably bewilder his partner, Lundquist. Lundquist was of the masculine school that believed women were not worth a second glance once they'd crossed the menopausal finish line. No doubt it was all rooted in biology. Males mustn't waste their energy or sperm on a non-reproductive female. No wonder Lundquist had looked so relieved when Katzka agreed to interview Brenda Hainey. Lundquist considered postmenopausal women to be Bernard Katzka's forte, by which he meant Katzka was the one detective in Homicide who had the patience and fortitude to hear them out.

And this was precisely what Katzka had been doing for the last fifteen minutes, listening patiently to Brenda Hainey's bizarre charges. She was not easy to follow. The woman mingled the mystical with the concrete, in the same breath telling him about signs from heaven and syringes of morphine. He might have been amused by the quirky nature of this encounter if the woman had been likable, but Brenda Hainey was not. There was no warmth in her blue eyes. She was angry, and angry people were not attractive.

'I've spoken to the hospital about this,' she said. 'I went straight to their president, Mr Parr. He promised he'd investigate, but that was five days ago, and so far I've heard nothing. I call every day. His office tells me they're still looking into it. Well, today I decided enough was enough. So I called your people. And *they* tried to put me off too, tried to make me talk to some rookie police officer first. Well I believe in going straight to the highest authority. I do it all the time, every morning when I pray. In this case, the highest authority would be *you*.'

Katzka suppressed a smile.

'I've seen your name in the newspaper,' Brenda said. 'In connection with that dead doctor from Bayside.'

'You're referring to Dr Levi?'

'Yes. I thought, since you already know about

294

the goings-on in that hospital, you're the one I should speak to.'

Katzka almost sighed, but caught himself. He knew she would take it for what it was, an expression of weariness. He said, 'May I see the note?'

She pulled a folded paper from her purse and handed it to him. It had one typewritten line: *Your aunt did not die a natural death. A friend.*

'Was there an envelope?'

This, too, she produced. On it was typed the name *Brenda Hainey*. The flap had been sealed, then torn open.

'Do you know who might have sent this?' he asked.

'I have no idea. Maybe one of the nurses. Someone who knew enough to tell me.'

'You say your aunt had terminal cancer. She could have died of natural causes.'

'Then why send me that note? Someone knew differently. Someone wants this looked into. *I* want it looked into.'

'Where is your aunt's body now?'

'Garden of Peace Mortuary. The hospital shipped it out pretty quick, if you ask me.'

'Whose decision was that? It must have been next of kin.'

'My aunt left instructions before she died. That's what the hospital told me, anyway.'

'Have you spoken to your aunt's doctors? Perhaps they can clear this up.'

'I'd prefer not to speak to them.'

'Why not?'

'Given the situation, I'm not sure I trust them.'

'I see.' Now Katzka did sigh. He picked up his pen and flipped to a fresh page in his notebook. 'Why don't you give me the names of all your aunt's doctors.'

'The physician in charge was Dr Colin Wettig. But the one who really seemed to be making all the decisions was that resident of his. I think she's the one you should look at.'

'Her name?'

'Dr DiMatteo.'

Katzka glanced up in surprise. 'Abigail DiMatteo?'

There was a brief silence. Katzka could see consternation clearly written on Brenda's face.

She said, cautiously, 'You know her.'

'I've spoken to her. On another matter.'

'It won't affect your judgment on this case, will it?'

'Not at all.'

'Are you certain?' She challenged him with a gaze he found irritating. He was not easily irritated, and he had to ask himself now why this woman so annoyed him.

Lundquist chose that moment to walk past the desk, and he flashed what could only be characterized as a sympathetic smirk. Lundquist should have interviewed this woman. It would have been good for him, an exercise in polite restraint, which Lundquist needed to develop.

Katzka said: 'I always try to be objective, Miss Hainey.'

'Then you should take a close look at Dr DiMatteo.'

'Why her in particular?'

'She's the one who wanted my aunt dead.'

Brenda's charges struck Katzka as improbable. Still, there was the matter of that note and who had sent it. One possibility was that Brenda had sent it to herself; stranger things had been done by people hungry for attention. That was easier for him to believe than what she was claiming had happened: that Mary Allen had been murdered by her doctors. Katzka had spent weeks watching his wife slowly die in the hospital, so he was well acquainted with cancer wards. He had witnessed the compassion of nurses, the dedication of oncologists. They knew when to keep fighting for a patient's life. They also knew when the fight was lost, when the suffering outweighed the benefits of one more day, one more week, of life. There had been times toward the end when Katzka had wanted desperately to ease Annie across the final threshold. Had the doctors suggested such a move, he would have agreed to it. But they never had. Cancer killed quickly enough; which doctor would risk his professional future to hurry along a patient's death? Even if Mary Allen's doctors had made such a move, could one truly consider it homicide?

It was with reluctance that he drove to Bayside

297

Hospital that afternoon after Brenda Hainey's visit. He was obligated to make a few inquiries. At the hospital's public information office, he confirmed that Mary Allen had indeed expired on the date Brenda said she had, and that the diagnosis had been undifferentiated metastatic carcinoma. The clerk could give him no other information. Dr Wettig, the attending, was in surgery and unavailable for the afternoon. So Katzka picked up the phone and paged Abby DiMatteo.

A moment later she called back.

'This is Detective Katzka,' he said. 'We spoke last week.'

'Yes, I remember.'

'I have some questions on an unrelated matter. Where can I meet you?'

'I'm in the medical library. Is this going to take a long time?'

'It shouldn't.'

He heard a sigh. Then a reluctant: 'Okay. The library's on the second floor, administrative wing.'

In Katzka's experience, the average person – provided he or she was not a suspect – enjoyed talking to homicide cops. People were curious about murder, about police work. He'd been astonished by the questions they asked *him*, even the sweetest-faced old ladies, everyone longing to hear the details, the bloodier the better. Dr DiMatteo, however, had sounded genuinely unwilling to speak to him. He wondered why.

He found the hospital library tucked between data processing and the financial office. Inside were a few aisles of bookshelves, a librarian's desk, and a half dozen study carrels along one wall. Dr DiMatteo was standing beside the photocopier, positioning a surgical journal on the plate. She'd already collated a number of papers into piles, and had stacked them on a nearby desk. It surprised him to see her performing such a clerical task. He was also surprised to see her dressed in a skirt and blouse rather than the scrub clothes he'd assumed was the uniform of all surgical residents. From the first day he'd met Abby DiMatteo, he'd thought her an attractive woman. Now, seeing her in a flattering skirt, with all that black hair hanging loose about her shoulders, he decided she was really quite stunning.

She looked up and gave a nod. That's when he noticed something else different about her today. She seemed nervous, even a little wary.

'I'm almost finished,' she said. 'I have one more article to copy.'

'Not on duty today?'

'Excuse me?'

'I thought surgeons lived in scrub suits.'

She placed another page on the Xerox machine and hit the Copy button. 'I'm not scheduled for the OR today. So I'm doing a literature search. Dr Wettig needs these for a conference.' She stared down at the copier, as though the flashing light, the machine's whir, required all her concentration. When the last pages rolled out, she took them to the table, where the other stacks lay waiting, and sat down. He pulled out the chair across from her.

She picked up a stapler, then set it back down again.

Still not looking at him, she asked: 'Have there been new developments?'

'In regard to Dr Levi, no.'

'I wish I could think of something new to tell you. But I can't.' She gathered up a few pages and stapled them together with a sharp snap of the wrist.

'I'm not here about Dr Levi,' he said. 'This is about a different matter. A patient of yours.'

'Oh?' She picked up another stack of papers and slid it between the stapler teeth. 'Which patient are we talking about?'

'A Mrs Mary Allen.'

Her hand paused for a second in midair. Then it came down, hard, on the stapler.

'Do you remember her?' he asked.

'Yes.'

'I understand she died last week. Here, at Bayside.'

'That's right.'

'Can you confirm that her diagnosis was undifferentiated metastatic carcinoma?'

'Yes.'

'And was she in the terminal stages?'

'Yes.'

'Then her death was expected?'

There was a hesitation. It was just long enough to notch up his alertness.

She said, slowly, 'I would say it was expected.'

He was watching her more closely, and she seemed to know it. He didn't say anything for a moment. Silence, in his experience, was far more unnerving. Quietly he asked: 'Was her death in any way unusual?'

At last she looked up at him. He realized she was sitting absolutely still. Almost rigid.

'In what way unusual?' she asked.

'The circumstances. The manner in which she expired.'

'Can I ask why you're pursuing this?'

'A relative of Mrs Allen's came to us with some concerns.'

'Are we talking about Brenda Hainey? The niece?'

'Yes. She thinks her aunt died of causes unrelated to her disease.'

'And you're trying to turn this into a homicide?'

'I'm trying to determine if there's anything worth investigating. Is there?'

She didn't answer.

'Brenda Hainey received an anonymous note. It claimed that Mary Allen didn't die of natural causes. Do you have any reason, any reason at all, to think there might be substance to that?'

He could have predicted several likely responses. She might have laughed and said this was all ridiculous. She might have told him that Brenda Hainey was crazy. Or she might show puzzlement, even a flash of anger, that she was being subjected to these questions. Any one of those reactions would have been appropriate. What he did not expect was her actual response.

She stared at him with a face suddenly drained

white. And she said softly: 'I refuse to answer any more questions, Detective Katzka.'

Seconds after the policeman left the library, Abby reached in panic for the nearest telephone and paged Mark. To her relief, he immediately answered her call.

'That detective was here again,' she whispered. 'Mark, they know about Mary Allen. Brenda's been talking to them. And this cop's asking questions about how she died.'

'You didn't tell him anything, did you?'

'No, I—' She took a deep breath. The sigh that followed was close to a sob. 'I didn't know what to say. Mark, I think I gave it away. I'm scared and I think he knows it.'

'Abby, listen. This is important. You didn't tell him about the morphine in your locker, did you?'

'I wanted to. Jesus, Mark, I was ready to spill my guts. Maybe I should. If I just came out and told him everything—'

'*Don't.*'

'Isn't it better to just tell him? He'll find out anyway. Sooner or later, he'll dig it all up. I'm sure he will.' She let out another breath, and felt the first flash of tears sting her eyes. She was going to be sobbing in a minute, right here in the library, where anyone could see her. 'I don't see any way around it. I have to go to the police.'

'What if they don't believe you? They take one look at the circumstantial evidence, that morphine in your locker, and they'll jump to the obvious conclusion.'

'So what am I supposed to do? Wait for them to arrest me? I can't stand this. I can't.' Her voice faltered. In a whisper she repeated, 'I can't.'

'So far the police have nothing. I won't tell them a thing. Neither will Wettig or Parr, I'm sure of it. They don't want this out in the open any more than you do. Just hold on, Abby. Wettig's doing everything he can to get you reinstated.'

It took her a moment to regain her composure. When at last she spoke again, her voice was quiet but steady. 'Mark, what if Mary Allen *was* murdered? Then there *should* be an investigation. We should bring this to the police ourselves.'

'Is that what you really want to do?'

'I don't know. I keep thinking it's what we *ought* to do. That we're obligated. Morally and ethically.'

'It's your decision. But I want you to think long and hard about the consequences.'

She already had. She'd thought about the publicity. The possibility of arrest. She'd gone back and forth on this, knowing what she *should* do, yet afraid to take action. *I'm a coward. My patient's dead, maybe murdered, and all I can worry about is saving my own goddamn skin.*

The hospital librarian walked into the room, wheeling a squeaky cart of books. She sat down at her desk and began stamping the inside covers. *Whap. Whap.*

'Abby,' said Mark. 'Before you do anything, *think.*'

'I'll talk to you later. I've got to go now.' She hung up and went back to the table, where she sat down and stared at the stack of photocopied journal articles. This was the extent of her work today. This was what she'd spent all morning doing, collecting this pile of paper. She was a physician who could no longer practice, a surgeon banished from the OR. The nurses and house staff didn't know what to make of it all. She was sure the rumors were already swirling thick and furious. This morning, when she'd walked through the wards looking for Dr Wettig, the nurses had all turned to look at her. What are they saying behind my back? she wondered.

She was afraid to find out.

The *whap, whap* had ceased. She realized the librarian had stopped stamping her book covers and was now eyeing Abby.

Like everyone else in this hospital, she, too, is wondering about me.

Flushing, Abby gathered up her papers and carried them to the librarian's desk.

'How many copies?'

'They're all for Dr Wettig. You can charge them to the residency office.'

'I need to know the exact count for the copier log. It's our standing policy.'

Abby set the stack of papers down and began counting pages. She should have known the librarian would insist. This woman had been at Bayside forever, and she'd never failed to inform each new crop of interns that, in this room, things were done *her* way. Abby was getting angry now, at this librarian, at the hospital, at the mess her life had become. She finished counting the last article.

'Two hundred fourteen pages,' she said, and slapped it down on the pile. The name *Aaron Levi, MD*, seemed to jump out at her from the top page. The article's title was 'Comparison of Cardiac Transplant Survival Rates Between Critically Ill and Outpatient Recipients.' The authors were Aaron, Rajiv Mohandas, and Lawrence Kunstler. She stared at Aaron's name, shaken by the unexpected reminder of his death.

The librarian, too, noticed Aaron's name and she shook her head. 'It's hard to believe Dr Levi's gone.'

'I know what you mean,' Abby murmured.

'And to see both those names on the same article.' The woman shook her head.

'Excuse me?'

'Dr Kunstler and Dr Levi.'

'I'm afraid I don't know Dr Kunstler.'

'Oh, he was here before you came.' The librarian closed the copier log and primly slid it back onto her bookshelf. 'It must have happened six years ago, at least.'

'What happened six years ago?'

'It was just like that Charles Stuart case. You know, the man who jumped off the Tobin Bridge. That's where Dr Kunstler jumped.'

Abby focused again on the article. On the two names at the top of the page. 'He killed himself?'

The librarian nodded. 'Just like Dr Levi.'

*   *   *

The clatter of mah-jongg tiles being stirred on the
dining table was too loud to talk over. Vivian shut
the kitchen door and went back to the sink, where
she'd set the colander of bean sprouts. She
resumed snapping off the shriveled tails and
throwing the tops into a bowl. Abby didn't know
anyone bothered to snap off bean sprout roots.
Only the goddamn nitpicky Chinese, Vivian told
her. The Chinese spent hours laboring over some
dish that's devoured in minutes. And who noticed
the tails, anyway? Vivian's grandmother did. And
her grandmother's friends did. Put a dish of bean
sprouts with the tails still attached in front of those
ladies, and they'd all wrinkle their noses. So here
was the obedient granddaughter, the gifted surgeon
soon to be opening her own practice, concentrating
on the weighty task of snapping sprouts. She did it
swiftly, efficiently, every movement vintage Vivian.
The whole time she listened to Abby's story, those
graceful hands of hers never fell still.

'Jesus,' Vivian kept murmuring. 'Jesus, you are
screwed.'

In the next room the clatter of tiles had stopped,
the new round of play begun. Every so often,
through the buzz of gossip, there'd be a clunk as
someone tossed a tile into the center.

'What do you think I should do?' said Abby.

'Either way, DiMatteo, he's got you.'

'That's why I'm talking to *you*. You've been
screwed by Victor Voss. You know what he's
capable of.'

306

'Yeah.' Vivian sighed. 'I know too well.'

'Do you think I should go to the police? Or should I ride this out and hope they don't dig any deeper?'

'What does Mark think?'

'He thinks I should keep my mouth shut.'

'I agree with him. Call it my inherent distrust of authority. You must have more faith in the police than I do, if you're thinking of turning yourself in and hoping for the best.' Vivian reached for a dish towel and dried her hands. She looked at Abby. 'Do you really think your patient was murdered?'

'How else do I explain that morphine level?'

'She was already getting it. And probably tolerant enough to need sky-high levels just to stay comfortable. Maybe the doses finally accumulated.'

'Only if she got an extra dose. Accidentally or intentionally.'

'Just to set you up?'

'No one ever checks morphine levels on terminal cancer patients! Someone wanted to make sure her murder didn't slip by unnoticed. Someone who knew it *was* murder. And sent that note to Brenda Hainey.'

'How do we know Victor Voss did it?'

'He's the one who wants me out of Bayside.'

'Is he the only one?'

Abby stared at Vivian. And wondered: *Who else wants me out?*

In the dining room, the thunderous clatter of mah-jongg tiles signalled the end of another round. The noise startled Abby. She began to pace the kitchen. Past the rice cooker burbling on the counter, past the stove where steam wafted, spicy and exotic, from cooking pots. 'This is crazy. I can't believe anyone else would do this, just to get me fired.'

'Jeremiah Parr's got his own neck to save. And Voss is probably breathing down it right this minute. Think about it. The hospital board is packed with Voss's rich buddies. They could have Parr fired. Unless he fires *you* first. Hey, you're not paranoid, DiMatteo. People really *are* out to get you.'

Abby sank into a chair at the kitchen table. The noise from the game in the next room was giving her a headache. That and all the old-lady chatter. This house was full of noise, visitors talking Cantonese at a near shout, friendly conversation raised to argument pitch. How could Vivian stand having her grandmother live with her? The din alone would drive Abby crazy.

'It still all comes back to Victor Voss,' said Abby. 'One way or the other, he'll have his revenge.'

'Then why did he drop those lawsuits? That part doesn't make sense. He sends steamrollers coming right at you. Then suddenly, they all stop.'

'Instead of being sued by everyone, I'm accused of murder. What a wonderful alternative.'

'But you do see that it doesn't make sense? Voss probably paid a lot to get those lawsuits rolling. He wouldn't just drop them. Not unless he was concerned about some possible consequence. A countersuit, for instance. Were you planning something like that?'

'I discussed it with my lawyer, but he advised against it.'

'So why *did* Voss drop the lawsuits?'

It didn't make sense to Abby, either.

She considered that question all the way home, driving back from Vivian's house in Melrose. It was late afternoon, and the traffic was heavy as usual on Route 1. Though it was drizzling outside, she kept her window open. The stench of rotting pig organs still lingered in her car. She didn't think the smell would ever disappear. It would always linger, a permanent reminder of Victor Voss's rage.

The Tobin Bridge was coming up – the place where Lawrence Kunstler had chosen to end his life. She slowed down. Perhaps it was a morbid compulsion that made her glance sideways, towards the water, as she drove onto the bridge. Under dreary skies, the river looked black, its surface stippled by wind. Drowning was not a death she would choose. The panic, the thrashing limbs. Throat closing against the rush of cold water. She wondered if Kunstler had been conscious after he hit the water. Or whether he had struggled against the current. She wondered, too, about Aaron. Two doctors, two suicides. She'd forgotten to ask Vivian about Kunstler. If he had died only six years ago, Vivian might have heard of him.

Abby's gaze was so drawn to the water, she

didn't notice that the car in front of her had slowed down, that traffic had backed up from the toll booth. When she glanced up at the road, she saw that the car in front was stopped dead.

Abby slammed on the brakes. An instant later, she was jolted by a rear-end thump. She glanced in the mirror and saw the woman behind her shaking her head apologetically. For the moment, traffic on the bridge was going nowhere. Abby stepped out of her car and ran back to survey the damage.

The other woman got out as well. She stood by nervously as Abby inspected the rear bumper.

'It looks okay,' said Abby. 'No harm done.'

'I'm sorry, I guess I wasn't paying attention.'

Abby glanced at the woman's car, and saw that her front bumper was equally undamaged.

'This is embarrassing,' the woman said. 'I was so busy watching that tailgater behind me.' She pointed at a maroon van idling behind her car. 'Then *I* go and bump someone.'

A horn honked. Traffic was moving again. Abby returned to her car and continued across. As she drove past the toll booth, she couldn't help one last backward glance at the bridge, where Lawrence Kunstler had made his fatal leap. *They knew each other, Aaron and Kunstler. They worked together. They wrote that article together.*

That thought kept going around in her mind as she navigated the streets back to Cambridge.

Two doctors on the same transplant team. And both of them commit suicide.

She wondered if Kunstler had left a widow.

Wondered if Mrs Kunstler had been just as bewildered as Elaine Levi was.

She looped around the Harvard Common. As she veered off onto Brattle Street, she happened to glance in the rearview mirror.

A maroon van was behind her. It, too, drove onto Brattle.

She drove another block, past Willard Street, and looked again at the mirror. The van was still there. Was it the tailgater from the bridge? She hadn't given that van more than a glance at the time, and all she'd taken in was its color. She didn't know why seeing it now made her feel uneasy. Maybe it was that recent crossing of the bridge, and that glimpse of the water. The reminder of Kunstler's death. Of Aaron's death.

On impulse, she turned left, onto Mercer.

So did the van.

She turned left again, onto Camden, then right onto Auburn. She kept glancing in the mirror, waiting for, almost expecting, the van to come into view. Only when she'd reached Brattle Street again, and the van hadn't reappeared, did she allow herself a sigh of relief. What a nervous Nellie.

She drove straight home and pulled into the driveway. Mark wasn't back yet. That didn't surprise her. Despite drizzly skies, he'd planned to take *Gimme Shelter* out for another round-the-buoy race against Archer. Bad weather, he'd told her, was no excuse not to sail, and short of a hurricane, the race would go on.

She stepped into the house. It was gloomy inside, the afternoon light gray and watery through the windows. She crossed to the tabletop lamp and was about to switch it on when she heard the low growl of a car on Brewster Street. She looked out the window.

A maroon van was moving past the house. As it approached her driveway, it slowed to a crawl, as though the driver was taking a long, careful look at Abby's car.

Lock the doors. Lock the doors.

She ran to the front door, turned the dead bolt, and slid the chain into place.

The back door. Was it locked?

She ran down the hall and through the kitchen. No dead bolt, just a button lock. She grabbed a chair and slid it against the door, propping it under the knob.

She ran back to the living room and, standing behind the curtain, she peeked outside.

The van was gone.

She looked in both directions, straining for a view toward each corner, but saw only empty street, slick with drizzle.

She left the curtains open and the lights off. Sitting in the dark living room, she stared out the windows and waited for the van to reappear. Wondered if she should call the police. With what complaint? No one had threatened her. She sat there for close to an hour, watching the street, hoping that Mark would come home.

The van didn't appear. Neither did Mark.

Come home. Get off your goddamn boat and come home.

She thought of him out on the bay, sails snapping overhead, boom slamming across in the wind. And the water, turbid and churning under gray skies. Like the river had been. The river where Kunstler died.

She picked up the phone and dialed Vivian. The clamor of the Chao household came through the line in a lively blast of noise. Over the sounds of laughter and shouted Cantonese, Vivian said: 'I'm having trouble hearing you. Can you say that again?'

'There was another doctor on the transplant team who died six years ago. Did you know him?'

Vivian's answer came back in a shout. 'Yeah. But I don't think it was that long ago. More like four years.'

'Do you have any idea why he committed suicide?'

'It wasn't a suicide.'

'What?'

'Look, can you hold on a minute? I'm going to change extensions.'

Abby heard the receiver clunk down and had to endure what seemed like an endless wait before Vivian picked up the extension. 'Okay, Grandma! You can hang up!' she yelled. The chatter of Cantonese was abruptly cut off.

'What do you mean, it wasn't a suicide?' Abby said.

'It was an accident. There was some defect in his

313

furnace and carbon monoxide collected in the house. It killed his wife and baby girl, too.'

'Wait. Wait a minute. I'm talking about a guy named Lawrence Kunstler.'

'I don't know anyone named Kunstler. That must have happened before I got to Bayside.'

'Who are *you* talking about?'

'An anesthesiologist. The one before they hired Zwick. I'm blocking on his name right now . . . Hennessy. That's the name.'

'He was on the transplant team?'

'Yeah. A young guy, right out of fellowship. He wasn't here very long. I remember he was thinking about moving back West when it happened.'

'Are you sure it was an accident?'

'What else would it be?'

Abby stared out the window at the empty street and said nothing.

'Abby, is something wrong?'

'Someone was following me today. A van.'

'Come on.'

'Mark isn't home yet. It's almost dark and he should be home by now. I keep thinking about Aaron. And Lawrence Kunstler. He jumped off the Tobin Bridge. And now you're telling me about Hennessy. That's three, Vivian.'

'Two suicides and an accident.'

'That's more than you'd expect in one hospital.'

'Statistical cluster? Or maybe there's something about working for Bayside that's really, really depressing.' Vivian's attempt at humor fell flat and she knew it. After a pause she said, 'Do you honestly think someone was following you?'

'What did you tell me? *You're not paranoid. Someone's really out to get you.*'

'I was referring to Victor Voss. Or Parr. They have reasons to harass you. But to follow you around in a van? And what does it have to do with Aaron or the other two guys?'

'I don't know.' Abby drew her legs up on the chair and hugged herself for warmth. For self-protection. 'But I'm getting scared. I keep thinking about Aaron. I told you what that detective said – that Aaron's death may not be a suicide.'

'Does he have any evidence?'

'If he did, he certainly wouldn't tell me.'

'He might tell Elaine.'

Of course. The widow. The one who'd want to know, who'd demand to know.

After she hung up, Abby looked up Elaine Levi's phone number. Then she sat gathering the nerve to actually make the call. It was now dark outside, and the drizzle had turned to a steady rain. Mark still wasn't home. She shut the curtains and turned on the lights. All of them. She needed brightness and warmth.

She picked up the phone and dialed Elaine.

It rang four times. She cleared her throat, preparing to leave a message on the inevitable answering machine. Then she heard three piercing tones, followed by a recording: 'The number you have dialed is no longer in service. Please check your listing and dial again . . .'

315

Abby redialed, painstakingly confirming each number as she punched it in.

Four rings were followed by the same piercing tones. 'The number you have dialed is no longer in service . . .'

She hung up and stared at the phone as if it had betrayed her. Why had Elaine changed her number? Who was she trying to avoid?

Outside, a car splashed through the rain. Abby ran to the window and peered through a crack in the curtains. A BMW was pulling into the driveway.

She offered up a silent prayer of thanks.

Mark was home.

Sixteen

Mark refilled his wine glass. 'Sure, I knew them both,' he said. 'I knew Larry Kunstler better than Hennessy. Hennessy wasn't with us very long. But Larry was one of the guys who recruited me here, straight from my fellowship. He was an okay guy.' Mark set the wine bottle down on the table. 'A really nice guy.'

The maître d' swept past, escorting a flamboyantly dressed woman to a nearby table, where she was greeted with a noisy chorus of 'There you are, darling,' and 'Love your dress!' Their high-pitched gaiety at that particular moment struck Abby as vulgar. Even obscene. She wished she and Mark had stayed home. But he had wanted to eat out. They had so few free evenings together, and they hadn't properly celebrated their engagement. He had ordered wine, had made the toast, and now he was finishing off the bottle – something he seemed to be doing more and more these days. She watched him drain the last of the wine, and she thought: All the stress of my legal problems is affecting Mark as well.

'Why didn't you ever tell me about them?' she asked.

'It never came up.'

'I would think *someone* would mention them. Especially after Aaron died. The team loses three colleagues in six years, and no one says a thing. It's almost as if you're all afraid to talk about it.'

'It's a pretty depressing thing to talk about. We try not to bring up the subject, especially around Marilee. She knew Hennessy's wife. She even arranged her baby shower.'

'The baby who died?'

Mark nodded. 'It was a shock when it happened. A whole family, just like that. Marilee went a little hysterical when she heard about it.'

'It was definitely an accident?'

'They'd bought the house a few months before. They never got the chance to replace the old furnace. Yes, it was an accident.'

'But Kunstler's death wasn't.'

Mark sighed. 'No. Larry's was not an accident.'

'Why do you think he did it?'

'Why did Aaron do it? Why does anyone commit suicide? We can come up with half a dozen possible reasons, but the truth is, Abby, we don't know. We never know. And we never understand. We look at the big picture and say, *things get better. They always get better.* Somehow, Larry lost that perspective. He couldn't see the long range anymore. And that's when people fall apart.

When they lose all sight of the future.' He took a sip of wine, then another, but he seemed to have lost any enjoyment in its taste. Or in the food.

They skipped dessert and left the restaurant, both of them silent and depressed.

Mark drove through thickening fog and intermittent rain. The whisk of the windshield wipers filled in for conversation. *That's when people fall apart*, Mark had said. *When they lose all sight of the future.*

Staring at the mist, she thought: *I'm reaching that point. I can't see it anymore. I can't see what's going to happen to me. Or even to us.*

Mark said, softly: 'I want to show you something, Abby. I want to know what you think about it. Maybe you'll think I'm just crazy. Or maybe you'll be wild about the idea.'

'What idea?'

'It's something I've been dreaming about. For a long time, now.'

They drove north, out of Boston, kept driving through Revere and Lynn and Swampscott. At Marblehead Marina, he parked the car and said, 'She's right there. At the end of the pier.'

She was a yacht.

Abby stood shivering and bewildered on the dock as Mark paced up and down the boat's length. His voice was animated now, more animated than it had been all evening, his arms gesturing with enthusiasm.

'She's a cruiser,' he said. 'Forty-eight feet, fully equipped, everything we'd need. Brand new sails, new nav equipment. Hell, she's hardly been used. She could take us anywhere we'd want to go. The Caribbean. The Pacific. You're looking at freedom, Abby!' He stood on the dock, arm raised as if in salute to the boat. 'Absolute freedom!'

She shook her head. 'I don't understand.'

'It's a way out! Fuck the city. Fuck the hospital. We buy this boat. Then we bail out of here and go.'

'Where?'

'Anywhere.'

'I don't want to go anywhere.'

'There's no reason to stay. Not now.'

'Yes there is. For *me* there is. I can't just pack up and leave! I've got three years left, Mark. I have to finish them now, or I'll never be a surgeon.'

'I *am* one, Abby. I'm what *you* want to be. What you *think* you want to be. And I'm telling you, *it's not worth it.*'

'I've worked so hard. I'm not going to give up now.'

'What about *me*?'

She stared at him. And realized that, of course, this *was* all about him. The boat, the escape to freedom. The soon-to-be-married man, suddenly seized with the urge to run away from home. It was a metaphor that perhaps even he did not understand.

'I want to do this, Abby,' he said. He went to her, his eyes glittering. Feverish. 'I put in an offer, on this boat. That's why I got home so late. I was meeting with the broker.'

'You made an offer without telling me? Without even calling me?'

'I know it sounds crazy—'

'How can we afford this thing? I'm way over my head in debt! It'll take me years to pay back my student loans. And you're buying a *boat*?'

'We can take out a mortgage. It's like buying a second home.'

'This isn't a home.'

'It's still an investment.'

'It's not what I'd invest my money in.'

'I'm not spending *your* money.'

She took a step back and stared at him. 'You're right,' she said quietly. 'It's not my money at all.'

'Abby.' He groaned. 'Jesus, Abby—'

The rain was starting to fall again, cold and numbing against her face. She walked back to the car and climbed inside.

He got into the car as well. For a moment, neither one of them spoke. The only sound was the rain on the roof.

He said, quietly, 'I'll withdraw the offer.'

'That's not what I want.'

'What do you want?'

'I thought we'd be sharing more. I don't mean the money. I don't care about that. What hurts is that you think of it as *your* money. Is that how it's going to be? Yours or mine? Should we call in the lawyers now and draw up the prenuptial agreement? Divide up the furniture and the kids?'

'You don't understand,' he said, and she heard a strange and unexpected note of desperation in his voice. He started the car.

They drove halfway home without speaking.

Then Abby said: 'Maybe we should rethink the engagement. Maybe getting married isn't really what you want, Mark.'

'Is it what you want?'

She looked out the window and sighed. 'I don't know,' she murmured. 'I don't know anymore.'

It was the truth. She didn't.

Tragedy Claims Family of Three

While Dr Alan Hennessy and his family slept through the night, a killer was creeping up the basement steps. Deadly carbon monoxide gas, produced by a faulty furnace, is blamed for the New Year's Day deaths of thirty-four-year-old Hennessy, his wife Gail, thirty-three, and their six-month-old daughter Linda. Their bodies were discovered late that afternoon by friends who'd been invited to the house for dinner . . .

Abby repositioned the microfiche, and photos of Hennessy and his wife appeared on the screen, his face pudgy and serious, hers seemingly snapped in mid-laugh. There was no photo of the baby. Perhaps the *Globe* thought all six-month-old babies looked alike anyway.

Abby changed microfiches to a date three and a half years before the Hennessy deaths. She found the article she was looking for on the front page of the Metro section.

Body of Missing Physician
Recovered from Inner Harbor

A body found floating Tuesday in Boston Harbor
was identified today as Dr Lawrence Kunstler, a
local thoracic surgeon. Dr Kunstler's car was
found abandoned last week in the southbound
Tobin Bridge breakdown lane. Police are
speculating that his death was a suicide. No
witnesses, however, have come forward, and the
investigation remains open . . .

Abby centered Kunstler's photograph on the
microfilm screen. It was a blandly formal pose,
complete with white coat and stethoscope, Dr
Kunstler gazing directly at the camera.

And now, directly at her.

Why did you do it? Why did you jump? she
wondered. And she couldn't suppress the after-
thought: *Or did you?*

The one advantage of being relieved of ward
duties was that Abby could skip out for the whole
afternoon and no one at Bayside would notice, or
even care. So when she walked out of the Boston
Public Library and into the bustle of Copley
Square, she felt a sense of both emptiness and
relief that she didn't have to return to the hospital.
The afternoon, if she so desired, was hers.

She decided to drive to Elaine's house.

For the past few days, she'd been asking around
for Elaine's new phone number. Neither Marilee

Archer nor any of the other transplant team wives had even known that Elaine's number had been changed.

Now, with the images of Kunstler and Hennessy still painfully sharp in her mind, she headed west on Route 9, to Newton. Talking to Elaine was not something she looked forward to, but over the last few days, whenever she thought about Kunstler and Hennessy, she couldn't help thinking about Aaron as well. She remembered the day of his funeral, and how no one had even mentioned the two previous deaths. Any other group of people would have found it an unavoidable topic. Someone would normally have remarked, *This makes number three.* or *Why is Bayside so unlucky?* or *Do you think there's a common factor here?* But no one had said a thing. Not even Elaine, who must have known about Kunstler and Hennessy.

Not even Mark.

If he kept this from me, what else hasn't he told me?

She pulled into Elaine's driveway and sat there for a moment, her head in her hands, trying to shake off her depression. But the pall remained. *It's all falling apart for me*, she thought. *My job. And now I'm losing Mark. The worst part about it is, I don't have any idea why it's happening.*

Ever since the night she'd brought up the subject of Kunstler and Hennessy, everything had changed between her and Mark. They lived in the same house and slept in the same bed, but their interactions had become purely automatic. Like the sex. In the dark, with her eyes closed, she could have been making love to anyone.

She looked up at the house. And thought: *Maybe Elaine knows something.*

She got out of the car and climbed the steps to the front door. There she noticed the newspapers, two of them, still rolled up and lying on the porch. They were a week old and already yellowed. Why hadn't Elaine picked them up?

She rang the doorbell. When no one answered, she tried knocking, then rang again. And again. She could hear the bell echoing inside the house, followed by silence. No footsteps, no voices. She looked down at the two newspapers and knew that something was wrong.

The front door was locked; she left the porch and circled around the side of the house, to the back garden. A stone path trailed off into curving beds of well-tended azaleas and hydrangeas. The lawn looked recently mown, the hedges clipped, but the flagstone patio seemed disconcertingly empty. Then she remembered the furniture, the umbrella table and chairs that she'd seen here the afternoon of the funeral. They were gone.

The kitchen door was locked, but just off the patio was a sliding glass door that hadn't been latched. Abby gave it a tug and it glided open. She called: 'Elaine?' and stepped inside.

The room was vacant. Furniture, rugs – it was all gone, even the pictures. She stared in bewilderment at the blank walls, at the floor where the missing rug had left a darker rectangle on the sun-faded wood. She went into the living room, her footsteps echoing in the bare rooms. The house was swept clean, vacant except for a few advertisement postcards lying just inside the front door mail slot. She picked one up and saw it was addressed to Occupant.

She went into the kitchen. Even the refrigerator was empty, the surfaces wiped down and smelling of disinfectant. The wall telephone had no dial tone.

She walked outside and stood in the driveway, feeling completely disoriented. Only two weeks ago she had been inside this very house. She had sat on the living room couch and eaten canapés and eyed the Levi family photos over the fireplace. Now she wondered if she'd hallucinated the whole scene.

Still in a daze, she got in her car and backed out of the driveway. She drove on automatic pilot, scarcely paying attention to the road, her mind focused on Elaine's bizarre disappearance. Where would she go? To uproot her life so abruptly after Aaron's death didn't seem rational. Rather, it seemed like something one did out of panic.

Suddenly uneasy, she glanced in the rearview mirror. She'd made it a habit to check the mirror, ever since Saturday, when she'd first glimpsed the maroon van.

There was a dark green Volvo driving behind her. Hadn't it been parked outside Elaine's house? She couldn't be sure. She hadn't really been paying attention.

The Volvo blinked its lights on and off.

She accelerated.

The Volvo did too.

She turned right, onto a major thoroughfare. Ahead stretched a suburban strip of gas stations and mini-malls. *Witnesses. Lots of witnesses.* Yet the Volvo was still right behind her, still blinking its lights.

She'd had enough of being pursued, enough of being frightened. To hell with this. If he wanted to harass her, she'd turn the tables and confront him.

She swerved into the parking lot of a shopping mall. He followed her. One glance outside told her there were plenty of people around, shoppers pushing carts, drivers searching for parking spots. Here was the place to do it.

She slammed on the brakes.

The Volvo screeched to a halt inches from her rear bumper.

She scrambled out of her car and ran back to the Volvo. Furiously she rapped at the driver's window. 'Open up, damn you! *Open up!*'

The driver rolled down his window and looked out at her. Then he removed his sunglasses. 'Dr DiMatteo?' said Bernard Katzka. 'I thought it was you.'

'Why have you been following me?'

'I saw you drive away from the house.'

'No, *before*. Why did you follow me before?'

'When?'

'Saturday. The van.'

He shook his head. 'I don't know about any van.'

She backed away. 'Forget it. Just quit tailing me, okay?'

'I was trying to get you to pull over. Didn't you see me flash my lights?'

'I didn't know it was you.'

'Mind telling me what you are doing at Dr Levi's house?'

'I stopped by to see Elaine. I didn't know she'd moved.'

'Why don't you pull into that parking space? I'd like to talk to you. Or are you going to refuse to answer questions again?'

'That depends on what you're going to ask me.'

'It's about Dr Levi.'

'That's all we're going to talk about? Just Aaron?'

He nodded.

She thought about it. And decided that questions could go both ways. That even the close-mouthed Detective Katzka might be induced to give out information.

She glanced toward the mall. 'I see a doughnut shop over there. Why don't we go in and have a cup of coffee?'

Cops and doughnuts. The association had become an urban joke, reinforced in the public's mind by every overweight cop, by every patrol car ever parked outside a Dunkin' Donuts. Bernard Katzka, however, did not appear to be a doughnut fan; he ordered only a cup of black coffee, which he sipped without any apparent pleasure. Katzka did not strike Abby as the sort of man who indulged in much of anything that was pleasurable, sinful, or even remotely unnecessary.

His first question came right to the point. 'Why were you at the house?'

'I came to see Elaine. I wanted to talk to her.'

'About what?'

'Personal matters.'

'It was my impression that you two were just acquaintances.'

'Did she tell you that?'

He ignored her question. 'Is that how you'd characterize the relationship?'

She let out a breath. 'Yes, I guess so. We know each other through Aaron. That's all.'

'So why did you come to see her?'

Again she took a deep breath. And realized she was probably clueing him in to her own nervousness. 'Some strange things have happened to me lately. I wanted to talk to Elaine about it.'

'What things?'

'Someone was following me last Saturday. A maroon van. I spotted it on the Tobin Bridge. Then I saw it again, when I got home.'

'Anything else?'

'Isn't that upsetting enough?' She looked straight at him. 'It scared me.'

He regarded her in silence, as though trying to decide if it really was fear he was seeing in her face. 'What does this have to do with Mrs Levi?'

'You're the one who got me wondering about Aaron. About whether he really committed

329

suicide. Then I found out two other Bayside doctors have died.'

Katzka's frown told her this was news to him.

'Six and a half years ago,' she said, 'there was a Dr Lawrence Kunstler. A thoracic surgeon. He jumped off the Tobin Bridge.'

Katzka said nothing, but he had shifted forward, almost imperceptibly, in his chair.

'Then three years ago, there was an anesthesiologist,' continued Abby. 'A Dr Hennessy. He and his wife and baby died of carbon monoxide poisoning. They called it an accident. A broken furnace.'

'Unfortunately, that kind of accident happens every winter.'

'And then there's Aaron. That makes three. All of them were on the transplant team. Doesn't that seem like a terribly unlucky coincidence to you?'

'What are you formulating here? That someone's stalking the transplant team? Killing them off one by one?'

'I'm just pointing out a pattern here. You're the policeman. You should investigate it.'

Katzka sat back. 'How is it you got involved in all this?'

'My boyfriend's on the team. Mark doesn't admit it, but I think he's worried. I think the whole team's worried, and they're wondering who's going to be next. But they never talk about it. The way people never talk about plane crashes when they're standing at the boarding gate.'

'So you're worried about your boyfriend's safety?'

'Yes,' she said simply, leaving out the larger truth: that she was doing this because she wanted Mark back. All of him. She didn't understand what had happened between them, but she knew their relationship was crumbling. And it had all started to deteriorate the night she'd mentioned Kunstler and Hennessy. None of this she shared with Katzka, because it was all based on feelings. Instinct. Katzka was the kind of man who worked with more tangible coinage.

Obviously, he'd expected her to say more. When she remained silent, he asked: 'Is there anything else you want to tell me? About anything at all?'

He's talking about Mary Allen, she thought with a flash of panic. Looking at him, she had the overwhelming urge to tell him everything. Here, now. Instead she quickly avoided his gaze. And responded with a question of her own.

'Why were you watching Elaine's house?' she asked. 'That's what you're doing, isn't it?'

'I was talking to the next-door neighbor. When I came out, I saw you pull out of the driveway.'

'You're questioning Elaine's neighbors?'

'It's routine.'

'I don't think so.'

Almost against her will, her gaze lifted to his. His gray eyes admitted nothing, gave nothing away.

'Why are you still investigating a suicide?'

'The widow packs up and leaves practically

331

overnight, with no forwarding address. That's unusual.'

'You're not saying Elaine's guilty of anything, are you?'

'No. I think she's scared.'

'Of what?'

'Do you know, Dr DiMatteo?'

She found she could not look away, found there was something about the quiet intensity of his eyes that held her transfixed. She felt a brief and completely unexpected flicker of attraction, and she had no idea why this man, of all people, should inspire it.

'No,' she said. 'I have no idea what Elaine's running from.'

'Maybe you can help me answer another question, then.'

'Which is?'

'How did Aaron Levi accumulate all his wealth?'

She shook her head. 'He wasn't particularly wealthy, as far as I knew. A cardiologist earns maybe two hundred thousand, tops. And he was sending a lot of that to his two kids in college.'

'Was there family money?'

'You mean like an inheritance?' She shrugged. 'I heard Aaron's father was an appliance repairman.'

Katzka sat back, thinking. He wasn't looking at her now, but was staring at his coffee cup. There was a depth of concentration to this man that intrigued her. He could drop out of a conversation just like that, leaving her feeling abandoned.

'Detective, how much wealth are we talking about?'

He looked up at her. 'Three million dollars.'

Stunned, Abby could only stare at him.

'After Mrs Levi vanished,' he said, 'I thought I should take a closer look at the family finances. So I spoke to their CPA. He told me that shortly after Dr Levi died, Elaine discovered her husband had a Cayman Islands bank account. An account she'd known nothing about. She asked the CPA how to access the money. And then, without warning, she skipped town.' Katzka gave her a questioning look.

'I have no idea how Aaron got that much money,' she murmured.

'Neither does his accountant.'

They were silent a moment. Abby reached for her coffee and found it had gone cold. So had she.

She asked, softly: 'Do you know where Elaine is?'

'We have an idea.'

'Can you tell me?'

He shook his head. 'At the moment, Dr DiMatteo,' he said, 'I don't think she wants to be found.'

Three million dollars. How had Aaron Levi accumulated three million dollars?

All the way home, she considered that question. She couldn't see how a cardiologist would be able to do it. Not with two kids in private universities and a wife with expensive taste in antiques. And why had he hidden his wealth? The Cayman Islands was where people stashed their money when they wanted it kept out of sight of the IRS. But even Elaine had not known about the account until after Aaron's death. What a shock it must have been to go through her dead husband's papers. To discover that he'd been hiding a fortune from her.

Three million dollars.

She pulled into the driveway. Found herself surveying the neighborhood for a maroon van. It was getting to be a habit, that quick glance up and down the street.

She walked in the front door and stepped over the usual pile of afternoon mail. Most of it was professional journals, two of everything for the two doctors in the house. She gathered them all up and lugged them into the kitchen. On the table she began sorting everything into two piles. His junk, her junk. His life, her life. Nothing here worth a second glance.

It was four o'clock. Tonight, she decided, she'd cook a nice dinner. Serve it with candlelight and wine. Why not? She was now a lady of leisure. While Bayside took its sweet time deciding her future as a surgeon, she could stay busy fixing things up between her and Mark with romantic dinners and feminine coddling. Lose the career but keep the man.

Shit, DiMatteo. You're starting to sound desperate.

She scooped up her half of the junk mail, carried

it to the trash can, and stepped on the pop-up-lid pedal. Just as the mail was tumbling in, she glimpsed a large brown envelope stuffed at the bottom. The word *yachts*, printed in bold letters in the return address, caught her eye. She dug out the envelope and brushed off the coffee grounds and egg shells.

At the top left was printed:

East Wind Yachts
Sales and Service
Marblehead Marina

It had been sent to Mark. But it was not addressed to their Brewster Street house. It had been sent to a P.O. box.

She looked again at the words: *East Wind Yachts Sales and Service.*

She left the kitchen and went to Mark's desk in the living room. The bottom drawer, where he kept his files, was locked, but she knew where the key was. She'd heard him plunk it into the pencil cup. She found the key and opened the drawer.

Inside were all his household files. Insurance papers, mortgage papers, car papers. She found a tab with *Boat* written on it. There was a folder for *Gimme Shelter*, his J-35. There was also a second folder. It looked new. On the tab was written *H-48*.

She pulled out the H-48 file. It was a sales contract from East Wind Yachts. *H-48* was an abbreviation for the boat's design. A Hinckley yacht, forty-eight feet long.

She sank into a chair, feeling sick. *You kept it a secret*, she thought. *You told me you'd withdraw the offer. Then you bought it anyway. It's your money, all right. I guess this makes it perfectly clear.*

Her gaze moved to the bottom of the page. To the terms of sale.

Moments later, she walked out of the house.

'Cash for organs. Is it possible?'

In the midst of stirring cream into his coffee, Dr Ivan Tarasoff stopped and glanced at Vivian. 'Do you have any proof this is going on?'

'Not yet. We're just asking you if it's possible. And if so, how could it be done?'

Dr Tarasoff sank back on the couch and sipped his coffee as he thought it over. It was four forty-five, and except for the occasional scrub-suited resident passing through to the adjoining locker room, the Mass Gen surgeons' lounge was quiet. Tarasoff, who'd come out of the OR only twenty minutes ago, still had a dusting of glove talc on his hands and a surgical mask dangling around his neck. Watching him, Abby was comforted, once again, by the image of her grandfather. The gentle blue eyes, the silver hair. The quiet voice. *The voice of ultimate authority*, she thought, *belongs to the man who never has to raise it.*

'There've been rumors, of course,' said Tarasoff. 'Every time a celebrity gets an organ, people

336

wonder if money was involved. But there's never been any proof. Only suspicions.'

'What rumors have you heard?'

'That one can buy a higher place on the waiting list. I myself have never seen it happen.'

'I have,' said Abby.

Tarasoff looked at her. 'When?'

'Two weeks ago. Mrs Victor Voss. She was third on the waiting list and she got a heart. The two people at the top of the list later died.'

'UNOS wouldn't allow that. Or NEOB. They have strict guidelines.'

'NEOB didn't know about it. In fact, they have no record of the donor in their system.'

Tarasoff shook his head. 'This is hard to believe. If the heart didn't come through UNOS or NEOB, where did it come from?'

'We think Voss paid to keep it out of the system. So it could go to his wife,' said Vivian.

'This is what we know so far,' said Abby. 'Hours before Mrs Voss's transplant, Bayside's transplant coordinator got a call from Wilcox Memorial in Burlington that they had a donor. The heart was harvested and flown to Boston. It arrived in our OR around one A.M., delivered by some doctor named Mapes. The donor papers came with it, but somehow they got misplaced. No one's seen them since. I looked up the name Mapes in the Surgery section of the *Directory of Medical Specialists*. There's no such surgeon.'

'Then who did the harvest?'

'We think it was a surgeon named Tim Nicholls.

337

His name *is* listed in the *Directory*, so we know he does exist. According to his CV, he trained a few years at Mass Gen. Do you remember him?'

'Nicholls,' murmured Tarasoff. He shook his head. 'When was he here?'

'Nineteen years ago.'

'I'd have to check the residency records.'

'We're thinking this is what happened,' said Vivian. 'Mrs Voss needed a heart, and her husband had the money to pay for it. Somehow the word went out. Grapevine, underground, I don't know how. Tim Nicholls happened to have a donor. So he funneled the heart directly to Bayside, bypassing NEOB. And various people got paid off. Including some of the Bayside staff.'

Tarasoff looked horrified. 'It's possible,' he said. 'You're right, it could happen that way.'

The lounge door suddenly swung open and two residents walked in, laughing, as they headed for the coffee pot. They seemed to take forever as they fussed with the cream and sugar. At last they left the room.

Tarasoff was still looking stunned. 'I've referred patients to Bayside myself. We're talking about one of the top transplant centers in the country. Why would they go outside the registry? Risk getting into trouble with NEOB and UNOS?'

'The answer's obvious,' said Vivian. 'Money.'

Again they fell silent when another surgeon walked into the lounge, his scrub top soaked with sweat. He gave a grunt of exhaustion and sank into one of the easy chairs. Leaning back, he closed his eyes.

Softly Abby said to Tarasoff: 'We need you to look up the residency file on Tim Nicholls. Find out what you can about him. Tell us if he really did train here. Or if his CV's a complete fabrication.'

'I'll just call him myself. Put the questions to him directly.'

'No, don't. We're not sure yet how far this reaches.'

'Dr DiMatteo, I believe in being blunt. If there's a shadow organ procurement network out there, I want to know about it.'

'So do we. But we have to be very careful, Dr Tarasoff.' Abby glanced uneasily at the dozing surgeon in the chair. She lowered her voice to a whisper. 'In the last six years, three Bayside doctors have died. Two suicides and an accident. All of them were on our transplant team.'

She saw, from the look of shock on his face, that her warning had had its intended effect. 'You're trying to scare me,' he said. 'Aren't you?'

Abby nodded. 'You should be scared. We all should.'

Outside, in the parking lot, Abby and Vivian stood together under a gray, drizzling sky. They had arrived in their separate cars, and now it was time to go their own ways. The days were growing so short now; only five o'clock, and already the light was fading. Shivering, Abby pulled her slicker tighter and glanced around the lot. No maroon vans.

'We don't have enough,' said Vivian. 'We can't force an investigation yet. And if we tried, Victor Voss could just cover his tracks.'

'Nina Voss wasn't the first one. I think Bayside's done this before. Aaron died with three million dollars in his account. He must have been getting payoffs for some time.'

'You think he got second thoughts?'

'I know he was trying to get out of Bayside. Out of Boston. Maybe they wouldn't let him go.'

'That could be what happened to Kunstler and Hennessy.'

Abby released a deep breath. Again she glanced around the lot, searching for the van. 'I'm afraid that's exactly what happened to them.'

'We need other names, other transplants. Or more donor information.'

'All the information about donors is locked up in the transplant coordinator's office. I'd have to break in and steal it. If it's even there. Remember how they misplaced the donor papers on Nina Voss?'

'Okay, so we go at it from the recipient side.'

'Medical Records?'

Vivian nodded. 'Let's find out the names of who got transplanted. And where they were on the waiting list when it happened.'

'We'll need NEOB's help.'

'Right. But first we need names and dates.'

Abby nodded. 'I can do that.'

'I'd help you out, but Bayside won't let me in its doors anymore. They think I'm their worst nightmare.'

'You and me both.'

Vivian grinned, as if it was something to be proud of. She seemed small, almost childlike in her oversize raincoat. Such a fragile-looking ally. But while her size didn't inspire much confidence, her gaze did. It was direct and uncompromising. And it saw too much.

'Okay, Abby,' sighed Vivian. 'Now tell me about Mark. And why we're keeping this from him.'

Abby released a deep breath. The answer spilled out in a rush of anguish. 'I think he's part of it.'

'*Mark?*'

Abby nodded. And looked up at the drizzling sky. 'He wants out of Bayside. He's been talking about sailing away. Escape. Just like Aaron did before he died.'

'You think Mark's been taking payoffs?'

'A few days ago, he bought a boat. I don't mean just a boat. A *yacht*.'

'He's always been crazy about boats.'

'This one cost half a million dollars.'

Vivian said nothing.

'Here's the worst part,' whispered Abby. 'He paid in cash.'

Seventeen

The Medical Records file room was in the hospital basement, just down the hall from Pathology and the morgue. It was a department well known to every physician at Bayside. This was where doctors signed off on charts, dictated discharge summaries, and initialed lab reports and verbal orders. The room was furnished with comfortable chairs and tables, and to accommodate the often erratic work hours of its physicians, the department stayed open until nine P.M. every night.

It was six that evening when Abby walked into Medical Records. As she'd expected, the room was nearly deserted for the dinner hour. The only other physician was a haggard-looking intern, his desk piled high with delinquent charts.

Heart pounding, Abby approached the clerk's desk and smiled. 'I'm compiling statistics for Dr Wettig. He's doing a study on heart transplant morbidity. Could you pull up a list on your computer? The names and record numbers of all heart transplants done here in the last two years.'

'For a records search like that, we need a request form from the department.'

'They've all gone home by now. Could I get that form to you some other time? I'd like to have this ready for him by the morning. You know how the General is.'

The clerk laughed. Yes, she knew exactly how the General was. She sat down at her keyboard and called up the Search screen. Under Diagnosis, she typed in *Cardiac Transplant*, then the years to be searched. She hit the Enter button.

One by one, a list of names and record numbers began to appear. Abby watched, mesmerized by what she saw scrolling down the screen. The clerk hit Print. Seconds later, the list rolled out of the printer. She handed the page to Abby.

There were twenty-nine names on the list. The last one was Nina Voss.

'Could I have the first ten charts?' Abby asked. 'I might as well start working on this tonight.'

The clerk vanished into the file room. A moment later she reemerged hugging a bulky armful of files. 'These are only the first two. I'll get you the rest.'

Abby lugged the charts to a desk. They landed with a heavy thud. Every heart transplant patient generated reams and reams of documentation, and these two were no different. She opened the first folder to the patient information sheet.

The name was Gerald Luray, age fifty-four. Source of payment was private insurance. Home address was in Worcester, Massachusetts. She didn't know how relevant any of this information was, so she copied it all down onto a yellow legal pad. She also copied the date and time of transplant and the names of the doctors in attendance. She recognized all the names: Aaron Levi, Bill Archer, Frank Zwick, Rajiv Mohandas. *And Mark*. As expected, there was no donor information anywhere in the chart. That was always kept separate from recipient records. However, among the nurses' notes, she found written: '0830 – Harvest reported complete. Donor heart now enroute from Norwalk, Connecticut. Patient wheeled to OR for prep . . .'

Abby wrote: 0830. Harvest in Norwalk, Conn.

The records clerk wheeled a cart to Abby's desk, deposited five more charts, and went back for more.

Abby worked straight through the supper hour. She didn't stop to eat, didn't allow herself even a break, except to call Mark to tell him she'd be home late.

By closing time, she was starving.

She stopped at a McDonald's on the way home and ordered a Big Mac and giant fries and a vanilla shake. Cholesterol to feed the brain. She ate it all while sitting in a corner booth, keeping an eye on the dining room. At that hour, the other patrons were mostly the postmovie crowd, teenagers on dates, and here and there a few depressed-looking bachelors. No one even seemed to notice she was there. She finished every last French fry, then left.

Before she started the car, she made a quick survey of the parking lot. No van.

At ten-fifteen, she arrived home to find that Mark was already in bed and the lights were out. She was relieved that she would not have to answer any questions. She undressed in the dark and climbed under the covers, but she didn't touch him. She was almost afraid to touch him.

When he suddenly stirred and reached out to her, she felt her whole body go rigid.

'I missed you tonight,' he murmured. He turned her face to his and gave her a long and intimate kiss. His hand slid down to her waist and caressed her hip. Stroked along her thigh. She didn't move; she felt as frozen as a mannequin, unable to respond or resist. She lay with her eyes closed, her pulse roaring in her ears, as he pulled her into his arms. As he slid inside her.

Who am I making love to? she wondered as he thrust again and again, their hips colliding with brutish force.

Then it was over, and he was sliding out of her.

'I love you,' he whispered.

It was a long time later, after he'd fallen asleep, that she whispered her answer.

'I love you too.'

At seven-forty A.M. she was back in Medical Records. Several of the desks were now occupied by physicians cleaning up paperwork before making their morning rounds. Abby requested five more charts. Quickly she took notes, gave the charts back to the clerk, and left.

She spent the morning in the medical library, looking up more articles for Dr Wettig. It wasn't until late that afternoon when she returned to Medical Records.

She requested ten more charts.

Vivian finished off the last slice of pizza. It was her fourth slice, and where she put it all was a mystery to Abby. That elfin body consumed calories like a fat-burning furnace. Since they'd sat down in the booth at Gianelli's, Abby had eaten only a few bites, and even those were an effort.

Vivian wiped her hands on a napkin. 'So Mark still doesn't know?'

'I haven't said a thing to him. I guess I'm afraid to.'

'How can you stand it? Living in the same house and not talking?'

'We talk. We just don't talk about *this*.' Abby touched the sheaf of notes on the table – the notes she'd been carrying around all day. She'd been careful to keep them where Mark wouldn't find them. Last night, when she'd returned home after McDonald's, she had hidden the notes under the couch. Lately it seemed she'd been hiding so many things from him, and she didn't know how long she could keep it up.

'Abby, you've got to talk to him about this eventually.'

'Not yet. Not until I know.'

'You're not afraid of *Mark*, are you?'

'I'm afraid he'll deny everything. And I'll have no way of knowing if he's telling the truth.' She ran her hands through her hair. 'God, it's like reality's completely shifted on me. I used to think I was standing on such solid ground. If I wanted something badly enough, I just worked like hell for it. Now I can't decide what to do, which move to make. All the things I counted on aren't there for me anymore.'

'Meaning Mark.'

Wearily, Abby rubbed her face. 'Especially Mark.'

'You look awful, Abby.'

'I haven't been sleeping very well. I've got so many things to think about. Not just Mark. But also that business with Mary Allen. I keep waiting for Detective Katzka to show up on my doorstep with his handcuffs.'

'You think he suspects you?'

'I think he's too bright not to.'

'You haven't heard anything from him. Maybe he'll let it slide. Maybe you're giving him too much credit.'

Abby thought of Bernard Katzka's calm gray eyes. And she said, 'He's a hard man to read. But I think Katzka's not only smart, he's persistent. I'm scared of him. And weirdly enough, fascinated by him too.'

Vivian sat back. 'Interesting. The prey intrigued by her hunter.'

'Sometimes I just want to call Katzka and blurt

347

out everything. Get it all over with.' Abby dropped her head in her hands. 'I'm so tired, I wish I could run away somewhere. Sleep for a whole week.'

'Maybe you should move out of Mark's house. I've got an extra bedroom. And my grandmother's leaving.'

'I thought she was a permanent houseguest.'

'She makes the rounds of all her grandkids. Right now I've got a cousin in Concord who's bracing herself for *the visit*.'

Abby shook her head. 'I don't know what to do. The thing is, I love Mark. I don't trust him anymore, but I love him. At the same time, I know that what we're doing could ruin him.'

'It could also save his life.'

Abby looked miserably at Vivian. 'I save his life. But I destroy his career. He may not thank me much for that.'

'Aaron would have thanked you. Kunstler would have. Certainly Hennessy's wife and baby would have thanked you.'

Abby said nothing.

'How certain are you that Mark's involved?'

'I'm *not* certain. That's what makes this so hard. *Wanting* to believe in him. And not having any evidence to tell me one way or the other.' She touched her notes. 'I've looked at twenty-five files so far. Some of the transplants go back to two years ago. Mark's name is on every one of them.'

'So is Archer's. And Aaron's. That doesn't tell us anything. What else have you learned?'

'All the records look pretty much the same. Nothing to distinguish one from any other.'

'Okay, what about the donors?'

'That's where things get a little interesting.' Abby glanced around the restaurant. Then she leaned toward Vivian. 'Not all of the charts mention which city the donor organ comes from. But a number of them do. And there seems to be a cluster. Four of them came from Burlington, Vermont.'

'Wilcox Memorial?'

'I don't know. The hospital was never specified in the nurses' notes. But I find it interesting that a relatively small town like Burlington ends up with so many brain-dead people.'

Vivian's gaze met hers in a stunned look. 'There's something really wrong here. We were hypothesizing nothing more than a shadow referral network. Donors who are simply kept out of the registry system. But that doesn't explain a cluster of donors in one town. Unless . . .'

'Unless donors are being generated.'

They fell silent.

Burlington is a university town, thought Abby. *Full of young, healthy college students. With young, healthy hearts.*

'Can I have the dates on those four Burlington harvests?' said Vivian.

'I have them right here. Why?'

'I'm going to check them against the Burlington obituaries. Find out who died on those dates. Maybe we can identify the names of the four

349

donors. And find out how they ended up brain-dead.'

'Not all obits list the cause of death.'

'Then we may have to go to the death certificates. Which means a trip to Burlington for one of us. A place I've been dying to visit. *Not*.' Vivian's tone of voice was almost breezy. That warrior woman bravado again; she had the act down pat. But this time it wasn't enough to hide the note of apprehension.

'Are you sure you want to do this?' said Abby.

'If we don't, then Victor Voss wins. And the losers are going to be people like Josh O'Day.' She paused. And asked, quietly: 'Is this what *you* want to do, Abby?'

Abby dropped her head in her hands. 'I don't think I have a choice any longer.'

Mark's car was in the driveway.

Abby pulled up behind it and turned off her engine. For a long time she simply sat there, scraping up the energy to get out of the car, to walk into the house. To face him.

At last she stepped out of the car and walked in the front door.

He was in the living room, watching the late night news. As soon as she came in, he clicked off the TV. 'How is Vivian doing these days?' he asked.

'She's fine. Landed right back on her feet. She's buying into a practice in Wakefield.' Abby hung up her coat in the closet. 'And how was your day?'

'We got a dissecting aorta. He bled out sixteen units just like that. I didn't get out till seven.'

'Did he make it?'

'No. We ended up losing him.'

'That's too bad. I'm sorry.' She shut the closet door. 'I'm kind of tired. I think I'll go up and take a bath.'

'Abby?'

She paused and looked at him. They were separated by the width of the living room. But the gulf between them seemed miles wider.

'What's happened to you?' he asked. 'What's wrong?'

'You know what's wrong. I'm worried about my job.'

'I'm talking about us. Something's wrong with *us*.'

She didn't say anything.

'I hardly see you anymore. You're at Vivian's more than you are here. When you are home, you act like you're somewhere else.'

'I'm preoccupied, that's all. Can't you understand why?'

He sank back, suddenly looking very tired. 'I have to know, Abby. Are you seeing someone else?'

She stared at him. Of all the things Mark might say to her, this was the last thing she'd expected. She almost felt like laughing at the trivial nature of his suspicions. *If only it were that simple. If only our problems were the same as every other couple's.*

'There's no one else,' she said. 'Believe me.'

'Then why aren't you talking to me anymore?'

'I'm talking to you now.'

'This isn't talking! This is *me* trying to get the old Abby back. Somewhere along the way I've lost her. I've lost *you*.' He shook his head and looked away. 'I just want you back again.'

She went to the couch and sat down beside him. Not close enough to touch, but close enough to feel connected, if only distantly.

'Talk to me, Abby. Please.' He looked at her, and suddenly it was the old Mark she saw. The same face that had smiled at her across the operating table. The face she loved. 'Please,' he repeated, softly. He took her hand and she didn't pull away. She let him take her into his arms. But even there, where she'd once felt safe, she could not relax. She lay stiff and uneasy against his chest.

'Tell me,' he said. 'What's wrong between us?'

She closed her eyes against the sting of fresh tears. 'Nothing's wrong,' she said.

She felt his arms go very still around her. Without even looking at his face, she knew that he could tell she was, once again, lying.

At seven-thirty the next morning, Abby pulled into her parking space at Bayside Hospital.

She sat in her car for a moment, eyeing the wet pavement, the steady drizzle. Only mid-October, she thought, and already this dreary foretaste of winter. She had not slept well last night. In fact, she could not remember the last good night's sleep she'd had. How long could a person hold up without sleep? How long before fatigue led to psychosis? Glancing in the rearview mirror, she scarcely recognized the haggard stranger staring back at her. In two weeks it seemed she had aged ten years. At this rate she'd be hitting menopause by November.

A flash of maroon in the mirror caught her eye.

She snapped her head around just in time to see a van retreating behind the next aisle of cars. She waited for another glimpse of it. It didn't reappear.

Quickly she stepped outside and began to walk toward the hospital. The weight of her briefcase felt like an anchor weighing her down. Off to her right, a car engine suddenly roared to life. She whirled, expecting to see the van, but it was a station wagon pulling out of a space.

Her heart was slamming against her chest. It didn't calm down until she was inside the building. She took the stairs down to the basement and walked into Medical Records. This would be her final visit; she was down to the last four names on the list.

She lay the request slip on the counter and said, 'Excuse me, may I have these charts please?'

The clerk turned to face her. Perhaps Abby was only imagining it, but the woman seemed to freeze momentarily. They had dealt with each other before, and the clerk usually seemed friendly enough. Today she wasn't even smiling.

'I need these four charts,' said Abby.

The clerk looked at the request slip. 'I'm sorry, Dr DiMatteo. I can't get these files for you.'

'Why not?'

'They're not available.'

'But you haven't even checked.'

'I've been told not to release any more files to you. It's Dr Wettig's orders. He said if you came in, we're to refer you to his office immediately.'

Abby felt the blood drain from her face. She said nothing.

'He said he never authorized any chart search.' The clerk's tone of voice was plainly accusatory. *You lied to us, Dr DiMatteo.*

Abby had no answer. It seemed to her the room had suddenly fallen silent. She turned and saw that three other doctors were in the room, and they were all watching her.

She walked out of Medical Records.

Her first impulse was to leave the building. To avoid the inevitable confrontation with Wettig and just drive away. To keep driving until this was a thousand miles behind her. She wondered how long it would take to reach Florida and the beach and palm trees. She'd never been to Florida. She'd never done so many things other people had done. She could do them all now if she'd just walk out of this goddamn hospital, climb in her car, and say: *Fuck it. You win. You all win.*

But she didn't walk out of the building. She stepped into the basement elevator and punched Two.

On that short ride to the administrative floor,

several things became instantly clear to her. The first was that she was too stubborn or too stupid to run. The second was that a beach was not really what she wanted. What she wanted was her dream back.

She got out of the elevator and walked up the carpeted hall. The residency office was around the corner, past Jeremiah Parr's suite. As she walked past Parr's secretary, she saw the woman sit up sharply and reach for the phone.

Abby turned the corner and walked into the residency office. There were two men standing by the secretary's desk, neither of whom Abby had ever seen before. The secretary looked up at Abby with that same stunned expression that had flashed across the face of Parr's secretary, and blurted: 'Oh! Dr DiMatteo—'

'I need to see Dr Wettig,' said Abby.

The two men turned to look at her. In the next instant, Abby was startled by a flash of light. She flinched away as the light went off again and again. A camera flashbulb.

'What are you doing?' she demanded.

'Doctor, would you care to comment on the death of Mary Allen?' one of the men said.

'What?'

'She was your patient, wasn't she?'

'Who the hell are you?'

'Gary Starke, *Boston Herald*. It is true you're an advocate of euthanasia? We know you've made statements to that effect.'

'I never said anything of the—'

'Why were you relieved of your ward duties?'

Abby took a step back. 'Get away from me. I'm not talking to you.'

'Dr DiMatteo—'

Abby turned to flee the office. She almost collided with Jeremiah Parr, who'd just walked in the door.

'I want you reporters out of my hospital *now*,' Parr snapped. Then he turned to Abby. 'Doctor, come with me.'

Abby followed Parr out of the room. They walked swiftly down the hall and into his office. He shut the door and turned to look at her.

'The *Herald* started calling half an hour ago,' he said. 'Then the *Globe* called, followed by about half a dozen other newspapers. It hasn't let up since.'

'Did Brenda Hainey tell them?'

'I don't think it was her. They seemed to know about the morphine. And the vial in your locker. Things she didn't know.'

She shook her head. 'How?'

'Somehow it leaked out.' Parr sank into the chair behind his desk. 'This is going to kill us. A criminal investigation. Police swarming up and down the halls.'

The police. Of course. By now it's leaked out to them as well.

Abby stared at Parr. Her throat felt too parched to produce a single word. She wondered if *he* was the source of the leak, then decided it was unlikely. This scandal would hurt him, too.

There was a sharp rap on the door, and Dr Wettig walked in. 'What the hell do I do about those reporters?' he said.

'You'll have to prepare a statement, General. Susan Casado's on her way over. She'll help you with the wording. Until then, no one talks to anyone.'

Wettig gave a curt nod. Then his gaze focused on Abby. 'May I see your briefcase, Dr DiMatteo?'

'Why?'

'You know why. You had no authority to search those patient records. They are private and confidential. I'm ordering you to turn over all the notes you took.'

She did nothing. Said nothing.

'I hardly think an additional charge of theft is going to help your case.'

'Theft?'

'Any information you gleaned from that illegal chart search was stolen. Give me the briefcase. *Give it to me.*'

Wordlessly she handed it to him. She watched him open it. Watched him shuffle through the papers and remove her notes. She could do nothing except hang her head in defeat. Once again they had beaten her. They had made the preemptive strike, and she hadn't been prepared. She should have known better. She should have stashed the notes before coming up here. But she'd been too focused on what she would say, how she would explain herself to Wettig.

He shut the briefcase and handed it back to her. 'Is that everything?' he asked.

She could only nod.

Wettig regarded her for a moment in silence. Then he shook his head. 'You would have made a fine surgeon, DiMatteo. But I think it's time to recognize the fact you need help. I'm recommending you seek psychiatric evaluation. And I'm releasing you from the residency program, effective today.' To her surprise, she heard a note of genuine regret in his voice when he added, quietly: 'I'm sorry.'

Eighteen

Detective Lundquist was a handsome blond, the ideal Teutonic specimen. He had interviewed Abby for two hours now, asking his questions while pacing around the cramped interview room. If it was a tactic designed to make her feel threatened, then it was working. In the small Maine town where Abby grew up, cops were the guys who waved at you from their cars, who walked cheerfully around town with keys clinking on their belts, and who handed out citizenship awards at high school graduations. They were not people you were supposed to be afraid of.

Abby was afraid of Lundquist. She'd been afraid of him from the moment he'd walked into the room and set a tape recorder on the table. She'd been even more afraid when he'd pulled out a card from his suit pocket and read her her rights. *She* was the one who'd walked into the police station of her own volition. She had asked to speak to Detective Katzka. Instead they had sent in Lundquist, and he had questioned her with the barely restrained aggression of an arresting officer.

The door opened, and at last Bernard Katzka walked into the room. To finally see someone she knew should have been a relief to Abby, but Katzka's impassive face offered no reassurance whatsoever. He stood across the table from her, regarding her with a weary expression.

'I understand you haven't called an attorney,' he said. 'Do you wish to call one now?'

'Am I under arrest?' she asked.

'Not at the moment.'

'Then I'm free to go at any time?'

He paused and looked at Lundquist, who shrugged. 'This is only a preliminary investigation.'

'Do you think I need an attorney, Detective?'

Again Katzka hesitated. 'That's really your decision, Dr DiMatteo.'

'Look, I walked in here on my own. I did it because I *wanted* to talk to you. To tell you what happened. I've willingly answered all this man's questions. If you're putting me under arrest, then yes, I'll call an attorney. But I want to make it clear from the start that it's not because I've done anything wrong.' She looked Katzka in the eye. 'So I guess my answer is, I don't need an attorney.'

Again Lundquist and Katzka exchanged glances, their meaning unclear to her. Then Lundquist said, 'She's all yours, Slug,' and he moved off into a corner.

Katzka sat down at the table.

'I suppose you're going to ask all the same questions he did,' said Abby.

'I missed the beginning. But I think I've already heard most of your answers.'

He nodded at the mirror in the far wall. It was a viewing window, she realized. He'd been listening to the session with Lundquist. She wondered how many others were standing behind that glass, watching her. It made her feel exposed. Violated. She shifted her chair, turning her face away from the mirror, and found she was now gazing directly at Katzka.

'So what are *you* going to ask me?'

'You said you think someone is setting you up. Can you tell us who?'

'I thought it was Victor Voss. Now I'm not so sure.'

'Do you have other enemies?'

'Obviously I do.'

'Someone who dislikes you enough to murder your patient? Just to set you up?'

'Maybe it wasn't murder. That morphine level was never confirmed.'

'It has been. Mrs Allen was exhumed a few days ago, at the request of Brenda Hainey. The medical examiner ran the quantitative test this morning.'

Abby absorbed this information in silence. She could hear the tape recorder, still whirring. She sank back in her chair. There was no question now. Mrs Allen had died of an OD.

'A few days ago, Dr DiMatteo, you told me you were being followed by a purple van.'

'Maroon,' she whispered. 'It was a maroon van. I saw it again, today.'

'Did you get a license number?'

'It was never close enough.'

'Let me see if I understand this correctly. Someone administers a morphine overdose to your patient, Mrs Allen. Then he – or she – plants a vial of morphine in your locker. And now you're being followed around town by a van. And you think these incidents were all engineered by Victor Voss?'

'That's what I thought. But maybe it's someone else.'

Katzka sat back and regarded her. His look of weariness had spread to his shoulders, which were now slumped forward.

'Tell us about the transplants again.'

'I've already told you everything.'

'I'm not entirely clear how it's connected to this case.'

She took a deep breath. She'd gone over this already with Lundquist, had told him the whole story of Josh O'Day and the suspicious circumstances of Nina Voss's transplant. Judging by Lundquist's disinterested response, it had been a waste of time. Now she was expected to repeat the story, and it would be a waste of more time. Defeated, she closed her eyes. 'I'd like a drink of water.'

Lundquist left the room. While he was gone, neither she nor Katzka said a word. She just sat with her eyes closed, wishing it were all over. But it would never be over. She would be in this room for eternity, answering the same questions forever.

Maybe she should have called an attorney after all. Maybe she should just walk out. Katzka had told her she was not under arrest. Not yet.

Lundquist returned with a paper cup of water. She drank it down in a few gulps and set the empty cup on the table.

'What about the heart transplants, Doctor?' prodded Katzka.

She sighed. 'I think that's how Aaron got his three million dollars. By finding donor hearts for rich recipients who didn't want to wait their turn on the list.'

'The list?'

She nodded. 'In this country alone, we have over five thousand people who need heart transplants. A lot of them are going to die because there's a shortage of donor hearts. Donors have to be young and in previously good health – which means the vast majority of donors are trauma victims with brain death. And there aren't enough of those to go around.'

'So who decides which patient gets a heart?'

'There's a computerized registry. Our regional system is run by New England Organ Bank. They're absolutely democratic. You're prioritized according to your condition. Not your wealth. Which means if you're way down the list, you have a long wait. Now let's say you're rich, and you're worried you'll die before they find you a heart. Obviously, you'll be tempted to go outside the system to get an organ.'

'Can it be done?'

'It would have to involve a shadow match-making service. A way to keep potential donors out of the system and funnel their hearts directly to wealthy patients. Or there's even a worse possibility.'

'Which is?'

'They're generating new donors.'

'You mean *killing* people?' said Lundquist. 'Then where are all the dead bodies? The missing persons reports?'

'I didn't say that's what's happening. I'm just telling you how it could be done.' She paused. 'I think Aaron Levi was part of it. That might explain his three million dollars.'

Katzka's expression had scarcely changed. His impassivity was beginning to irritate her.

She said, more animated now: 'Don't you see? It makes sense to me now, why those lawsuits against me were dropped. They probably hoped I'd stop asking questions. But I didn't stop. I just kept asking more and more. And now they *have* to discredit me, because I can blow the whistle on them. I could ruin everything.'

'So why don't they just kill you?' It was Lundquist asking the question in a plainly skeptical tone of voice.

She paused. 'I don't know. Maybe they don't think I know enough yet. Or they're afraid of how it'd look. So soon after Aaron's death.'

'This is very creative,' said Lunquist, and he laughed.

Katzka lifted his hand in a terse gesture to

Lundquist to shut up. 'Dr DiMatteo,' he said, 'I'll be honest with you. This is not coming across as a likely scenario.'

'It's the only one I can think of.'

'Can I offer one?' said Lundquist. 'One that makes perfect sense?' He stepped toward the table, his gaze on Abby. 'Your patient Mary Allen was suffering. Maybe she asked you to help her over the edge. Maybe you thought it was the humane thing to do. And it was humane. Something any caring physician would consider doing. So you slipped her an extra dose of morphine. Problem is, one of the nurses saw you do it. And she sends an anonymous note to Mary Allen's niece. Suddenly you're in trouble, and all because you were trying to be humane. Now you're looking at charges of homicide. Prison time. It's all getting pretty scary, isn't it? So you cobble together a conspiracy theory. One that can't be proved – or disproved. Doesn't that make more sense, Doctor? It makes more sense to me.'

'But that's not what happened.'

'What did happen?'

'I told you. I've told you everything—'

'Did you kill Mary Allen?'

'No.' She leaned forward, her hands clenched in fists on the table. 'I did not kill my patient.'

Lundquist looked at Katzka. 'She's not a very good liar, is she?' he said, and he walked out of the room.

For a moment neither Abby nor Katzka spoke. Then she asked, softly, 'Am I under arrest now?'

'No. You can leave.' He rose to his feet.

So did she. They stood looking at each other as though neither one of them had quite decided that the interview was over.

'Why am I being released?' she asked.

'Pending further investigation.'

'Do you think I'm guilty?'

He hesitated. She knew it was not a question he should answer, yet he seemed to be struggling for some measure of honesty in his reply. In the end, he chose to avoid the question entirely.

'Dr Hodell's been waiting for you,' he said. 'You'll find him at the front desk.' He turned to open the door. 'I'll be talking to you again, Dr DiMatteo,' he said, and left the room.

She walked down the hall and into the waiting area.

Mark was standing there. 'Abby?' he said softly.

She let him take her into his arms, but her body registered his touch with a strange sense of numbness. Detachment. As if she herself were floating above them both, observing from a distance two strangers embracing, kissing.

And from across that same distance, she heard him say: 'Let's go home.'

Through the security partition, Bernard Katzka watched the couple walk toward the door, observing how closely Hodell held the woman. It was not something a cop saw every day. Affection. Love. More often it was couples wrangling away, bruised faces, cut lips, fingers pointed in accusation. Or it was pure lust. Lust he saw all the time. It was out in full view, as blatant as the whores walking the streets of Boston's Combat Zone. Katzka himself was not immune to it, to that occasional need for a woman's body.

But love was something he had not felt in a long time. And at that moment, he envied Mark Hodell.

'Hey, Slug!' someone called. 'Call on line three.'

Katzka reached for the telephone. 'Detective Katzka,' he said.

'This is the ME's office. Hold for Dr Rowbotham, please.'

As Katzka waited, his gaze shifted back toward the waiting area, and he saw that Abby DiMatteo and Hodell were gone. The couple with everything, he thought. Looks. Money. High-powered careers. Would a woman in her enviable position risk it all, just to ease the pain of a dying patient?

Rowbotham came on the line. 'Slug?'

'Yeah. What's up?'

'A surprise.'

'Good or bad?'

'Let's just call it unexpected. I have the tissue GC-MS results back on Dr Levi.'

GC-MS, or gas chromatography-mass spectrometry, was a method used by the crime lab for identification of drugs and toxins.

'I thought you already ruled out everything,' said Katzka.

'We ruled out the usual drugs. Narcotics, barbs. But that was using immunoassay and thin-layer chromatography. This is a doctor we're talking about, so I figured we couldn't go with just the usual screen. I also checked for fentanyl, phencyclidine, some of the volatiles. I came up with a positive in the muscle tissue. Succinylcholine.'

'What's that?'

'It's a neuromuscular blocking agent. Competes with the body's neurotransmitter, acetylcholine. The effect is sort of like *d*-tubocurarine.'

'Curare?'

'Right, but succinylcholine has a different chemical mechanism. It's used in the OR all the time. To immobilize muscles for surgery. Allow easier ventilation.'

'Are you saying he was paralyzed?'

'Completely helpless. The worst part of it is, he would've been conscious, but unable to struggle.' Rowbotham paused. 'It's a terrible way to die, Slug.'

'How is the drug administered?'

'Injection.'

'We didn't see any needle marks on the body.'

'It could have been in the scalp. Hidden in the hair. It's just a pinprick we're talking about. We could easily have missed it with all the postmortem skin changes.'

Katzka thought it over for a moment. And he remembered something Abby DiMatteo had told him only a few days ago, something he hadn't completely followed up on.

He said, 'Could you look up two old autopsy reports for me? One would be from about six years ago. A jumper off the Tobin Bridge. The name was Lawrence Kunstler.'

'Spell it for me . . . Okay, got it. And the next name?'

'Dr Hennessy. I'm not sure about his first name. That one was three years ago. Accidental carbon monoxide poisoning. The whole family died as well.'

'I think I remember that one. There was a baby.'

'That's the one. I'll see if I can't get exhumation orders rolling.'

'What are you looking for, Slug?'

'I don't know. Something that might've been missed before. Something we might pick up now.'

'In a corpse that's been dead six years?' Rowbotham's laugh was plainly skeptical. 'You must be turning into an optimist.'

'More flowers, Mrs Voss. They were just delivered. Do you want them in here? Or shall I put them in the parlor?'

'Bring them in here, please.' Sitting in a chair by her favorite window, Nina watched the maid carry the vase into the bedroom and set it down on a night table. Now she was fussing with the arrangement, moving stems around, and the fragrance of sage and phlox wafted toward Nina.

'Put them here, next to me.'

'Of course, ma'am.' The maid moved the vase to the small tea table beside Nina's chair. She had to make room for it by taking away another vase of Oriental lilies. 'They're not your usual flowers, are they?' the maid said, and her tone of voice was not entirely approving as she regarded the usurping vase.

'No.' Nina smiled at the unruly arrangement. Already her gardener's eye had picked out and identified each splash of color. Russian sage and pink phlox. Purple coneflowers and yellow heliopsis. And daisies. Lots and lots of daisies. Such common, undistinguished flowers. How did one find daisies so late in the season?

She brushed her hand across the blossoms and inhaled the scents of late summer, the remembered fragrance of the garden she had been too ill to tend. Now summer was gone, and their house in Newport was closed for the winter. How she disliked this time of year! The fading of the garden. The return to Boston, to this house with its gold-leafed ceilings and carved doorways and bathrooms of Carrara marble. She found all the dark wood oppressive. Their summer home was blessed with light and warm breezes and the smell of the sea. But this house made her think of winter. She picked out a daisy and breathed in its pungent scent.

'Wouldn't you rather have the lilies next to you?' the maid asked. 'They smell so lovely.'

'They were giving me a headache. Who are these flowers from?'

The maid pulled off the tiny envelope taped to the vase and opened the flap. ' "To Mrs Voss. A speedy recovery. Joy." That's all it says.'

Nina frowned. 'I don't know anyone named Joy.'

'Maybe it'll come to you. Would you like to go back to bed now? Mr Voss says you should rest.'

'I've had enough of lying in bed.'

'But Mr Voss says—'

'I'll go to bed later. I'd like to sit here for a while. By myself.'

The maid hesitated. Then, with a nod, she reluctantly left the room.

At last, thought Nina. *At last I'm alone.*

For the past week, ever since she'd left the hospital, she had been surrounded by people. Private duty nurses and doctors and maids. And Victor. Most of all, Victor, hovering at her bedside. Reading aloud all her get-well cards, screening all her phone calls. Protecting her, insulating her. Imprisoning her in this house.

All because he loved her. Perhaps he loved her too much.

Wearily she leaned back in the chair and found herself staring at the portrait hanging on the opposite wall. It was her portrait, painted soon after their marriage. Victor had commissioned it, had even chosen which gown she should wear, a long mauve silk patterned faintly with roses. In the painting she was standing under a vine-covered arbor, a single white rose clutched in one hand, her other hand dangling awkwardly at her side. Her smile was shy, uncertain, as though she were thinking to herself: *I am only standing in for someone else.*

Now, as she studied that portrait of her younger self, she realized how little she'd changed since that day she'd posed as a young bride in the garden. The years had altered her physically, of course. She'd lost her robust good health. In so many ways, though, she was unchanged. Still shy, still awkward. Still the woman Victor Voss had claimed as his possession.

She heard his footsteps and looked up as he came into the bedroom.

'Louisa told me you were still up,' he said. 'You should be taking your nap.'

'I'm fine, Victor.'

'You don't look strong enough yet.'

'It's been three and a half weeks. Dr Archer says his other patients are already walking on tread-mills by now.'

'You're not like any other patient. I think you should take a nap.'

She met his gaze. Firmly she said: 'I'm going to sit here, Victor. I want to look out the window.'

'Nina, I'm only thinking of what's best for you.'

But she had already turned away from him, and was staring down at the park. At the trees, their fall brilliance fading to winter brown. 'I'd like to go for a drive.'

'It's too soon.'

'. . . to the park. The river. Anywhere, just away from this house.'

'You're not listening to me, Nina.'

She sighed. And said, sadly, 'You're the one who's not listening.'

There was a silence. 'What are these?' he said, pointing to the vase of flowers by her chair.

'They just arrived.'

'Who sent them?'

She shrugged. 'Someone named Joy.'

'You can pick these kinds of flowers at the roadside.'

'That's why they're called wildflowers.'

He lifted the vase and carried it to a table in a far corner. Then he brought the Oriental lilies back and set them beside her. 'At least these aren't weeds,' he said, and left the room.

She stared at the lilies. They *were* beautiful. Exotic and perfect. Their cloying fragrance sickened her.

She blinked away an unexpected film of tears and focused on the tiny envelope lying on the table. The one that had come with the wildflowers.

Joy. Who was Joy?

She opened the flap and took out the enclosed card. Only then did she notice that something was written on the back of the card.

Some doctors always tell the truth, it said.

And beneath that was a phone number.

Abby was home alone when Nina Voss called at five P.M.

'Is this Dr DiMatteo?' said a soft voice. 'The one who always tells the truth?'

'Mrs Voss? You got my flowers.'

'Yes, thank you. And I got your rather odd note.'

'I've tried every other way to contact you. Letters. Phone calls.'

'I've been home over a week.'

'But you haven't been available.'

There was a pause. Then a quiet, 'I see.'

She has no idea how isolated she's been, thought Abby. *No idea how her husband has cut her off from the outside.*

'Is anyone else listening to this?' asked Abby.

'I'm alone in my room. What is this all about?'

'I have to see you, Mrs Voss. And it has to be without your husband's knowledge. Can you arrange it?'

'First tell me why.'

'It's not an easy thing to say over the phone.'

'I won't meet with you until you tell me.'

Abby hesitated. 'It's about your heart. The one you got at Bayside.'

'Yes?'

'No one seems to know whose heart it was. Or where it came from.' She paused. And asked quietly: 'Do you know, Mrs Voss?'

The silence that followed was broken only by the sound of Nina's breathing, rapid and irregular.

'Mrs Voss?'

'I have to go.'

'Wait. When can I see you?'

'Tomorrow.'

'How? Where?'

There was another pause. Just before the line went dead, Nina said: 'I'll find a way.'

The rain beat a relentless tattoo on the striped awning over Abby's head. For forty minutes now she had been standing in front of Cellucci's Grocery, shivering beneath the narrow overhang of canvas. A succession of delivery trucks had pulled up to unload, the men wheeling in dollies and cartons. Snapple and Frito-Lay and Winston cigarettes. Little Debbie had a snack for you.

At four-twenty the rain began coming down harder, swirling with the wind. Gusts of it angled under the awning, splattering her shoes. Her feet were freezing. An hour had passed; Nina Voss was not going to show up.

Abby flinched as a Progresso Foods truck suddenly roared away from the curb, spewing exhaust. When she looked up again, she saw that a black limousine had stopped across the street. The driver's window rolled down a few inches and a man called: 'Dr DiMatteo? Come into the car.'

She hesitated. The windows were too darkly tinted for Abby to see inside, but she could make out the silhouette of a single rear-seat passenger.

'We haven't much time,' urged the driver.

She crossed the street, head bent under the beating rain, and opened the rear door. Blinking water from her eyes, she focused on the backseat passenger. What she saw dismayed her.

In the gloom of the car, Nina Voss looked pale and shrunken. Her skin was a powdery white. 'Please get in, Doctor,' said Nina.

Abby slid in beside her and shut the door. The limousine pulled away from the curb and glided noiselessly into the stream of traffic.

Nina was so completely bundled up in a black

coat and scarf that her face seemed to be floating, bodyless, in the car's shadows. This was not the picture of a recovering transplant patient. Abby remembered Josh O'Day's ruddy face, remembered his liveliness, his laughter.

Nina Voss looked like a talking corpse.

'I'm sorry we're late,' said Nina. 'We had a problem leaving the house.'

'Does your husband know you're meeting me?'

'No.' Nina sat back, her face almost swallowed up in all that black wool. 'I've learned, over the years, that one doesn't tell Victor certain things. The real secret of a happy marriage, Dr DiMatteo, is silence.'

'That hardly sounds like a happy marriage.'

'It is. Strangely enough.' Nina smiled and looked out the window. The watery light cast distorted shadows on her face. 'Men have to be protected from so many things. Most of all from themselves. That's why they need us, you know. The funny thing is, they'll never admit it. They think they're taking care of *us*. And all the time, we know the truth.' She turned to Abby, and her smile faded. 'Now I need to know. What has Victor done?'

'I was hoping you could tell me.'

'You said it had to do with my heart.' Nina touched her hand to her chest. In the gloom of the car, her gesture seemed almost religious. Father, Son, Holy Ghost. 'What do you know about it?'

'I know your heart didn't come through normal channels. Almost all transplant organs are matched to recipients through a central registry. Yours wasn't. According to the organ bank, you never got a heart at all.'

Nina's hand, still resting on her chest, had squeezed into a tense white ball. 'Then where did this one come from?'

'I don't know. Do you?'

The corpselike face stared at her in silence.

'I think your husband knows,' said Abby.

'How would he?'

'He bought it.'

'People can't just buy hearts.'

'With enough money, people can buy anything.'

Nina said nothing. By her silence, she admitted her acceptance of that fundamental truth. *Money can buy anything.*

The limousine turned onto Embankment Road. They were driving west along the Charles River. Its surface was gray and stippled by falling rain.

Nina asked, 'How did you learn about this?'

'Lately I seem to have a lot of free time on my hands. It's amazing what you can accomplish when you find yourself suddenly unemployed. In just the last few days, I've found out a lot of things. Not just about your transplant, but about others as well. And the more I learn, Mrs Voss, the more scared I get.'

'Why come to me about this? Why not go to the authorities?'

'Haven't you heard? I have a new nickname these days. *Dr Hemlock.* They're saying I kill my patients with kindness. None of it's true, of course, but people are always ready to believe the worst.' Wearily Abby gazed out at the river. 'I have no job. No credibility. And no proof.'

'What do you have?'

Abby looked at her. 'I know the truth.'

The limousine dipped through a puddle. The spray of water drummed the underside of the car. They had veered away from the river and the road to the Back Bay Fens now curved ahead of them.

'At ten P.M. on the night of your transplant,' said Abby, 'Bayside Hospital got a call that a donor had been found in Burlington, Vermont. Three hours later, the heart was delivered to our OR. The harvest was supposedly done at Wilcox Memorial Hospital, by a surgeon named Timothy Nicholls. Your transplant was performed, and there was nothing out of the ordinary about it. In so many ways, it was like every other transplant done at Bayside.' She paused. 'With one major difference. No one knows where your donor heart came from.'

'You said it came from Burlington.'

'I said it supposedly did. But Dr Nicholls has vanished. He may be hiding. Or he may be dead. And Wilcox Memorial denies any knowledge of a harvest on that night.'

Nina had retreated into silence. She seemed to be shrinking away into the woolen coat.

'You weren't the first one,' said Abby.

The white face stared back with a numb expression. 'There were others?'

'At least four. I've seen the records from the past

378

two years. It always happened the same way. Bayside would get a call from Burlington that there's a donor. The heart is delivered to our OR sometime after midnight. The transplant's done, and it's all routine. But something's wrong with this picture. We're talking about four hearts, four dead people. A friend and I have searched the Burlington obituaries for those dates. None of the donors appear.'

'Then where are the hearts coming from?'

Abby paused. Meeting Nina's disbelieving gaze, she said, 'I don't know.'

The limousine had looped north and was once again skirting the Charles River. They were heading back toward Beacon Hill.

'I have no proof,' said Abby. 'I can't get through to New England Organ Bank, or anyone else. They all know I'm under investigation. They think of me as the crazy lady. That's why I came to you. That night we met in the ICU, I thought: *There's a woman I'd want as a friend.*' She paused. 'I need your help, Mrs Voss.'

For a long time, Nina said nothing. She was not looking at Abby, but was staring straight ahead, her face white as bleached bone. At last she seemed to come to a decision. She released a deep breath and said, 'I'm going to drop you off now. Would this corner be all right?'

'Mrs Voss, your husband bought that heart. If he did it, so can other people. We don't know who the donors are! We don't know how they're getting them—'

'*Here*,' Nina said to the driver.

The limousine pulled over to the curb.

'Please get out,' said Nina.

Abby didn't move. She sat for a moment, not speaking. The rain tapped monotonously on the roof.

'Please,' whispered Nina.

'I thought I could trust you. I thought . . .' Slowly Abby shook her head. 'Goodbye, Mrs Voss.'

A hand touched her arm. Abby glanced back, into the other woman's haunted eyes.

'I love my husband,' said Nina. 'And he loves me.'

'Does that make it right?'

Nina didn't answer.

Abby climbed out and shut the door. The limousine drove away. As she watched the car glide into the dusk, she thought: *I'll never see her again*.

Then, shoulders slumped, she turned and walked away through the rain.

'Home now, Mrs Voss?' The chauffeur's voice, flat and tinny through the speaker phone, startled Nina from her trance.

'Yes,' she said. 'Take me home.'

She wrapped herself tighter in her cocoon of black wool and stared at the rain streaking across her window. She thought of what she would say to Victor. And what she would not, could not, say. *This is what has become of our love*, she thought.

Secrets upon secrets. And he is keeping the most terrible secret of all.

She lowered her head and began to cry, for Victor, and for what had happened to their marriage. She wept for herself as well, because she knew what had to be done, and she was afraid.

The rain streamed like tears down the window. And the limousine carried her home, to Victor.

Nineteen

Shu-Shu needed a bath. The older boys had been saying this for days, had even threatened to toss Shu-Shu into the sea if Aleksei did not give her a good cleaning. She stinks, they said, and no wonder, with all your snot on her. Aleksei did not think Shu-Shu stank. He liked the way she smelled. She had not been washed, ever, and each scent she wore was like a different memory. The smell of gravy, which he'd spilled on the tail, reminded him of last night's supper, when Nadiya had served him double portions of everything. (And smiled at him, too!) The odor of cigarettes was Uncle Misha's smell, gruff but warm. The sour beet smell was from last Easter morning, when they had laughed and eaten boiled eggs and he had spilled soup on Shu-Shu's head. And if he closed his eyes and inhaled deeply, he could sometimes detect another scent, fainter, but still there after all the years. It was not something he could classify as sour or sweet. Rather, he recognized it by the feelings it stirred in him. By the smell it brought to his heart. It was the smell of his babyhood. The smell of being caressed and sung to and loved.

Hugging Shu-Shu, Aleksei burrowed deeper under his blanket. I'll never let them give you a bath, he thought.

Anyway, there weren't so many of *them* left to torment him. Five days ago, another boat had appeared through the fog, and had drifted alongside them. While all the boys had scrambled to the rail to watch, Nadiya and Gregor had walked back and forth, calling out name after name. *Nikolai Alekseyenko! Pavel Prebrazhensky!* There were whoops of triumph, fists punched in the air as each name was called. *Yes! I have been chosen!*

Later, the ones not chosen, the ones left behind, remained huddled at the rail, watching in silence as the motor launch carried the chosen boys to the other ship.

'Where do they go?' Aleksei asked.

'To families in the West,' Nadiya answered. 'Now come away from the rail. It's getting cold up here.'

The boys didn't move. After a while Nadiya didn't seem to care if they stayed up on deck or not, and she left to go below.

'Families in the West must be stupid,' said Yakov.

Aleksei turned to look at him. Yakov was staring fiercely out to sea, his chin jutted out like someone hungry for a fight. 'You think everyone's stupid,' said Aleksei.

383

'They are. Everyone on this boat is.'

'That means you too.'

Yakov didn't answer. He simply clutched the rail with his one hand, his gaze directed at the other ship as it glided back into the fog. Then he walked away.

Over the next few days, Aleksei scarcely saw him.

Tonight, as usual, Yakov had disappeared right after supper. He was probably in his stupid Wonderland, Aleksei thought. Hiding out in that crate with all the mouse turds.

Aleksei pulled the blanket over his head. And that was how he fell asleep, curled up in his bunk with dirty Shu-Shu cradled against his face.

A hand shook him. A voice called softly in the night: 'Aleksei, Aleksei.'

'Mommy,' he said.

'Aleksei, it's time to wake up. I have a surprise for you.'

Slowly he drifted up through layers of sleep, surfacing into darkness. The hand was still shaking him. He recognized Nadiya's scent.

'It's time to go,' she whispered.

'Where am I going?'

'You must get ready to meet your new mother.'

'Is she here?'

'I'll take you to her, Aleksei. Out of all the boys, you've been chosen. You're very lucky. Now come. But be quiet.'

Aleksei sat up. He was not quite awake yet, not

quite certain if he was dreaming. Nadiya reached up and helped him off the bunk.

'Shu-Shu,' he said.

Nadiya put the dog in his arms. 'Of course you can bring your Shu-Shu.' She took his hand. She had never held his hand before. The sudden rush of happiness shook him fully awake. He was holding her hand and they were walking together, to meet his mother. It was dark and he was scared of the dark, but Nadiya would see to it that nothing happened to him. He remembered, somehow he remembered: *This is how it feels to hold your mother's hand.*

They left the cabin and walked down a dimly lit corridor. He was stumbling through a joyous daze, not paying attention to where they were going, because Nadiya was taking care of everything. They turned down another corridor. This one he did not recognize. They pushed through a door.

Into Wonderland.

The steel walkway stretched before them. Beyond it stood the blue door.

Aleksei stopped.

'What is it?' asked Nadiya.

'I don't want to go in there.'

'But you have to.'

'There are people living there.'

'Aleksei, don't be difficult.' Nadiya gripped his hand more firmly. 'This is where you must go.'

'*Why?*'

Suddenly she seemed to understand that a different tactic was called for. She crouched down so that they were eye to eye, and took him firmly by the shoulders. 'Do you want to ruin everything? Do you want to make her angry? She expects an obedient little boy, and now you are being very disagreeable.'

His lips trembled. He tried so hard not to cry, because he knew how much adults hated children's tears. But the tears were starting to fall anyway, and now he'd probably ruined everything. Just as Nadiya had said he would. He was always ruining everything.

'Nothing is settled yet,' said Nadiya. 'She can still choose another boy. Is that what you want?'

Aleksei sobbed. 'No.'

'Then why aren't you behaving?'

'I'm afraid of the quail people.'

'What? You are ridiculous. I wouldn't be surprised if *no one* ever wanted you.' She straightened and snatched his hand again. '*Come.*'

Aleksei looked at the blue door. He whispered: 'Carry me.'

'You're too big. You'll hurt my back.'

'Please carry me.'

'You have to walk, Aleksei. Now hurry, or we'll be late.' She put her arm around him.

He began to walk, only because she was there beside him, hugging him close. The way he was hugging Shu-Shu close. As long as they held each other, the three of them, nothing bad would happen.

Nadiya knocked at the blue door.

It swung open.

Yakov heard them on the walkway above. Aleksei's whining. Nadiya's impatient coaxing. He crawled to the edge of the crate and cautiously peered up at them. They were crossing to the blue door now. A moment later, they vanished through it.

Why does Aleksei get to go in there, and not me?

Yakov slipped out of the crate and up the stairs to the blue door. He tried to open it, but as always, it was locked.

Defeated, he went back to his crate. It was quite a comfortable hiding place now. Over the last week, he had scavenged a blanket, a flashlight, and a number of magazines with naked ladies in them. He had also lifted a lighter and a pack of cigarettes from Koubichev. Sometimes Yakov would smoke one, but there were so few cigarettes, he was careful to save them. Once he'd accidentally set the shavings on fire. That had been exciting. Most of the time, though, he just liked having the cigarettes around, liked holding the pack, reading and rereading the label under the beam of the flashlight.

That's what he'd been doing when he'd heard Aleksei and Nadiya on the walkway.

Now he waited for them to come back out of the blue door. It was taking a long time. What were they doing in there?

Yakov threw the cigarettes down. It wasn't fair.

He looked at a few pictures in the magazines.

Practiced flicking the lighter on and off. Then he decided he was sleepy. He curled up in the blanket and dozed off.

Sometime later, he was awakened by a rumbling sound. At first he thought something was wrong with the ship's engines, then he realized the sound was growing louder, and that it was not coming from Hell, but from the deck above.

It was a helicopter.

Gregor tied the twist top and set the plastic bag in the cooler. He handed it to Nadiya. 'Well, take it.'

At first she didn't seem to hear. Then she looked at him, her face drained white, and he thought: *The bitch can't handle it.* 'It needs ice. Go on, do it.' He shoved the cooler toward her.

She seemed to recoil in horror. Then, breathing deeply, she took it, carried it across the room, and set it on the countertop. She began scooping ice into the cooler. He noticed that her legs were not quite steady. The first time around was always a shock to the system. Even Gregor had had his queasy moments the first time. Nadiya would get over it.

He turned to the operating table. The anesthetist had already zipped up the shroud and was now gathering up the bloodied drapes. The surgeon had made no move to help. Instead, he was slumped back against the counter, as though trying to catch his breath. Gregor regarded him with distaste. There was something especially disgusting about a doctor who let himself get so

388

grotesquely fat. The surgeon did not look well tonight. He had wheezed his way through the entire procedure, and his hands had seemed more tremulous than usual.

'My head hurts,' the surgeon groaned.

'You've been drinking too much. Probably got yourself a fucking hangover.' Gregor moved to the table and grasped one end of the shroud. Together, he and the anesthetist lifted their burden and slid it onto the gurney. Next, Gregor picked up the pile of dirty clothes and set those on the gurney as well. He almost overlooked the stuffed dog. It was lying on the floor, the ratty fur soaked with blood. He tossed it on top of the dirty clothes, then he and the anesthetist wheeled the gurney to the disposal chute. They opened the hatch and deposited the shroud, the clothes, and the dog into the chute.

The surgeon moaned. 'This is the worst fucking headache . . .'

Gregor ignored him. He stripped off his gloves and went to the sink to wash his hands. One never knew what one might pick up handling those filthy clothes. Lice, perhaps. He scrubbed as thoroughly as a doctor preparing to operate.

There was a loud crash, the clatter of falling metal instruments. Gregor turned.

The surgeon was lying on the floor, his face bright red, his limbs jerking like a puppet gone out of control.

Nadiya and the anesthetist stood frozen in horror.

'What's wrong with him?' demanded Gregor.

'I don't know!' said the anesthetist.

'Well do something about it!'

The anesthetist knelt beside the convulsing man and made a few helpless attempts to revive him. He loosened the man's surgical gown, clapped an oxygen mask on his face. The convulsions were worse now, the arms flapping like goose wings.

'Hold the mask on for me!' said the anesthetist. 'I'm going to give him an injection!'

Gregor knelt at the man's head and took hold of the mask. The surgeon's face felt repulsive, doughy and oily. Spittle had dribbled out of his mouth, turning the oxygen mask slippery. His skin was beginning to turn blue. Gregor knew then, looking at the darkening cyanosis, that their efforts were futile.

Moments later, the man was dead.

For a long time, the three of them stood around staring at the corpse. It seemed to have ballooned even larger and more grotesque. The stomach was distended and the fleshy folds of the face had spread out like a boneless jellyfish.

'What the fuck do we do now?' said the anesthetist.

'We need another surgeon,' Gregor said.

'You can't exactly pull one out of the sea. We'll have to head into port sooner than planned.'

'Or transfer the live cargo . . .' Gregor suddenly glanced upward. So did Nadiya and the anesthetist. They all heard it now: the *whup-whup* of the helicopter. He looked at the cooler on the countertop. 'Is it ready?'

'I packed it with ice,' said Nadiya.

'Go, then. Bring it up to them.' Gregor looked back down at the carcass of the dead surgeon. He gave it a kick of disgust. 'We'll take care of the whale.'

The blue eye was shining on deck.

From his hiding place under the bridge stairway, Yakov had watched the blue light flare on first, followed by the surrounding circle of white lights. They were all blazing now, so brightly he could not look directly at them. Instead he looked up at the sky, at the helicopter hovering overhead. It descended from the darkness, and Yakov closed his eyes as the wash of the rotors whipped his face. When he opened his eyes again, he saw that the helicopter had landed.

The door swung open, but no one emerged. It was waiting for someone to board.

Yakov crept forward so that he was gazing through the gap between two steps, straight at the helicopter. *Lucky Aleksei*, he thought. *Aleksei must be leaving tonight.*

He heard the clang of a door shutting and a figure appeared at the edge of the lit circle. It was Nadiya. She crossed the deck, her body bent forward at the waist, her ass sticking in the air. She was scared those rotors would chop off her stupid head. She leaned inside the helicopter door, her ass still poking out as she spoke to the pilot. Then she backed out and retreated to the edge of the lights.

A moment later, the helicopter lifted off.

The lights shut off, plunging the deck into darkness.

Yakov eased around the stairway to watch as the helicopter rose. He saw the tail swing away like a giant pendulum on a string. Then the craft thundered away, swooping low over the water, and vanished into the night.

A hand grabbed Yakov's arm. He gave a cry as he was yanked backward and spun around.

'What the fuck are you doing up here?' said Gregor.

'Nothing!'

'What did you see?'

'Just a helicopter—'

'*What did you see?*'

Yakov only stared at him, too terrified to answer.

Nadiya had heard their voices. Now she crossed the deck toward them. 'What is it?'

'The boy's been watching again. I thought you locked the cabin.'

'I did. He must have slipped out earlier.' She looked at Yakov. 'It's always *him*. I can't watch him every second.'

'I've had enough of this one anyway.' Gregor gave Yakov's arm a jerk, pulling him toward the stairway hatch. 'He can't go back with the others.' He turned to open the hatch.

Yakov kicked him in the back of the knee.

Gregor shrieked, releasing his grip.

Yakov ran. He heard Nadiya's shouts, heard footsteps pounding after him. Then more footsteps, clanging down the bridge stairway. He darted forward, toward the bow. Too late, he realized he had run straight onto the landing deck.

There was a loud *clank*, and the deck lights flared on.

Yakov was trapped in the very center of their brilliance. Shielding his eyes, he stumbled blindly away from the sounds of pursuit. But they were all around him now, moving in. Grabbing his shirt. He flailed.

Someone slapped him across the face. The blow sent Yakov sprawling. He tried to crawl away, but his legs were kicked out from under him.

'That's enough!' said Nadiya. 'You don't want to kill him!'

'Little motherfucker,' Gregor grunted.

Yakov was yanked up by the hair. Gregor shoved him forward across the deck, toward the stairwell hatch. Yakov kept stumbling, only to be dragged back up again by the hair. He couldn't see where they were going. He knew only that they were going down some steps, moving along a corridor. Gregor was cursing the whole way. He was also limping a little, which gave Yakov some small measure of satisfaction.

A door swung open and Yakov was tossed over the threshold.

'You can rot in there for a while,' said Gregor. And he slammed the door shut.

Yakov heard the latch close. Heard footsteps fade away. He was alone in the darkness.

He drew his knees to his chest and lay hugging himself. A strange trembling seized his body, and he tried to stop it but couldn't. He could hear his own teeth chattering, not from the cold, but from some quaking deep in his soul. He closed his eyes and was confronted with the images of what he'd seen tonight. Nadiya crossing the deck, gliding, floating through an unearthly field of light. The helicopter door open and waiting. Now Nadiya bending over, reaching out as she hands something to the pilot.

A box.

Yakov drew his legs more tightly to his chest, but the trembling didn't ease.

Whimpering, he put his thumb in his mouth and began to suck.

Twenty

For Abby, mornings were the worst. She would awaken feeling that first sleepy flush of anticipation for the day ahead. Then suddenly she'd remember: *I have nowhere to go.* That realization would strike as cruelly as any physical blow. She would lie in bed, listening to Mark getting dressed. She'd hear him moving around in the still-dark bedroom, and she would feel so engulfed by depression she could not say a word to him. They shared a house and a bed, yet they'd scarcely spoken to each other in days. *This is how love dies*, thought Abby, hearing him walk out the front door. *Not with angry words, but with silence.*

When Abby was twelve years old, her father was laid off from his job at the tannery. For weeks afterward, he'd drive away each morning, as though heading for work as usual. Abby never found out where he went, or what he did. Till the day he died, he never told her. All Abby knew was that her father was terrified of staying home and confronting his own failure. So he'd continued the charade, fleeing the house every morning.

Just as Abby was doing today.

She left the car at home and walked instead, blocks and blocks, not really caring where she went. Last night the weather had turned cold, and by the time she finally stopped in at a bagel shop, her face was numb. She bought coffee and a sesame seed bagel and slid into one of the booths. She'd taken only two bites when she happened to glance at the man at the next table. He was reading a *Boston Herald*.

Abby's photo was on the front page.

She felt like crawling out the door. Furtively she glanced around the café, half expecting everyone to be looking at her, but no one was.

She bolted out of the booth, tossed her bagel in the trash, and walked out. Her appetite was gone. At a newsstand a block away, she purchased a copy of the *Herald* and huddled shivering in a doorway while she scanned the article.

Rigors of Surgical Training
May Have Led to Tragedy

By all accounts, Dr Abigail DiMatteo was an outstanding resident – one of the best at Bayside Medical Center, according to Department Chairman Dr Colin Wettig. But sometime in the last few months, soon after Dr DiMatteo entered her second year in the program, things began to go terribly wrong . . .

Abby had to stop reading; her breaths were coming too hard and fast. It took her a few moments to calm down enough to finish the article. When she finally did, she felt truly sick.

The reporter had included everything. The lawsuits. Mary Allen's death. The shouting match with Brenda. None of it was deniable. All the elements, taken together, painted the picture of an unstable, even dangerous personality. It fed right into the public's secret horror of being at the mercy of a deranged physician.

I can't believe it's me they're writing about.

Even if she managed to retain her medical license, even if she finished a residency, an article like this would follow her forever. So would the doubts. No patient in his right mind would go under the knife of a psychopath.

She didn't know how long she walked around with that newspaper clutched in her hand. When she finally came to a halt, she was standing on the Harvard University Common, and her ears were aching from the cold. She realized it was already well past lunchtime. She'd been walking around all morning, and now half the day was gone. She didn't know where to go next. Everyone else on the Common – students with backpacks, shaggy professors in tweeds – seemed to have a destination. But not her.

She looked down again, at the newspaper. The photograph they'd used for her was from the residency directory, a shot taken when she was an intern. She'd smiled straight at the camera, her face fresh and eager, the look of a young woman ready and willing to work for her dream.

She threw the newspaper into the nearest trash receptacle and walked home, thinking: *Fight back. I have to fight back.*

But she and Vivian had run out of leads. Yesterday, Vivian had flown to Burlington. When she'd called Abby last night, it had been with bad news: Tim Nicholls's practice had closed down, and no one knew where he was. Dead end. Also, Wilcox Memorial had no records of any harvests on those four dates. Another dead end. Finally, Vivian had checked with the local police and had found no records of missing persons or unidentified bodies with their hearts cut out. Final dead end.

They've covered their tracks. We'll never beat them.

As soon as she stepped in the front door, she saw the answering machine was blinking. It was a message from Vivian to call back. She'd left a Burlington number. Abby dialed the number, but got no answer, so she hung up.

Next she called NEOB, but as usual, they wouldn't put her through to Helen Lewis. No one, it seemed, wanted to hear the latest theories of the psychopathic Dr DiMatteo. She didn't know who else to call. She ran through the list of all the people she knew at Bayside. Dr Wettig. Mark. Mohandas and Zwick. Susan Casado. Jeremiah Parr. She didn't trust any of them. *Any* of them.

She'd just picked up the phone to try calling

Vivian again when she happened to glance out the window. Parked at the far end of the street was a maroon van.

You bastard. This time you're mine!

She ran to the hall closet and pulled out the binoculars. Focusing from the window, she could just make out the license plate.

I got you, she thought in triumph. *I got you.*

She grabbed the phone and dialed Katzka. It struck her then, as she was waiting for him to come on the line, how strange it was that *he* should be the one she'd call. Maybe it was an automatic response. You need help, you call a cop. And he was the only cop she knew.

'Detective Katzka,' he said in his usual flat and businesslike voice.

'The van is back!' she blurted.

'Excuse me?'

'This is Abby DiMatteo. The van that was following me – it's parked right outside my house. The license number's five-three-nine, TDV. Massachusetts plate.'

There was a pause as he wrote it down. 'You live on Brewster Street, right?'

'Yes. Please send someone right away. I don't know what he's going to do.'

'Just sit tight and keep the doors locked. Got that?'

'Okay.' She let out a nervous breath. 'Okay.'

She knew the doors were already locked, but she rechecked them anyway. Everything was secure. She returned to the living room and sat near the curtain, every so often glancing outside to make sure the van was still there. She wanted it to stay right where it was. She wanted to see the driver's reaction when the cops arrived.

Fifteen minutes later, a familiar green Volvo drove by and pulled over at the curb, right across the street from the van. She hadn't expected Katzka himself to show up, but there he was, stepping out of his car. At her first glimpse of him, she felt an overwhelming sense of relief. He'll know what to do, she thought. Katzka was clever enough to deal with anything.

He crossed the street and slowly approached the van.

Abby pressed closer to the window, her heart suddenly pounding. She wondered if Katzka's pulse was racing as fast as hers was. He moved with almost casual grace toward the driver's door. Only as he shifted, turning slightly toward Abby, did she notice that he'd drawn his gun. She hadn't even seen him reach for it.

She was almost afraid to watch now. Afraid for *him.*

He edged forward and glanced in the window. Apparently he saw nothing suspicious. He circled around to the rear of the van and peered through the back window. Then he reholstered his gun and looked up and down the street.

At a nearby house, the front door suddenly swung open and a man in gray overalls stormed down the porch steps, yelling and waving. Katzka responded with his trademark unflappability and produced his badge. The other man took a look at it and handed it back. Then he took out his wallet and showed *his* ID.

For a while the two men stood talking, gesturing every so often toward the van and the house. At last the man in the overalls went back inside.

Katzka walked toward Abby's.

She let him in the front door. 'What happened?'

'Nothing.'

'Who's the driver? Why's he been following me?'

'He says he has no idea what you're talking about.'

She followed him into the living room. 'I'm not blind! I've seen that van here before. On this street.'

'The driver says he's never been here before.'

'Who *is* the driver, anyway?'

Katzka pulled out his notebook. 'John Doherty, age thirty-six, Massachusetts resident. Licensed plumber. He says this is the first call he's ever made to Brewster Street. The van is registered to Back Bay Plumbing. And it's full of tools.' He closed his notebook and slid it into his coat pocket. Then he regarded her with his usual detachment.

'I was so sure,' she murmured. 'I was so sure it was the same one.'

'You still insist there was a van?'

'Yes, Goddamn it!' she snapped. 'There *was* a van!'

He reacted to her outburst with a slightly raised

eyebrow. She forced herself to take a deep breath. A burst of temper was the last thing this man would respond to. He was all logic, all reason. Mr Spock with a badge.

She said, more calmly now, 'I am not imagining things. And I'm not making them up.'

'If you think you see the van again, get the license number.'

'If I *think* I see it?'

'I'll call Back Bay Plumbing, to confirm Doherty's information. But I really do believe he's just a plumber.' Katzka glanced toward her living room. The phone was ringing. 'Aren't you going to answer it?'

'Please don't leave. Not yet. I have a few things to tell you.'

He had already reached for the doorknob. Now he paused, watching as she picked up the phone.

'Hello?' she said.

A woman's voice responded softly, 'Dr DiMatteo?'

Instantly Abby's gaze shot to Katzka's. He seemed to understand, just from her glance, that this call was important. 'Mrs Voss?' said Abby.

'I've learned something,' said Nina. 'I don't know what it means. If it means anything at all.'

Katzka moved to Abby's side. He had done it so quickly, so quietly, she'd barely registered his approach. He bent his head toward the receiver to listen in.

'What did you find out?' said Abby.

'I made some calls. To the bank, and to our

accountant. On September twenty-third, Victor transferred funds to a company called the Amity Corporation. In Boston.'

'You're sure about that date?'

'Yes.'

September twenty-third, thought Abby. One day before Nina Voss's transplant.

'What do you know about Amity?' asked Abby.

'Nothing. Victor's never mentioned the name. With a transaction this large, he'd normally discuss it . . .' There was a silence. Abby heard voices in the background, then the sounds of frantic shuffling. Nina's voice came back on. Tenser. Softer. 'I have to get off the phone.'

'You said it was a large transaction. How large?'

For a moment there was no reply. Abby thought perhaps Nina had already hung up. Then she heard the whispered answer.

'Five million,' said Nina. 'He transferred five million dollars.'

Nina hung up the telephone. She heard Victor's footsteps, but she did not look up as he came into the bedroom.

'Who were you talking to?' he asked.

'Cynthia. I called to thank her for the flowers.'

'Which flowers were those again?'

'The orchids.'

He glanced at the vase on the dresser. 'Oh, yes. Very nice.'

'Cynthia says they're going to Greece next spring. I guess they're tired of the Caribbean.'

How easily she lied to him. When had it started? When had they stopped speaking the truth to each other?

He sat down beside her on the bed. She felt him studying her. 'When you're all better,' he said, 'maybe we'll go back to Greece. Maybe we'll even go with Cynthia and Robert. Wouldn't you like that?'

She nodded and looked down at the bedspread. At her hands, the fingers bony and wasting away. *But I am never getting better. We both know that.*

She slid her legs out from under the covers. 'I have to use the bathroom,' she said.

'Shall I help you?'

'No. I'm fine.' Rising to her feet, she felt a brief spell of light-headedness. Lately she'd been having the spells often, whenever she stood up or exerted herself in even the slightest way. She said nothing about it to Victor, but just waited for the feeling to pass. Then she continued slowly into the bathroom.

She heard him pick up the telephone.

Only when she'd shut the bathroom door did she suddenly realize her mistake. The last number she'd called was still in the phone's memory system. All Victor had to do was press Redial, and he would know she'd lied to him. It was just the sort of thing Victor would do. He'd learn she hadn't called Cynthia. He'd find out, somehow he'd find out, that it was Abby DiMatteo she'd called.

Nina stood with her back pressed to the

bathroom door, listening. She heard him hang up the phone again. Heard him say, 'Nina?'

Another wave of light-headedness hit her. She dropped her head, fighting the darkness that was beginning to cloud her vision. Her legs seemed to melt away beneath her. She felt herself sliding downward.

He rattled the door. 'Nina, I need to speak to you.'

'Victor,' she whispered, but knew he couldn't hear her. No one could hear her.

She lay on the bathroom floor, too weak to move, too weak to call out to him.

She felt her heart flutter like a butterfly's wings in her chest.

'This has to be the wrong place,' said Abby.

She and Katzka were parked on a run-down street in Roxbury. It was a neighborhood of barred storefronts and businesses on the verge of collapse. The only apparently thriving enterprise was a bodybuilding gym a few doors down. Through the gym's open windows, they could hear the clank of weights and occasional masculine laughter. Adjacent to the gym was an unoccupied building with a FOR LEASE sign. And next to that was the Amity building, a four-story brownstone. Over the entrance hung the sign:

Amity Medical Supplies
Sales and Service

Behind the barred front windows was a tired-looking display of company products: Crutches and canes. Oxygen tanks. Foam mattress pads to prevent bedsores. Beside commodes. A mannequin wearing a nurse's uniform and cap straight out of the sixties.

Abby gazed across the street at the shabby display window and said, 'This can't be the right Amity.'

'It's the only listing in the phone book,' said Katzka.

'Why would he transfer five million dollars to *this* business?'

'It could be just one branch of a larger corporation. Maybe he saw an investment opportunity.'

She shook her head. 'The timing's all wrong. Put yourself in Victor Voss's place. His wife is dying. He's desperate to get her the operation she needs. He's not going to be thinking about his investments.'

'It depends how much he cares about his wife.'

'He cares a lot.'

'How do you know?'

She looked at him. 'I know.'

He regarded her in that quiet way of his. How strange, she thought, that his gaze no longer made her feel uncomfortable.

He opened his door. 'I'll see what I can find out.'

'What are you going to do?'

'Look around. Ask a few questions.'

'I'll go in with you.'

'No, you stay in the car.' He started to step out, but she pulled him back.

'Look,' she said. 'I'm the one with everything to lose. I've already lost my job. I'm losing my license. And now people are calling me a murderer or a psychotic or both. It's *my* life they've fucked up. This could be my one chance to fight back.'

'Then let's not screw it up, okay? Someone in there could recognize you. That would certainly tip them off. Do you want to risk that?'

She sank back. Katzka was right. Goddamn it, he was right. He hadn't wanted her to come along on this ride in the first place, but she'd insisted. She'd told him she could drive here on her own, with or without him. So here she was, and she couldn't even walk into the building. She couldn't even fight her own battles anymore. They'd taken that away from her, too. She sat shaking her head, angry about her own impotence. Angry at Katzka for having pointed it out.

He said, 'Lock the doors.' And he stepped out of the car.

She watched him cross the street, watched him walk into the shabby entrance. She could picture what he'd find inside. Depressing displays of wheelchairs and emesis basins. Racks of nurses' uniforms under dustcovers of yellowing plastic. Boxes of orthopedic shoes. She could imagine every detail because she had been in shops just like it when she'd purchased her first set of uniforms.

Five minutes passed. Then ten.

Katzka, Katzka. What are you doing in there?

He'd said he was going to ask questions, that he would try not to tip them off. She trusted his judgment. The average homicide cop, she decided, was probably smarter than the average surgeon. But maybe not smarter than the average internist. That was the running joke among hospital house staff: the stupidity of surgeons. Internists relied on their brains, surgeons on their precious hands. If an internist is in an elevator and the door starts to shut prematurely, he'll stick in his hand to stop it. A surgeon will stick in his head. Ha, ha.

Twenty minutes had gone by. It was after five now, and the anemic sunshine had already faded to a gloomy dusk. Through the window crack, she could hear the continual whoosh of cars on Martin Luther King Boulevard. Rush hour. Up the street, two men with biceps of heroic proportions came out of the gym and lumbered to their cars.

She kept watching the entrance, waiting for Katzka to emerge.

It was five-twenty.

The traffic was beginning to thicken even on this street. Through the flow of cars, she caught only intermittent glimpses of the front entrance. Then, suddenly, there was a gap in the traffic and she was looking straight across the street as a man emerged from the side door of the Amity building. He paused on the sidewalk and glanced at his watch. When he looked up again, Abby felt her heart kick into a gallop. She recognized that face. The grotesquely heavy brow. The hawklike nose.

It was Dr Mapes. The courier who'd delivered

Nina Voss's donor heart to the operating room.

Mapes began walking. Halfway up the street, he stopped at the blue Trans Am parked at the curb. He took out a set of car keys.

Abby looked back at the Amity building, hoping, praying for Katzka to appear. *Come on, come on. I'm going to lose Mapes!* She looked back at the Trans Am. Mapes had climbed inside now, and was fastening his seat belt. He started the engine. Easing slightly away from the curb, he waited for a break in the traffic.

Abby cast a frantic glance down at the ignition and saw that Katzka had left his keys dangling there.

This could be her one chance. Her only chance.

The blue Trans Am pulled into the street.

There was no time left to think it over.

Abby scrambled into the driver's seat and started Katzka's car. She lurched into traffic, eliciting a screech of tires and an angry honk from another car behind her.

A block ahead, Mapes glided through the intersection just as the light turned red.

Abby squealed to a stop. There were four cars between her and the intersection and no way to get around them. By the time the light turned green again, Mapes could be blocks away. She sat counting the seconds, cursing Boston traffic lights and Boston drivers and her own indecision. If only she'd pulled away from the curb earlier! The Trans Am was barely in view now, just a glint of blue in a river of cars. What the hell was wrong with this light?

At last it turned green, but still no one was moving. The driver in front must be asleep at the wheel. Abby leaned on her horn, releasing a deafening blast. The cars ahead of her finally began to move. She stepped on the accelerator, then let up on it.

Someone was pounding at the side of her car.

Glancing right, she saw Katzka running alongside the passenger door. She braked and hit the lock-release button.

He yanked open the door. 'What the hell are you doing?'

'Get in.'

'No, first you pull over—'

'*Get the fuck in!*'

He blinked in surprise. And got in.

At once she goosed the accelerator, and they shot through the intersection. Two blocks ahead, a flash of blue streaked rightward. The Trans Am was turning onto Cottage Street. If she didn't stay right on his tail, she could lose him in the traffic coming up. She swerved left across a double line, raced past three cars in a row, and screeched back into her lane just in time. She heard Katzka snap on his seat belt. Good. Because this could be one hell of a wild ride. They turned onto Cottage.

'Are you going to tell me?' he said.

'He came out the side door of the Amity building. The guy in the blue car.'

'Who is he?'

'The organ courier. He said his name was Mapes.' She spotted another break in traffic, made another passing swoop into the left lane, then back again.

Katzka said, 'I think I should drive.'

'He's heading into the traffic circle. Now which way? Which way's he going . . .'

The Trans Am looped around the circle, then cut away east.

'He's heading for the expressway,' said Katzka.

'Then so are we.' Abby entered the traffic circle and peeled off after the Trans Am.

Katzka had guessed correctly. Mapes was heading onto the expressway ramp. She followed him, her heart ramming her chest, her hands slick on the steering wheel. Here's where she could lose him. The expressway at five-thirty was like a bumper car ride at sixty miles an hour, every driver a maniac intent on getting home. She merged into traffic and spotted Mapes way ahead, switching to the left lane.

She tried to make the same lane change, only to find a truck muscling in, refusing to yield. Abby signaled, nudged closer to his lane. The truck only tightened the gap. This had turned into a dangerous game of chicken now, Abby veering toward the truck, the truck holding fast. She was too pumped up on adrenaline to be afraid, too intent on keeping up with Mapes. Behind the wheel, she had transformed into some other woman, a desperate, foul-mouthed stranger she scarcely recognized. She was fighting back at them, and it felt good. It felt powerful. Abby DiMatteo on fucking testosterone.

She floored the accelerator and shot left, right in front of the truck.

'Jesus Christ!' yelled Katzka. 'Are you trying to get us killed?'

'I don't give a shit. I want this guy.'

'Are you like this in the OR?'

'Oh, yeah. I'm a real fucking terror. Haven't you heard?'

'Remind me not to get sick.'

'Now what's he doing?'

Up ahead the Trans Am had switched lanes again. It peeled to the right, onto the turnoff for the Callahan Tunnel.

'*Shit*,' said Abby, cutting right as well. She shot across two lanes and they entered the cavelike gloom of the tunnel. Graffiti whipped past. Concrete walls echoed back the grinding of tires over pavement, the whoosh-whoosh of cars slicing the air. Their reemergence into the gray light of dusk was a shock to their eyes.

The Trans Am left the expressway. Abby followed.

They were in East Boston now, the gateway to Logan International Airport. That must be where Mapes was headed, she thought. The airport.

She was surprised when, instead, he rattled across a railroad track and worked his way west, away from the airport. He headed into a maze of streets.

Abby slowed down, gave him some space. That surge of adrenaline she'd felt during the frantic chase on the expressway was fading. The Trans

Am wasn't going to get away from her in this neighborhood. Now her challenge was to avoid being noticed.

They were heading along the wharves of Boston's Inner Harbor. Behind a chain-link fence, rows and rows of unused ship's containers were stacked three deep like giant Legos. And beyond the container yard was the industrial waterfront. Against the setting sun loomed the silhouettes of loading cranes and ships in port. The Trans Am turned left, drove through an open gate and into the container yard.

Abby pulled up beside the fence and parked. Peering through a gap between a forklift and a container, she saw the Trans Am drive to the foot of the pier and stop. Mapes got out of his car. He strode onto the dock, where a ship was moored. It looked like a small freighter – a two-hundred footer, she estimated.

Mapes gave a shout. After a moment, a man appeared on deck and waved him aboard. Mapes climbed the gangplank and disappeared into the vessel.

'Why did he come here?' she said. 'Why a boat?'

'Are you sure it's the same man?'

'If it isn't, then Mapes has a double working at Amity.' She paused, suddenly remembering where Katzka had just spent the last half hour. 'What did you find out about the place, anyway?'

'You mean before I noticed someone stealing my car?' He shrugged. 'It looked like what it's supposed to be. A medical supply business. I told them I needed a hospital bed for my wife, and they demonstrated some of the latest models.'

'How many people in the building?'

'I saw three. One guy in the showroom. Two on the second floor handling phone orders. None of them looked very happy to be working there.'

'What about the upper two floors?'

'Warehouse space, I assume. There's really nothing about that building worth pursuing.'

She looked past the fence, at the blue Trans Am. 'You could subpoena their financial records. Find out where Voss's five million dollars went to.'

'We have no basis on which to subpoena any records.'

'How much evidence do you need? I *know* that was the courier! I know what these people are doing.'

'Your testimony isn't going to sway any judge. Certainly not under the circumstances.' His answer was honest – brutally so. 'I'm sorry, Abby. But you know as well as I do that you have a whopping credibility problem.'

She felt herself closing off against him, withdrawing in anger. 'You're absolutely right,' she shot back. 'Who'd believe me? It's just the psychotic Dr DiMatteo, babbling nonsense again.'

He didn't respond to that self-pitying statement. In the silence that followed, she regretted having said it. The sound of her own voice, wounded and sarcastic, seemed to hang between them.

They said nothing for a while. Overhead a jet screamed, the shadow of its wings swooping past like a raptor's. It climbed, glittering in the last light of the setting sun. Only as the jet's roar faded away did Katzka speak again.

'It's not that I don't believe you,' he said.

She looked at him. 'No one else does. Why would you?'

'Because of Dr Levi. And the way he died.' He gazed straight ahead at the darkening road. 'It wasn't the way people usually kill themselves. In a room where no one will find you for days. We don't like to think of our bodies decomposing. We want to be found before the maggots get to us. Before we're black and bloated. While we can still be recognized as human. Then there were all the plans he'd made. The trip to the Caribbean. Thanksgiving with his son. He was looking ahead, expecting a future.' Katzka glanced sideways, at a streetlamp that had just flickered on in the gathering dusk. 'Finally there's his wife, Elaine. I often have to talk to surviving spouses. Some of them are shocked, some of them grieving. Some of them are just plain relieved. I'm a widower myself. I remember, after my wife died, that it was all I could manage just to crawl out of bed every morning. But what does Elaine Levi do? She calls a moving company, packs up her furniture, and leaves town. It's not the act of a grieving spouse. It's what someone does when they're guilty. Or they're scared.'

Abby nodded. It's what she'd thought as well. That Elaine was afraid.

'Then you told me about Kunstler and

Hennessy,' he said. 'And suddenly I'm not looking at a single death. I'm dealing with a series of them. And Aaron Levi's is beginning to look less and less like a suicide.'

Another jet took off, the scream of its engines making conversation impossible. It banked left, skimming the evening mist now gathering over the harbor. Even after the jet had vanished into the western sky, Abby could still hear the roar in her ears.

'Dr Levi didn't hang himself,' said Katzka.

Abby frowned at him. 'I thought the autopsy was confirmatory.'

'We found something on toxicology. We got the results back just last week from the crime lab.'

'Something turned up?'

'In his muscle tissue. They found traces of succinylcholine.'

She stared at him. *Succinylcholine*. It was used every day by anesthesiologists to induce muscle relaxation during surgery. In the OR, it was a vitally useful drug. Outside the OR, its administration would cause the most horrible of deaths. Complete paralysis in a fully conscious subject. Though awake and aware, one would be unable to move or breathe. Like drowning in a sea of air.

She swallowed, her throat suddenly dry. 'It wasn't a suicide.'

'No.'

She took a breath and slowly let it out. For a moment she was too horrified to speak. She didn't dare even consider what Aaron's death must have been like. She looked through the fence, toward the pier. Evening fog was forming over the harbor and starting to drift in wispy fingers across the waterfront. Mapes had not reappeared. The freighter loomed, black and silent in the fading light.

'I want to know what's on that boat,' she said. 'I want to know why he's gone there.' She reached for the door.

He stopped her. 'Not yet.'

'When?'

'Let's drive up a block and pull over. We can wait there.' He glanced at the sky, then at the fog thickening over the water. 'It'll be dark soon.'

Twenty-one

'How long has it been?'

'Only about an hour,' said Katzka.

Abby hugged herself and shivered. The evening had turned even colder, and inside the car, their breaths fogged the windows. In the mist outside, the distant streetlamp gave off a sulfurous yellow glow.

'Interesting you should put it that way. *Only an hour.* To me it feels like all night.'

'It's a matter of perspective. I've put in a lot of time in surveillance. Early in my career.'

Katzka as a young man – she couldn't picture that, couldn't imagine him as a fresh-faced rookie. 'What made you become a policeman?' she asked.

He shrugged, a blip of shadow in the gloom of the car. 'It suited me.'

'I guess that explains everything.'

'What made you become a doctor?'

She wiped a streak across the fogged windshield and stared out at the boxy canyons formed by ships' containers. 'I don't quite know how to answer that.'

'Is it such a difficult question?'

'The answer's complicated.'

'So it wasn't something simple. Like for the good of humanity.'

Now it was her turn to shrug. 'Humanity will scarcely notice my absence.'

'You go to school for eight years. You train for another five years. It has to be a pretty compelling reason.'

The window had fogged up again. She wiped her hand across it and the condensation felt strangely warm against her skin. 'I guess, if I had to give you a reason, it would be my brother. When he was ten years old, he had to be hospitalized. I spent a lot of time watching his doctors. Seeing how they worked.'

Katzka waited for her to elaborate. When she didn't, he said softly, 'Your brother didn't live?'

She shook her head. 'It was a long time ago.' She looked down at the moisture glistening on her hand. Warm as tears, she thought. And for one precarious moment she thought she might shed real tears. She was glad Katzka remained silent; she did not feel up to answering any more questions, not up to reviving the images of the ER, of Pete lying on a gurney, the blood splashed on his brand new tennis shoes. How small those shoes had seemed, far too small for a ten-year-old boy. And then there'd been the months of watching him lie in a coma, his flesh shrinking away, his limbs contracting into a permanent self-embrace. The night he'd died, Abby had lifted him from the bed and had sat rocking him in her arms. He'd felt weightless, and as fragile as an infant.

She told Katzka none of this, yet she sensed he understood all he needed to know. Communication by empathy. It was not a talent she'd suspected he possessed. But then, there were so many things about Katzka that she found surprising.

He looked out at the night. And he said: 'I think it's dark enough.'

They stepped out of the car and walked through the open gate, into the container yard. The freighter loomed in the mist. The only light aboard the vessel was a weirdly greenish glow from one of the lower portholes. Otherwise the ship seemed abandoned. They walked onto the pier, passing a tower of empty crates stacked on a loading pallet.

At the ship's gangplank they paused, listening to the slap of water on the hull, to the myriad groans of steel and cable. The shriek of another jet taking off startled them both. Abby glanced up at the sky, and as she watched the jet's lights lift away she had the disorienting sensation that she was the one moving through space and time. She almost reached out to Katzka for a steadying grip. *How did I end up standing on this pier, with this man?* she wondered. *What strange chain of events has brought me to this unexpected moment in my life?*

Katzka touched her arm, his contact warm and

solid. 'I'm going to look around on board.' He stepped onto the gangplank. He'd taken only a few paces toward the vessel when he halted and glanced back up the pier.

A pair of headlights had just swung through the gate. The vehicle was now rolling toward them, across the container yard. It was a van.

Abby had no chance to duck for cover behind the crates. The headlights' beams had already caught her, trapped at the end of the pier.

The van skidded to a halt. Shielding her eyes against the glare, Abby could see almost nothing, but she heard doors open and slam shut. Heard footsteps crunching across the gravel as the men moved in to cut off any escape.

Katzka materialized right beside her. She hadn't even heard him scramble off the gangplank, but suddenly there he was, stepping between her and the van. 'Okay, just back off,' he said. 'We're not here to cause any trouble.'

The two men, silhouetted by the headlights, hesitated only a second. Then they began to advance.

'Let us by!' Katzka said.

Abby's view of the men was partially blocked by Katzka's back. She didn't see what happened next. All she knew was that he suddenly dropped to a crouch, that there was a simultaneous crack of gunfire and the zing of something ricocheting off the concrete pier behind her.

She and Katzka lunged at the same time for the cover of the crates. He shoved her head to the ground as more gunfire rang out, chunking out splinters of wood.

Katzka returned fire. Three quick blasts.

There was a tattoo of retreating footsteps. A terse exchange of voices.

Then the sound of the van being started, the engine revving and tires spitting up gravel.

Abby raised her head to look. To her horror she saw the van was rolling toward them, bearing down on the crates like a battering ram.

Katzka took aim and fired. Four bursts that shattered the windshield.

The van bumped crazily onto the pier, swerved right, then left, a battering ram gone out of control.

Katzka fired two last, desperate blasts.

The van kept coming.

Abby registered a blinding glimpse of headlights. Then she flung herself off the pier and hurtled into pitch darkness.

The plunge into icy water was shocking. She sputtered back to the surface, choking on brine and spilled diesel fuel, her limbs flailing at the black water. She heard men shouting on the pier above, then a thunderous splash. Water boiled up and washed over her head. She surfaced again, coughing. At the end of the pier the water seemed to be glowing a phosphorescent green. The van. It was sliding under the surface, its headlights casting two watery beams of light. As it sank, the greenish glow faded to black.

Katzka. Where was Katzka?

She whirled around in the water, stroking as she scanned the blackness. The surface was still churning, wavelets slapping her face, and she was struggling to see through the sting of salt in her eyes.

She heard a soft splash and a head popped out of the brine a few feet away. Treading water, Katzka glanced in her direction, and saw that she was holding her own. Then he looked up, at the sound of more voices – from the ship? There were two men, maybe three, their footsteps thudding up and down the pier. They were yelling to each other, but their shouts seemed garbled and unintelligible.

Not English, thought Abby, but she could not identify the language.

Overhead a light appeared, the beam cutting through the mist and slowly skimming the water.

Katzka dove. So did Abby. She swam as far as her breath would carry her, away from the pier, toward the blackness of open water. Again and again she came up, gasped in a breath, then dove again. When she resurfaced a fifth time, she was treading in darkness.

There were now two lights moving on the pier, the beams scanning the mist like a pair of relentless eyes. She heard the splash of water somewhere close, and then a quick intake of breath, and she knew Katzka had surfaced nearby.

'Lost my gun,' he panted.

'What the hell's going on?'

'Just keep swimming. The next pier.'

The night suddenly lit up with shocking brilliance. The freighter had turned on its deck lights, illuminating every detail on the pier. There was one man on the gangplank, and one crouching at the pier's edge with a searchlight. Towering beside them was a third man, his rifle aimed at the water.

'*Go*,' said Katzka.

Abby dove, clawing her way through liquid blackness. She'd never been a good swimmer. Deep water scared her. Now she was swimming through water so dark it might as well be bottomless. She came up for another breath, but could not seem to get enough air, no matter how deeply she gasped.

'Abby, keep moving!' urged Katzka. 'Just get to that next pier!'

Abby glanced back toward the freighter. She saw that the searchlights were tracing an ever-larger circle on the water. That the beam was flitting toward them.

She slipped, once again, underwater.

By the time she and Katzka finally clambered out onto land, Abby could barely move her limbs. She crawled up rocks slippery with oil and seaweed. Crouching in the darkness, the barnacles biting into her knees, she vomited into the water.

Katzka took her arm, steadied her. She was shaking so hard from exertion she thought she might shatter were it not for his grip.

At last there was nothing left in her stomach. Weakly she raised her head.

'Better?' he whispered.

'I'm freezing.'

'Then let's get someplace warm.' He glanced up at the pier, looming above them. 'I think we can make it up those pilings. Come on.'

Together they scrambled up the rocks, slipping and sliding on moss and seaweed. Katzka made it up onto the pier first, then he reached down and hauled her up after him. They rose to a crouch.

The searchlight sliced through the mist, trapping them in its glare.

A bullet ricocheted off the concrete right behind Abby.

'*Move!*' said Katzka.

They sprinted away. The searchlight pursued them, the beam zigzagging through the darkness. They were off the concrete pier now, running toward the container yard. Bullets spat up gravel all around them. Ahead loomed the containers, stacked up in a giant maze of shadows. They ducked down the nearest row, heard bullets pinging on metal. Then the gunfire ceased.

Abby slowed down to catch her breath. She was still exhausted from the swim, still weak from retching up seawater. And now she was shaking so hard her feet were stumbling.

Voices drew near. They seemed to come from two directions at once.

Katzka grabbed her hand and pulled her deeper into the maze of containers.

They ran to the end of the row, turned left, and kept running. Then both of them halted.

At the far end of the row, a light winked.

They're in front of us!

Katzka veered right, turned down another row. Stacked containers towered on both sides of them like the walls of a chasm. They heard voices and corrected course again. By now they'd made so many turns, Abby couldn't tell if they were moving in circles, couldn't tell if they'd fled this way seconds earlier.

A light danced ahead of them.

They halted, spun around to retrace their steps. And saw another flashlight beam winking. It swept back and forth, moving toward them.

They're ahead of us. And behind us.

In panic she stumbled backward. Reaching out to steady herself, she felt the cleft between two containers. The gap was barely wide enough to fit into.

The flashlight beam winked closer.

Grabbing Katzka's arm, she squeezed into the opening, pulling him after her. Deeper and deeper she wormed, through a filigree of cobwebs, until she bumped up against the wall of an adjacent container. No way forward. They were trapped here, wedged tightly into a space narrower than a coffin.

The crunch of footsteps on gravel approached.

Katzka's hand reached out to grip hers, but his touch did nothing to ease her panic. Her heart was slamming against her chest. The footsteps drew closer.

She heard voices, now – one man hailing

another, then a second man answering in some unrecognizable tongue. Or was it the blood roaring through her ears that made their words seem garbled beyond comprehension?

A light danced past the cleft opening. The two men were standing close by, conversing in puzzled tones. They had only to shine their flashlights into the gap, and they'd spot their prey in the crevice. Someone kicked at the ground and gravel skittered and clanged against the container.

Abby closed her eyes, too terrified to look. She didn't want to be watching when that beam of light flooded into their hiding place. Katzka's grip tightened around her hand. Her limbs were rigid with tension, her breath coming in short, shallow gasps. She heard another scrape of shoes across the ground, another skittering of gravel.

Then the footsteps moved away.

Abby didn't dare move. She wasn't sure she *could* move; her legs felt locked in position. *Years from now*, she thought, *they'll find me standing here, my skeleton frozen stiff in terror.*

It was Katzka who made the first move. He eased toward the opening and was about to poke his head out for a look when they heard a soft *whick*. A light flared and went out. Someone had lit a match. Katzka went dead still. The smell of cigarette smoke wafted through the darkness.

Somewhere, faintly, a man was calling.

The cigarette smoker grunted out a reply, and then his footsteps faded away.

Katzka didn't move.

They remained frozen, hands clasped together, neither one daring to whisper a word. Twice they heard their pursuers pass by; both times, the men moved on.

There was a distant rumble, like the growl of thunder somewhere over the horizon.

Then, for a long time, they heard nothing.

It was hours later when they finally emerged from their hiding place. They crept down the row of containers and stopped to scan the waterfront. The night had turned unnervingly silent. The mist had lifted, and overhead, stars twinkled faintly in a sky washed by city lights.

The next pier was dark. They saw no men, no lights, not even the glow of a porthole. There was only the long low silhouette of the concrete pier jutting out, and the sparkle of moonlight on the water.

The freighter was gone.

Twenty-two

The alarm on the heart monitor was going crazy, squealing as the line traced a chaotic dance of death across the screen.

'Mr Voss.' A nurse grasped Victor's arm, tried to pull him away from Nina's bed. 'The doctors need room to work.'

'I'm not leaving her.'

'Mr Voss, they can't do their job if you're here!'

Victor shook off the woman's hand with a violence that made her cringe, as though struck. He remained standing at the end of his wife's bed, gripping the footrail so tightly his knuckles looked like exposed bone.

'Back!' came a command. 'Everyone back!'

'Mr Voss!' It was Dr Archer speaking now, his voice slicing through the bedlam. 'We need to shock your wife's heart! You have to move away from the bed *now*.'

Victor released the footrail and stepped back.

The shock was delivered. It coursed through Nina's body in a single, barbaric jolt. She was too small, too fragile to be abused this way! Enraged, he took a step forward, ready to snatch the paddles away. Then he stopped.

On the monitor above the bed, the jagged line had transformed to a calmly rhythmic series of blips. He heard someone release a sigh, and felt his own breath escape in a single rush.

'Systolic's sixty. Up to sixty-five . . .'

'Rhythm seems to be holding.'

'Up to seventy-five systolic.'

'Okay, turn down that IV.'

'She's moving her arm. Can we get a wrist restraint over here?'

Victor pushed past the nurses to Nina's side. No one tried to stop him. He took her hand and pressed it to his lips. And he tasted, on her skin, the salt of his own tears.

Stay with me. Please, please, stay with me.

'Mr Voss?' The voice seemed to call to him from across a long distance. Turning, he focused on Dr Archer's face.

'Can we step outside?' said Archer.

Victor shook his head.

'She's all right for the moment,' said Archer. 'All these people are taking good care of her. We'll be just outside the room. I need to speak to you. Now.'

At last Victor nodded. Tenderly he lay down Nina's hand and followed Archer out of the cubicle.

They stood together in a quiet corner of the ICU. The lights had been dimmed for the evening, and against the bank of green screens, the silhouette of the monitor nurse sat silent and motionless.

'The transplant's been postponed,' said Archer. 'There was a problem with the harvest.'

'What do you mean?'

'It couldn't be done tonight. We'll have to reschedule for tomorrow.'

Victor looked at his wife's cubicle. Through the uncurtained window, he could see her head moving. She was waking up. She needed him at her side.

He said, 'Nothing can go wrong tomorrow night.'

'It won't.'

'That's what you told me after the first transplant.'

'Organ rejection is something we can't always stop. No matter how hard we try to prevent it, it happens.'

'How do I know it won't happen again? With a second heart?'

'I can't make promises. But at this point, Mr Voss, we don't have an alternative. Cyclosporine's failed. And she had an anaphylactic reaction to OKT-3. There's nothing left except another transplant.'

'It *will* be done tomorrow?'

Archer nodded. 'We'll make sure it's done tomorrow.'

Nina was not yet fully conscious when Victor returned to her bedside. So many times before, he had watched her as she slept. Over the years he had taken note of the changes in her face. The delicate lines that had formed at the corners of her mouth. The gradual sagging of the jawline. The new whisper of white in her hair. Each and every change he had mourned, because it reminded him that their journey together was but a temporary passage through a cold and lonely eternity.

And yet, because it was *her* face, each and every change he had loved.

It was hours later when she opened her eyes. At first he did not realize she was awake. He was sitting in a chair by her bed, his shoulders slumped with fatigue, when something made him raise his head and turn to her.

She was looking at him. She opened her hand in a silent request for his touch. He grasped it, kissed it.

'Everything,' she whispered, 'will be all right.'

He smiled. 'Yes. Yes, of course it will.'

'I've been lucky, Victor. So very lucky . . .'

'We both have.'

'But now you have to learn to let me go.'

Victor's smile faded. He shook his head. 'Don't say that.'

'You have so much ahead of you.'

'What about *us*?' He was grasping her hand in both of his now, like a man trying to hold on to water as it trickles away. 'You and I, Nina, we're not like everyone else! We always used to say that to each other. Don't you remember? How we were different. We were special. And nothing could ever happen to us?'

'But something has, Victor,' she murmured. 'Something has happened to me.'

'And *I will take care of it.*'

She said nothing, only shook her head sadly.

It seemed to Victor that the last thing he saw, as Nina's eyelids closed again, was a look of quiet defiance. He gazed down at her hand, the one he'd been holding so possessively. And he saw that it was closed, in a fist.

It was nearly midnight when Detective Lundquist dropped off an exhausted Abby at her front door. She saw that Mark's car was not parked in the driveway. When she stepped inside the house, she could feel its emptiness as clearly as one senses a chasm yawning at one's feet. He's had an emergency at the hospital, she thought. It was not unusual for him to leave the house late at night, called into Bayside to tend to a gunshot wound or a stabbing. She tried to visualize him as she had seen him so many times before in the OR, his face masked in blue, his gaze focused downward, but she could not seem to come up with the image. It was as though the memory, the old reality, had been erased.

She went to the answering machine, hoping he'd left a voice memo on the recorder. All she found were two phone messages. Both were from Vivian, and the number she'd left had an out-of-state area code. She was still in Burlington. It was too late now to call her back. She'd try in the morning.

Upstairs, she stripped off her wet clothes, threw them in the washing machine, and stepped into the shower. She noticed the tiles were dry; Mark hadn't used the shower tonight. Had he even been home?

As the hot water beat down on her shoulders, she stood with her eyes closed, thinking. Dreading what she'd have to say to Mark. This was why she had returned to his house tonight. The time had come to confront him, to demand answers. The uncertainty had become unbearable.

After she got out of the shower, she sat down on the bed and called in a page for Mark. She was startled when the phone rang almost immediately.

'Abby?' It wasn't Mark, but Katzka. 'Just checking to see if you're okay. I called a little while ago and there was no answer.'

'I was in the shower. I'm fine, Katzka. I'm just waiting for Mark to get home.'

A pause. 'You're by yourself?'

His note of concern brought a faint smile to her lips. Scratch that armor of his, and you'd find a real man under there after all.

'I locked all the doors and windows,' she said. 'Just like you told me.' Over the phone, she could hear a background buzz of voices, along with the squeal of a police radio, and she could picture him standing on that dock, the blue emergency lights flashing on his face. 'What's happening over there?' she asked.

'We're waiting for the divers. The equipment's already in position.'

'You really think the driver's still trapped in the van?'

434

'I'm afraid so.' He sighed, and it was a sound of such profound weariness, she gave a murmur of concern.

'You should go home, Katzka. You need a hot shower and some chicken soup. That's my prescription.'

He laughed. It was a surprising sound, one she'd never heard from him before. 'Now if I could just find a pharmacy to fill it.' Someone spoke to him. It sounded like another cop, asking about bullet trajectories. Katzka turned to answer the man, then he came back on the line. 'I have to go. You sure you're okay there? You wouldn't rather stay in a hotel?'

'I'll be fine.'

'Okay.' Again, she heard Katzka sigh. 'But I want you to call a locksmith in the morning. Have him install deadbolts on all the doors. Especially if you're going to be spending a lot of nights home alone.'

'I'll do that.'

There was a brief silence. He had pressing matters to attend to, yet he seemed reluctant to hang up. At last he said, 'I'll check back with you in the morning.'

'Thanks, Katzka.' She hung up.

Again she paged Mark. Then she lay down on the bed and waited for him to call back. He didn't.

As the hours passed, she tried to calm her growing fears by tallying up all the possible reasons he wasn't answering. He could be asleep in one of the hospital call rooms. His beeper could be broken.

He could be scrubbed and unavailable in the OR.

Or he could be dead. Like Aaron Levi. Like Kunstler and Hennessy.

She paged him again. And again.

At three A.M., the phone finally rang. In an instant she was wide awake and reaching for the receiver.

'Abby, it's me.' Mark's voice crackled on the wire, as though he were calling from across a long distance.

'I've been paging you for hours,' she said. 'Where are you?'

'I'm in the car, heading to the hospital right now.' He paused. 'Abby, we need to talk. Things have . . . changed.'

She said, softly: 'Between us, you mean.'

'No. No, this has nothing to do with you. It never did. It has to do with *me*. You just got sucked into it, Abby. I tried to get them to back off, but now they've taken it too far.'

'*Who* has?'

'The team.'

She was afraid to ask the next question, but she had no choice now. 'All of you? You're all involved?'

'Not anymore.' The connection briefly faded, and she heard what sounded like the whoosh of traffic. His voice regained its volume. 'Mohandas and I came to a decision tonight. That's where I've been, at his house. We've been talking, comparing notes. Abby, we're putting our heads on the block. But we decided it's time to end this. We can't do it any longer. We're going to blow this thing wide open, Mohandas and me. And fuck everyone else. Fuck Bayside.' He paused, his voice suddenly breaking. 'I've been a coward. I'm sorry.'

She closed her eyes. 'You knew. All this time you knew.'

'I knew *some* of it – not all. I had no idea how far Archer was taking it. I didn't *want* to know. Then you started asking all those questions. And I couldn't hide from the truth any longer . . .' He released a deep breath and whispered, 'This is going to ruin me, Abby.'

She still had her eyes closed. She could see him in the darkness of his car, one hand on the wheel, the other gripping the cellular phone. Could imagine the misery on his face. And the courage; most of all, the courage.

'I love you,' he whispered.

'Come home, Mark. Please.'

'Not yet. I'm meeting Mohandas at the hospital. We're going to get those donor records.'

'Do you know where they're kept?'

'We have an idea. With just two of us, it could take us a while to search all the files. If you helped us out, we might be able to get through them by morning.'

She sat up in bed. 'I won't be getting much sleep tonight anyway. Where are you meeting Mohandas?'

'Medical Records. He has the key.' Mark hesitated. 'Are you sure you want to be in on this, Abby?'

'I want to be wherever *you* are. We'll do this together. Okay?'

'Okay,' he said softly. 'See you soon.'

Five minutes later, Abby walked out the front door and climbed into her car.

The streets of West Cambridge were deserted. She turned onto Memorial Drive, skirting the Charles River as she headed southeast, toward the River Street bridge. It was three-fifteen A.M., but she could not remember feeling so awake. So alive.

At last we're going to beat them! she thought. *And we're going to do it together. The way we should have done it from the start.*

She crossed the bridge and headed onto the ramp for the turnpike. There were few cars traveling at that hour, and she merged easily with sparse eastbound traffic.

Three and a half miles later, the turnpike came to an end. She changed lanes, preparing to turn off onto the Southeast Expressway ramp. As she curved onto it, she suddenly became aware of a pair of headlights bearing down on her.

She accelerated, merging onto the southbound expressway.

The headlights pulled closer, high beams glaring off her rearview mirror. How long had they been behind her? She had no idea. But they were zooming in now like twin bats out of hell.

She sped up.

So did the other car. Suddenly it swooped left into the next lane. It pulled up beside her until they were almost neck and neck.

She glanced sideways. Saw the other car's window roll down. Glimpsed the silhouette of a man in the right passenger seat.

In panic, she floored the accelerator.

Too late she spotted the car stalled ahead of her. She slammed on the brakes. Her car spun and caromed off the concrete barrier. Suddenly the world tilted sideways. Then everything was tumbling over and over. She saw darkness and light. Darkness, light.

Darkness.

'. . . repeat, this is Mobile Unit Forty-one. Our ETA is three minutes. Copy?'

'Copy, Forty-one. How're the vitals?'

'Systolic holding at ninety-five. Pulse one ten. We've got normal saline going in one peripheral line. Hey, looks like she's starting to move.'

'Keep her immobilized.'

'We've got her in a collar and a spinal board.'

'Okay, we're ready and waiting for you.'

'See you in a minute, Bayside . . .'

. . . Light.

And pain. Short, sharp explosions of it in her head.

She tried to scream, but no sound came out. She tried to turn away from that piercing light, but her neck seemed trapped in a chokehold. She thought if she could just escape that light and burrow back into darkness, the pain would go away. With all her strength she twisted, straining to break free of the paralysis that had seized her limbs.

'Abby. Abby, hold still!' a voice commanded. 'I have to look in your eyes.'

She twisted the other way, felt restraints chafing her wrists, her ankles. And she realized that it was not paralysis that prevented her movement. She was tied down, all four limbs strapped to the gurney.

'Abby, it's Dr Wettig. Look at me. Look at the light. Come on, open your eyes. *Open.*'

She opened her eyes, forced herself to keep them open, even though the beam of his penlight felt like a blade piercing straight through her skull.

'Follow the light. Come on. That's good, Abby. Okay, both pupils are reactive. EOMs are normal.' The penlight, mercifully, shut off. 'I still want that CT.'

Abby could make out shapes now. She could see the shadow of Dr Wettig's head against the diffuse brightness of the overhead lights. There were other heads moving around on the periphery of her vision, and a white privacy curtain billowing like a cloud off in the distance. Pain pricked her left arm; she gave a jerk.

'Easy, Abby.' It was a woman's voice, soft, soothing. 'I have to draw some blood. Hold very still. I have a lot of tubes to collect.'

Now a third voice: 'Dr Wettig, X-ray's ready for her.'

'In a minute,' said Wettig. 'I want a bigger-bore IV in. Sixteen gauge. Come on, people.'

Abby felt another stab, this time in her right arm. The pain drove straight through her confusion and brought her mind into startling focus. She knew exactly where she was. She couldn't recall how she'd arrived, but she knew this was Bayside Emergency Room, and that something terrible must have happened.

'Mark,' she said, and tried to sit up. 'Where's Mark?'

'Don't move! We'll lose this IV!'

A hand closed over her elbow, pinning her arm to the gurney. The grasp was too firm to be gentle. They were all hurting her, stabbing her with their needles, holding her down like some captive animal.

'Mark!' she cried.

'Abby, listen to me.' It was Wettig again, his voice low and impatient. 'We're trying to reach Mark. I'm sure he'll be here soon. Right now, you have to cooperate or we can't help you. Do you understand? Abby, do you understand?'

She stared up at his face and she went very still. So many times before, as a resident, she had felt intimidated by his flat blue eyes. Now, strapped down and helpless under that gaze, she felt more than intimidated. She felt truly, deeply frightened. She glanced around the room, seeking a friendly face, but everyone was too busy attending to IVs and blood tubes and vital signs.

She heard the curtain whisk open, felt a lurch as the gurney began to move. Now the ceiling was rushing past in a flashing succession of lights, and she knew they were taking her deeper into the hospital. Into the heart of the enemy. She didn't even try to struggle; the restraints were impossible to fight. *Think*, she thought. *I have to think.*

They turned the corner, into X-ray. Now another face, a man's, appeared over her gurney. The CT technician. Friend or enemy? She couldn't tell anymore. They moved her onto the table and buckled straps across her chest and hips.

'Hold very still,' the tech commanded, 'or we'll have to do this all over again.'

As the scanner slid over her head, she felt a sudden rush of claustrophobia. She remembered how other patients had described CT scans: *like having your head jammed into a pencil sharpener.* Abby closed her eyes. Machinery clicked and whirred around her head. She tried to think, to remember the accident.

She remembered getting into her car. Driving onto the turnpike. Then her memory tape had a gap. Retrograde amnesia; the accident itself was a complete blank. But the events leading up to it were slowly coming back into focus.

By the time the scan was completed, she'd managed to piece together enough memory fragments to understand what she had to do next. If she wanted to stay alive.

She was quietly cooperative as the CT technician transferred her back onto the gurney – so cooperative, in fact, that he left off the wrist restraints and buckled on only the chest strap. Then he wheeled her into the X-ray anteroom.

'The ER's coming to get you,' he said. 'If you need me, just call. I'm right in the next room.'

Through the open doorway she could hear him talking on the telephone.

'Yeah, this is CT. We're all done here. Dr Blaise is looking over the scan now. You want to come get her?'

Abby reached up and quietly unbuckled the chest strap. As she sat up, she felt the room begin to whirl. She pressed her hands to her temples and everything seemed to settle back into focus.

The IV.

She ripped the tape off her arm, wincing at the sting, and pulled out the catheter. Saline dribbled out of the tubing, onto the floor. She ignored the saline, concentrating instead on stopping the flow of blood from her vein. A sixteen-gauge puncture is a big hole. Though she taped over it tightly, it continued to ooze. She couldn't worry about that now. They were coming to get her.

She climbed off the gurney, her bare feet landing in a pool of saline. In the next room, the tech was cleaning up the CT table. She could hear the rattle of tissue paper, the clang of a trash can.

She took a lab coat off the door hook and pulled it on over her hospital gown. Just that effort seemed to drain her. She was struggling to think, to see through a white haze of pain as she moved to the door. Her legs felt sluggish, as though she were wading through quicksand. She pushed into the hallway.

It was empty.

Still slogging through quicksand, she moved up the corridor, reaching out every so often to steady herself against the wall. She turned a corner. At the far end of the hallway was an emergency exit. She struggled toward it, thinking: *If I can just reach that door, I'll be safe.*

Somewhere behind her, from what seemed like a great distance, she heard voices. The sound of hurrying footsteps.

She lunged against the emergency exit bar and pushed out, into the night. Alarm bells started ringing. At once she began to run, fleeing in panic into the darkness. She stumbled off the curb into the parking lot. Broken glass and gravel cut into her bare feet. She had no plan of escape, no destination in mind; she knew only that she had to get away from Bayside.

There were voices behind her. A shout.

Glancing back, she saw three security guards run out the ER entrance.

She ducked behind a car – too late. They had spotted her.

She lurched to her feet and began to run again. Her legs still didn't work right. She was stumbling as she dodged between parked cars.

Her pursuers' footsteps pounded closer, moving in from two directions at once.

She turned left, between two parked cars.

They surrounded her. One guard grabbed her left arm, another her right. She kicked, punched. Tried to bite them.

But now there were three of them, and they

were dragging her back to the Emergency Room. Back to Dr Wettig.

'They'll kill me!' she screamed. 'Let me go! They're going to kill me!'

'No one's going to hurt you, lady.'

'You don't understand. *You don't understand!*'

The ER doors whisked open. She was swept inside, into the light, and lifted onto a gurney. Strapped down, even as she kicked and thrashed.

Dr Wettig's face appeared, white and taut above hers. 'Five milligrams Haldol IM,' he snapped.

'No!' shrieked Abby. '*No!*'

'Come on, I want it given *stat*.'

A nurse materialized, syringe in hand. She uncapped the needle.

Abby lurched, trying to buck free of the restraints.

'Hold her down,' said Wettig. 'Goddamn it, can we get her immobilized here?'

Hands clamped over her wrists. She was twisted sideways, her right buttock bared.

'Please,' begged Abby, looking up at the nurse. 'Don't let him hurt me. Don't let him.'

She felt the icy lick of alcohol, then the prick of the needle plunging into her buttock.

'Please,' she whispered. But she knew it was already too late.

'It will be all right,' said the nurse. And she smiled at Abby. 'Everything will be all right.'

Twenty-three

'No skid marks on the pier,' said Detective Carrier. 'The windshield's shattered. And the driver's got what looked to me like a bullet hole over the right eye. You know the drill, Slug. I'm sorry, but we're going to need your gun.'

Katzka nodded. And he gazed, wearily, down at the water. 'Tell the diver he'll find my gun right about there. Unless the current's moved it.'

'You think you fired off eight rounds?'

'Maybe more. I know I started with a full clip.'

Carrier nodded, then he gave Katzka a pat on the shoulder. 'Go home. You look like shit warmed over, Slug.'

'As good as that?' said Katzka. And he walked back up the pier, through the gathering of crime lab personnel. The van had been pulled out of the water hours before, and it now sat at the edge of the container yard. Streamers of seaweed had snagged on the axle. Because of the air in the tires, the van had turned over underwater, and its roof had sunk into the bottom ooze. The windshield was caked with mud. They'd already traced its registration to Bayside Hospital, Operations and Facilities. According to the Facilities manager, the van was one of three owned and operated by the hospital for the purpose of shuttling supplies and personnel to outlying clinics. The manager had not noticed any of his vans were missing until the police had called him an hour ago.

The driver's door now hung open, and a photographer was leaning inside, shooting pictures of the dashboard. The body had been removed half an hour ago. His driver's license had identified him as Oleg Boravoy, age thirty-nine, a resident of Newark, New Jersey. They were still awaiting further information.

Katzka knew better than to approach the vehicle. His actions were being called into question, and he had to keep his distance from the evidence. He crossed the container yard to where his own car was parked, outside the fence, and slid inside. Groaning, he dropped his face in his hands. At two A.M. he'd gone home to shower and catch a few hours of sleep. Shortly after sunrise, he'd been back on the pier. *I'm too old for this*, he thought, *too old by at least a decade*. All this running around and shooting in the dark was for the young lions, not for a middle-aged cop. And he was feeling very middle-aged.

Someone tapped on his window. He looked up and saw it was Lundquist. Katzka rolled down the glass.

'Hey, Slug. You okay?'

'I'm going home to get some sleep.'

'Yeah, well before you do, I thought you'd want to hear about the driver.'

'We have something back?'

'They ran the name Oleg Boravoy through the computer. Bingo, he's in there. Russian immigrant, came here in eighty-nine. Last known residence Newark, New Jersey. Three arrests, no convictions.'

'What charges?'

'Kidnapping and extortion. The charges never stick because the witnesses keep disappearing.' Lundquist leaned forward, his voice dropping to a murmur. 'You ran into some really bad shit last night. The Newark cops say Boravoy's Russian mafia.'

'How sure are they?'

'They ought to know. New Jersey's where Russian mafia has its home base. Slug, those guys make the Colombians look like the fucking Rotary Club. They don't just make a hit. They chop off your fingers and toes first, for the fun of it.'

Katzka frowned, remembering the panic of last night. Treading water in the darkness as men ran on the pier above, shouting words in a language he didn't understand. He was having visions now of dismembered fingers and toes, of Boston streets littered with random body parts. Which made him think of scalpels. Operating rooms.

'What's Boravoy's connection to Bayside?' he asked.

'We don't know.'

'He was driving their vehicle.'

'And the van's full of medical supplies,' said Lundquist. 'Couple thousand dollars' worth. Maybe we're talking black market. Boravoy could have partners at Bayside siphoning off drugs and supplies. And you just caught him delivering the goods to their freighter.'

'What about that freighter? You talk to the harbormaster?'

'The ship's owned by some New Jersey firm called the Sigayev Company. Panamanian registry. Her last known port of call was Riga.'

'Where's that?'

'Latvia. I think it's some breakaway Russian republic.'

The Russians again, thought Katzka. If this was indeed Russian mafia, then they were dealing with criminals known for pure and bloody viciousness. With every legitimate wave of immigrants rode a shadow wave of predators, criminal networks that followed their countrymen to the land of opportunity. The land of easy prey.

He thought of Abby DiMatteo, and his anxiety suddenly sharpened. He hadn't spoken to her since that one A.M. phone call. Just an hour ago, he'd been about to call her again. But as he was dialing her number, he'd realized that his pulse had quickened. And he'd recognized that sign for what it was. Anticipation. A joyful, aching, completely irrational eagerness to hear her voice. They were feelings he had not experienced in years, and he understood, only too painfully, what they meant.

He had quickly disconnected. And had spent the last hour in a deepening depression.

He gazed off toward the pier. By now the ship could be a hundred miles out to sea. Even if they located it, there would be a jurisdiction problem.

He said to Lundquist, 'I want anything there is on the Sigayev Company. I want any links to Amity and to Bayside Hospital.'

'On my list, Slug.'

Katzka started his car. He looked at Lundquist. 'Your brother still in the Coast Guard?'

'No. But he's got buddies who're still in.'

'Run this by them. See if they've boarded that freighter lately.'

'Doubt it. If she just sailed in from Riga.' Lundquist paused, glancing up. Detective Carrier was crossing toward them, waving.

'Hey, Slug,' said Carrier. 'Did you get the message about Dr DiMatteo?'

Instantly Katzka turned off the engine. But he couldn't shut off the sudden roar of his own pulse. He stared at Carrier, expecting the worst.

'There's been an accident.'

A lunch cart rattled down the hallway. Abby woke up with a start and found she was lying in sheets damp with sweat. Her heart was still pounding from the nightmare. She tried to turn in bed, but found she couldn't; her hands were tied down, her wrists sore from chafing. And she realized that she had not been dreaming at all. This *was* the nightmare, and it was one from which she could not wake up.

With a sob of frustration she sank back against the pillow and stared at the ceiling. She heard the creak of a chair. She turned her head.

Katzka was sitting by the window. In the glare of midday, his unshaven face looked older and wearier than she had ever seen him before.

'I asked them to take off the restraints,' he said. 'But they told me you'd pulled out a few too many IVs.' He rose and came to her bedside. There he stood gazing down at her. 'Welcome back, Abby. You're a very lucky young lady.'

'I don't remember what happened.'

'You had an accident. Your car rolled over on the Southeast Expressway.'

'Was there anyone else . . .'

He shook his head. 'No one else was hurt. But your car was pretty much totaled.' There was a silence. She realized he was no longer looking at her. He was looking somewhere at her pillow instead.

'Katzka?' she asked softly. 'Was it my fault?'

Reluctantly he nodded. 'Based on the skid marks, it appears you were traveling at a high rate of speed. You must have braked to avoid a vehicle stalled in your lane. Your car veered into a highway barrier. And rolled over, across two lanes.'

She closed her eyes. 'Oh my God.'

Again there was a pause. 'I guess you haven't heard the rest,' he said. 'I spoke to the investigating officer. I'm afraid they found a shattered container of vodka in your car.'

She opened her eyes and stared at him. 'That's impossible.'

'Abby, you can't remember what happened. Last night, on the pier, was a traumatic experience. Maybe you felt the need to unwind. To have a few drinks at home.'

'I'd remember *that*! I'd remember if I'd been drinking—'

'Look, what's important right now is—'

'*This* is important! Can't you see, Katzka? They're setting me up again!'

He rubbed his hand over his eyes, the unfocused gesture of a man struggling to stay awake. 'I'm sorry, Abby,' he murmured. 'I know this can't be an easy thing for you to acknowledge. But Dr Wettig just showed me your blood alcohol level. They drew it last night in the ER. It was point two-one.'

He wasn't facing her now, but was gazing blankly out the window, as though just the act of looking at her had taken too much out of him. She could not even turn her body to confront him face to face; the restraints wouldn't allow it. She gave a violent yank on her bonds, and the pain that stung her chafed wrists almost brought tears to her eyes. She was not going to cry. Damn it, she was not going to cry.

She closed her eyes and concentrated on channeling her rage. It was all she had left, the only weapon with which she could fight back.

They had taken everything else away from her. They had taken even Katzka.

She said, slowly: 'I was not drinking. You have to believe me. I was not drunk.'

'Can you tell me where you were going at three in the morning?'

'I was coming here, to Bayside. I remember that much. Mark called me, and I was coming to . . .' She stopped. 'Has he been here? Why isn't he here?'

His silence was chilling. She turned her head to look at him, but could not see his face.

'Katzka?'

'Mark Hodell hasn't been answering his pages.'

'What?'

'His car's not in the hospital parking lot. No one seems to know where he is.'

She tried to speak, but her throat felt as if it had swollen shut, and the only sound that came out was a whispered: 'No.'

'It's too early to draw any conclusions, Abby. His pager may be broken. We don't know anything yet.'

But Abby knew. She knew with a certainty that was both immediate and shattering. Her whole body suddenly felt numb. Lifeless. She didn't realize she was crying, didn't even feel the tears sliding down until Katzka rose, tissue in hand, and gently wiped her cheek.

'I'm sorry,' he murmured. He brushed her hair off her face, and just for a moment, his hand lingered there, fingers resting protectively on her forehead. He said, more softly, 'I'm so sorry.'

'Find him for me,' she whispered. 'Please. Please, find him for me.'

'I will.'

A moment later she heard him walk out of the room. Only then did she realize he had untied the restraints. She was free to leave the bed, to walk out of the room. But she didn't.

She turned her face into the pillow and wept.

At noon a nurse came in to remove the IV and to leave a lunch tray. Abby didn't even look at the food. The tray was later removed, untouched.

At two o'clock, Dr Wettig walked in. He stood by her bed, flipping through the pages of her chart, making clucking sounds as he reviewed the lab results. At last he looked down at her. 'Dr DiMatteo?'

She didn't answer him.

'Detective Katzka tells me you deny drinking any alcohol last night,' he said.

She said nothing.

Wettig sighed. 'The first step toward recovery is acknowledging you have a problem. Now, I should have been more aware. I should have realized what you were struggling with all this time. But now it's all out in the open. It's time to deal with the problem.'

She looked up at him. 'What would be the point?' she said dully.

'The point is, you have some sort of future worth salvaging. A DUI is a serious setback, but you're an intelligent woman. There will

454

be other careers open to you besides medicine.'

Her response was silence. The loss of her career felt almost insignificant at that moment, compared to the greater grief she felt over Mark's vanishing.

'I've asked Dr O'Connor to evaluate you,' said Wettig. 'He'll be in sometime this evening.'

'I don't need a psychiatrist.'

'I think you do, Abby. I think you need a lot of help. You have to get beyond these delusions of persecution. I'm not going to approve your release until O'Connor clears it. He may decide to transfer you to the Psychiatry Unit. That's his call. We can't have you hurting yourself, the way you tried to last night. We're all very concerned about you, Abby. *I'm* concerned about you. That's why I'm ordering a psychiatric evaluation. It's for your own good, believe me.'

She looked straight up at him. 'Fuck you, General.'

To her immense satisfaction, he flinched and stepped away from the bed. He slapped the chart shut. 'I'll check in on you later, Dr DiMatteo,' he said, and left the room.

For a long time she stared at the ceiling. Only moments ago, before Wettig had walked in, she had felt too weary to fight. Now every muscle had tensed and her stomach was in turmoil. Her hands ached. She looked down and realized they were knotted into fists.

Fuck all of you.

She sat up. The dizziness lasted only a few seconds, then passed. She'd been lying in bed too long. It was time to get moving. To regain control of her life.

She crossed the room and opened the door a crack.

A nurse looked up from her desk and stared directly at Abby. Her name tag said W. SORIANO, R.N. 'Do you need something?'

'Uh, no,' said Abby, and quickly retreated back behind her closed door.

Shit. Shit, they were keeping her a prisoner.

In bare feet she paced a circle around the room, trying to plan her next move. She couldn't think about Mark right now. If she did, she'd just curl up in bed again, crying. That's what they wanted her to do, what they expected her to do.

She went to the chair by the window and sat down to think. She considered the moves open to her, but couldn't come up with any. Last night, Mark had said Mohandas was on their side, but now Mark was missing. She wasn't going to trust Mohandas. She wasn't going to trust anyone in this hospital.

She went to the nightstand and picked up the phone. There was a dial tone. She called Vivian's number, and got a recording. Then she remembered that Vivian was still in Burlington.

She called her own home, punched in her access code, and listened to the messages from her answering machine. There had been another call from Vivian, and by the tone of her voice, the call had been urgent. She'd left a Burlington number.

Abby dialed it.

This time Vivian answered. 'You barely caught me. I was just about to check out of here.'

'You're coming home?'

'I've got a six o'clock flight to Logan. Listen, this trip has been nothing but a wild goose chase. There were no harvests done in Burlington.'

'How do you know?'

'I checked the airport here. And every other airstrip in the area. On the nights of those transplants, there were no midnight flights logged out of here to Boston. Not a single dinky plane. Burlington's just a cover for them. And Tim Nicholls provided the official paperwork.'

'And now Nicholls has vanished.'

'Or they got rid of him.'

They both fell momentarily silent. Then Abby said, softly: 'Mark's missing.'

'What?'

'No one knows where he is. Detective Katzka says they can't find his car. And Mark doesn't answer his pages.' She paused, her throat closing over.

'Oh, Abby. Abby . . .' Vivian's voice faltered.

In the brief silence, Abby heard a click on the line. She was gripping the receiver so tightly her fingers ached.

'Vivian?' she said.

There was another click. And then the line went dead.

She hung up and tried to call again, but there was no dial tone. She tried the operator, tried hanging up again and again. Still no dial tone.

The hospital had disconnected her telephone.

Katzka stood on the narrow walkway of the Tobin Bridge and stared down at the water far below. From the west ran the Mystic River, on its way to join the waters of the Chelsea River before flowing out to Boston Harbor and the sea. It was a long drop, thought Katzka, imagining the force with which a body would impact on that water. Almost certainly a fatal drop.

Turning, he gazed past the late afternoon traffic whizzing by and focused on the downriver side of the bridge. He traced the hypothetical sequence of events that would follow a body's plunge. The corpse would be carried by the current into the harbor. At first, it would drift along below the water's surface, perhaps scraping across the bottom silt. Eventually the body's internal gases would expand. This would happen over a time span of hours to days. It depended on the water temperature and the speed with which the gas-forming bacteria multiplied in the rotting intestines. At a certain point, the corpse would float to the surface.

That's when it would be found. In a day or two. Bloated and unrecognizable.

Katzka turned to the patrolman standing beside him. He had to shout over the sound of traffic. 'What time did you notice the car?'

'Around five A.M. It was pulled over in the northbound breakdown lane. Right over there.'

He pointed across the lanes of whizzing cars. 'Nice green BMW. I stopped right away.'

'You didn't see anyone near the BMW?'

'No, sir. It looked abandoned. I called in the license number and confirmed it wasn't reported stolen. I figured maybe the driver had engine trouble and left to get help. It was a hazard to traffic, sitting there. So I called the tow truck.'

'No keys in the car? No note?'

'No, sir. Nothing. It was clean as a whistle inside.'

Katzka looked back down at the water. He wondered how deep the river was at this point, and how fast the current was moving.

'I did try calling Dr Hodell's home, but no one answered,' said the patrolman. 'I didn't know at the time that he was missing.'

Katzka said nothing. He just kept gazing down at the river, thinking about Abby, wondering what he should tell her. She had looked so heart-breakingly fragile in that hospital bed, and he couldn't bear the thought of inflicting any more blows. Any more pain.

I won't tell her. Not yet, he decided. *Not until we find a body.*

The patrolman looked down at the river, too. 'Jesus. Do you think he jumped?'

'If he's down there,' said Katzka, 'it wasn't because he jumped.'

The phones had been ringing all day, two LPNs had called in sick, and charge nurse Wendy

Soriano had missed lunch. She was in no mood to be pulling a double shift. Yet here she was at three thirty P.M., facing the prospect of another eight hours on duty.

Her kids had already called twice. *Mommy, Jeffy's hitting me again. Mommy, what time is Daddy coming home? Mommy, can we use the microwave? We promise we won't burn the house down.* Mommy, Mommy, Mommy.

Why didn't they ever bother Daddy at work?

Because Daddy's job is so much more fucking important.

Wendy dropped her head in her hands and stared down at the stack of charts flagged with doctors' orders. The residents loved to write orders. They breezed in with their fancy Cross pens and scribbled such earthshattering instructions as: 'Milk of magnesia for constipation,' or 'bedrails up at night.' Then they presented the flagged charts to the nurses like God passing instructions to Moses. *Thou shalt not tolerate constipation.*

With a sigh, Wendy reached for the first chart.

The phone rang. It better not be the kids again, she thought. Not another *Mommy he's hitting me* call. She answered it with an irritated: 'Six East, Wendy.'

'This is Dr Wettig.'

'Oh.' Automatically she sat up straight. One didn't slouch when speaking to Dr Wettig. Even if it was on the phone. 'Yes, Doctor?'

'I want to follow up that blood alcohol level on

460

Dr DiMatteo. And I want it sent out to MedMark Labs.'

'Not our lab?'

'No. Route it directly to MedMark.'

'Certainly, Doctor,' said Wendy, scribbling down the order. It was an unusual request, but one didn't question the General.

'How's she doing?' he asked.

'A little restless.'

'Has she tried to leave?'

'No. She hasn't even come out of the room.'

'Good. Make sure she stays there. And absolutely no visitors. That includes all medical personnel, except for the ones I specify in my orders.'

'Yes, Dr Wettig.'

Wendy hung up and stared at her desk. During that call, three more flagged charts had been deposited there. Damn. She'd be taking off order sheets all evening. Suddenly she felt dizzy from hunger. She still hadn't had lunch, hadn't even had a break in hours.

She glanced around, and saw two LPNs chatting in the hallway. Was she the only person working her butt off here?

She tore off the order for the blood alcohol level and deposited it in the lab tech's box. As she rose from the desk, the phone began to ring. She ignored it; after all, that's what ward clerks were for.

She walked away to the sound of two lines jangling.

For once, someone else could answer the damn phone.

The vampire was back, carrying her tray of blood tubes and lab slips and needles. 'I'm sorry, Dr DiMatteo. But I need to stick you again.'

Abby, standing at the window, merely glanced at the phlebotomist. Then she turned back to the view. 'This hospital's sucked all the blood I have to give,' she said, and stared at the dreary view beyond the window. In the parking lot below, nurses scurried for the hospital doors, hair flying, raincoats flapping in the wind. In the east, clouds had gathered, black and threatening. Will the skies never clear? wondered Abby.

Behind her came the clatter of glass tubes. 'Doctor, I really do have to get this blood.'

'I don't need any more tests.'

'But Dr Wettig ordered it.' The phlebotomist added, with a quiet note of desperation, 'Please don't make things hard for me.'

Abby turned and looked at the woman. She seemed very young. Abby was reminded of herself at some long-ago time. A time when she, too, was terrified of Wettig, of doing the wrong thing, of losing all she'd worked for. She was afraid of none of these things now. But this woman was.

Sighing, Abby went to the bed and sat down.

The phlebotomist set her blood tray on the bedside table and began opening sterile packets containing gauze, a disposable needle, and a Vacutainer syringe. Judging by the number of filled blood tubes in her tray, she had already gone through the motions dozens of times today. There were only a few empty slots remaining.

'Okay, which arm would you prefer?'

Abbey held out her arm and watched impassively as the rubber tourniquet was tucked into place with a snap. She made a fist. The antecubital vein swelled into view, bruised by all the earlier venipunctures. As the needle pierced her skin, Abby turned away. She looked, instead, at the phlebotomist's tray, at all the neatly labeled tubes of blood. A vampire's candy box.

Suddenly she focused on one specimen in particular, a purple-topped tube with the label facing toward her. She stared at the name.

VOSS, NINA
SICU BED 8

'There we go,' said the vampire, withdrawing the needle. 'Can you hold that gauze in place?'

Abby looked up. 'What?'

'Hold the gauze while I get you a Band-Aid.'

Automatically Abby pressed the gauze to her arm. She looked back at the tube containing Nina Voss's blood. The attending physician's name was just visible, at the corner of the label. *Dr Archer*.

Nina Voss is back in the hospital, thought Abby. *Back on cardiothoracic service*.

The phlebotomist left.

Abby paced over to the window and stared out at the darkening clouds. Scraps of paper were flying around the parking lot. The window rattled, buffeted by a fresh gust of wind.

Something has gone wrong with the new heart.

She should have realized that days ago, when they'd met in the limousine. She remembered Nina's appearance in the gloom of the car. The pale face, the bluish tinge of her lips. Even then, her transplant was already failing.

Abby went to the closet. There she found a bulging plastic bag labeled PATIENT BELONGINGS. It contained her shoes, her blood-stained slacks, and her purse. Her wallet was missing; it was probably locked up in the hospital safe. A thorough search of the purse turned up a few loose nickels and dimes in the bottom. She would need every last one.

She zipped on the slacks, tucked in her hospital gown top, and stepped into the shoes. Then she went to the door and peeked out.

Nurse Soriano wasn't at the desk. However, two other nurses were in the station, one talking on the phone, another bent over paperwork. Neither was looking in Abby's direction.

She glanced down the hall and saw the cart with the evening meal trays come rattling into the ward, pushed by an elderly volunteer in pink. The cart came to a stop in front of the nurses' desk. The volunteer pulled out two meal trays and carried them into a nearby patient room.

That's when Abby slipped out into the hall. The meal cart blocked the nurses' view as Abby walked calmly past their desk and out of the ward.

She couldn't risk being spotted on the elevators; she headed straight for the stairwell.

Six flights up she emerged on the twelfth floor. Straight ahead was the OR wing; around the corner was the SICU. From the linen cart in the OR hallway, she picked up a surgical gown, a flowered cap, and shoe covers. Completely garbed in blue like everyone else, she just might pass unnoticed.

She turned the corner and walked into the SICU.

Inside she found chaos. The patient in Bed 2 was coding. Judging by the tensely staccato voices and by all the personnel frantically pressing into the cubicle, the resuscitation was not going well. No one even glanced in Abby's direction as she walked past the monitor station and crossed to Cubicle 8.

She paused outside the viewing window just long enough to confirm that it was, indeed, Nina Voss in the bed. Then she pushed into the cubicle. The door swung shut behind her, muffling the voices of the code team. She pulled the curtains over the window, to shut off all view of the room, and turned to the bed.

Nina was sleeping, serenely unaware of the frantic activity going on beyond her closed door. She seemed to have shrunk since Abby had last seen her, like a candle slowly being consumed by the flame of her illness. The body beneath those sheets looked as small as a child's.

Abby picked up the nurses' clipboard hanging

at the foot of the bed. In a glance she took in all the parameters recorded there. The rising pulmonary wedge pressure. The slowly falling cardiac output. The upward titration of dobutamine in a futile attempt to boost cardiac performance.

Abby hung the clipboard back on the hook. As she straightened, she saw that Nina's eyes were open and staring at her.

'Hello, Mrs Voss,' said Abby.

Nina smiled and murmured, 'It's the doctor who always tells the truth.'

'How are you feeling?'

'Content.' Nina sighed. 'I am content.'

Abby moved to her bedside. They looked at each other, neither one speaking.

Then Nina said, 'You don't have to tell me. I already know.'

'Know what, Mrs Voss?'

'That it's almost over.' Nina closed her eyes and took a deep breath.

Abby took the other woman's hand. 'I never got the chance to thank you. For trying to help me.'

'It was Victor I was trying to help.'

'I don't understand.'

'He's like that man in the Greek myth. The one who went into Hades to bring back his wife.'

'Orpheus.'

'Yes. Victor is like Orpheus. He wants to bring me back. He doesn't care what it takes. What it costs.' She opened her eyes and her gaze was

466

startlingly clear. 'In the end,' she whispered, 'it will cost him too much.'

They were not speaking of money. Abby understood that at once. They were speaking of souls.

The cubicle door suddenly opened. Abby turned to see a nurse staring at her in surprise.

'Oh! Dr DiMatteo, what are you . . .' She glanced at the closed curtains, then her gaze swiftly assessed all the monitors and IV lines. *Checking for signs of sabotage.*

'I haven't touched anything,' said Abby.

'Would you please leave?'

'I was only visiting. I heard she was back in SICU and—'

'Mrs Voss needs her rest.' The nurse opened the door and swiftly ushered Abby out of the cubicle. 'Didn't you see the NO VISITORS sign? She's scheduled for surgery tonight. She can't be disturbed.'

'What surgery?'

'The retransplant. They found a donor.'

Abby stared at the closed door to Cubicle 8. She asked, softly, 'Does Mrs Voss know?'

'What?'

'Did she sign the consent form for surgery?'

'Her husband's already signed it for her. Now please leave *immediately.*'

Without another word, Abby turned and walked out of the unit. She didn't know if anyone noticed her departure; she just kept walking down the hall until she'd reached the elevators. The door opened; the car was filled with people. She stepped

467

inside and quickly turned her back to the other passengers and faced the door.

They found a donor, she thought, as the elevator descended. *Somehow they found a donor. Tonight, Nina Voss will have a new heart.*

By the time the car reached the lobby, she had already worked out the sequence of events that would be taking place tonight. She had read the records of other Bayside transplants; she knew what was going to happen. Sometime around midnight, they would wheel Nina into the OR, where Archer's team would prep and drape her. There they would wait for the call. And at that precise moment, a different surgical team in a different OR would already be gathered around another patient. They would reach for scalpels and begin to slice skin and muscle. Bone saws would grind. Ribs would be lifted, exposing the treasure within. A living, beating heart.

The harvest would be swift and clean.

Tonight, she thought, *it will happen just the way it has before.*

The elevator door opened. She stepped out, head bowed, eyes focused on the floor. She walked out the front doors and into a driving wind.

Two blocks away, cold and shaking, she ducked into a phone booth. Using her precious cache of nickels and dimes, she called Katzka's number.

He wasn't at his desk. The policeman who answered the extension offered to take a message.

'This is Abby DiMatteo,' she said. 'I have to talk to him now! Doesn't he have a pager or something?'

'Let me transfer you to the operator.'

She heard two transfer clicks, then the operator came on. 'I'll have Dispatch radio his car now,' she said.

A moment later, the operator came back on. 'I'm sorry, we're still waiting for Detective Katzka to respond. Can he reach you at your current number?'

'Yes. I mean, I don't know. I'll try calling him later.' Abby hung up. She was out of coins, out of phone calls.

She turned and looked out the phone booth, and saw scraps of newspapers tumbling by. She didn't want to step out into that wind again, but she didn't know what else to do.

There was one more person she could call.

Half the phone book had been torn away. With a sense of futility, she flipped through the white pages anyway. She was startled to actually find the listing: *I. Tarasoff.*

Her hands were shaking as she dialed collect. *Please talk to me. Please take my call.*

After four rings she heard his gentle 'Hello?' She could hear chinaware clattering, the sounds of a dinner table being set, the sweet strains of classical music. Then: 'Yes, I'll accept the charges.'

She was so relieved, her words spilled out in a rush. 'I didn't know who else to call! I can't reach Vivian. And no one else will listen to me. *You* have to go to the police. *Make* them listen!'

'Now slow down, Abby. Tell me what's happening.'

She took a deep breath. Felt her heart thudding with the need to share her burden. 'Nina Voss is getting a second transplant tonight,' she said. 'Dr Tarasoff, I think I know how it works. They don't fly the hearts in from somewhere else. The harvests are done right *here*. In *Boston*.'

'Where? Which hospital?'

Her gaze suddenly focused on a car moving slowly up the street. She held her breath until the car continued around the corner and vanished.

'Abby?'

'Yes. I'm still here.'

'Now Abby, I understand from Mr Parr that you've been under a great strain lately. Isn't it possible this is—'

'*Listen. Please listen to me!*' She closed her eyes, forcing herself to stay calm. To sound rational. He must not have any doubts at all about her sanity. 'Vivian called me today from Burlington. She found out there weren't any harvests done there. The organs didn't come from Vermont.'

'Then where are the harvests done?'

'I'm not entirely sure. But I'm guessing they're done in a building in Roxbury. Amity Medical Supplies. The police have to get there before midnight. Before the harvest can be done.'

'I don't know if I can convince them.'

'You *have* to! There's a Detective Katzka, in Homicide. If we can reach him, I think he'll listen to us. Dr Tarasoff, this isn't just an organ matchmaking service. They're generating donors. They're *killing* people.'

In the background, Abby heard a woman call out: 'Ivan, aren't you going to eat your dinner? It's getting cold.'

'I'll have to skip it, dear,' said Tarasoff. 'There's been an emergency . . .' His voice came back on the line, soft and urgent. 'I don't think I need to tell you that this whole thing scares me, Abby.'

'It scares the hell out of me, too.'

'Then let's just drive straight to the police. Drop it in *their* laps. It's too dangerous for us to handle.'

'Agreed. One hundred percent.'

'We'll do it together. The bigger the chorus, the more convincing our message.'

She hesitated. 'I'm afraid that having me along may hurt the cause.'

'I don't know all the details, Abby. *You* do.'

'Okay,' she said, after a pause. 'Okay. We'll go together. Could you come and get me? I'm freezing. And I'm scared.'

'Where are you?'

She glanced out the phone booth window. Two blocks away, the lights of the hospital towers seemed to pulsate in the blowing darkness. 'I'm in a phone booth. I don't know which street it's on. I'm a few blocks west of Bayside.'

'I'll find you.'

'Dr Tarasoff?'

'Yes?'

'Please,' she whispered. 'Hurry.'

471

Twenty-four

As Vivian Chao's plane touched down at Logan International, she felt her anxiety tighten another notch. It wasn't the flight that had rattled her. Vivian was a fearless flyer, able to sleep soundly through even the worst turbulence. No, what was worrying her now, as the plane pulled up at the gate and as she gathered her carry-on from the overhead bin, was that last phone conversation with Abby. The abrupt disconnection. The fact that Abby had never called back.

Vivian had tried calling Abby at home, but there'd been no answer. Thinking about it during the flight, she'd realized that she didn't know where Abby had been calling from. Their connection had been severed too quickly for her to find out.

Lugging her carry-on, she walked off the plane and into the terminal. She was startled to find a huge crowd waiting at the gate. There was a forest of bright balloons and mobs of teenagers holding up signs that read *Welcome home, Dave!* and *Atta*

Boy and *Local Hero!* Whoever Dave was, he had an adoring public. She heard cheers, and glancing back, she saw a grinning young man stride out of the elevated walkway right behind her. The crowd surged forward, practically swallowing up Vivian in their eagerness to greet Dave, the local hero. Vivian had to navigate through a crush of squealing kids.

Kids, hell. They all towered over her by at least a head.

It took good old quarterback drive to shove her way through. By the time she emerged from the mob, she was pushing ahead with so much momentum, she practically bowled over a man standing on the periphery. She muttered a quick apology and kept walking. It took her a few paces to realize he hadn't said a word in exchange.

Her first stop was the restroom. All this anxiety was putting the squeeze on her bladder. She ducked inside to use the toilet and came back out.

That's when she saw the man again – the one she'd bumped into only moments ago. He was standing by the gift shop across from the women's restroom. He appeared to be reading a newspaper. She knew it was him because the collar of his raincoat was turned under. When she'd collided with him earlier, that inside-out flap was what her eyes had focused on.

She continued walking, toward baggage claim.

It was during that long hike past an endless succession of airline gates that her brain finally clicked on. Why was the man waiting at her gate unless he was there to meet someone? And if he *had* met a passenger, why was he now by himself?

She stopped at a newsstand, randomly picked up a magazine, and took it to the cashier. As the woman rang up the purchase, Vivian shifted just enough to cast a furtive glance around her.

The man was standing by a do-it yourself flight insurance counter. He seemed to be reading the instructions.

Okay, Chao, so he's following you. Maybe it's a case of love at first sight. Maybe he took one look at you and decided he couldn't let you walk out of his life.

As she paid for the magazine, she could feel her heart hammering. *Think. Why is he following you?*

That one was easy. The phone call from Abby. If anyone had been listening in, they'd know that Vivian was arriving at Logan on a six P.M. flight from Burlington. Just before the call was disconnected, she'd heard clicks on the line.

She decided to hang around the newsstand shop for a while. She browsed among the paperbacks, her eyes scanning the covers, her mind racing. The man probably didn't have a weapon on him; he would have had to bring it through the security check. As long as she didn't leave the airport's secured area, she should be safe.

Cautiously she peered over the paperback shelf.

The man wasn't there.

She came out of the shop and glanced around. There was no sign of him anywhere.

You are such an idiot. No one's following you.

She continued walking, past the security check and down the steps to baggage claim.

The suitcases from the Burlington flight were just rolling onto the carousel. She spotted her red Samsonite sliding down the ramp. She was about to push closer when she spotted the man in the raincoat. He was standing near the terminal exit, reading his newspaper.

At once she looked away, her pulse battering her throat. He was waiting for her to pick up her luggage. To walk past him out that exit, into the night.

Her red Samsonite made another revolution.

She took a deep breath and edged into the crowd of passengers waiting for their baggage. Her Samsonite was coming past again. She didn't pick it up but casually followed it around as it made its slow circle. When she was standing on the other side of the carousel, the crowd blocked her view of the man in the raincoat.

She dropped her carry-on bag and ran.

There were two carousels ahead of her, both of them unused at the moment. She sprinted past them, then darted out the far exit doors.

She emerged into the windblown night. Off to her left she heard a commotion. The man in the raincoat had just pushed his way out of the other exit. A second man came out a few steps behind him. One of them pointed at Vivian and barked out something incomprehensible.

Vivian took off, fleeing up the sidewalk. She

knew the men were chasing her; she could hear the thud of a luggage cart toppling and the angry shouts of a porter.

There was a *pop*, and she felt something flick through her hair.

A bullet.

Her heart was banging, her lungs gasping in air thick with bus fumes.

She saw a doorway ahead. She ducked in it and raced for the nearest escalator. The moving stairs were going the wrong way. She ran up them two at a time. As she reached the upper level, she heard another *pop*. This time pain sliced her temple, and she felt a dribble of warmth on her cheek.

The American Airlines ticket counter was straight ahead. It was fully manned, a line of people snaking in front of it.

She heard footsteps pounding on the escalator behind her. Heard one of the men shouting words she couldn't understand.

She sprinted for the ticket counter, bowled over a man and a suitcase dolly, and leaped onto the countertop. Her momentum carried her straight over. She landed on the other side, her body slamming against the luggage loading belt.

Four astonished airline reps were staring down at her.

Her legs were shaking as she rose to her feet. Cautiously she peered across the countertop. She saw only a crowd of stunned bystanders. The men had vanished.

Vivian looked at the reps, who were still frozen

in place. 'Well, aren't you going to call Security?'

Wordlessly, one of the women reached for the phone.

'And while you're at it,' said Vivian, 'dial nine-one-one.'

A dark Mercedes crawled along the road and came to a stop beside the phone booth. Abby could just make out the driver's profile, backlit by the lights of a passing car. It was Tarasoff.

She ran to the passenger door and climbed inside. 'Thank God you're here.'

'You must be freezing. Why don't you take my coat? It's on the back seat.'

'Please, just go! Let's get out of here.'

As Tarasoff pulled away from the curb, she glanced back to see if anyone was following them. The road behind them was dark.

'Do you see any cars?' he asked.

'No. I think we're okay.'

Tarasoff released a shaky breath. 'I'm not very good at this. I don't even like to watch crime shows.'

'You're doing fine. Just get us to the police station. We can call Vivian to meet us there.'

Tarasoff glanced nervously in the rearview mirror. 'I think I just saw a car.'

'What?' Abby looked back, but saw nothing.

'I'm going to turn here. Let's see what happens.'

'Go ahead. I'll keep watching.'

As they rounded the corner, Abby kept her gaze focused on the road behind them. She saw no headlights, no other cars at all. Only when they slowed to a stop did she turn and face forward. 'What's wrong?'

'Nothing's wrong.' Tarasoff cut the headlights.

'Why are you . . .' Abby's words froze in her throat.

Tarasoff had just pressed the lock release button.

She glanced right in panic as her door swung open. A gust of wind swept in. Suddenly hands reached in and she was being dragged out into the night. Her hair fell across her eyes, obscuring her vision. She fought blindly against her captors but could not succeed in loosening their grips. Her hands were yanked behind her back and the wrists bound together. Her mouth was taped. Then she was lifted and thrust into the trunk of a nearby car.

The hood slammed shut, trapping her in darkness.

They were moving.

She rolled onto her back and kicked upward. Again and again she slammed her feet against the trunk lid, kicking until her thighs ached, until she could scarcely lift her legs. It was useless; no one could hear her.

Exhausted, she curled up on her side and forced herself to think.

Tarasoff. How is Tarasoff involved?

Slowly the puzzle came together, piece by piece. Lying in the cramped darkness, with the road rumbling beneath her, she began to understand.

Tarasoff was chief of one of the most respected cardiac transplant teams on the East Coast. His reputation attracted desperately ill patients from around the world, patients with the wherewithal to go to any surgeon they chose. They demanded the best, and they could afford to pay for it.

What they could not buy, what the system would never allow them to buy, was what they needed to stay alive: hearts. Human hearts.

That's what the Bayside transplant team could provide. She remembered what Tarasoff had once said: '*I refer patients to Bayside all the time.*'

He was Bayside's go-between. He was their matchmaker.

She felt the car brake and turn. The tires rolled across gravel, then stopped. There was a distant roar, a sound she recognized as a jet taking off. She knew exactly where they were.

The trunk hood opened. She was lifted out, into a buffeting wind that smelled of diesel fuel and the sea. They half-carried, half-dragged her down the pier and up the gangplank. Her screams were muffled by the tape over her mouth and lost in the thunder of the jet's takeoff. She caught only a glimpse of the freighter deck, of shifting blackness and geometric shadows, and then she was dragged below, down steps that rattled and clanged. One flight, then another.

A door screeched open and she was thrust inside, into darkness. Her hands were still bound behind her back; she could not break her fall. Her chin slammed to the metal floor and the impact was blinding. She was too stunned to move, to utter even a whimper as pain drove like a stake through her skull.

Another set of footsteps clanged down the stairway. Dimly she heard Tarasoff say: 'At least it's not a total waste. Take the tape off her mouth. We can't have her suffocating.'

She rolled onto her back and struggled to focus. She could make out Tarasoff's silhouette, standing in the faintly lit doorway. She flinched as one of the men bent down and ripped off the tape.

'Why?' she whispered. It was the only question she could think of. '*Why?*'

The silhouette gave a faint shrug, as though her question was irrelevant. The other two men backed out of the room. They were preparing to shut her inside.

'Is it the money?' she cried. 'Is it that simple an answer?'

'Money means nothing,' Tarasoff said, 'if it can't buy you what you need.'

'Like a heart?'

'Like the life of your own child. Or your own wife, your own sister or brother. You, of all people, should understand that, Dr DiMatteo. We know all about little Pete and his accident. Only ten years old, wasn't he? We know you've lived through your own private tragedy. Think, Doctor, what would you have given to have saved your brother's life?'

She said nothing. By her silence, he knew her answer.

'Wouldn't you have given anything? Done everything?'

Yes, she thought, and that admission took no reflection at all. *Yes*.

'Imagine what it's like,' he said, 'to watch your own child dying. To have all the money in the world and know that she still has to wait her turn in line. Behind the alcoholics and the drug abusers. And the mentally incompetent. And the welfare cheats who haven't worked a single day in their lives.' He paused. And said, softly, 'Imagine.'

The door swung shut. The latch squealed into place.

She was lying in pitch darkness. She heard the rattle of the stairway as the three men climbed back to deck level, heard the faint thud of a hatch closing. Then, for a time, she heard only the wind and the groan of the ship straining at its lines.

Imagine.

She closed her eyes and tried not to think of Pete. But there he was standing in front of her, proudly dressed in his Cub Scout uniform. She thought of what he'd said when he was five: that Abby was the only girl he wanted to marry. And she thought of how upset he'd been to learn that he could not marry his own sister . . .

What would I have done to save you? Anything. Everything.

In the darkness, something rustled.

Abby froze. She heard it again, the barest whisper of movement. *Rats.*

She squirmed away from the sound and

managed to rise up onto her knees. She could see nothing, could only imagine giant rodents scurrying on the floor all around her. She struggled to her feet.

There was a soft *click*.

The sudden flare of light flooded her retinas. She jerked backward. A bare bulb swung overhead, clinking softly against the dangling pull-chain.

It was not a rat she had heard moving in the darkness. It was a boy.

They stared at each other, neither one of them saying a word. Though he stood very still, she could see the wariness in his eyes. His legs, thin and bare beneath shorts, were tensed for flight. But there was nowhere to run.

He looked about ten, very pale and very blond, his hair almost silver under the swaying lightbulb. She noticed a bluish smudge on his cheek, and realized with a sudden start of outrage that the smudge was not dirt, but a bruise. His deep-set eyes were like two more bruises in his white face.

She took a step toward him. At once he backed away. 'I won't hurt you,' she said. 'I just want to talk to you.'

A frown flickered across his forehead. He shook his head.

'I promise. I won't hurt you.'

The boy said something, but his answer was incomprehensible to her. Now it was her turn to frown and shake her head.

They looked at each other in shared bewilderment.

Suddenly they both glanced upward. The ship's engines had just started up.

Abby tensed, listening to the rattle of chain, the squeal of hydraulics. Moments later, she felt the rocking of the hull as it cut through the water. They had left the dock and were now under way.

Even if I get out of these bonds, out of this room, there's nowhere for me to run.

In despair, she looked back at the boy.

He was no longer paying any attention to the sound of the engines. Instead, his gaze had dropped to her waist. Slowly he edged sideways and stared at her bound wrists, tucked close to her back. He looked down at his own arm. Only then did Abby see that his left hand was missing, that his forearm ended in a stump. He had held it close to his body, concealing the deformity from her view. Now he seemed to be studying it.

He looked back at her and spoke again.

'I can't understand what you're saying,' she said.

He repeated himself, this time with an edge of petulance in his voice. Why *couldn't* she understand? What was wrong with her?

She simply shook her head.

They regarded each other in mutual frustration. Then the boy lifted his chin. She realized that he had come to some sort of decision. He circled around to her back and tugged at her wrists, trying to loosen the bonds with his one hand. The cord was too tightly knotted. Now he knelt on the floor behind her. She felt the nip of his teeth, the heat of his breath against her skin. As the light-bulb swayed overhead, he began to gnaw, like a small but determined mouse, at her bonds.

'I'm sorry, but visiting hours are over,' said a nurse. 'Wait, you can't go in there. Stop!'

Katzka and Vivian walked straight past the nurses' desk and pushed into Room 621. 'Where's Abby?' demanded Katzka.

Dr Colin Wettig turned to look at them. 'Dr DiMatteo is missing.'

'You told me she'd be watched here,' said Katzka. 'You assured me nothing could happen to her.'

'She *was* watched. No one came in here without my express orders.'

'Then what happened to her?'

'That's a question you'll have to ask Dr DiMatteo.'

It was Wettig's flat voice that angered Katzka. That and the emotionless gaze. Here was a man who revealed nothing, a man in control. Staring at Wettig's unreadable face, Katzka suddenly recognized himself, and the revelation was startling.

'She was under *your* care, Doctor. What've you people done with her?'

'I don't like your implications.'

Katzka crossed the room, grabbed the lapels of Wettig's lab coat, and shoved him backward against the wall. 'Goddamn you,' he said, '*Where did you take her?*'

Wettig's blue eyes at last betrayed a flicker of fear. 'I told you, I don't know where she is! The nurses called me at six-thirty to tell me she was gone. We've alerted Security. They've already searched the hospital but they can't find her.'

'You know where she is, don't you?'

Wettig shook his head.

'*Don't you?*' Katzka gave him another shove.

'I don't know!' gasped Wettig.

Vivian stepped forward and tried to pull them apart. 'Stop it! You're choking him! Katzka, let him *go!*'

Abruptly Katzka released Wettig. The older man swayed backward against the wall, breathing heavily. 'I thought, given her delusional state, she'd be safer in the hospital.' Wettig straightened and rubbed his neck where the collar of the lab coat had left a bright red strangulation mark. Katzka stared at the mark, shocked by the evidence of his own violence.

'I didn't realize,' said Wettig, 'that she might be telling the truth after all.' Wettig pulled a slip of paper from his pocket and handed it to Vivian. 'The nurses just gave that to me.'

'What is it?' said Katzka.

Vivian frowned. 'This is Abby's blood alcohol level. It says here it's zero.'

'I had it redrawn this afternoon and sent to an independent lab,' Wettig explained. 'She kept insisting she hadn't been intoxicated. I thought, if

I could confront her with undeniable evidence, that I could break through her denial . . .'

'This result is from an outside lab?'

Wettig nodded. 'Completely independent of Bayside.'

'You told me her alcohol was point two-one.'

'That was the one done at four A.M. in Bayside's lab.'

Vivian said, 'The half-life of blood alcohol ranges anywhere from two to fourteen hours. If it was that high at four A.M., then this test should show at least a trace left.'

'But there's no alcohol in her system,' said Katzka.

'Which tells me that either her liver is amazingly fast at metabolizing it,' said Wettig, 'or Bayside's lab made a mistake.'

'Is that what you're calling it?' said Katzka. 'A mistake?'

Wettig said nothing. He looked drained. And very old. He sat down on the rumpled bed. 'I didn't realize . . . didn't want to consider the possibility . . .'

'That Abby was telling the truth?' said Vivian.

Wettig shook his head. 'My God,' he murmured. 'This hospital should be shut down. If what she's been saying is true.'

Katzka felt Vivian's gaze. He looked at her.

She said, softly: 'Now do you have any doubts?'

For hours the boy had slept in her arms, his breath puffing out warm whispers against her neck. He lay limp, arms and legs askew, the way children do when they are deeply, trustingly asleep. He had been shivering when she'd first embraced him. She'd massaged his bare legs, and it was like rubbing cold, dry sticks. Eventually his shaking had stopped, and as his breathing slowed, she'd felt that flush of warmth that children give off when they finally fall asleep.

She, too, slept for a while.

When she woke up, the wind was blowing harder. She could hear it in the groaning of the ship. Overhead, the bare lightbulb swayed back and forth.

The boy whimpered and stirred. There was something touching about the smell of young boys, she thought, like the scent of warm grass. Something about the sweet androgyny of their bodies. She remembered how her brother Pete had felt, sagging against her shoulder as he slept in the backseat of the family car. For miles and miles, while their father drove, Abby had felt the gentle drumming of Pete's heart. Just as she was feeling this boy's heart now, beating in its cagelike chest.

He gave a soft moan and shuddered awake. Looking up at her, recognition slowly dawned in his eyes.

'Ah-bee,' he whispered.

She nodded. 'That's right. Abby. You remembered.' Smiling, she stroked his face, her finger tracing across the bruise. 'And you're . . . Yakov.'

He nodded.

They both smiled.

Outside, the wind groaned and Abby felt the floor rock beneath them. Shadows swayed across the boy's face. He was watching her with an almost hungry look.

'Yakov,' she said again. She brushed her mouth across one silky blond eyebrow. When she lifted her head, she felt the wetness on her lips. Not the boy's tears, but hers. She turned her face against her shoulder to wipe away the tears. When she looked back at him, she saw he was still watching her with that strange, rapt silence of his.

'I'm right here,' she murmured. And, smiling, she brushed her fingers through his hair.

After a while his eyelids drifted shut and his body relaxed once again into the trusting limpness of sleep.

'So much for the search warrant,' said Lundquist, and he kicked the door. It flew open and banged against the wall. Cautiously he edged into the room and froze. 'What the fuck is all this?'

Katzka flipped on the wall switch.

Both men blinked as light flooded their eyes. It shone down with blinding intensity from three overhead lamps. Everywhere Katzka looked, he saw gleaming surfaces. Stainless steel cabinets. Instrument trays and IV poles. Monitors studded with knobs and switches.

In the center of the room was an operating table.

Katzka approached the table and stared down at the straps hanging from the sides. Two for the wrists, two for the ankles, two longer straps for the waist and chest.

His gaze moved to the anesthesia cart set up at the head of the table. He went to it and slid open the top drawer. Inside lay a row of glass syringes and needles capped in plastic.

'What the hell is this doing here?' said Lundquist.

Katzka closed the drawer and opened the next one. Inside he saw small glass vials. He took one out. *Potassium chloride*. It was half empty. 'This equipment's being used,' he said.

'This is bizarre. What kind of surgery were they doing up here?'

Katzka looked at the table again. At the straps. Suddenly he thought of Abby, her wrists tied down on the bed, tears trickling down her face. The memory was so painful he gave his head a shake to dispel the image. Fear was making it hard for him to think. If he couldn't think, he couldn't help her. He couldn't save her. Abruptly he moved away from the table.

'Slug?' Lundquist was eyeing him in puzzlement. 'You okay?'

'Yeah.' Katzka turned and walked out the door. 'I'm fine.'

Back outside on the sidewalk, he stood in the gusting wind and looked up at the Amity building. From street level, one saw nothing unusual about it. It was just another run-down building on a rundown street. Dirty brownstone façade, windows with air conditioners jutting out. When he had been inside it the day before, he had seen only what he'd expected to see. What he was supposed to see. The dingy showroom, the battered desks piled high with supply catalogs. A few salesmen listlessly talking on telephones. He had not seen the top floor, had never suspected that a single elevator ride would bring him to that room.

To that table with its straps.

Less than an hour ago, Lundquist had traced the building's ownership to the Sigayev Company – the same New Jersey company to which the freighter was registered. That Russian mafia connection again. How deep into Bayside did it reach? Or were the Russians merely allied with someone inside the hospital? A trading partner, perhaps, in black market goods?

Lundquist's beeper chirped. He glanced at the readout, and reached into the car for the cellular phone.

Katzka remained in front of the building, his thoughts shifting back to Abby and where he should look next. Every room of the hospital had already been searched. So had the parking lot and the surrounding areas. It appeared that Abby had left the hospital on her own. Where would she go? Whom would she have called? It would have been someone she trusted.

'Slug!'

Katzka turned to see Lundquist waving the telephone. 'Who's on the line?'

'The Coast Guard. They've got a chopper waiting for us.'

* * *

Footsteps clanged on the stairway.

Abby's head snapped up. In her arms, Yakov slept on, unaware. Her heart was thundering so hard she thought it would surely wake him, but he didn't stir.

The door swung open. Tarasoff, flanked by two men, stood looking in at her. 'It's time to go.'

'Where?' she said.

'Only a short walk.' Tarasoff glanced at Yakov. 'Wake him up. He comes too.'

Abby hugged Yakov closer. 'Not the boy,' she said.

'Especially the boy.'

She shook her head. 'Why?'

'He's AB positive. The only AB we happen to have in stock at the moment.'

She stared at Tarasoff. Then she looked down at Yakov, his face flushed with sleep. Through his thin chest she could feel the beating of his heart. *Nina Voss*, she thought. *Nina Voss is AB positive . . .*

One of the men grabbed her arm and hauled her to her feet. She lost her grip on the boy; he tumbled to the floor where he lay blinking in confusion. The other man gave Yakov a sharp prod with his foot and barked a command in Russian.

The boy sleepily stumbled to his feet.

Tarasoff led the way. Down a dim corridor, then through a locked hatch. Up a staircase and through another hatch, to a steel walkway. Straight ahead was a blue door. Tarasoff started toward it, the walkway rattling under his weight.

Suddenly the boy balked. He twisted free and started to run back the way they'd come. One of the men snagged him by the shirt. Yakov spun around and sank his teeth into the man's arm. Howling in pain, the man slapped Yakov across the face. The impact was so brutal it sent the boy sprawling.

'Stop it!' screamed Abby.

The man jerked Yakov to his feet and gave him another slap. Now the boy stumbled toward Abby. At once she swept him up into her arms. Yakov clung to her, sobbing into her shoulder. The man moved toward her, as though to separate them.

'You stay the fuck away from him!' Abby yelled.

Yakov was shaking, whimpering incomprehensibly. She pressed her lips to his hair and whispered: 'Sweetheart, I'm with you. I'm right here with you.'

The boy raised his head. Looking into his terrified eyes, she thought: *He knows what's going to happen to us.*

She was shoved forward, across the walkway, and through the blue door.

They passed into a different world.

The corridor beyond was paneled in bleached wood, the floor was white linoleum. Overhead glowed a haze of softly diffused light. Their footsteps echoed as they walked past a spiral staircase and turned a corner. At the end of the passage was a wide door.

The boy was shaking even harder now. And he was getting heavy. She set him down on his feet and cupped his face in her hand. Just for a second their gazes met, and what could not be communicated in words was now shared in that single look. She took Yakov's hand and gave it a squeeze. Together they walked toward the door. One man was in front of them, one behind them. Tarasoff was in the lead. As he unlocked the door, Abby shifted her weight forward, every muscle tensing for the next move. Already she had released Yakov's hand.

Tarasoff pushed the door and it swung open, revealing a room of stark white.

Abby lunged. Her shoulder slammed into the man in front of her, shoving him against Tarasoff, who stumbled across the threshold to his knees.

'You bastards!' yelled Abby, flailing at them. '*You bastards!*'

The man behind her tried to seize her arms. She twisted around and swung at his face, her fist connecting in a satisfying thud. She spied a flash of movement. It was Yakov, darting away and vanishing around the corner. Now the man she'd shoved was on his feet again, coming at her from the other direction. Together the two men trapped her between them and lifted her from the floor. She didn't stop fighting and thrashing as they carried her through the doorway into the white room.

'You've got to control her!' said Tarasoff.

'The boy—'

'Forget the boy! He can't go anywhere. Get her up on the table!'

'She won't hold still!'

'*Bastards!*' Abby screamed, kicking one leg free.

She heard Tarasoff fumbling in cabinets. He snapped: 'Give me her arm! I need to get at her arm!'

Tarasoff approached, syringe in hand. Abby cried out as the needle plunged in. She twisted, but couldn't break free. She twisted again, and this time her limbs barely responded. She was having trouble seeing now. Her eyelids wouldn't stay open. Her voice came out barely a sigh. She tried to scream, but could not even draw the next breath.

What is wrong with me? Why can't I move?

'Get her in the next room!' said Tarasoff. 'We have to intubate now or we're going to lose her.'

The men carried her into the adjoining room and slid her onto a table. Lights came on overhead, searingly bright. Though fully awake, fully aware, she could not move a muscle. But she could feel everything. The straps tightening around her wrists and ankles. The pressure of Tarasoff's hand on her forehead, tipping her head back. The cold steel blade of the laryngoscope sliding into her throat. Her shriek of horror echoed only in her head; no sound came out. She felt the plastic ET tube snaking down her throat, gagging, suffocating her as it moved past her vocal cords and into her trachea. She could not turn away, could not even fight for air. The tube was taped to her face and connected to an ambubag. Tarasoff squeezed the bag and Abby's chest rose and fell in three quick, lifesaving breaths. Now he took off the ambubag and connected the ET tube to a ventilator. The machine took over, pumping air into her lungs at regular intervals.

'Now go get the boy!' snapped Tarasoff. 'No, not both of you. I need someone to assist.'

One of the men left. The other stepped closer to the table.

'Fasten that chest strap,' said Tarasoff. 'The succinylcholine will wear off in another minute or two. We can't have her thrashing around while I start the IV.'

Succinylcholine. This is how Aaron died. Unable to struggle. Unable to breathe.

Already the drug's effect was starting to fade. She could feel her chest muscles begin to spasm against the insult of that tube. And she could raise her eyelids now, could see the face of the man standing above her. He was cutting away her clothes, his gaze flickering with interest as he bared her breasts, then her abdomen.

Tarasoff started the IV in her arm. As he straightened, he saw that Abby's eyes were fully open now and staring at him. He read the question in her gaze.

'A healthy liver,' he said, 'is not something we can take for granted. There's a gentleman in Connecticut who's been waiting over a year for a donor.' Tarasoff reached for a second IV bag and he hung it on the pole. Then he looked at her. 'He was delighted to hear we've finally found a match.'

All that blood they drew from me in the ER, she thought. *They used it for tissue typing.*

He continued with his tasks. Connecting the second bag to the line. Drawing medications into syringes. She could only look at him mutely as the ventilator pumped air into her lungs. Her muscle function was beginning to return. Already she could wiggle her fingers, could shrug her shoulders. A drop of perspiration slid down her temple. She was sweating with the effort to move. To regain control of her body. A clock on the wall read eleven-fifteen.

Tarasoff had finished laying out the tray of syringes. He heard the sound of the door open and shut again, and he turned. 'The boy's loose,' he said. 'They're still hunting him down. So we'll take the liver first.'

Footsteps approached the table. Another face came into view and stared down at Abby.

So many times before she had looked across the operating table at that face. So many times before, she had seen those eyes smiling at her above a surgical mask. They were not smiling now.

No, she sobbed, but the only sound that came out was the soft rush of air through the ET tube. *No . . .*

It was Mark.

Twenty-five

Gregor knew that the only way out of the ship's aft section was through the blue door, and it was locked. The boy must have gone up the spiral staircase.

Gregor peered up at the steps, but he saw only curving shadows. He began to climb, the flimsy staircase ringing with his weight. His arm still throbbed where the boy had bit him. The little bastard. This one had caused trouble from the start.

He reached the next level and stepped off the staircase, onto thick carpet. He was now in the living quarters of the surgeon and the surgeon's assistant. To the aft were two private cabins with a shared head and a shower. At the forward end was a well-appointed saloon. The only way out of this section was back down the staircase. The boy was trapped.

Gregor headed aft first.

The first cabin he came to was the dead surgeon's. It stank of tobacco. He flicked on the light and saw an unmade bed, a locker with the door hanging open, a desk with an overflowing ashtray. He crossed to the locker. Inside he found clothes reeking of smoke, an empty vodka bottle, and a secret stash of pornographic magazines. No boy.

Gregor next searched the surgical assistant's cabin. It was far more orderly, the bed made, the clothes in the locker neatly pressed. No boy in here either.

He glanced in the head, then started toward the saloon. Before he reached it, he heard the noise. It was a muffled whine.

He entered the saloon and turned on the lights. Quickly his gaze swept the room, taking in the couch, the dining table and chairs, and the television set with its stack of videotapes. Where was the boy? He circled the room, then stopped, staring at the forward wall.

The dumbwaiter.

He ran to it and pried open the doors. All he saw were cables. He slapped the Up button, and the cables began to move, groaning as they lifted their burden. Gregor leaned forward, ready to snatch hold of the boy.

Instead he found himself staring at the empty dumbwaiter.

The boy had already escaped into the galley.

Gregor headed back down the staircase. This was not a catastrophe. The galley was already secured. Gregor had started padlocking it every night, after discovering that the crew was sneaking food out of the pantry. The boy was still trapped.

Gregor pushed through the blue door and started across the walkway.

'I'm sorry, Abby,' said Mark. 'I never thought it would go this far.'

Please, she thought. *Please don't do this . . .*

'If there was any other way . . .' He shook his head. 'You pushed it too hard. And then I couldn't stop you. I couldn't control you.'

A tear slid from her eye and trickled into her hair. Just for an instant, she saw a flash of pain in his face. He turned away.

'It's time to gown up,' said Tarasoff. 'Will you do the honors?' He held out a syringe to Mark. 'Pentobarb. We want to be humane about this, after all.'

Mark hesitated. Then he took the syringe and turned to the IV pole. He uncapped the needle and poked it into the injection port. Again he hesitated. He looked at Abby.

I loved you, she thought. *I loved you so much.*

He pushed the plunger.

The lights began to dim. She saw his face waver, then fade into a deepening pool of gray.

I loved you.

I loved you . . .

The galley door was locked.

Yakov tugged again and again at the knob, but the door would not budge. What now? The dumbwaiter again? He scurried back to it and pressed the button. Nothing happened.

Frantically he glanced around the galley, considering all the possible hiding places. The pantry. The cupboards. The walk-in refrigerator. All of them offered only temporary concealment. Eventually the men would look in all those places. Eventually they would find him.

He would have to make it difficult for them.

He looked up at the lights. There were three bare bulbs shining overhead. He ran to the cupboard and plucked out a heavy ceramic coffee cup. He threw it at the nearest light.

The bulb shattered and went dark.

He fished out more cups. Three throws and the second bulb shattered.

He was about to aim at the last bulb when his gaze suddenly fell on the cook's radio. It was set in its usual place on top of the cupboard. His gaze followed the radio's extension cord as it trailed down to the countertop, where the toaster sat.

Yakov glanced at the stove and spotted an empty soup pot. He dragged the pot off the burner and carried it to the sink. He turned on the faucet.

A radio was playing at full volume.

Gregor pushed open the galley door and stepped inside. Music blasted away in the darkness. Drums and electric guitars. He felt for the wall switch and flicked it on. No lights. He tried it a few more times, but nothing happened. He took a step forward and his leather sole crunched on glass.

The little bastard's smashed out the lights. He's going to try to slip by me in the dark.

Gregor pushed the door shut. By the light of a match, he inserted his key in the lock and turned the deadbolt. No escape now. The match went out.

He turned to the darkness. 'Come on, boy!' he yelled. 'Nothing's going to happen to you!'

He heard only the radio blaring away, drowning out any other noise. He moved toward the sound, then paused to light another match. The radio was sitting on the countertop, right in front of him. As he switched off the music, he noticed the meat cleaver lying on the countertop. Beside it lay scraps of what looked like brown rubber.

So he's got his hands on the cook's knives, has he?

The match flickered out.

Gregor took out his gun and called out: 'Boy?'

Only then did he notice that his feet were wet.

He lit a third match and looked down.

He was standing in a pool of water. Already it had soaked into his leather shoes, certainly ruining them. Where was the water coming from? In the wavering light of the flame, he scanned the area around his feet and saw that the water had spread halfway across the floor. Then he saw the extension cord, the end sliced off, one coil glistening at the edge of the pool. In bewilderment he scanned the length of the cord as it snaked across the floor and looped upward, to a chair.

Just before his match flickered out, the last

image that Gregor registered was the faint gleam of blond hair, and the figure of the boy, his arm stretched toward the wall socket.

The end of the cord was dangling from his hand.

Tarasoff held out the scalpel. 'You make the first incision,' he said, and saw the look of dismay in the other man's eyes. *You have no choice, Hodell,* he thought. *You're the one who tried to recruit her into the fold. You're the one who made the mistake. Now you have to correct it.*

Hodell took the scalpel. They had not even begun to operate, and already sweat had broken out on his forehead. He paused, the blade poised over the exposed abdomen. They both knew this was a test – perhaps the ultimate one.

Go ahead. Archer did his part by taking care of Mary Allen. Just as Zwick did with Aaron Levi. Now it's your turn. Prove you're still part of the team, still one of us. Cut open the woman you once made love to.

Do it.

Mark shifted the scalpel in his hand, as though trying to get a better grip. Then he took a breath and pressed the blade to the skin.

Do it.

Mark sliced. A long, curving incision. The skin parted and a line of blood welled up and dribbled onto the surgical drapes.

Tarasoff relaxed. Hodell was not going to be a problem after all. He had, in fact, passed the point

502

of no return years ago, as a surgical fellow. A night of heavy drinking, a few snorts of cocaine. The next morning, a strange bed, and a pretty nursing student strangled to death on the pillow beside him. And Hodell with no memory of what had really happened. It was all very persuasive.

And there'd been the money to cement the recruitment.

The carrot and the stick. It worked almost every time. It had worked with Archer and Zwick and Mohandas. And with Aaron Levi too – for a while. Theirs had been a closed society, meticulous about guarding their secrets. And their profits. No one else at Bayside, not Colin Wettig, not even Jeremiah Parr, could even begin to guess how much money had changed hands. It was enough money to buy the very best doctors, the very best team – a team Tarasoff had created. The Russians merely supplied the parts and, when necessary, the brute force. In the OR, it was the team that performed the miracles.

Money alone had not been enough to keep Aaron Levi in their fold. But Hodell was still theirs. He was proving it now with every slice of his scalpel.

Tarasoff assisted, positioning retractors, clamping bleeders. It was a pleasure to work with such young and healthy tissue. The woman was in excellent condition. She had a minimum of subcutaneous fat and her abdominal muscles were flat and tight – so tight that their assistant, standing at the head of the table, had to infuse more succinylcholine to relax them for easier retraction.

The scalpel blade penetrated the muscle layer. They were in the abdominal cavity now. Tarasoff widened the retractors. Beneath a thin veil of peritoneal tissue glistened the liver and loops of small intestine. All of it healthy, so healthy! The human organism was a beautiful sight to behold.

The lights flickered and almost went off altogether.

'What's going on?' said Hodell.

They both looked up at the lamps. The lights brightened again to full intensity.

'Just a glitch,' said Tarasoff. 'I can still hear the generator.'

'This is not an optimal setup. A rocking ship. The power going off—'

'It's a temporary arrangement. Until we find a replacement for the Amity building.' He nodded at the surgical site. 'Proceed.'

Hodell raised his scalpel and paused. He'd been trained as a thoracic surgeon; a liver resection was a procedure he'd performed only a few times before. Perhaps he needed extra guidance.

Or perhaps the reality of what he was doing was starting to sink in.

'Is there a problem?' Tarasoff asked.

'No.' Mark swallowed. Once again he began to cut, but his hand was shaking. He lifted the scalpel and took a few deep breaths.

'We haven't a lot of time, Dr Hodell. There's another donor to harvest.'

'It's just . . . isn't it hot in here?'

'I hadn't noticed. Proceed.'

Hodell nodded. Gripping the scalpel, he was about to make another incision when he suddenly froze.

Tarasoff heard a sound behind him – the sigh of the door as it whished shut.

Mark, staring straight ahead, lifted his scalpel.

The explosion seemed to punch him in the face. Hodell's head snapped backward. Blood and bone fragments sprayed across the table.

Tarasoff spun around to look at the door, and he caught a glimpse of blond hair and the boy's white face.

The gun fired a second time.

The shot went wild, the bullet shattering a glass door in the supply cabinet. Shards rained onto the floor.

The anesthetist ducked for cover behind the ventilator.

Tarasoff backed away, his gaze never leaving the gun. It was Gregor's gun, compact enough, light enough, for even a child to hold. But the hand clutching that gun was shaking too hard now to shoot straight. *He's only a boy*, thought Tarasoff. A frightened boy whose aim kept wavering indecisively between the anesthetist and Tarasoff.

Tarasoff glanced sideways at the instrument tray, and he spotted the syringe of succinylcholine. It still contained more than enough to subdue the child. Slowly he edged sideways, stepping over Hodell's body and through the spreading pool of blood. Then the gun swung back toward him, and he froze.

The boy was crying now, his breath coming in quick, tearful gasps.

'It's all right,' soothed Tarasoff. And he smiled. 'Don't be afraid. I'm only helping your friend. Making her well again. She's very sick. Don't you know that? She needs a doctor.'

The boy's gaze focused on the table. On the woman. He took a step forward, then another. His breath suddenly escaped in a high, keening wail. He did not hear the anesthetist slip past him and flee from the room. Nor did he seem to hear the faint rumble of the helicopter. It was approaching, preparing to land for the pickup.

Tarasoff took the syringe from the tray. Quietly he moved closer to the table.

The boy lifted his head and his cry rose to a despairing shriek.

Tarasoff raised the syringe.

At that instant the boy looked up at him. And it was no longer fear, but rage that shone in the boy's eyes as he aimed Gregor's gun.

And fired one last time.

Twenty-six

The boy would not leave her bedside. From the moment the nurses had wheeled her out of Recovery and into the SICU, he had stayed right beside her, a pale little ghost haunting her bed. Twice the nurses had taken him by the hand and led him out of the cubicle. Twice the boy had found his way back in again. Now he stood gripping the siderail, his gaze silently pleading with her to wake up. At least he was no longer hysterical, the way he'd been when Katzka had come across him on the ship. He'd found the boy leaning over Abby's butchered body, sobbing, imploring her to live. Katzka had not understood a word of what the boy was saying. But he'd understood perfectly his panic. His despair.

There was a tapping on the cubicle window. Turning, Katzka saw Vivian Chao motioning to him. He opened the door and joined her outside the cubicle.

'That kid can't stay here all night,' she said.

'He's getting in their way. Plus, he doesn't look very clean.'

'Every time they try to take him away, he starts screaming.'

'Can't you talk to him?'

'I don't know any Russian. Do you?'

'We're still waiting for the hospital translator. Why don't you exert some male authority? Just pull him out.'

'Give the boy some time with her, okay?' Katzka turned and gazed through the window at the bed. And he found himself struggling to shake off the superimposed image that would haunt him for the rest of his days: Abby lying on the table, her abdomen slit open, her intestines glistening under the OR lights. The boy whimpering, cradling her face. And on the floor, lying in a lake of their own blood, the two men – Hodell already dead, Tarasoff unconscious and bleeding but still alive. Like everyone else aboard that freighter, Tarasoff had been taken into custody.

Soon there would be more arrests. The investigation was just beginning. Even now, federal authorities were closing in on the Sigayev Company. Based on what the freighter's crew had already told them, the scope of the organ-selling operation was wider – and far more horrifying – than Katzka could have imagined.

He blinked and refocused on the here and now: Abby, lying on the other side of that window, her abdomen swathed in bandages. Her chest rising and falling. The monitor tracing the steady rhythm of her heart. Just for an instant, he felt the same flash of panic he'd experienced on the ship, when Abby's heartbeat had started skipping wildly across the monitor. When he'd thought he was about to lose her, and the chopper bringing Vivian and Wettig to the ship had still been miles away. He touched the glass and found himself blinking again. And again.

Behind him, Vivian said softly, 'Katzka, she'll be okay. The General and I do good work.'

Katzka nodded. Without a word, he slipped back into the cubicle.

The boy looked up at him, his gaze as moist as Katzka's. 'Ah-bee,' he whispered.

'Yeah, kid. That's her name.' Katzka smiled.

They both looked at the bed. A long time seemed to pass. The silence was broken only by the soft and steady beep of the cardiac monitor. They stood side by side, sharing a vigil over this woman whom neither of them knew well, but about whom they already cared so deeply.

At last Katzka held out his hand. 'Come on. You need your sleep, son. And so does she.'

The boy hesitated. For a moment he studied Katzka. Then, reluctantly, he took the offered hand.

They walked together through the SICU, the boy's plastic shoes scuffling across the linoleum. Without warning, the boy slowed down.

'What is it?' said Katzka.

The boy had paused outside another cubicle. Katzka, too, looked through the glass.

Beyond the window, a silver-haired man sat in a chair by the patient's bed. His head was bowed in his hands, his whole body was quaking with silent sobs. *There are things even Victor Voss cannot buy*, thought Katzka. *Now he's about to lose everything. His wife. His freedom.* Katzka looked at the woman lying in the bed. Her face was as white and fragile-looking as porcelain. Her eyes, half-opened, had the dull sheen of impending death.

The boy pressed closer to the glass.

In that instant, as he leaned forward, the woman's eyes seemed to register one last flicker of life. She focused on the boy. Slowly her lips curved into a silent smile. And then she closed her eyes.

Katzka murmured, 'It's time to go.'

The boy looked up. Firmly, he shook his head. As Katzka watched in helpless silence, the boy turned and walked back into Abby's cubicle.

Suddenly Katzka felt weary beyond belief. He looked at Victor Voss, a ruined man who now sat with his body crumpled forward in despair. He looked at the woman in the bed, her soul slipping away even as he watched. And he thought: *So little time. We have so little time on this earth with the people we love.*

He sighed. Then he, too, turned and walked into Abby's cubicle.

And took his place beside the boy.

THE END

LIFE SUPPORT
By Tess Gerritsen

*Control was the word Dr Toby Harper lived by.
She strove to keep her life in order, her ER in order.*

But no one could have been prepared for the man she
admits one quiet night to the Springer Hospital.
Delirious and in a critical condition from a possible
viral infection of the brain, he barely responds to
treatment. And then he disappears without trace.

Toby must find her patient. The hunt leads her to a
second patient with the same infection and reveals an
unsettling twist – the infection can only be spread
through direct tissue exchange.

As unexpected tragedy hits close to home, Toby
discovers the unthinkable: a terrifying and deadly
epidemic is about to be unleashed . . .

'IT'S SCARY JUST HOW GOOD
TESS GERRITSEN IS'
Harlan Coben

'Richly drawn hospital scenes . . . chilling science . . .
and breathless ER style pacing make *Life Support* a
quick, delightfully scary read'
People

0553817736

BANTAM BOOKS

VANISH
By Tess Gerritsen

Those who vanish sometimes come back to us.

The beautiful woman appears to be just another corpse in the morgue. But when medical examiner Maura Isles looks down at the body, she gets the fright of her life.

The corpse opens its eyes.

Now very much alive, the woman is rushed to the hospital, where she murders a security guard and seizes hostages, one of whom is the heavily pregnant homicide detective Jane Rizzoli.

But who is this woman, and what does she want? Only Jane can solve the mystery – if she survives the night.

'GERRITSEN IS A CRAFTSWOMAN'
Daily Mirror

'YOU ARE GOING TO BE UP ALL NIGHT'
Stephen King

0593053516

NOW AVAILABLE FROM BANTAM PRESS

BANTAM PRESS